The Judge's Lawyer

ALSO BY DYLAN H. JONES

DI TUDOR MANX
Book 1: Anglesey Blue
Book 2: Doll Face
Book 3: Shadow Soul

STANDALONES
What Follows
Hear Her Scream
The Judge's Lawyer

THE JUDGE'S LAWYER

DYLAN H. JONES

LUME BOOKS
A JOFFE BOOKS COMPANY

Lume Books, London
A Joffe Books Company
www.lumebooks.co.uk

First published in Great Britain in 2025

Cover art by Cherie Chapman

ISBN: 978-1-83901-616-5

I owe a huge debt of gratitude to my beta readers for their dedication in ensuring all the legal elements in the book were correct. Thank you for stopping me from stepping on those legal landmines!

This book is dedicated to you, along with my extraordinary wife, Laura, and my beautiful daughter, Bella, who are both endless sources of support, inspiration, and laughter.

CHAPTER 1

I wait for the Captain to pass out from his nightly cocktail of alcohol and drugs before I make my move: the drunk, high, and sleeping make for easy targets.

Captain? The name sticks like a tumor in my throat, but tonight, he'll pay the price for his sins, and out of the many promises I've made and broken, this will be the one I keep.

The streets of La Cruz are dusty and dark, and I walk them like a ghost lingering between one life and the next. In the distance, the discordant notes of a car alarm pierce through the darkness, pulsing with the impatience of an agitated heartbeat. I ignore the sound, continue over the potholed streets and think back to a warm September day, another glorious Northern Californian fall when the fading embers of summer made you feel good to be alive, made you grateful for every damned thing you ever had. Here on the Riviera Nayarit, the same sun cracks down like a thousand lashes on your back, shows no mercy, beats you with everything it has.

But for now, there's a reprieve. For the next few hours, the sun's tucked under the flip side of the world, and when it rises again over the bare backbone of the Sierra Madres, it will do so lazily, in no hurry to birth the day, just like everything else here in Mexico: *mañana*, always *mañana*.

At two in the morning, La Cruz seems abandoned. One bar remains open, Pancho's, a filthy hole-in-the-wall. Outside the bar stands a white horse with the poise of a thoroughbred champion. It looks out of place in the dust and poverty, tied to the wall and scraping its front right hoof along the dirt as if preparing to bolt. The beast snorts, lifts its nostrils in my direction, sweeps its tail across its hindquarters, and bows its head as if in sympathy of or maybe in resignation to its own fate.

Two men, one older and dressed in a business suit, the other much younger and scrawnier, sit at a table outside the bar, pulling on thick cigars and shuffling dominoes across a red checkered tablecloth. Traditional Mexican folk music spills from the bar; it sounds like the mariachi I've heard in the streets, but this is harder-edged, grittier. At the table next to the men, a young couple pay their tab. The man wears a cream linen suit; the woman a white dress and red scarf that looks like a wrap of blood around her neck. They stand, look around, and scurry down a dimly lit alleyway.

After the couple leave, the two men slap wads of cash on the table and look up, study for a moment the stocky, six-foot-two American wearing a *Bad Brains* T-shirt, shake their heads, laugh, then continue laying down their wagers. I'm just another *gringo* passing through, not worth their time. Many gringos had arrived in La Cruz since the construction of the new marina. More gringos meant more trouble, always. As far as I could tell, thus was written the history of Mexico.

Minutes later, I'm at the dockside, trudging down the asphalt road leading down to the moorings. The yellow lights from the Casa Genoa hotel nestled into the hillside spills onto the jungle foliage behind me. I could only imagine what the locals made of this place: two hundred luxury rooms, costing more a night than many people here would earn in a year, with views that span the sandy crescent of Banderas Bay and westerly to the rocky point of

Punta Mita. Or maybe the locals are all good with it, get on with their lives while all around them changes.

The stench of brine and diesel catches in my throat as I clamber down the iron staircase bolted to the dockside. My sneakers slip from the greasy metal rungs.

A creak of timbers as I jump from the stairs and land crisply on the jetty.

Pushing my back against the cold, damp brickwork of the harbor wall, I listen and watch in the shadows.

Nothing stirs, but that means shit. This place is thick with shadows.

I listen to the gentle slap of water against hulls and anxious notes of the car alarm closer now, as if it's caught on the breeze and followed me here.

After a five-minute walk along the jetty, I reach my destination, *El Gordo Loco*, a sleek, white catamaran at least fifty feet from aft to stern. Violet-colored lights loop around the rigging, casting an artificial glow over the timber deck.

I haul my tired body aboard and listen to the low groan of ropes pulling against iron cleats as the vessel yields to my weight. Soft-shoeing over the deck, I head to the central cabin area.

I count six steps down to the galley. From here, another five steps to the starboard stateroom.

Before I forget, I check my handgun, a bronze-colored .45 stuffed into the waistband of my jeans. It feels awkward in my hand, like I shouldn't be carrying it. At the same time, it's a necessity, a means to a bloody end.

As I edge down the steps, music spills from the cabin-mounted speakers: "Mexican Radio" by *Wall of Voodoo*. A bitter irony I have no time to dwell on.

Inside, the catamaran is spotless. The wood polished until it gleams, and violet lighting reflects off the fat chrome fittings.

Squeezing through the narrow galley, my elbow pushes a shot glass to the floor. As the glass rumbles across the timber, it sounds like a freight train rolling through the boat.

I hold my breath. Nothing stirs. Reaching down, I retrieve the glass, set it back in the sink, and hear the car alarm again, punching holes in the stillness like it's desperate for my attention.

I push open the door leading to the Captain's stateroom and steady the .45 in my hands, just like they do in the movies.

The artifice isn't necessary. My weapon is surplus to requirements. It feels ridiculous, overkill, a misjudged strategy.

It takes a few seconds to process the scene.

Empty bottle of Código Tequila on the table, a half-smoked cigar, its end still ashen and warm, and a discarded pizza box, the restaurant's bright red logo obscured by a wedge of American dollar bills. Next to the tequila bottle, a pyramid of white powder waiting to be cut by the razor lying close by. But it's the tableau played out on the bed that sends a spike through my stomach; it takes all my willpower to keep the bile from rising.

The Captain lies on his back, left arm exposed under a white sheet. I recognize the tattoo inked onto the back of the hand: *Sangre Norteña* in red cursive.

The room is a theater of red, like the handiwork of a vengeful God. Blood splatters cover the portholes and the ceiling in an abstract of human vermilion. If the Captain's eyes were still in their sockets, they might tell the story of what had gone down, but they're gone, pecked away and discarded on the floor like battle spoils of a sack of vultures.

Astride the Captain, a young girl, way too young to be here. Her throat is surgically slit, her neck a damp choker of red dripping onto her shoulders. I notice the adolescent fullness of her hips, the puppy fat around her belly, the red-and-green jaguar tattoo inked into her right shoulder, its tail coiling around her arm. She's probably from one of the shadier bars in Sayulita, the kind of backstreet bars respectable gringos fear to tread. Unlike the Captain, the girl's eyes are still in their sockets. Even so, they tell me nothing. Those deep brown pools have no secrets to proffer, no story to recite. They stare at the ceiling, maybe someplace way above that to the stars and the great celestial fairytale of the afterlife.

Mother Mary, full of grace, bestow thy eternal grace on me and save my wretched soul.

Sorry, honey, not tonight.

I run a tentative finger over the Captain's arm. Warm skin, as if he might still possess a molecule of life.

I listen for one last death-rattle shiver, but that time has passed. All I hear is the bleating of the car alarm plucking at the wires in my head.

Amidst the bloody carnage, I have a single thought: precise, clear, unsettling.

If the body's still warm, the killer must be close by.

I step away, rush onto the deck, fall to my knees, just about stop myself from throwing up.

When I raise my head, a bright white light shines, bleaching out everything around me. The sound of a gun pin cocking tightens the skin around my bones, echoes with a terrible intensity deep in my gut.

A voice, low and steady: "Never one for taking good advice when it was given, were you, Sweeney?"

I struggle to make out the face. It's blurred and silhouetted behind the light. The overwhelming smell of menthol curls up my nostrils as the man speaks.

"Best you take it easy and tell me everything. That is, if you want to see your wife and son again."

PART 1:
BAD JUDGMENT

CHAPTER 2

Three Weeks Previously

The pre-coffee drama I could have lived without. But that was just the future warming up for the main event, leaving clues like breadcrumbs for me to follow. Not that I paid attention. I'd regret that down the line, but I couldn't beat myself up too much. Few people notice life's beats until it's too late.

That future began on a perfect Bay Area fall morning, another Indian summer lifting the hem of her sari with a promise of warmer days before the season slipped into winter. I woke with a yellow smudge of dawn loitering at my window, seagulls cackling like fishwives, my cell phone buzzing across the dresser, and the distant stirrings of a hangover in the making.

My sleep's hardly deep or restorative on the best of nights; a cocktail of hard liquor and ear-throbbing music before lights out all but guarantees Mr. Sandman won't be making a house call, but like most things in life, it's a compromise. Mope around my apartment like a moody teenager or make the adult decision, pour myself another Calo Isla single malt and max the volume on Joy Division's "Unknown Pleasures" (one of the greatest post-punk albums ever pressed to vinyl, in my not-so-humble opinion).

I checked the caller ID: *Sierra*, as predictable as the day is long. She sounded tired.

"I heard gunshots last night. I was worried about Kurt."

That figured. Sierra had requested I move out of the family home six months ago. I moved into an apartment in Oakland's Jack London Square, owned by my good friend, Victor Santiago. I'd known Victor since we'd attended law school; he was the best man at my wedding and godfather to my son, Kurt. In our small legal circle, trial by Victor was known as the Santiago Ambush. The man never went into court without a bullet primed in the chamber and had the uncanny ability to gauge the pitch-perfect moment to pull the trigger and send that bullet ripping through the prosecution's evidence. Victor dressed the part of the successful defense attorney: Brioni suits, Armani shirts, Gucci Oxfords, and a shit-eating grin, even on the days he lost, which were rare. Framing that grin, a studiously handsome face. He possessed that lethal combination of boyish charm and scholarly logic that had jurors hanging on his every word.

"Mitch, are you listening?"

"Probably delinquents with firecrackers."

"I know gunfire when I hear it."

"That you do, Sierra. So, what do you want me to do about it?"

"I want you to figure out a way to pay our debts . . . your debts."

"Nicely done, Sierra. Slip in the knife before six in the morning. Thanks for that."

Of course, I said none of this. There's no advantage in twisting the blade when it's already buried deep; best to give Sierra the satisfaction of drawing it out when she was good and ready. She continued.

"I'm calling a realtor."

9

I refused to be drawn in on this point of order. Every few years, Sierra would decide she was done with city living and start checking the listings for single-family homes out in the East Bay suburbs. As I kept insisting to my beautiful but misguided wife, North Oakland wasn't exactly Hell's Kitchen. In realtor parlance, the area was *up and coming, colorful, diverse, mid-rejuvenation*. A young gay couple had bought the house across the street, renovated from the floorboards up: solar roof, new windows, a front yard straight out of *Sunset* magazine.

"Welcome to the gayborhood," I'd joked at the time.

"One rainbow flag and a begonia gazebo do not make a safe neighborhood, Mitch," Sierra had responded.

Fair point, but Sierra never had an eye for the bigger picture. She was a detail person, loved minutia, hated surprises and listening to music on anything other than vinyl. I could have loved her for that alone. Sierra worked as the senior features editor of our local newspaper. Journalism suited her intellect, made her feel she could corral the world into some sort of order, if she could get her words down on paper. I'd always been less concerned with order. You can try your best to control fate, but it's a fool's errand, and as some wise-ass lawyer keeps telling me, "Fate is its own river. Try stopping that flow, and she'll find another way to get where she's meant to be."

Injustice, however . . . that was a splinter that had burrowed its way under my skin as far back as I could remember, and was probably the reason I became a lawyer; that, and the sorry state of my bank balance after two years of cash jobs in the UK after my student visa expired. I'd met a girl out there, the love of my life, or so I imagined. She ditched my ass six months later. I stayed on, tried to heal the wound, and found grunt work with a private security outfit looking for a dumb American who didn't ask too many questions. Two years later, my heart just about healed, I returned to California, begged a loan from my parents, enrolled in law school, and figured it was about time I did some good in the world, try one small beat at a time to make a difference. Beats: I figure you make enough of them, the rhythm's gotta start changing at some point.

"I'm serious, Mitch. What about the sideshows and the shootings? It's not safe."

"You're too close to it, Sierra. Turn off your Citizen app."

"That's your solution? Ignore it?"

I didn't say as much, but ignoring shit I had no control over usually worked for me. As the Serenity Prayer states: *God, grant me the serenity to accept the things I cannot change, courage to change the things I can, and wisdom to know the difference.*

I'd never bought into religion, but that proverb spoke to me when I first heard it. Lost some of its sheen when I discovered the prayer was one of the core tenets of the twelve steps to recovery: I'm not a fan, witnessed my brother pass through that whole AA circus. He kicked the booze but got addicted to the program, balls-deep in the whole happy clappy, tambourines and holy roller-gang bang, living the sober life. Good luck to him. *When I need a conversion, I'll call you, brother, but don't hold your breath.*

"Mitch?"

"Do what you need to do, Sierra."

"Is that all you've got to say?"

"No, got a bunch more to say, just not this morning. Tell Kurt I'll see him tomorrow night."

I felt bad cutting Sierra off, but my attendance was required at the Alameda Superior Courtroom that morning. Thirty minutes later, I was showered and dressed.

If I knew what lay ahead that day, I'd have stayed in bed, feigned some illness, and avoided the whole shit show that was about to rain down on me.

CHAPTER 3

Back in the day, Jack London Square was just another Oakland neighborhood best avoided after sundown. Recently, that had all changed. Jack London was now prime waterfront real estate, and my apartment — *muchas gracias*, Victor — was located two blocks from the San Francisco ferry terminal, close to the Amtrak line. The trains rattled and jangled into town all hours of the day until midnight when a blessed peace descended, broken only by police sirens and the cough of foghorns carrying across the bay.

Most days I cycled to work. The courthouse was an easy ten-minute bike ride, and I figured I needed the exercise. At Second Street, I snagged a double espresso, sipping and watched the day break into motion. Forklifts hummed and puttered in and out of the doorways of the produce warehouses across the street and wizened old men barked orders to the younger men hauling crates from the trucks. A Chinese guy standing on the corner flashed his black, toothless smile at me; he must have been a hundred and two if he was a day.

"Good morning, sir," he said, with a smoker's rasp. "Gonna be a bright, sunshiny day."

"Sure is," I said, gesturing my coffee to the cloudless blue sky. "Jimmy Cliff wasn't far wrong."

"Hey, you know Jimmy Cliff?"

12

"Sure, me and Jimmy go way back."

The old man hacked like his lungs were about to rocket out of his throat, then serenaded me as I passed.

That right, old man? Gotta be honest, I'm finding a severe shortage in the "nothing but blue skies" department these days, but who was I to burst his bubble? The old guy probably didn't have many "bright sunshiny days" to look forward to. God love him for wanting to point out every last one of them to passing strangers.

I cycled off, leaving 'Jimmy Cliff' to his solo.

* * *

I was due at the courthouse at nine thirty to attend the second part of the suppression motion in the case of the People versus Francisco Castillo. Last week, the prosecution had presented its case. Now it was the defense's day in court, and representing the defendant — Victor Santiago.

Typically, I'd pass Victor's cases to a colleague to avoid any conflict of interest. But this was a request by the Assistant Presiding Judge at the Alameda Superior Court, Harriet Croft; a request where a *No thank you, your honor, I'm busy* wouldn't fly.

Heading to the courthouse, I took the side streets to avoid the foul stench drifting from Lake Merritt, a hundred-and-forty-acre tidal lagoon east of downtown. Typically, the lakeside would be a scurry of joggers and commuters, but foot traffic was close to zero due to a rare, late-summer algae bloom. In just a few days, the bloom had spread its poisonous tentacles through the water, leaving tens of thousands of piscine corpses in its wake. The stench from the rotting carcasses of mudsuckers, striped bass, and sticklebacks lying belly-up and dead-eyed at the shoreline drifted for several blocks, a post-apocalyptic marine life carnage that, looking back, was as ominous a sign I would get that my life was about to suffer a similar fate, all because of one man, Paco Magic.

* * *

Paco Magic — given name Francisco Miguel Castillo — sat next to Victor Santiago at the defense table, cucumber cool, examining his fingernails as if the morning's proceedings were keeping him from his manicure appointment. Bald, mid-sixties, muscular, Zapata mustache, wearing a tailored suit that failed to hide his deep tan, and a leathery and expensive cologne I could smell from across the courtroom.

For those who didn't know him, Paco Castillo resembled your average Bay Area multimillionaire CEO, a dime a dozen around these parts, except he wasn't. Paco Magic was the alleged *patrón* of *La Sangre Norteña*, an organized crime gang affiliated with the Sinaloa Cartel. I guess if you want a successful criminal enterprise, you learn from the best.

La Sangre ran California's narcotics trafficking from Eureka down to San Diego and rose to prominence in the late '80s when cultivating and distributing weed was still illegal in the state. The organization had set up business deep in Humboldt County, buying land and property like they were playing Monopoly for keeps. I'd heard from a contact at the Oakland Police Department that *La Sangre* had ditched the weed business once Proposition 64 passed and California legalized cannabis. I'd also heard rumors they'd held onto their weed farms and labs, cultivating more potent strains and selling them on the black market. It made sense. The paperwork and filings in setting up a legal weed business were time-consuming and costly, and profits were marginal. I figured the truth, as in most things, lay somewhere in between.

Pot cultivation and distribution needs a system, a bureaucracy of logistics to keep the machinery running, the same logistics it takes to traffic weapons, distribute narcotics across state lines, enforce protection rackets, and manage sex trafficking rings. Once the system's in place, swap out the product, and it's business as usual.

"Paco Magic" had earned his moniker for never having spent a night in jail. This was no conjuring trick, no glitzy Las Vegas magic show. Paco had a cadre of overpaid, whip-smart lawyers at his disposal. Victor Santiago was one of them.

I said Victor was good; I never claimed he was a saint.

"Mitch," he'd tell me, "every American citizen has a right to a lawyer in a court of law. All I do is serve the people. If it's not me, then some half-assed lawyer's going to take the case, and you know this already, *amigo*, nobody's going to do a better job defending you than Victor Santiago."

It was the kind of logic Victor excelled at. No wiggle room for personal feelings, ethical dilemmas, and bleeding hearts. Just the facts, pure and simple.

A row behind Paco Castillo sat his wife, Oksana. She was at least three decades younger, early thirties. Oksana was as stunning as she was composed, with gunmetal-gray eyes, cheekbones you could sharpen knives on, and dressed as if she had far more glamorous places to be. That place was likely the VIP section of an exclusive nightclub, hanging off the arm of some aging oligarch like an over-priced accessory. Either side of Oksana, like stone pillars, sat two Latino men in suits, all torso and no neck; they looked like the perps who'd shot the sheriff, the deputy, and then returned fire on the posse hunting them down.

I was aware of Paco Castillo through my job as a Judicial Staff Attorney, which gave me access to the trickier criminal cases passing through the courts. They called grunts like me a "Judge's Lawyer." I'd worked there for twenty years, closing in on retirement in another eight, with a team of three researchers working under me.

Judges are busy people; they don't have the time to research every case that arrives on their docket. Our job is to make the time. Truth be told, without us, the whole judicial process grinds to a screeching halt. On the best days, the machinery of justice chugs along slowly and methodically, a network of moving parts ticking away like a perfectly engineered Swiss watch. At least, that's how it's meant to work. In reality, the machinery runs more like an old grandfather clock: a few ticks behind the times, regularly a tock late, and too often, the pendulum skews counter to the direction it's meant to swing.

Sometimes, I'd catch an error the defense team had overlooked, or some chain of evidence error the prosecution had tried to sneak past the judge. Those days, I felt like I was sending a handful of good karma back into the world, and despite the daily grind, the work appealed to my analytic and contrary nature. In a former life, I got my kicks by flipping authority the bird. The urge hadn't left me; I was just smarter at disguising it, kept that upright middle finger hidden under my desk. On the flip side of that bird, as a state employee, my benefits were generous, and my paycheck steady. Most days, I left the office by five and didn't bring the job home. Maybe with some serious focus and ambition, like Victor, I could have set up my own criminal law practice. Truth was, I preferred the quiet life, got the job done, rallied against injustice when it reared its ugly boot in my face, planned to retire at fifty-eight with a generous pension and dedicate the rest of my days to making music.

Problem was, fate hadn't received that memo. And like the old Hebrew proverb says, man plans, God laughs. I should have heard the Almighty chuckling his holy ass off when I stepped into Alameda court number three that morning and kicked off a chain of events that put myself and everyone I cared for in Paco Castillo's line of fire.

CHAPTER 4

The clerk addressed the courtroom and asked everyone to stand.

I expected Judge Harriet Croft to walk in. Instead, Alameda Superior Court Presiding Judge Griffin Harper lumbered in, papers in one hand, water bottle in the other. Rumor had it this judge's water bottle was a Trojan horse — short on water, long on vodka. Harper was severely overweight, with a mop of slicked-back silver hair and a face that gave the impression it had just been pulled from a hot oven. Seventy-eight years old, Harper had been diagnosed with lung cancer and was set to retire at the end of the year. He grunted and addressed both lawyers in that no-nonsense manner he'd sharpened at the whetstone of the courts.

"Yes, gentlemen, I am not the judge you were expecting," he said. "Judge Croft is dealing with a family emergency. I have read a transcript of the prior proceedings. And I want to again thank the court reporter for getting that to me on such short notice. Now, if everyone is as thrilled with this interruption to their morning as I am, I recommend you do others here the courtesy of making this brief."

A response was surplus to requirements.

Victor and Paco sat at the defense table alongside Victor's private investigator, Alma Torres. At the opposing table sat deputy DA Max Hale, and next to him, the officer involved in

Paco's arrest, Theodore Connor. Late forties, Van Dyke goatee and square-faced, Connor resembled an inflatable gorilla you see flapping in the wind outside car dealerships. Seated behind Connor was his partner, Officer Darlene Mason, thin as wire, copper-colored hair. Mason looked nervous, repeatedly wiping her palms down her thighs like some modern-day Lady Macbeth, trying to rid herself of an incriminating stain.

Harper took a swig from his bottle and spoke. "Mr. Santiago, this is day two of the suppression motion. Your reputation precedes you, I prepare to be wowed."

Victor stood. "I'll try not to disappoint, your honor." He tugged at his shirt cuffs and fastened the center button on his jacket. "The defense's intention today is to prove the evidence presented by the prosecution in last week's hearing is fruit of the poisonous tree. We believe the search of my client's vehicle was illegal, which renders any evidence found at the scene inadmissible in this court."

"An accusation the prosecution strongly objects to, your honor," Max Hale said, easing himself to his full six feet three. Hale was early thirties, a rising star in the Alameda DA's office, dressed well, his suit a step up from the usual off-the-rack DA uniform.

"Noted, but the DA's office has already presented its case." Harper gestured Hale should sit his ass back down.

Victor continued. "Last week, the prosecution told the court officers Connor and Mason pulled over Mr. Castillo for a minor traffic infraction. The prosecution then informed the court a weapon was found in plain view as Officer Connor searched the vehicle, which led to my client's arrest. Today, we will prove that the weapon was not in plain view and that the search conducted by Officer Connor was illegal. As stated by the prosecution in the same hearing, the forensic report matched the ballistics of the gun to the slaying of a young schoolteacher, Masie Howard. A tragedy, in which my client had no part. He has an alibi for the day in question."

"Mr. Santiago, is your client on trial?"

"No, your honor, I just—"

"Then stick to the facts surrounding the search of your client's vehicle."

Judge Harper had made the right call. This was an evidentiary hearing; Victor had tried to sneak in a defense of Castillo to cast him in a more favorable light. Acknowledging the judge's call, Victor nodded and checked his notes. "In the first hearing, Officer Connor testified that a nine-millimeter Glock 19 was found in plain view in Mr. Castillo's vehicle, a Tesla Model X. My client insists not only was the weapon not in plain view, but in the glove compartment, and that he also had no previous knowledge that the weapon was there. And, pursuant to California's automobile exception to the warrant requirement, police officers may only search a vehicle with probable cause — if there are exigent circumstances, or if the evidence is in plain view. But none of these, in truth, applied here, your honor."

Harper grunted. "Are you implying both officers are lying?"

"Just presenting the facts, which also include the failure of the officers' body cameras to record the specious stop and subsequent arrest. And as a reminder, it is public record that Officer Connor already has several racial profiling accusations leveled against him."

"Final warning," Harper said, waving his pen. "Limit your comments directly to the search of your client's vehicle."

Victor continued. "Both officers state they stopped Mr. Castillo at 3:43 p.m. on July 17 for failing to signal one hundred feet before making a turn. After approaching the vehicle, they asked Mr. Castillo to exit, and he immediately complied. While Mr. Castillo sat on the curb, supervised by Officer Mason, Officer

Connor was alone in the vehicle. It was during this time the illegal search occurred."

"Do you have evidence that proves this search was illegal?" Harper asked.

"I do, your honor. I have evidence that proves both officers lied to cover up their actions."

I noticed Officer Mason bristle as if someone had walked over her grave. Hale, too, seemed flushed with concern.

Victor cleared his throat. "Mr. Castillo, no stranger to this manner of harassment from the Oakland Police Department, had the presence of mind to record the audio of the interaction via his cell phone. I'd like my investigator, Alma Torres, to take the stand and play you this recording, your honor."

Harper gestured for Alma to step forward. She stomped to the stand, fiddled with her ear piercings, and switched on a small Bluetooth speaker.

"Ms. Torres, can you tell the judge what he's about to hear?" Victor asked.

"Yeah, sure," Alma said, brushing a strand of hair to reveal several neck tattoos. "Mr. Castillo switched on the voice memo function on this phone as Officer Connor approached his vehicle and put the phone under his seat."

Alma pressed play.

The first voice was Officer Connor requesting Paco's license and registration. After some radio static, Connor called out. *"We got us a hot tamale here, Darlene. Gonna need you to watch his ass."*

"Sure, I got ya back, Teddy. Do what you need to do."

Connor then addressed Paco. *"Seems you got a bunch of frequent flyer miles with the OPD, Mr. Castillo. Now, I figure a Mexican man like yourself, driving a real expensive electric vehicle like this, you gotta be hiding something, am I right?"*

"Nothing to hide, officer. And I am an American citizen."

"That so? Seems to me every time I pull over one of you people, you've got something to hide. Narcotics, weapons . . . you hiding anything like that in there?"

I imagined Paco sitting with his hands at two and ten, gripping the wheel. This was probably the moment he figured the smartest move was keeping his mouth shut.

"What? You no hablo inglés all of a sudden?" Connor exhaled, his frustration audible. *"Sir, I need you to exit the car, hands where I can see them. Nice and easy, wouldn't want you tripping and hurting yourself. Darlene, escort him to the curb. He's gone mute on us, unless you want to try practicing your Spanish . . ."*

"I don't speak fucking Spanish."

"Make sure his ass stays on the sidewalk. If he tries anything, you got your taser close by?"

"Got that shit locked and loaded, Teddy."

The next few seconds comprised a series of clicks and the solid clunk of something opening. Connor muttered a triumphant, *"Bingo, motherfucker."*

Victor gestured Alma should stop the playback. "There is more, your honor, but I think we've heard the most pertinent sections."

Connor turned to his partner, Mason, and mouthed something. Hale tapped Connor's shoulder, giving him the *calm down* motion. Connor made a gesture that implied he wanted him to stand up and object, but Hale's hands were tied. This wasn't a trial; the prosecution had the burden of proof and had presented its evidence last week. Harper would have shot him down before he got his words out.

"Thank you for your testimony, Ms. Torres," Victor said. "What, in your opinion, is happening in that recording?"

"Well, it's pretty obvious. Officer Connor's opening the glove compartment. Doesn't take a genius to figure it out."

"How can you be sure?"

"Because the only way to open the Tesla's glove compartment is with the touch screen. Connor opens it within seconds of entering the car."

"Which means?"

"It means he's familiar with the interior of a Tesla. Most people would go straight for the glove compartment, push the lock or something."

"But Officer Connor opened the compartment within seconds of entering the car?"

"Fifteen. I timed it."

"Does Officer Connor own a Tesla?"

"No, he owns a Dodge 500 Ram, six liter. Nice truck if you've got the cash to gas her up."

"So, the opposite of a Tesla?"

"Guess you could say that."

"So how could Officer Connor have opened the glove compartment so quickly?"

"His wife, Barbara Connor, owns a Tesla Model 3. The glove compartment functions the same in all Teslas."

Victor turned to Harper. "What you heard, your honor, were the sounds of Officer Connor accessing the glove compartment, which proves this was an illegal search. And as stated earlier, my client had no previous knowledge of the presence of a weapon in his vehicle."

Harper sat back. "I commend your research, Mr. Santiago, but it's hardly wowing me. This recording could be open to multiple interpretations. Without clear visuals, how can we be sure Officer Connor is conducting an illegal search?"

Hale gave a sly smile as he turned to both officers, who seemed to breathe a sigh of relief. Their relief was short-lived.

Harper leaned forward. "But what is bugging the biscuits out of me, Mr. Hale, are the faulty body cams. If Officers

Connor and Mason had forgotten to switch them on, I'd say that was negligence, but both failing at the same time looks to me a lot like convenience. I'd like your take on this, especially as the burden of proof falls on the prosecution to prove the legality of the search."

Hale cleared his throat. "Your honor, mechanical failure of body cams is not unusual."

Victor stood and gestured at Hale. "Does the prosecution have any evidence to support that fact? The number of times body cams fail? The results of these failures? Any verified statistics to support Mr. Hale's assumption? 'It's not unusual' is not a legal argument, your honor . . . I believe it's a Tom Jones song."

A ripple of laughter passed through the courtroom. Paco had a Cheshire-cat-sized smile pasted on his face.

"Do you have specifics to support your claim, Mr. Hale?" Harper asked.

Hale rifled through his papers, searching for a line item of hope buried in there. "If Mr. Santiago had provided his findings in good time, we would have secured an expert witness to speak to the facts."

That's when I noticed the predatory glint in Victor's eyes.

"Actually, your honor, there is such an expert here in the courtroom. Someone at the Superior Court who can verify or repudiate these facts. If he were willing and you were open, I'd like to call Mitchum Sweeney to the stand."

I sat bolt upright. Was Victor really going there?

"This is just theatrics, your honor," Hale complained.

Victor pressed on. "The prosecution made an assumption with no evidence to support their claims. By calling an expert witness, we can test the prosecution's hypothesis to everyone's satisfaction." He paused and turned to the judge. "I am putting my client's defense on the line here, your honor."

Paco stiffened and threw Victor a look that said, *You better know what you're doing, cabrón.*

"Mr. Sweeney and I have not discussed this case," Victor insisted. "Calling an impartial witness to the stand is fair to the defense and the prosecution. I'd also argue it's critical for you, your honor, to make a decision on suppressing the evidence in question."

Harper turned to me. "Mr. Sweeney, are you willing to take the stand and provide an expert opinion based on your experience?"

Victor's eyes were almost pleading with me. I had no choice. I already owed Victor more than I could ever repay him. "Yes, I'd be willing," I said and walked to the stand.

Victor wasted no time in diving in. "Your work at the Alameda Superior Court involves researching criminal cases, correct, Mr. Sweeney?"

"My team analyzes criminal evidence and provides this legal research to the judges hearing the motions or trying the cases."

"And how long have you worked in your current position?"

"Twenty years."

"And you've provided this kind of legal research for Judge Harper?"

"Yes. Yes, I have."

"So, he trusts you?"

"I can't speak for the judge, but I'd hope so."

Harper grunted and sipped his water bottle.

Victor turned to me. "How many hours of body-cam footage have you reviewed in your career? Ballpark is fine."

"We review police body-cam footage every week. Each recording is about an hour, and there could be multiple cameras to review. Ballpark, I'd estimate over a hundred hours a year."

"So, we can safely assume you've analyzed hundreds of hours of body-cam footage in your time at the court?"

"Between my colleagues and myself, I'd say that's about right."

"Tell me, how often does a body-cam failure occur?"

"The cameras are extremely reliable. I've only seen it occur twice in my career."

"That's very specific."

"I remember them because they're the anomalies. They stick with you."

"What did you see on the footage on the day of my client's arrest?"

"My colleague, Katie Pearson, reviewed the incident and brought it to my attention."

"And what was it specifically that your colleague was concerned about?"

"She was concerned both Officers Connor and Mason's body cams had captured footage earlier that day but failed to record Mr. Castillo's arrest."

"Were the body cams engaged at the scene at any time?"

"No, they were not. Cameras fail, but more often than not, it's human error."

Victor addressed the judge. "But that's not what the prosecution is arguing. Both officers swore under oath that their body cams malfunctioned, a mechanical failure." He turned to face me. "In all these hundreds of hours of footage you've analyzed, how many times have both police officers' body cams failed simultaneously during an arrest?"

"Never. I've never encountered two body cams failing at the same time, and given the work my department does for the judges, I would have heard about it."

Victor nodded. "Now, I'd like to ask you some hypothetical questions. In your expert opinion, would you consider the search of my client's vehicle to be illegal?"

"Based on the evidence of the recording and the failure of the body cams to record the search properly, it's my expert opinion that Officer Connor probably conducted an illegal search."

"Concerning Officer Connor's prejudicial language you heard on the recording, hypothetically, could this have played a part in the arrest of my client?"

Hale stood. "Objection, your honor. Officer Connor is not on trial here."

"I'll rephrase. In your years of experience, have you encountered racial profiling in detentions?"

"I can't say it's what happened here, but yes, it's a real problem for OPD, for sure."

Victor nodded. "So, to recap, Mr. Castillo was arrested by an officer with a history of racial intolerance, evidenced in the derogatory language he used toward my client. Second, the search was illegal. The weapon was not in plain view but inside the glove compartment, which Officer Connor had no cause to search. Third, an expert witness, with twenty years of court service, has never encountered two body cams failing simultaneously."

Victor gestured at the prosecution's table. "This leads to only one conclusion. Both officers colluded to ensure their cameras were disengaged during the arrest with the intent of conducting a fishing expedition that led to the unlawful arrest of Mr. Castillo."

He turned to the judge. "Your honor, this evidence was found illegally and should be suppressed. I've already stated three areas of concern. Who knows how many more my team could dig up between now and a trial date? My client is not guilty of possessing a deadly weapon, and he certainly should not be charged with killing that young teacher. This was a pretext stop, made by a racially prejudiced officer who conducted an illegal search to find something incriminating on my client because he didn't like the color of his skin."

The judge sighed and addressed the prosecution. "Mr. Hale, do you have questions for the witness?"

Hale turned to me. "You and Mr. Santiago are good friends, correct?"

"Which is why I recuse myself from his cases. And, as I stated earlier, after I realized this was Mr. Santiago's case, I handed the footage over to a colleague."

"But you're here today as an expert witness for Mr. Santiago?"

"I was here at Judge Croft's request. I wasn't expecting to be called to the stand."

"Did you and Mr. Santiago conspire? Did he share evidence with you?"

"No. I would never do that, it's—"

Before I finished, Harper interrupted. "Mr. Hale, all I'm hearing are spurious allegations, not questions. I'm ready to make my ruling."

He turned to Victor. "Mr. Santiago, your case was well-researched and presented. There's little doubt in my mind the search of your client's vehicle was unlawful. No judge in his right mind would allow this evidence into trial. The evidence is suppressed. Your client is free to go."

He turned to the prosecutor, whose face bore the scars of another Victor Santiago ambush. "Mr. Hale, you and I need to confer. I have serious concerns about Officers Connor and Mason's conduct and want a full account of why these public servants are still patrolling the streets of my city. Thank you for your time. The court is adjourned."

CHAPTER 5

Outside the courtroom, it was just another busy day in Justice Town, framed in a rainbow of bureaucratic beige. I was about to head back to the office when I noticed an African American man standing across from me, almost as tall as the doorway he leaned against. His stiff stance made me think military, the "permanently on standby" type, primed for any emergency that would compel him to wade in, guns blazing, to save the day. His hair was a millimeter above a buzz cut, and his nose had a prominent kink as if someone had broken it in some past messed-up situation he was sworn to secrecy about. I'd noticed him in the courtroom, lingering in the shadows. From fifty feet away, the man's steady gaze, as he casually unwrapped a pack of mints, unnerved me.

There was no time to dwell on this. Someone had sidled up to my right shoulder. Catching the stale odor of Marlboro Lights, I knew without turning this was Ron Boone, head of the SEIU 1021, the union representing the Superior Court employees. Ron was straight out of union leader central casting, with ruddy Irish skin and a comb-over. Ron would look scruffy in an Armani tuxedo, not that his socialist leanings would allow him that indulgence.

He scowled at me with a half-squint. "You fucked up in there, Sweeney."

"You were in the courtroom?"

"Stepped in while you were testifying." He poked me in the chest. "Why d'ya have to take the stand? That prick's walking away like he's OJ fucking Simpson."

I raised my arms. "Ron, I was as surprised as the DA. I didn't expect to be called as a witness. You know how it goes."

Ron shook his head. "I'm more than familiar with how shit works. One law for the rich, another for the rest of us. That ain't justice, that's corruption. The man slamming his fist down on good working people."

"Still the revolutionary? Fighting the good fight?"

"People forget we built this country on the backs of working folk."

"I haven't."

Ron backed off a little. "Yeah, I know. You've always been good to us, and the union's grateful 'n' all, but Castillo? He's a piece of work. Should be locked up for life for what he did."

"What's the deal?" I asked, noticing his eyes moistening.

He scratched the back of his neck. "That young teacher, Masie Howard? She was my niece. Twenty-three years old, sweetest girl you ever met."

"I had no idea."

"Yeah, well, I don't go running my mouth off. It's personal."

"I'm sorry for your loss."

"Words ain't gonna bring Masie back, but I appreciate you sayin' it."

I sensed Ron was about to ask me something else when the courtroom door swung open. Paco, Victor, and Oksana marched out, the two pillars of colossus flanking them.

Ron's face flushed; I sensed he was rumbling inside, like a volcano building to an eruption. Paco must have caught on to the same tremor and shot Ron a stare that doused that fire without a

29

word spoken. The action was impressive as it was unnerving. I'd only met a few men like Paco before, men who held their past in their eyes, made sure you knew what they'd done, what they were capable of if you as much as glanced at them the wrong way.

"Yeah, well," Ron said, stepping back like a dog who'd stepped out of line. "We got business to discuss," he added, breaking Paco's stare. "Got something you need to hear." He shuffled away and headed to the bowels of the courts.

As we all stood there, the defense team glorious in victory, another man came running over — Latino, skinny as a two-dollar hamburger, white socks, baggy gray board shorts, black shower slides, the back of his hand inked with *Sangres Norteñas* in crimson cursive.

"*Patrón*, got the car waiting," he said, chin up, proud, like he'd just solved for *pi*.

Paco, seemingly more intimidating than in the courtroom, puffed out his chest. The man carried some serious presence; maybe in another lifetime, he could have been a scene-stealing character actor whose name you never remember but with a face you never forget. His eyes were coal-black pools, giving the impression that nothing existed behind them, as if they were there just for show.

He looked the man up and down. "You know what this place is, *cabrón*?"

The man laughed nervously. "Sure, the courthouse. Everyone knows that, *patrón*."

Paco rested a hand on his shoulder. "Right, the house of American justice, Jorge. The reason we live in freedom is because of the institutions that uphold the law. Do you understand?"

"Yeah, *claro*, I get it," Jorge said, stepping from foot to foot like he needed to sprint to the restroom. "Can we go now? 'Cause I'm double parked. Don't need no more tickets."

Paco massaged his fingers into Jorge's shoulder. "If you know that, why did you come to pick up Francisco Castillo looking like a cheap gangbanger?"

"*Patrón*, I—"

Paco gestured to the group. "Do any of us look like gangsters?"

"No, I just—"

"Now, tell me, what does it look like when a successful businessman gets picked up by someone who looks like you?"

"I don't know."

"Sure you do. Think about it."

"Erm . . ." Jorge bit his lower lip, brain churning until he found an answer that might placate his boss. "Don't look good?" he finally offered.

Paco squeezed Jorge's shoulder tighter. I could see it took all of the man's willpower not to buckle under the pressure of Paco's grip. "Worse, it shows you have no respect. If you want to drive for Paco Castillo, you dress like a professional, *comprendes*?"

Jorge nodded as Paco dug his thumb into the shallow dip between his neck and collarbone. He winced. "Won't happen again, *patrón*. I'll go buy a suit this afternoon, swear to God."

Paco removed his hand, wiped his face like he was done with that bit of business, and moved on to the next agenda item, which happened to be me.

"My apologies, Mr. Sweeney; Jorge is new, comes highly recommended, but still has much to learn."

Jorge stepped back, wiping his nose with his sleeve. I noticed a faint twitch of resentment in his eyes, as if the dressing down had offended him, but he was in no position to argue his point.

"My family and I are grateful you stood up and told the truth, Mr. Sweeney." Paco extended his hand. I took it, figuring a handshake wasn't optional. He slipped a business card into my lapel pocket and tapped an index finger just above my heart. "If you ever need anything from Paco Castillo, let me know." He placed a palm on his own heart. "I am now in your debt."

"No debt owed. Just doing my job."

Paco patted my cheek with his enormous palm, which I was sure could crush my skull in a single clench. "A debt is a debt. Now, you will come to my home tomorrow and will celebrate. I have the very best tequila, right, Victor?"

Victor grinned. "Top shelf."

"Erm, thanks, but I promised to take my son to the hockey game tomorrow night. He's a huge fan."

This made Paco smile. "It is good to keep promises to your children. Come afterward, dress code smart. Victor has my address."

I glanced at Victor, whose look said, *Whatever the fuck you do, Mitch, don't say no. Do. Not. Say. No.*

"Sure," I said as casually as I could. "I can always make time for tequila."

Satisfied, Paco and his entourage walked out into the late-morning sunshine.

I exhaled the breath I'd been holding, looked to the water cooler and noticed the African American man had gone.

I took the card from my pocket, studied the finely embossed print, and had the unsettling feeling Old Nick himself had handed me his calling card, and I'd entered a non-negotiable contract that would end badly for me or anyone who knew me.

Yeah, as Robert Johnson discovered, you make a pact with the devil at the crossroads, and eventually, the debt comes due.

CHAPTER 6

I'm not a fan of hockey. I could imagine plenty more fulfilling ways to spend three hours than watching twelve grown men in fat suits chase three inches of vulcanized rubber. But that was okay; I was there for my son, and when it came to Kurt, there was little I wouldn't do for the kid.

Not that I considered on-ice, gladiatorial combat appropriate entertainment for a ten-year-old, but I figured when those gorillas start piling on top of each other like an eighth-grade fight at recess, the violence quickly spirals into cartoon territory. Not that I'll be vocalizing my opinions anytime soon. Those guys don't look the jocular types, and I'm too partial to my features — serious, with innate intensity and a well-practiced scowl that brings to mind a bargain-basement Black Flag frontman, Henry Rollins (at least, according to a low-tier music mag that once profiled one of my more successful bands) — to have them re-organized in any fashion.

If you were in the market to observe some serious violence played out in the name of sport, stand on the sidelines on a cold morning in Edinburgh, the grass hard from dawn frost, the air like a wet rag to your face, and watch a game of field hockey. That shit's not for the faint of heart. No fat suits here, pal, just a pair of threadbare shin guards and a shot of single malt before you

33

run on the field, all the time praying to your merciful protestant God you wouldn't end up the unfortunate bawbag with a concussion because Hamish "The Hammer" Hamilton swiped you clean around the temple with the butt of his hockey stick.

I'd seen it happen. Spent my junior year at the University of Edinburgh. I was twenty-one, a stupid kid from Northern California who thought he was hot shit. It took me a few years to realize I was actually the original rebel without a clue, the BMX easy rider, the air guitar hero. I formed my first band in Edinburgh, a post-punk, three-man outfit called Einstein's Relatives — we were probably drunker than a Scottish uncle at a wake when we came up with that name. We played two gigs before the lead singer quit after an acid trip that revealed to him the power of the universe within. He bought a one-way ticket to India to find himself. Last I heard, he was still searching.

In Edinburgh, I developed a taste for single malt Scotch and a passion for red-headed, fair-skinned women. My wife, Sierra, rarely ventured out in the sun without a wide-brimmed hat, sunscreen, and a promise to hit the shade between the hours of eleven and three. Kurt was much the same: fair of skin and fair of nature, loved stargazing, watching sunsets, and hockey. Couldn't get enough of it when those fat suits started tumbling across the ice.

Kurt and I were in the bleachers at the Oakland Ice Center, watching the puck drop in the fourth quarter of an exhibition game between the San Jose Sharks and the Anaheim Ducks. It was the day after my court appearance, and the whole Paco Magic circus had cast a long shadow on my well-being. I'd called Victor and asked about bailing on Paco's invitation; his nervous laughter gave me my answer.

Kurt was enjoying the hell out of himself, digging into his cheesy nachos, jumping up and down with every stick foul, skate trip, and high-stick. Damn, it made me feel good. There's a crazy sense of satisfaction you get when your kid's just a kid, not a care in the world, a smile beaming across his face like the sunrise on a spring morning. I wrapped an arm around him, determined to catch some of those rays for myself.

He turned to me and spoke with wide-eyed earnestness: "You know, Dad, it's not your fault what happened."

Kids, they take your damn breath away when you least expect it. I ran a hand through his blond hair, his blue eyes looking at me like I had all the answers. "Yeah, well, you know, it was my fault. All of it."

He crunched on a nacho. "Is that why you had to move out?"

I wasn't expecting this, but I guess that's how it goes with kids; they'll open up when they're good and ready. I rolled with the flow. "Your mom was right to ask me to leave, at least for a little while. Sometimes grown-ups need some space."

"Like a timeout?"

"Yeah, something like that," I said, failing to disguise the crack in my voice.

He looked up at me. "But Dad, when I get a timeout, it's not like for ever or anything."

Sure, I hoped this was all just an adult timeout, and Sierra would forgive me and embrace me again in the warm bosom of her love. But then again, that uneasy sensation that things might not play out as I hoped haunted me like the spirit of bad news yet to come.

I patted Kurt on the knee. "You're right, Kurt, nothing's for ever."

"What did you do, Dad? Was it bad?"

How the hell was I meant to answer that? I could tell him the whole family history of addiction that led to Sierra asking me to move out, how my mother's father had been a drunk of the worst kind: abusive, violent, died at forty-three. But addiction, like prominent foreheads and male pattern baldness, were passed down from one generation to the next in our family. I could handle my alcohol, never had a problem stopping when I'd had enough. Gambling, however, was a sad-sack addiction story all of its own; all of *my* own.

Sports wagers, Indian casinos, online gambling: if it lit up my dopamine, I'd lay my money down. I was dumb enough to think I had it under control; tomorrow, I'd quit the habit tomorrow. Sierra felt otherwise, especially when she discovered the Texas-sized debt hole I'd dug for myself. A gambler can only hide his addiction for so long, and I was deluded enough to think Sierra would never find out, figuring, as all gamblers do, I'd hit a lucky streak and pay off my debts before my wife realized anything was amiss.

The final demands, which landed in the mailbox before I could retrieve them from Sierra's curious hands, sealed the deal. Thirty-three thousand dollars in credit card debt, with an interest rate of twenty-nine percent, would take several life reincarnations on the eternal path to enlightenment to pay back. That's when Sierra asked me to move out. I couldn't blame her, but it still stung like hell, knowing I only had myself to blame.

But honestly, that debt was the least of my worries.

Spin a convincing enough story, and credit card companies help you figure out a payment plan, be damned polite about it, too. Problem was — and I'd neglected to inform Sierra of this item of breaking news — I was another forty-eight thousand dollars in debt to a local entrepreneur named Errol Capriani, who owned several nightclubs around town. Errol wasn't anywhere near as polite as the credit card companies; his method of debt retrieval fell more on the medieval side. I'd avoided him for the past few weeks and had nowhere close to forty-eight grand in my savings account. If Sierra knew, I was sure she'd have divorce papers sent within the hour.

I'd spent too many sleepless nights churning over what I could have done differently: regret, the most futile of human pursuits. Drinking to blunt the pain and anxiety wasn't a long-term solution, but with little else in my toolbox, it was the easiest solution at hand. I expected a visit from Errol or his goons any day. The knock on the door hadn't come, but the future's a bitch, comes after you when the lights are off, when you've stopped paying attention.

How could I explain any of this to a ten-year-old boy? I couldn't. "It's complicated, Kurt. Grown-ups do stupid stuff sometimes," was the best I had.

He seemed satisfied with that answer and turned his attention back to the Human Carnage Ice Capades. I sensed he had a bunch of follow-up questions, but this was as far as he was willing to push for now. Maybe, like most of the human race, he'd stopped short of digging too deep in case he didn't like the answers; this was Daddy's timeout, and he could deal with that. I bit on the inside of my lower lip, hoped he didn't notice the moisture in my eyes, and stood.

"Hot dog?"

Kurt nodded. "Extra ketchup."

"Be right back. And easy on the nachos, save some for your old man."

***

The hot dog stand smelled of sweating onions, stewed meat, and damp dollar bills passed through clammy palms. It reminded me of how hungry I was. I hadn't eaten since sharing a tuna sandwich at lunchtime with one of my researchers. Katie was in her early thirties with dyed pink hair, always dressed in black, and an ardent fan of the board game Settlers of Catan, with the T-shirts, figurines, and coffee mugs to prove it. She spent her lunch break spilling her guts about her boyfriend, asking my advice if she should break up with the guy. I offered some clichéd responses and made my excuses: *Really, Kat, things must be desperate if you're asking me for relationship advice.*

I'd just placed my order with the sullen youth behind the counter when I sensed someone standing close to me before they elbowed me in the ribs. I spun around.

"Jesus, Ron, quit sneaking up on people."

It was Ron Boone, attacking his hot dog with the ferocity of a man who hadn't eaten for days. "Bit jumpy tonight," he said, wiping a smear of ketchup from his chin. "Something on your mind?"

I stuffed the change into my pocket. "Didn't take you for a hockey fan."

"I'm from Boston. It's a goddamn religion out there. One of the last true sports of the working man. You can thank the Northern Irish for that, brought the game over when they emigrated to Canada."

"The Irish have a lot to answer for."

"This country was built on the broken backs of Irish laborers."

"Might get pushback from the Italians and Chinese on that front, Ron."

"Aye, all good, hard-working people, too. I got nothing but solidarity with those folks. United, we will prevail."

I heard my order being called. "Great catching up, Ron; enjoy the game."

He placed a hand on my arm. "That thing I mentioned yesterday after you took the stand for Castillo?"

"I didn't take the stand for him. I was called as an expert witness."

"Whatever, we still gotta talk."

"Not a good time. Can it wait?"

"Not for long, it can't." He shoved a legal-sized manila envelope in my hands. "You know the Union's been negotiating for a fair pay raise. Cost of living's out of control. I've got people commuting in from Martinez and freakin' Tracy because they can't afford to live in the city anymore."

"I don't hold the purse strings, Ron, I just work for the people pulling them."

Ron bunched his free hand into a fist. "Yeah, and those bastards pull 'em real tight. But I watched you in court, not that I agreed with what you did, that's no secret, but you ain't afraid to say what's right."

I grabbed both my hot dogs and squeezed extra ketchup over Kurt's. "What's the angle here?"

"Management keeps saying they don't have the money for cost-of-living raises; I'm calling bullshit." Ron tapped the envelope. "I figured out why they're stalling, and it ain't pretty."

"Summary?" I asked, cradling two dogs in one hand.

"The retired judges. You gotta start digging there, but you got the inside track, access I don't have."

"Access to what?"

Ron screwed up his napkin. "Enjoy the game, Mitch. Shaping up to be a tough scramble till the final whistle, I reckon."

CHAPTER 7

I pulled up to Paco Castillo's driveway in my 2002 eggplant-colored Saab 900 turbo. The valet collected my keys and parked my car in the shadows, hidden behind the Bentleys, Range Rovers, and two Lamborghini Huracans afforded pole position in the social rankings.

Paco lived in the Oakland Hills. The air up there is thick with the aroma of eucalyptus trees and new money. It's a nice place to call home, but you're shoulder-deep in wildfire country. Maybe, like me, Paco refused to dwell on things he couldn't control.

Security was tight. A pat-down with a metal detector, arms extended like da Vinci's *Vitruvian Man*, before entering the gargantuan foyer with a teardrop chandelier the size of a mid-sized family car. A scattering of what I assumed were original oil paintings set in heavy frames peppered the walls. I'm no expert, but glancing at the ornate gold trim and the red-and-black furnishings, I guessed the interior design vibe was Rococo or late Baroque.

Hanging over the wide, curving staircase was a comically oversized portrait of the happy couple: Paco in a suit, Oksana wearing some puffy white ensemble that spoke to me of poodle. It brought to mind the last days of the Russian tsars, where a little more self-awareness might have saved the Romanovs from their eventual doom. Or maybe that's how the fates were meant to play out, and no amount of capitulation to the revolting hordes of peasants would have saved the dynasty from the firing squad.

I wore my only suit, dark blue, matched with a gray shirt. I'd never felt comfortable in a suit, always imagined I resembled an out-of-work bouncer: too broad-shouldered, chest too bulky, neck too thick. On the drive up, I devised a simple game plan for the evening: sip tequila, engage in small talk, assure Paco he owed me no debt, make my excuses, job done, respects paid.

As I walked through the foyer, an attractive young woman in a shimmering gold leotard handed me a glass of chilled champagne. I'm no connoisseur, but it was the best damned champagne I'd ever had. It tasted of wealth, opulence, and the fading last days of an imperial dynasty. In rapid succession, I was offered five different appetizers, which danced on my taste buds like tiny ballerinas.

Looking around, I recognized a handful of guests: a couple of point guards for the Golden State Warriors and a minor celebrity I'd seen on the local talk show circuit, whose name eluded me. I was about to search for Victor and Paco when I felt a tap on my shoulder: Oksana Castillo, looking even more stunning than when I'd seen her in the courtroom, wearing a backless crimson dress that swept over her stilettos like bloodied ocean waves. Her stance, one leg crossed in front of the other, made me think she'd maybe been a dancer in a former life, a life long before Paco Castillo swept her off her feet to a life of unbridled luxury and fire hazard in the Oakland Hills.

"Are you enjoying the party, Mr. Sweeney?" Her accent was eastern European — Russian, I suspected.

"Please, the name's Mitch." I glanced around the room. "Bit more upscale than I'm used to."

"A wife should always know how to make her husband happy. I make sure Paco is happy on his birthday."

"I didn't realize. I would have brought a gift."

Oksana extended a pitying smile. "It was not expected. Paco has everything he needs."

I shrugged off the slight with the good grace it was intended. "Is he here?" I asked, eager to get a jump on my game plan.

"Follow me," she said, heels clicking along the marble floor.

I followed in the downdraft of her perfume. "You like?" she asked, gesturing over the room.

"Erm, it's very . . . regal," I said, aiming for maximum diplomacy.

She shrugged. "Ah, then you don't like."

"No, I like . . . I mean, I admire what you've done with the place, just not my taste, I guess."

"And what is your taste, Mitch?"

"Never really given it much thought. Post-Ikea chic? Mid-century Craigslist?"

By her vague smile, I figured my quip had landed with a dull thud in the teardrop chandelier.

Oksana stopped at the glass door that led outside and stepped back. "Paco is waiting for you."

Through the mottled darkness, I made out the azure shimmer of a swimming pool and loops of yellow lights illuminating the patio. A thick plume of smoke rose from behind an outdoor sectional like the announcement of a new Pope.

Oksana extended her arm. I took her hand; her bones felt brittle, her skin tepid.

"Thank you for what you did for my Paco." She leaned in close and positioned her lips an inch from my ear. "Mr. Sweeney," she said, slipping back into the formal. "If my husband asks you to do something for him, I want you to reject his request. Paco is a happier man without her in his life. She is poison, the worst kind of poison. Do you understand?"

I had no understanding whatsoever but played along anyway. "I'm just here for the tequila," I assured her.

Satisfied, Oksana drew back and floated, a vision in bloody crimson, back to her guests.

CHAPTER 8

Walking onto the patio, the air had a chilled, salty edge, like the rim of a margarita glass, the glistening campfire lights of the East Bay flickering below. As I approached, Paco stood, set his palms on my shoulders, and embraced me like a long-lost son. For a moment, I wondered if he was patting me down for a wire.

"You clean up well."

"Only suit I've got. Take it or leave it."

"We'll take it." Paco reached into a humidor, took out a cigar, and blow-torched the tip. "1956 pre-embargo Churchill," he said, handing me the smoldering cigar. "Fidel's loss is our gain."

I drew seventy years of perfectly preserved Cuban legacy pressed against my lips, the tobacco warm and smooth, the barest secretion of oil dampening the tip.

"Good?" Paco said.

I nodded.

"Hey, take a load off," Victor said, dragging a chair toward me. He was in casual mode: cream linen suit, black linen shirt, feet sans socks in his Gucci loafers.

Paco gestured to a server, an athletic young woman with a ponytail and intelligent eyes. She scuttled away and reappeared a few minutes later with a tequila bottle and three glasses. Paco smiled at her — Finley, according to her name tag — as she set the bottle and glasses on the table. He dismissed her with a curt wave, then lifted the bottle as if about to bestow it with a blessing.

"Código Añejo, 1530," he explained, pouring a generous measure into each glass. "Matured for thirteen years in the belly of a cognac cask. I assure you, my friend, you have never tasted a tequila like this."

"Won't be needing the salt and lime, then?"

"A liquor of this quality demands respect." Paco sat forward and raised his glass. "We toast now — to freedom and American justice."

"Amen to that," Victor agreed.

The sound of three glasses chinking drifted toward the hills.

"Victor tells me you are living in one of his apartments," Paco said.

I shot Victor a concerned look. I was already paranoid enough about this arrangement without Paco Castillo knowing the inside track on my personal life.

Victor laid a hand on my shoulder. "Paco's a careful man, likes to know who he's doing business with."

"I wasn't aware this was a business meeting. Should I be taking notes?"

Paco leaned forward. "Tell me, Mitch, why are you not living at home with your wife and son?"

"It's just temporary," I explained. "I'll leave Victor's as soon as . . ." I was at a loss to finish that sentence, just as I was at a loss a few hours ago speaking with Kurt.

Paco nodded. "We are very different, men and women," he said, considering the curtain of smoke rising from his cigar. "Sometimes, we are tides pulling in opposite directions; other times, we are the ocean waves rushing to the shore in harmony. As men, we must recognize both, and understand that each state is temporary."

"Go with the flow?" I offered.

"It is so. Somewhere, we find harmony, but it is not always so easy."

Under the soft fall of the garden lights, Paco resembled a Mexican grandfather conferring wisdom on his younger family members. But I had to keep matters in perspective. Paco, despite his efforts to present himself as a legitimate businessman, was the head of a brutal criminal organization that he ran with an iron fist. There I was, an Alameda Superior Court official sipping his expensive tequila like we were drinking buddies. I took a generous mouthful and focused on my exit strategy. Paco, though, had other plans.

"Where I am from, we have a saying. *A fuerza, ni los zapatos entran.*"

"Something about shoes?" I asked. My grasp of Spanish was loose at best.

"Literally, Mitch," Victor explained. "You can't force your shoes to fit."

Paco exhaled a plume of cigar smoke from the corner of his mouth, leaving me to draw my own conclusions as Victor slid a legal-sized manila envelope onto the table. The second one I'd received today.

"I find most men I admire have an interesting past," Paco said, looking at the envelope. "Before you studied law, you were a private investigator, correct?"

I pointed at the envelope. "Is that what it says in that file you've pulled on me?" I said, a prickle of irritation burrowing deep: what else had Victor told him? Paco's information was semi-correct. After getting dumped by the woman I imagined was the love of my life, I decamped to Brighton on the south coast of England. After meeting three shady guys in a pub on a rainy Saturday night, I found myself working for a private security company, Knight

Arrow Security, mostly tracking down runaway teenagers. I was good at this. My success rate was one hundred percent. The pay was good, cash in hand, but I ended up blowing most of it at the local racetrack . . . ground zero for my gambling addiction.

"You enjoyed being a private investigator?" Paco asked.

"I liked it well enough. Couldn't see making a career of it."

Paco spread his arms behind the couch. "*Sí*, the past is of no consequence. Now, we look to the future." He pointed his cigar my way. "I have a proposition for you, Mitch. A proposition that could benefit both of us."

I looked to the patio doors where Oksana held court with three men. She craned her neck toward me, no doubt checking to make sure I was compliant.

Paco spotted her looking my way. "Oksana is exquisite, no?"

"You're a lucky man," I said, breaking her glance.

"True, but Oksana is a worrier. I find Russian women to be loyal, but also very possessive. The Soviet times were not so good for women like Oksana, very harsh conditions, husbands and fathers drinking themselves to death." He paused. "When you come from nothing, you will do anything to make sure you never fall back there. I understand this better than anyone. I reassure Oksana, but all that worry? It will age her prematurely."

He sat forward. "Now, we talk business." He slid the envelope across the table and gestured I should open it.

I slipped out several prints of a woman who looked to be in her early forties, tall, with blonde hair past her shoulders, her eyes hidden behind sunglasses the size of saucers. The photographs were taken at a polo match, and judging by the palm trees and cloudless skies, maybe in Southern California, Florida, or some Middle Eastern petro-state. The woman wore what I assumed was regulation polo wear for the season: a white, ankle-length cotton dress, a scarf wound around her neck, and a wide-brimmed blue sun hat. In every photograph, she had a black, gold-tipped cigarette either dangling from the corner of her lips or poised elegantly at the end of her fingers. Paco had a type, I thought: tall, glacial-looking, cold even. Maybe the man enjoyed the challenge of icebergs, then discarded them once he'd carved them into a decent image of himself.

"My wife, Charlotte," Paco explained.

"You mean your ex-wife?"

He shrugged. "It is a complicated situation."

I studied Charlotte's photograph. "English?" I asked. Something about how she dressed made me think she wasn't American. Or maybe it was her haughty, nose-in-the-air attitude. Then again, I figured that kind of aristocratic affectation came with the territory when watching the sport of kings.

Paco chuckled. "English? *Sí*. You know your women?"

"I dated a few Brits back in my day," I explained, then pointed to a photograph where a black cigarette pack with gold lettering poked up from the side pocket of Charlotte's Louis Vuitton handbag. "Those are Sobranie Black Russians, not your liquor store Lucky Strike menthols," I said, dragging the reference from the debris of my mind. Some people have a memory palace. I have a memory dumpster full of useless facts. *The New Yorker* had run an article several years ago concerning a scandal around counterfeit Sobranies produced in China. I had a knack for remembering those kinds of details. Less of a photographic memory; more like a Polaroid memory, where the recollection would fade if I didn't haul it out from time and give it a good shaking.

"Expensive habit," I continued. "You don't see them much in the States."

Paco nodded, impressed. I had to admit I was enjoying myself, exercising that part of my brain again. I'd missed that during the past few years, shuffling papers around a dusty courtroom office. Not that the job wasn't without its perks; they were just becoming less *perkier*.

"Charlotte bore me two children," Paco explained. "Both educated at the best English schools. I don't see them as often as I'd like. Maybe after all that education, they are not so taken with a father who runs a construction business."

I didn't challenge him on this and executed a quick mental calculation. Paco was sixty-five. Charlotte couldn't be more than forty-five, which meant they must have married when Paco was forty and Charlotte was still in her twenties.

I laid the photographs on the table. "Why are you showing me these?"

"Last weekend, Charlotte was at an international polo match at the Empire Polo Club in Palm Springs. Do you know it?"

"Not the social circles I move in."

"Of course," he agreed. "Something is not right. She has not been seen for four days. This is not like Charlotte."

"Maybe she's on vacation?"

"I would know."

"Visiting your children?"

"That I would also know."

"Have you called the police?"

Paco's eyebrows raised in the *are you fucking kidding me, cabrón?* manner.

"Okay, you've been divorced for a while. Does Charlotte tell you everywhere she goes?"

Paco looked toward the house. "Divorced? Not officially. Charlotte refuses to sign the papers."

"Oh, but Oksana said—"

"Oksana has a mind of her own," Paco interrupted. "If it makes her feel better to call me her husband, then so be it. In spirit, we are married. It is just paperwork. It will come in time."

"When was the last time you spoke to Charlotte?"

"Eight years ago. We have lawyers talk for us." He gestured at Victor. "It is better that way."

The penny suddenly dropped with a loud clang. "So, you have your ex-wife — sorry, wife — followed?"

"Understand, Mitch, a man in my position needs to exercise extreme caution."

"Four days isn't that long. I'm sure she'll turn up, but you still haven't answered my question. Why are you showing me these?"

Paco leaned forward and pinned me with those serious-as-fuck eyes of his. "Mitch, I would like you to find Charlotte for me."

I just about choked on my cigar smoke. "Track her down, you mean? No, erm, I think you've mistaken me for someone else. I can't . . . Victor?"

Victor puffed on his cigar, his silence speaking volumes.

"I'm a lawyer at the Superior Court. I can't be seen . . . I'm not your man, Mr. Castillo." I downed the last sip of my tequila and stood. "Thank you for the hospitality, but it's getting late."

Paco waved his hand. "Two more minutes, please. The valet will bring your car. It will take him that long, anyway. Sit, *por favor*."

He called over to the server. Finley mumbled into her radio as she scurried back across the lawn.

"I was a private detective for a heartbeat. I was young; barely knew what the hell I was doing."

"But now you have over twenty years of experience at the Superior Court. You research and make conclusions based on the evidence you have. You know the right questions to ask. Successful investigations begin with asking the right questions, correct?"

"Mr. Castillo, I really think you're better off asking someone who's not part of the criminal justice system to help you. You must have plenty of people in your payroll who can do this kind of . . . research."

Victor laid down his cigar and gave me that professorial look he liked to give a jury at closing statements. "Paco needs someone discreet, an outsider."

Paco placed a hand on my knee. "When you are in the seat of power, there are always those who imagine you are only keeping it warm for them. I must always be looking out for the knife in my heart or the bullet in my back. You understand?"

"Another of your sayings?"

"No, it is my reality."

"Paco is finding it difficult to trust people in his organization," Victor said, sounding like some corporate PR spin doctor. "People talk, or they're forced into talking. An outsider like you? Nobody would suspect you, because no one knows you exist."

My exasperation reached its peak. "You know I can't do this, right? Victor, tell him."

"It wouldn't come without its rewards," Victor explained.

His answer took me aback. "Are you serious? This is insanity, really."

Paco pointed at me. "There is a path out of every bad situation, would you agree?"

"I guess. Depends on how bad the situation is."

"Good. Now, can we also agree that for every problem, if you look hard enough, there is a solution?"

"Where's this going?" I asked.

Victor said, "Paco was impressed with what you did for him in the courtroom yesterday. He would like to make sure you're compensated."

"I already said, no debt owed. Just doing my job."

"How does the number forty-eight thousand sound?" Paco said, leaning back.

My chest tightened, the tequila souring in my stomach. Forty-eight thousand dollars; the exact amount of money I owed Errol Capriani. "How—?" I began.

51

"The Capriani family and I have history," Paco explained. "We have our territory, they have theirs. It's an agreement that has flourished for many years. You do this small task for me, and I assure you, Errol Capriani will not be an issue."

"Let me get this straight," I said. "You're offering me forty-eight thousand dollars to locate Charlotte?"

"It's a small price to pay. You have shown yourself to be upstanding. You have no interest in me or my organization; in fact, deep down, I suspect you might despise a man like me. That is okay; we do not have to fall in love with the people we work with." He smiled. "If we did, matters would get complicated very quickly, no?"

"Bottom line, nobody can know Charlotte's missing," Victor interjected. "That's why we're asking you. You're smart, resourceful, and, most importantly, anonymous. And it's nothing you haven't done before. Just research."

"What about your private investigator, Alma? Isn't that what you pay her for?"

"Alma . . ." Victor paused. "Alma can be a blunt instrument. This needs careful handling from someone not formally attached to Paco or me."

"I wouldn't know where to even start," I said, surprised that I was even considering the proposal. Still, I couldn't deny the temptation of paying my debt to Capriani before Sierra found out had its allure.

"Which means you are thinking about it," Paco said.

Before I could clarify what I meant, Victor pulled a flash drive from his pocket. "All the information you need is here. Photographs, videos, reports. It's a starting point."

"I can't do this, Victor. If someone at the courts found out, I'd lose my job. You know that."

"Who else knows you owe money to Errol?"

"Just me, I guess, and his goons."

"Good. Paco pays Errol in cash. Deal done. You research, ask the right questions, and we keep this between the three of us. You've probably got some vacation time coming up. Use it if you need to. And remember, you'd be doing this for your family, for Kurt and Sierra, not for yourself."

Damn Victor; he always had a way of spinning the intangible so it made sense. Everything was a closing statement for him.

But before I could formulate a suitable comeback, all shades of hell broke loose from their chains at the Castillo residence.

CHAPTER 9

As Victor continued his closing statement, I noticed a squad of ninja-like figures slither from the bushes behind Paco's left shoulder and sweep across the lawn in a disciplined, military formation toward the house.

"Victor, Paco," I said. "I think there's . . ."

The cacophony of helicopter rotors slicing open the air above finished my sentence. A searing searchlight washed the night into a reverse negative of itself. As the downdraft pounded the garden, iron bistro tables, timber-framed lounge chairs, patio umbrellas, and fake cherub statues on plastic plinths took flight, as if scrambling for an escape route.

Under the blast of the searchlights, I lost sight of Paco and Victor. I shouted into the wind. My words were handed right back to me.

As the searchlight panned, more black-clad figures scuttled from the undergrowth. Orders were bellowed and complied with. Several explosions, flash bombs, like giant firecrackers, ignited inside the main house. I could only imagine the panic happening fifty feet beyond the swimming pool, which was now home to several lounge chairs. This was chaos at war with order; for now, chaos had the upper hand.

The grenade smoke billowing into the garden made it hard to see more than a hand's width in front of me. I wondered if this was an attack by a rival of Paco's, then figured it couldn't be. This was too much attention for a rival, too much noise; a hit would have been more subtle — like Paco had said, a knife in the heart or a bullet in the back.

I looked over to where Paco and Victor were sitting; nothing but cigar smoke and expensive cologne. They'd disappeared into the fog. The only other exit I knew of was through the house, and I figured they'd been smart enough to stay well clear of the eye of the storm.

Coughing, I extended a hand and stumbled around. A hand gripped my wrist and wrenched it back until the tendons almost snapped under the strain. My legs buckled, forcing me to my knees to the grass. I looked up. The stark blue eyes of Finley, the server, looked down at me.

She gave a wry smile. "Enjoy your tequila, motherfucker?"

Before I could reply, another hand, much stronger than Finley's, yanked back my head to forty-five degrees. Boots circled me, squishing into the lawn, then a big, ill-humored face grinned at me.

My nostrils twitched at the overwhelming smell of mint-tinged breath coming from the man's mouth. Regaining my focus, I recognized the face; the tall black man I'd seen hanging around the courthouse after Paco's hearing.

He flashed his badge and spoke with a calm, measured disposition, at odds with the surrounding chaos.

"Hell of an end to a nice evening, huh, Mr. Sweeney?" He crouched so his eyes were level with mine. "Special Agent in Charge Eric Landry," he said, flashing his badge. "The FBI look forward to your cooperation in our ongoing investigation into Francisco Castillo."

CHAPTER 10

After being handcuffed to the pool ladder, I was bundled like a sack of meat into the rear of an FBI Ballistic Armored Tactical Transport truck, then escorted in a freight elevator up to the ninetieth floor of the Ron Dellums Building in downtown Oakland.

The fluorescent lights in the FBI field office were harsh, with rows of soulless gray cubicles plotted out like cheap gravestones. Four offices occupied the right wall, their blinds drawn to maintain the impression of secrecy and no doubt provide the cubicle-dwellers a place to aspire to when promotions were being handed out. If it wasn't for the SWAT team drinking coffee outside the breakroom, looking about as celebratory as a conference of funeral directors, it could have passed for an insurance broker's or the office of a moderately successful CPA.

Landry guided me into one of the side offices. After removing his Kevlar vest and utility belt, he still exuded an intimidating presence, bulky, veiny biceps bulging under his black T-shirt. He kept his gun strapped to his hip and looked at me from under the brim of his FBI baseball cap. Up close, the crook in his nose was more prominent, his chin square like the edges of a Rubik's cube, one eye lazier than the other. Special Agent Eric Landry was hardly your leading-man handsome; more disagreeable-looking in the way of a third henchman who gets bumped off in the second act. An excellent face for podcasts. Flipping the light switch, he gestured for me to sit.

"Am I—?"

"No, Mr. Sweeney, you are not under arrest." He threw himself into a chair and stretched for a Diet Coke from a mini fridge. "Unless you're gonna tell me something to significantly change that state of affairs."

"Doubtful. That would entail entering into a conversation, and I'm not doing that without an attorney present."

Landry popped the ring pull. "You're a lawyer, Mr. Sweeney; I don't figure you for a fool."

"Good to know." I gestured at his can.

Message received, he reached for another and sent it sliding down the table Wild West saloon-style.

"Two days ago, you appeared as an expert witness in Paco Castillo's defense. What are you two, best buddies? Was that why he invited you to his residence? Return the favor?"

"No favor, sir; just doing my job as a staff attorney. And, to clarify, I wasn't a paid witness, and I was as surprised as anyone I was called to the stand. Can I go now?"

Landry took a fat swig and sat back. "Now, the way I figure it, this conversation could go one of two ways, Mr. Sweeney. Or can I call you Mitchum? Unusual name, by the way."

"Father was a die-hard Robert Mitchum fan. Most people call me Mitch."

"Right, Mitch, road number one. You refuse to talk until your attorney gets here. It's now, what, one thirty a.m.? If they're even in the mood to pick up the phone, it's gonna be a few hours before they arrive. The tight security checks at the building will delay them some. We'll begin questioning, which should take several hours. In the meantime, we'll make a call and secure a detention notice, which gets you out of this building sometime tomorrow evening at the earliest."

I took a sip of my Coke and had the unshakable feeling I wouldn't warm to the alternative option, either. "Road number two?"

"Easy street. I throw you a few softballs, and you help me out. If I like the answers, you'll be out of here in a few hours, get some sleep, and be back in the courthouse like none of this ever happened. How does that sound?"

"Like it's got a catch the size of a North Atlantic cod haul."

Landry smiled. "You're a smart guy, right?"

"Probably wouldn't be in here if I was."

"You know, Mitch, people end up on the other side of this table for a bunch of reasons. Some are just downright bad people. Others, they've made a dumbass mistake, made a wrong call, trusted the wrong person, found themselves knee-deep in a shit pile that lands them a long stay in a federal institution."

"And you're trying to figure out why I'm here?"

"No. I know why you're here. You're here because you're what I like to call a Dunkey."

"What's that? Like an ass or something?"

"Ever heard of the Dunning Kruger Effect?"

"No, but you're probably about to FBIsplain it to me."

"Cute. Think of it as the opposite of impostor syndrome. It's when people think they're smarter than they are. For instance, the less someone knows about a subject, the more opinions they're gonna have about that particular subject. The peak of Mount Stupidity, it's called. Now, does that make them an expert, the smartest guy in the room?"

"I'd have to guess that's a no."

"Exactly. So, when I get a Dunkey like yourself sitting across from me, my gut tells me he thinks he's got some angle to play the system. What that guy forgets is that the system's survived as long as it has because it is a lot smarter than he is. Are you one of those, Mitch? Think you can game the system?"

"No, sir."

"Of course you're not. Hell, you're a court lawyer, you're practically married to the system, which is why I'd bet my last dime you'll make the right choice here."

I looked through the glass to the anxious faces wandering like ghosts around the gravestones. "You fucked up tonight, right?" I said. "You and the ninjas out there."

A twitch of irritation flicked at Landry's cheek. "Okay, seeing as we're both on the same side, how about you ask me a question, and, if I can, I'll give you an honest answer. Then, I ask you a question—"

"Quid pro quo, Hannibal Lecter-style?" I interrupted. "You guys really do that?"

"Like I said, we're on the same team."

Landry wanted something from me; I just didn't know what. I also figured I was on solid ground. I'd done nothing illegal, but I was as curious as hell to know what had gone down "Okay," I agreed, "but I take the first swing. Why did the FBI raid Paco Castillo's house?"

Landry shuffled, unaccustomed to riding shotgun instead of sitting in the driver's seat. "We received intelligence that a shipment of valuable paintings was being delivered from their holding warehouse to Castillo's residence."

"Were the paintings stolen?"

"Why were you, a state court lawyer, at the home of a suspected gang leader?"

"He invited me."

"To thank you for getting the evidence against him suppressed?"

"Why the paintings?" I asked.

"Castillo has several rare collections stored in various free-ports around the country. The intel suggested he was moving them to his residence. The IRS was extremely interested in this development and called us in to help."

"Because freeports allow storage with no import tax," I said. "If he moves them, Castillo gets hit with a huge tax import bill from the IRS."

"Correct."

"So, you thought you could pull an Al Capone? Nail Castillo on tax fraud? Must be a real disappointment to you guys Alcatraz is closed for business."

"What did you talk about with Castillo?"

"We swapped recipes."

"You're acting pretty damn casual about all this, Mitch," Landry said. "Which makes me think you don't fully realize the implications of your actions." He sat back and pointed a finger at me. "You know what I see? I see a court lawyer getting cozy with a known criminal who just happened to have dodged a very public trial because of your expert opinion when called to do so by Paco Castillo's defense attorney — who, as we've recently discovered, is also a good friend of yours. And let's not forget you're also staying at Victor Santiago's apartment. Might be my FBI training, but that stinks like last week's sushi."

"Then arrest me."

"Who said anything about an arrest? We're just shooting the shit here."

"Sure we are. How did Castillo get away?"

"Our intel was incomplete. Castillo had a fire route to the north of the house and an all-wheel drive vehicle packed and ready to go."

I mentally kicked myself for not figuring it out sooner. Paco may not have worried about shit he had no control over, but he and I differed in one respect: he made preparations for when that shit pile eventually came rumbling downhill. I guess he didn't get to his position without putting some Houdini-level escape strategies in place.

"That must have got you guys pissed. All that taxpayer money on surveillance, agents, the helicopters? I guess you'll be the one answering for that fuckup."

"Is that your question?"

"Just an observation. My question is, why am I here? Your consolation prize?"

Landry tapped his fingers on the table. "Fair question. In the eyes of the law, you've done nothing illegal, though questionable maybe. A government lawyer attending the birthday party of a key FBI suspect. Did you bring him a gift?"

"Wasn't expected," I said, echoing Oksana's words.

"Figures. What do you give the man who has everything, right?"

"An FBI raid and a nice bouquet of fuck-yous?" I offered, though a reply was not required. Another one of my less endearing traits: the compulsion to answer rhetorical questions for the sheer hell of it.

"So, the paintings?" I asked.

"Faulty intel. No paintings, no arrest."

"Guess they don't call him Paco Magic for nothing."

Landry made the *enter* gesture at the doorway. "You met Agent Finley earlier."

The server at Paco's party made her way to the table.

"Yeah. Nearly tore my damn arm off."

"Only nearly?" Finley said, looking my way. "Must be losing my touch."

She laid a deck of photographs on the table before turning and leaving.

"I figured as you're here, you could help us out, off the record," Landry said, turning the photographs my way. "These were taken at Castillo's residence this evening. The FBI would appreciate your help in identifying some attendees."

I looked at the photographs. The quality wasn't great; no doubt taken with a small hidden camera.

"Not really my kind of people."

"Try."

I looked closer. "Okay, two point guards for the Golden Gate Warriors. Oksana Castillo, Paco, Victor Santiago . . . some minor celebrity; don't recall her name."

Landry sighed, gave me that *Are you fucking joking me?* eye roll.

I nodded and zoned in on a pale reflection in the window, and quickly recognized the bulldog posture, the thick mane of gray hair, the huge, ham-sculpted head: Presiding Judge Griffin Harper.

I diverted my gaze to the next photo. Landry obviously hadn't had the time to study the image to any degree, and I didn't feel a burning urge to help him out. I was sure Harper had a damned good reason for being at Paco's birthday bash, just as I did.

"Sorry. Not the kind of parties I usually get invited to. I'm more of a hot-dog-at-the-hockey-game kind of guy."

Landry gathered the photographs. "You know, Mitch, cooperating with the FBI does come with its advantages."

"Like what? Frequent FBI flyer miles? You guys have reward cards?"

"Protection, for one."

"Protection against what?"

"Wrong question. Protection against who?"

"I think you mean 'whom,'" I snarked. "Anyway, why would I need protection?"

"Not saying you do . . . yet."

"But you think I might?"

"No telling what kind of trouble people get themselves into associating with someone like Paco Castillo."

"Like I said, no association. Just a one-off invitation to the man's house. Now, if you keep pushing me on this, maybe I will call my lawyer after all."

Landry nodded. "We've detained you long enough. I'll walk you out."

* * *

We stood for a few minutes, waiting for the elevator. Through the hallway window, the first blades of sunlight broke like shards of gold over the San Francisco skyline twelve miles west. As the elevator opened, Landry popped a fresh mint in his mouth. "A word of advice. Paco Castillo's a dangerous man to be friends with, let alone his enemy."

He let his words sink in as he chewed on his mint.

"And your advice?"

"Don't be his friend or his enemy. Whatever he wants from you, say no, walk away." He handed me his card. "That's my cell. Call it, day or night, I'll answer."

As I stepped into the elevator, I had the terrifying sensation it wouldn't stop falling, would maintain its decent velocity and dump me directly into the bowels of hell, where I was sure Paco Castillo would be waiting, cigar in hand, to deliver me to my fate.

CHAPTER 11

Landry's prediction that I would get some sleep before heading to the office was way off target. My brain was in overdrive, and sleep would have been a faint, wonderful fantasy.

I trudged like a lonesome figure in an Edward Hopper painting through downtown Oakland's dawn-speckled sidewalks. The only other souls out at this hour were the invisible masses who make city living more comfortable for the rest of us: bleary-eyed office cleaners braving the cold and dark to a thankless job, street sweepers brushing gutters with a dull, dead-eyed routine.

Short on alternatives to hang before heading to the court-house, I remembered a hole-in-the-wall bar off 13th Street where the barman mixed a martini that could double as a Molotov cocktail. Back in the day, I'd spent more nights there than I cared to remember. The owner ran an illegal gambling den out of his upper-floor apartment; strictly invitation only. A friend of mine, Jimmy Spanks, who owned Spanky's Vinyl Pantry, out in Berkeley, vouched for me. Jim died a year ago after his addictions got the better of him. It was the wake-up call I needed to get my shit together. It just sucked that it took a good friend hanging himself from the garage rafters to see the error of my ways. I texted Victor to get his lawyer ass down there, ready to take the stand and answer some burning questions.

* * *

The Oriental Oasis was about as *oriental* as a kung pao chicken burrito with a side order of fries. The Double O, as it was called by those in the know, hadn't changed one bit since I last stepped through the doorway ten years ago. Two tubby Chinese men sat at a table Pacman, staring at the screen with the intensity of Rabbis studying the Talmud. An older African American woman spun back and forth on her bar stool, rubbing a cocktail olive around the rim of her glass as if hoping a genie might appear and grant her three wishes.

The stairs up to the gaming lounge were through the back, entry via a password that changed weekly. I'd be lying if I said those buried urges didn't tug at my gut like someone had thrown a rope around them and was dragging me toward that back room. I stood my ground and made a bee-line for the bar.

The owner was called Meng. I had no idea if this was his first or last name; never thought to ask. Meng was dozing behind the bar, fat face resting on his chest, drool unspooling from his lips. He rubbed his cheeks as he stood, his eyes narrowing as he rummaged through his memory to match the face to the drink. Eventually, he offered me a sleep-disturbed scowl.

"Single malt, one rock?" he mumbled.

"Good memory skills," I said, taking a seat. The lady three stools away briefly looked up, decided I wasn't worth the effort, and returned to conjuring up her genie.

"Always remember customers' drinks." Meng poked his temple with an index finger. "It's a gift."

"You don't say. All the same, too early for me, Meng. Just tonic water."

He poured the tonic over a glass of ice and pointed a potsticker-thick finger my way. "Long time no drink?" He laughed like this was the wittiest thing he'd come up with for months.

"Good one. Just killing some time."

He gestured around his tiny kingdom of sadness. "Everyone in here killing time."

"And you?"

"Me? Ha! Too tired to kill time. Let time kill me, easier that way."

I sipped my tonic. It was flat as Kansas. "You know, for a barman, you're no ray of sunshine."

"You want sunshine?" He gestured at the door. "Go outside. Three fifty . . . please."

"For tonic water?"

He shrugged. "Inflation. Blame government monetary policy."

Just then, the door swung open. Victor sauntered in, freshly groomed and suited up, Gucci shoes polished within an inch of their soft, leathery lives.

"I'm glad one of us had a good night's sleep," I snapped.

Victor scouted the establishment. "Well, this is swanky," he said, running a finger over the layer of dust covering the bar. "Your local?"

"Once upon a lifetime."

I noticed the woman three stools down adjusting her skirt and throwing a wide, lipstick-blotted smile Victor's way, her wish to meet a tall, dark, handsome stranger granted.

"You want a drink?" Meng asked Victor. "You look like a man who likes Scotch, the expensive kind, am I right?"

"Only after six in the evening, and before a medium-rare ribeye. You got one of those?"

Meng shrugged. "I got chips, peanuts. Maybe find some *chicharrones* in the back for my Mexican clients. You want some *chicharrones*?"

"I'm all good on the pig fat, thanks."

66

As Meng shuffled back to his stool, I lowered my voice. "What the fuck is going on? I've just spent hours being interrogated by the FBI because of your client, Paco fucking Castillo."

"Yeah, sorry we ran out on you last night. I was going to call you, but you know how it goes."

"No, I don't know how it goes. Explain to me why I'm caught in the middle of whatever the fuck it is you've got me involved in."

"Paco's only trying to help." Avoiding touching anything on the bar, Victor used his foot to hook a stool and dragged it closer to me. "Look, this is an easy win. You perform some light detective work for Paco; no big deal. In return, he pays your debt to Capriani, and Paco and Charlotte figure out their disagreement. I'll be honest: it's the best offer you're going to get."

"The best offer I'm going to get? Putting my career on the line working for the head of a criminal gang?"

"Legitimate businessman. Paco's never been convicted of anything illegal, not even a parking ticket. And dial down the drama. No one's losing their job over this, because no one will ever find out."

"You know I can't agree to this."

"Paco's very insistent. Thinks you're the man for the job."

Victor looked at me with that earnestness he reserved when addressing a jury. "Look, I can tell you're conflicted. I get that, but you're not looking at the upside. Debt cleared; Sierra never finds out. Isn't that what you want?"

"What's in this for you, Vic? You've always got an angle; there's no way you're doing this out of the kindness of your heart."

He took a moment. "Okay, we've been friends way longer than I care to remember. Let's say I'd prefer if you were the one who found Charlotte, not the usual dumb muscle Paco hires in these situations."

"Why?"

"Oksana's desperate for that ring on her finger, and Paco wants to keep her happy. If Charlotte's missing, then that's a problem for everyone."

"Because a missing person can't sign divorce papers."

"Which leaves me with one very unhappy client."

"I still don't understand why you can't just hire a private investigator."

"Like I said, Paco likes to keep things discreet, in the family."

"I'm family now?"

"You've got no skin in the game, and Paco likes you. Accept the offer, locate Charlotte, get your debts paid, and focus on repairing your marriage. Don't tell me you're not tempted."

I couldn't deny the temptation was strong, but I wasn't about to let Victor know that. "Not the point."

"At least you haven't said no," he said, scooching himself off the stool. "If you won't do it for Paco, do it for me."

I caught the subtext: *After all I've done for you, buddy, it's payback time.*

From his pocket, Victor took out the flash drive he'd shown me last night and slipped it into my hand. "You'll make the right choice," he said, and tapped my shoulder.

"Even if I agreed, Vic, this is way too risky."

He flashed that way too-charming grin my way. "Was a time you'd jump at this kind of risk."

As he walked toward the door, I called out, "And if I refuse?"

"Tempting as that might sound, I really don't think it's an option." He waved his arm like he was dismissing a courtier. "And find yourself a new local. This place is depressing as hell."

As the door snapped into its frame, the woman three stools down spoke up. "Hey, honey, your friend leave already? He was one good-looking man."

"Married, three kids," I said. "His husband's a real nice guy, though."

She mumbled into her cocktail. "Shoot, why all the fine ones gotta be gay or married these days?"

I figured she didn't expect an answer.

I downed my drink and regretted not taking Meng up on his offer of a Scotch on the rocks, then slapped a five-dollar bill on the bar.

He snatched the bill, didn't ask if I required change. "You leaving already? Got a game tonight, high rollers. You want the password?"

"I'm a changed man, Ming. Keep that password to yourself."

"Okay, see you in another ten years . . . if I still here. By the way, my name not Meng, it's Mikey," he said, laughing.

He was still chuckling as I pulled the door shut. *Yeah*, I thought, *if I say no to Paco Castillo's offer, gotta hope we're both still shooting the shit and laughing in ten years, Mikey boy.*

PART 2:
COURTING FAVORS

CHAPTER 12

I'd been shuffling around the office for a couple of hours before my team slunk in. Katie was first, skin sallow, eyes bloodshot, dyed pink hair unkempt. I guessed she'd been up all night playing Settlers of Catan or arguing with her boyfriend. Neither bode well for a productive day's work.

Tye, the newbie on the team, was next in. African American, puppy-dog handsome, always dressed like he was out to impress, with a tailored suit, crisp shirt, and a pocket square to finish the ensemble. Tye had a solid work ethic, had put himself through law school working a series of dead-end jobs.

Last in was Muriel, the matriarch of the team. Muriel was five years closer to retirement than I was, highlighted blonde hair with a middle parting as if channeling the spirit of 1990s-peak Jennifer Aniston. She always wore slacks and a sensible blouse just loose enough to disguise her ongoing weight problem. She was part of the office furniture. I couldn't imagine the place without her.

We exchanged pleasantries. Muriel brewed coffee and handed out leftover cookies from her book club, like she did every week. I scarfed three. I hadn't eaten since the finger food at Paco's, and when the sugar hit my blood, it mainlined straight into my brain. My mind shot off someplace else as I reached into my jacket pocket for the flash drive Victor had handed me.

"You good, boss?" Tye asked, looking at me through narrowed eyes.

"Top notch," I assured him, forcing my focus back into the room, then gave them a minor pep talk. Not that they needed it. The cases they were working on needed little handholding, and besides, I had somewhere else to be. Bundling under my arm the files I'd been collating since dawn, I headed out.

* * *

"Come to grace my day with a ray of sunshine, Sweeney, or piss all over it?" Presiding Judge Harper said as I entered his chambers. "Because if it's the latter, get in line." He was sitting behind his mahogany desk, which was stacked with papers and a collection of framed family photographs.

"Already hit the bathroom earlier, your honor."

He cleared his throat with a sharp cough. "Sit, you've got three minutes."

I laid the folder on his desk. "Thought you might need this."

His eyebrows rose like two curious caterpillars.

"Officer Theodore Connor's conduct record? Three sustained complaints for racial profiling. He completed the mandatory training and psych eval, but he was back on the job within a week on each occasion. His wife reported two accusations of spousal assault to the OPD in the past year. Both charges were dropped. We don't know if she dropped them voluntarily or someone persuaded her." I paused. "And the icing on the cake: the illegal search of Paco Castillo's vehicle. Figured you'd want to read them over when you've got an idle moment."

"Sweeney, what in God's name is an 'idle moment'?" he said, waving an arm over the mountain of files. "Why are you here, exactly? No bull crap. I'm way too old and crabby for bull crap."

"The suppression of evidence motion?" I said, scooting forward. "You raised concerns about Officer Connor's conduct. He's a liability to the force. The OPD has a duty to suspend and fire Connor. The sooner, the better, in my opinion."

Harper suppressed another cough and leaned back, his enormous girth spreading across his chair. "Not my call. It's a matter for the Oakland Police Oversight Board. Until Officer Connor commits a crime and gets hauled in front of a judge in my court, my hands are bound tighter than my prostate. Figured you knew all this already, what with you being an expert witness these days."

I did know that. I was fully aware of the due process, but Connor was my Trojan horse. "Of course, but I figured the files might save some time when they eventually haul Connor's ass in here for something a lot worse than harassing people of color."

Harper nodded. "That it? That's my ray of sunshine?"

"I heard the FBI raided Castillo's house last night. Thought that might brighten your day."

"It would if the Feds hadn't bungled the entire operation."

"Kicker is," I said, steering the conversation back on track, "Castillo gets raided the same night as his sixty-fifth birthday party. The place was full of his family and friends. What are the odds?"

Harper kept his gaze steady, no overt body language or tell that might give him away. "One hell of a birthday surprise," he said. "Now, do you have any other urgent news bulletins to share that I'm already aware of? The Titanic hit an iceberg? Brangelina no longer a couple? Michael Jackson liked young boys?"

"You might want to update your cultural references. You know, for the young people in the courthouse."

"I'll bear that in mind. Any other sage words of advice?"

"No, just dropping off the files, you know, just in case they need to find their way somewhere else."

Walking out, I figured I'd got the information I was fishing for. Harper had a solid poker face. He'd played it cool as an ice-carving when I brought up Paco's party. He hadn't mentioned being there, even though I'd seen the photographs to prove otherwise. I'd arrived late at Paco's that night. He must have left early, before the shit went down with the FBI. Still, the question pricked at the back of my brain; why was Alameda's Presiding Judge attending a birthday party for a suspected leader of an organized crime gang?

* * *

Later, at the courthouse café, I was still mulling the question over while chomping on a ham and cheese sandwich. Midway through my second bite, someone pulled up a chair across from me, sat, and settled a tray of food on the table that could have fed three.

"Ron," I said, gesturing at the tray. "Diet's right on track, then?"

He ignored the remark. "So, you read what I gave you?"

"Been a busy couple of days. I'll get to it."

"Make sure you do," he said, forking his side of mac and cheese. "Got people counting on me to do the right thing for our members."

"I don't know what you think I can do."

He jabbed his fork at me. "Do something. What I gave you is gonna set you on the right course. We're on a tight deadline. Negotiations start up in a couple of months, and I'm not wading in there on the back foot like some rookie. You don't win labor negotiations with hope and goodwill; you win them with information. Information your opponent doesn't know you have."

"Promise, I'll take a look after lunch," I assured him.

"You do that." He dug into his mashed potato as if he were looking for a gold nugget buried in the mountain of starch. "Nice suit, by the way. Job interview?"

"Going to an event at Kurt's school," I lied. "I won't have time to get home and change."

"Don't forget to shave. It looks like you haven't slept for a week. Not a good look on you, buddy."

"Always a bonus getting sartorial advice from you, Ron."

He smiled. "Here to help, that's Ron Boone."

He stopped eating for a moment. I could tell it took some serious willpower on his behalf. "Heard the Feds raided Castillo's house last night," he said, diving back into his food as soon as the question left his lips.

"You heard right."

"A bust, right? That cocksucker's got the luck of the Irish about him."

"I think he's Mexican."

"You know what I mean." He stuffed a wedge of meatloaf into his mouth. "Someday, though, right? I mean, the man's luck's gotta run out. Everyone's does."

CHAPTER 13

Later that afternoon, Sierra called and asked me over to the house "to talk stuff through." She didn't elaborate; I didn't push. Sometimes the questions we don't ask are the only things keeping hope alive.

She'd ordered pizza, a bad omen. If she'd asked me over to discuss reconciliation, I was sure she would have made the effort and cooked a meal. As Sierra cleared the plates, she granted me the privilege of tucking the little guy into his bed. I milked this for all it was worth, delaying the inevitable, whatever "stuff" Sierra intended to talk through.

The evening was warm, and we sat on the front porch overlooking the street. *God, I missed this*, I thought as Sierra sat across from me. I missed my home, missed Sierra; missed Kurt like someone had torn a limb right off me. I would have gladly blurted all this out, but I knew better. Full disclosure has its place, but not at nine o'clock at night under a waning moon, a sky full of stars, and a faint stirring of hope warming the heart.

I took a sip of the Scotch I'd poured earlier. "So, why the invite?"

Sierra looked at the street. "I meant what I said, Mitch."

"You say a lot of things," I said, fishing for exactly what she was referring to.

She tucked her legs under her and brushed the hair from her face. She looked so damned radiant under the fall of the porch light I could have proposed to her all over again. The dark blue sweater she wore loosely across her bare shoulders brought out the emerald shimmer of her eyes, the porch light falling softly on her face. It took all of my willpower not to jump out of my seat, lift her in my arms, carry her into the bedroom, strip off her clothes, lose myself in her body.

I still couldn't believe it had come to this. My wife of fifteen years was ten feet away from me, and I was sitting there like a nervous teenager. It was as if we'd never known each other, never laid skin on bare skin, never looked into each other's eyes as we made love. All that seemed distant now, a memory I was certain was real, but was so out of reach I was clueless about how to trace my way back to it. And worst of all, I knew I was to blame.

"I don't think you're taking this seriously. I've talked to a realtor."

Taking another swig, I tempered my response. "And?"

"I'm concerned about Kurt. He starts high school in a few years. You know the state of schools in Oakland. Three shootings last year, and the education's one of the worst in the state. He's our only child. We should do right by him."

"We could try private."

Sierra laughed. "Oh right, you just came into an unexpected windfall?"

I bristled at the comment. If only she knew how close to the bone she'd picked.

"St Jude's, then. Holy Names? Small classes, third of the price of private, kids wear uniforms."

"Seriously? We haven't set foot in a church for years, and we sure as hell aren't Catholic."

"I carry a lot of guilt. That's gotta count for something," I said, hoping to lighten the mood.

Sierra shook her head. "And when they start looking into me? Dig up all those articles I wrote on those Vatican One nut-jobs sheltering in a bunker in Mountain View waiting for the apocalypse? I doubt a confession and a few Hail Mary's will get us within spitting distance of a Catholic school. You are seriously delusional if you think that's going to happen."

That remark stung. I tried not to let it leave a mark and U-turned the conversation. "You can't sell the house without me. We're both on the deed."

"We also share a bank account. That didn't stop you from running up fifty thousand dollars of gambling debts."

"I'm figuring out how to pay that back."

"Figure harder, I'm—"

Our conversation was suddenly interrupted by a swarm of pocket rockets; miniature replicas of full-sized motorcycles around two feet high and sounding like high-pitched sewing machines buzzing the street. There must have been fifty of them, ridden by grown men pulling wheelies as they puttered past. They'd have appeared more threatening if they didn't remind me of those tiny cycles ridden by clowns around a circus ring.

"Case in point." She gestured to the street. "Who knows what weapons they're carrying?"

"Big leap there, Sierra."

She looked toward Kurt's bedroom as if to stress her point.

"There's something else?" I said, picking up on Sierra's body language, a skill I had down pat by now. "The real reason you asked me here?"

"I've been speaking with an attorney."

The sentence needed no modifier.

I rested my drink on the table. "Seriously? It's only been a few months. 'Let's see how things play out, time apart for a while,' that's what you said. And what about Kurt?"

"I owe it to you to let you know where things stand," she said, the buzz of bikes dissolving into the night. "No rash decisions, just weighing my options, that's all."

"You mean you're weighing up your exit strategy," I said, holding my anger back as best I could, though I sensed it leaking out of me like sweat.

"It's not like that."

"Then tell me what it's like. From where I'm sitting, you just told me you want to sell, move away, and you've hired a lawyer. Sounds pretty cut and dry to me."

"You're overreacting."

"Me?" I slugged back another. "Jesus, I'm making amends, Sierra. Seriously. I've got the credit card companies off my back and haven't gambled for eight months. I'm fixing this."

She took a moment, as if figuring out how to phrase what she had to say next. "Do you think you're looking for an escape? Because if that's the case, I need to know."

"An escape? From what?"

"Your job? Me? Kurt? I'm having a hard time understanding that if you love us, like you keep insisting you do, why do you do everything you can to push us away?"

"You guys are all I've ever wanted."

"So why put it all on the line? I don't get it."

I took another sip. "Honestly? The thrill, probably. You know, things could fall either way, good or bad, win or lose."

"Mostly lose."

I took that one on the chin.

"Mitch, I really think you should take some time to figure out what you want."

"I know what I want. I want you; Kurt. This, I want this, all of it."

"You might want it, but you need the gambling more. I think you've always had this restlessness. I don't know, maybe you imagined your life would turn out differently, and gambling is your way of dealing with that."

I wanted to argue with Sierra, tell her she was all shades of wrong, but deep down, she'd hit a seam of truth, I just hadn't had the guts to admit it to myself yet. I chugged the last of my Scotch, the ice cube clanking against my teeth. "Seems you've already decided. Not much else to say, is there?"

"No, I haven't, it's—"

"Look, I can't deal with this right now," I interrupted, slamming the glass down with greater force than I intended, startling Sierra. "Sorry, didn't mean . . . it's just that I've had a couple of days from hell."

"Want to talk about it?"

Sure, I wanted to talk about it, wanted to pour my heart out right there on the porch, lay it at Sierra's feet like some kind of sacrificial offering, tell her about the forty-eight grand I owed, Paco's offer, and the FBI grilling. But I held back. Spilling all that was as good as throwing gasoline on the fire, and I wasn't ready to torch my entire life just yet.

"Have it your way," she said, uncurling herself from the seat. "Oh, I almost forgot, someone left you something on the porch yesterday. I'll go get it."

Sierra headed to the kitchen. A few moments later, she came back with a brown paper bag. I reached inside. My stomach twisted in on itself as I removed the box of meat tortellini, the bright red Capriani's Deli logo screaming from the packaging.

"Found it on the doorstep when I came home. The note just said it's for you, nothing else."

Errol Capriani was sending me about as subtle a message as he knew how to send; payment was due. I dug my nails into my palms to give my panic someplace else to be.

"You okay?" Sierra asked.

"Yeah, all good. I did a favor for someone at the courthouse. They're just saying thanks."

"Right," Sierra said, with a look that indicated she didn't believe a word, but played along anyway, because she was too tired to argue.

I grabbed the package and stood. "Tell Kurt I'll see him next week — unless your lawyer's already advising you to take out a restraining order."

That last remark was unnecessarily callous, but I had the childish compulsion to snatch back the narrative with a killer closing line before I left, another one of my less attractive qualities.

"Mitch, don't—"

I didn't hear the rest of Sierra's words. I'd already zipped up my jacket and hoofed it down the same road as the pocket rockets.

* * *

Back at my apartment, I downed two Old Fashioneds and prepared myself a third. I was exhausted, but I knew any attempt at sleep would be an exercise in futility. Sierra's words played on repeat. Maybe she was right. Maybe I had become restless, and maybe I gambled because I was spiraling into some clichéd, middle-aged-man drama that made me yearn for the days when things were less predictable, less rote. The thought set me on edge. I needed something else to focus on, so I dropped the needle on PJ Harvey's "Rid of Me". As I let the gritty guitar riffs shake away the cobwebs, my phone buzzed. In my half-drunken stupor, I picked up, "Yeah?"

"Mitch," the voice said. "Maybe you should look outside."

I moved to the window and drew back an inch of blinds. My Saab, which I'd left at Paco's the night of the raid, was parked outside. Leaning on the hood of the car was Jorge, Paco's driver, wearing a suit that seemed tailored for a man twice his size and status.

Jorge looked up, tilted his hand to the shape of a handgun, shook it twice at me, miming what I imagined was the sound *pop pop*, then smiled, his gold-tipped teeth glinting under the streetlights.

"A working man needs his car, no?"

I watched Jorge climb into the black SUV waiting for him, then looked over to the box of Capriani's finest meat tortellini taunting me over the breakfast bar.

"My offer still stands," Paco Castillo said. "But remember, Mitch, everything has an expiration date."

CHAPTER 14

Shuffling into the office the following morning, I sensed something was off kilter. Work an office job long enough, and your spidey senses start tingling at the tiniest fluctuation in moods. Like a fisherman searching for answers in the ebb and flow of tides and the shifting clouds, they all pointed to something deeper: a calm fishing day ahead, an unsettled weather front, unpredictable swells looming from the depths. That morning, my immediate sense was that of a gathering storm. I'd ignored it for most of the morning until just before my lunch break, when I looked up and noticed Muriel loitering at my office door, with Katie and Tye flanking her.

"The three musketeers," I said, offering a smile. I made a big deal of looking at my watch. "Lunchtime already? What we thinking? Tacos?"

Muriel cleared her throat. She glanced nervously at Aramis (Kat) and D'Artagnan (Tye); Muriel would have to be Athos, which would make me the swashbuckling lush, Porthos; a fantasy I entertained for a few seconds before the absurdity kicked in. Still, once the idea had taken root, I couldn't dig it out.

"Okay, I'm no psychic, but I'm figuring this isn't taco-related." I fixed my gaze on Athos. "Muriel, you're obviously the spokesman. Shoot."

"Spokesperson," Aramis snapped. "It's spokesperson."

I nodded. "Right, as usual, Kat."

Muriel straightened her posture. "We just want to let you know that we know, Mitch."

I remained calm, gave nothing away. "Know about what, Muriel?"

Between her fingers, like a rosary, Muriel twirled the sea-blue evil eye pendant she'd bought while on vacation in Turkey. She'd given me a similar souvenir, which I'd hung off my desk lamp. Judging by recent events, the object was blissfully unaware of its limited function in life, or else its nascent charm had by now worn off.

"I think I speak for all of us," she said, gesturing to her sides like a flight attendant directing me to the emergency exits. "You should have told us about this. It's not right. Well, I . . . we, we all have an opinion, because we think it's only fair we're allowed opinions. Even though we report to you, we should have the freedom to speak out. And I know maybe we shouldn't have done what we did, and it's privileged information, but when it's something that directly affects us, then we have to speak up because if we don't—"

I held my hand up. "Muriel, would you like a bigger stick?"

Athos looked at me, momentarily derailed from her ramblings.

"To poke around that bush you've been beating around for the last two minutes?"

Katie, who had lost her patience, leaned in and stabbed an index finger on the envelope Ron Boone had handed me at the hockey game. With the Paco Castillo incident weighing heavy, I hadn't gotten around to reading it, but had slipped out the first page of the document, which had the words *Alameda Superior Court Staffing and Pay Review* in red type across the top. I had forgotten to tuck the document back inside the envelope. I couldn't blame the three musketeers for looking, I'd have done the same, but I was on the back foot. They'd read the document; I hadn't.

"Snooping, huh?" I said, tapping the envelope. "Got to say I'm a little disappointed, and—"

"You want to explain?" Katie interrupted, folding her arms across her *Nobody Wants Your Frickin' Sheep* T-shirt, which I picked up on as a Settlers of Catan reference, having played the game only once, coming in last with a surplus of sheep that could have heralded the beginning of the settlement's most profitable woolen mill.

"I'd love to explain, but I don't have a clue what this is about."

"Don't treat us like children," Muriel said, throwing some Athos badassery my way. "You really thought you could keep this from us?"

"Yeah, and how did you, like, even get that information?" Katie asked. "Isn't it confidential?"

I had a choice: feign ignorance or come clean. They were a dedicated team and deserved the truth. "Ron Boone. He gave me the documents."

"Boone?" Tye asked. "The SEIU union guy? Looks like he fell into a clothes dumpster outside a homeless shelter?"

"Yes, Tye, that guy," I said. "Now, apart from Ron's obvious lacking in the sartorial department, he's been a good friend of the court staff, fought for all our raises over the years."

"Yeah? What did he negotiate last year? Not even close to a cost-of-living raise," Katie protested. "May as well just piss that two percent into a bucket, throw it in the bay."

"It's been a challenging year, no doubt. Tax revenues are down," I countered, though my sympathies were firmly aligned with my team.

Katie scowled. "Maybe Alameda County could start taxing big tech. Get those rich fucks to pony up for affordable housing, community outreach. You know, stuff that actually helps people."

"It's a delicate balance," Muriel said. "Tax them too much, and they pull up stakes, move to Texas or someplace with low taxes, and take all the jobs with them. Fiscal responsibility; you've got to consider that."

Tye cocked his head. "Damn, all this time, and I've been sharing an office with a Republican," he said, leaning back as if shedding some extra distance between him and Muriel. "You got a MAGA hat stuck in your desk drawer, Miss M?"

He'd always called Muriel that since his first day on the job. I thought he'd grow out of it at some point. Three years later, he was still calling her Miss M. I figured his mom had brought him up right, probably proud as punch he was working at the court.

Muriel turned to Tye. "It would be none of your business if I did. And, for your information, no, I do not have a MAGA hat hidden in my desk or anyplace else."

"Yeah, well, I wouldn't give a flying shit if those tech bros fucked off to Texas or wherever," Katie said. "Entitled, arrogant dipshits who don't give a fuck about anyone else's feelings."

I sensed her subtext was less a subtext and more of a glaring, bold font headline, especially since only a couple of days ago, she'd complained to me about an app developer she'd been dating who was now ghosting her.

"So, what do we do?" Muriel asked. "We can't just ignore it."

"What would you like to do about it?" I asked, playing for time. "Not just Muriel, all of you."

Katie snatched the baton. "Go to the papers; expose the corruption. I mean, that's, like, millions of dollars in taxpayer money they're wasting. Bet if we dug deeper, we'd find this shit goes way back."

"Okay," I said, more curious than ever as to the contents of the documents. I made a promise to myself that I'd read them that night. "A little aggressive as a first step, but I can't fault your enthusiasm."

"There's no concrete evidence," Muriel said. "Nothing we could take to a journalist if we wanted to go that route, which I'm not sure we do."

"I agree with Miss M. Don't rock the boat yet. We don't want to get our asses fired over this."

I sensed Tye had been roped into this against his better judgment. But he was young; this was his first job, and his hesitation in confronting management came with the territory.

"What do you think, Mitch?" Muriel asked.

"You all make valid points," I said, my ass getting sore from sitting on the fence. "Let's regroup after the weekend. Something like this needs careful consideration, a strategy. Sound good?"

The three musketeers looked at each other, nodded, and slipped their rapiers back into their sheaths, at least for now. As the lead musketeer's privilege, Athos had the last word.

"Okay," Muriel said. "But we can't brush this under the carpet. We trust you to do the right thing, Mitch. Will you do that?"

CHAPTER 15

Didn't see the car that hit me. Failed to note the license plate, make, or model, nor was I granted the satisfaction of flipping off the driver.

I was homeward bound, five thirty, the fading rays of a low sun bestowing a hazy yellow glaze over Lake Merritt. The foot traffic remained light: no joggers or cyclists threading the fine spaces between each other, no office workers enjoying the last of the day's sunlight. The only activity came from a gaggle of Canada geese strutting the shoreline and two East Bay Municipal trucks dipping curious elephant trunks into the water to suck up the remains of the marine life that had perished in the algae bloom.

I'd just crossed onto Sixth Street, when a vehicle pulled dangerously close, scraping my rear seat stay. The bike wobbled. I braced for the worst. In those micro-seconds between the hit and landing on the sidewalk, I had no profound vision of my life passing before me, just a banal observation of how damned hungry I was. Had the most surreal of thoughts: would I die hungry? And when I arrived at my forever location, would they offer dinner or at least a light snack before calling up or down to the administrative corridors of the afterlife to alert them to my arrival?

I catapulted over the handlebars, smacked onto the sidewalk, and felt the skin scrape from my right cheek like a match across sandpaper. Scrambling to my feet, I scanned the traffic for the car that hit me, but all I heard was the throaty roar of a V8 making its getaway into the black hole of the Webster tunnel.

A handful of good Samaritans offered help and swore they'd seen the offending vehicle, before arguing amongst themselves about its color and make. I left them to it and pushed my bike four blocks to Jack London Square, handlebars askew, cheek aflame, ego bruised to hell, all the time doubting the decision I'd made the previous night to accept Paco's offer.

* * *

Pushing open my apartment door, I smelled expensive cologne and coffee brewing, sure signs that I had uninvited company.

Victor had made himself comfortable on the couch while Paco flipped aimlessly through the collection of vinyl albums I'd carted from the family home. Shrugging, he picked up a family photo taken in Yosemite last year. It reminded me of better times, but in my darkest of nights I wondered if I'd placed the photo there just to torture myself.

"Very nice family," Paco said. "You must miss them." His tailored suit and hulking presence seemed at odds with the compact apartment. Watching him pace the floor was like observing a great white trapped in an aquarium; I half expected him to nudge his forehead against the floor-to-ceiling windows, looking for a way out.

I glared at Victor. "Just let yourself in?"

He lifted his jangle of keys, then sat up as he noticed the trickle of scarlet running onto my collar. "What the holy fuck happened to you?"

"Minor disagreement with a car," I said, touching the blood, now drying on my cheek like toasted cheese.

Paco called into the kitchen. "Jorge, bring him a wet towel. Not white. Dark if he's got one."

Jorge, wearing a dark blue suit and white high-ball sneakers, lumbered from the kitchen, my coffee press in one hand, mug in the other.

"Make yourself at home, Jorge," I said, throwing myself into a chair, my bones still vibrating from the shock.

"Yeah, sure, just getting the boss a coffee."

Paco nodded at Jorge, who set down the coffee tray with a sigh I took for irritation; the guy was probably at Paco's beck and call 24/7. "Sorry, homie," he said, gesturing for me to stand back up. "Boss's orders."

He rummaged in my pockets, took my cell phone, and asked me to enter the passcode, then checked the phone was working and frisked me. "Did you get beat up or something?"

"Or something," I said.

"Right on." He turned to Paco. "All clean, boss." Then turned to me. "I'll go get a rag. Where—?"

"My rags? Kitchen island, third drawer."

Jorge shuffled into the kitchen and returned with a damp towel. "So, you sure you didn't get your ass kicked?"

"Like I just said, got hit by a car."

The information sunk in slowly, like a fly drowning in molasses. He gestured at my helmet on the table. "You should get yourself a real bike, a big-ass Italian one, get you the fuck out of trouble. That cycling shit's way too dangerous."

"Thanks for the advice."

"Eh, you're welcome," he said, tapping my shoulder, which recoiled back into my body as if in search of more pain.

Paco gestured for Jorge to stop talking.

"Going to leave a mark, no?" Paco said, pointing at my face.

"Traumatic events have a habit of doing that."

"You saw who did this? The car, driver?"

"Hit and run. I figured I'd get sideswiped at some point; it was just a matter of time."

"You know, Mitch, if this happened to me, I would wonder, why did this person drive away? Why be in such a rush? As you said, it was an accident. A good citizen would stop and make sure you were okay, no?"

I hadn't considered it until then, but once the idea slipped in there, it burrowed deep like a splinter. "You think it was deliberate?" I asked.

Paco shrugged as Jorge handed him his coffee. "When you are in my position, you cannot afford to take anything at face value, you understand?"

"Well, I'm not you."

"No, you are not. But you are now working with me, so we must look at every angle of every accident, anything that is out of the ordinary."

"I'm sure it was just an accident. I don't know anyone who'd want to—"

"*Sí, claro,*" Paco interrupted. "It was a coincidence, maybe? You believe in coincidences, Mitch?"

"They happen."

He sipped his coffee and smiled. "Okay, if you say so."

"Why the surprise visit?" I asked, hoping to change the subject, though I suspected the seed Paco had just planted would sprout roots at some point.

Victor said, "Just wanted to apologize for running out on you the other night at Paco's party, but you know—"

"I get it. Self-preservation. Anything else?"

Paco leaned forward. "The FBI questioned you, yes?"

"Me and about a hundred of your closest friends and family. Let me go after a few hours. Big fishing expedition. I'm a lawyer. There's only so far they're going to push."

Paco looked at Victor, nodded, and seemed satisfied with my response.

"We also wanted to thank you for agreeing to help us find Charlotte. It means a lot to Paco," Victor said.

"I wasn't aware I had a choice."

Victor continued. "There are only a handful of people Paco can trust right now."

I damped my cheek. "Well, guess I'm the lucky one."

"It is a comfort to me you agreed to this," Paco said. "And, of course, we have set everything in motion for your compensation package, but we must move quickly. You have the flash drive?"

"Haven't let it out of my sight."

"Then you have what you need to start. You will fly to Palm Springs, the last place Charlotte was seen. Your ticket and hotel are already booked. You leave tomorrow evening, Friday, so no need to take time off work." He gestured for Jorge to hand me the tickets. "I imagine this won't be a problem for you?"

"No problem at all," I assured him, a thin smile underlining my commitment.

Paco extracted a burner phone from his pocket. "Victor's number is the only one you will need. Only use this phone to contact him, understand?" He laid a roll of cash — it had to be at least a thousand bucks in twenties — on the coffee table.

"For expenses," he said, then stood, patting my injured shoulder. I winced.

"And Mitch, be very careful. We don't need more of these coincidences, *sí*?"

CHAPTER 16

Despite his abrasive nature, I harbored a soft spot for Ron Boone. He was old-school decent, a straight shooter, always had the union members' backs. Management held the opposite view. He'd been a courthouse fixture for decades, knew where the bodies were buried and who to ask when they required digging up. Management had never had the balls or cause to sideline Ron Boone or try to clip his wings. He was a pain in the ass, but at least he was their pain in the ass, and as such, somewhat manageable. But the pages he'd handed me were a fuse waiting to be lit. I now understood why the three musketeers were so riled up. The gist was as follows.

For years, Alameda Superior Court management had refused to give the court employees any significant annual raises, offering the predictable litany of excuses: falling tax revenues, reduced state assistance, more generous grants thrown at the feet of big tech to lure them to the delights of downtown Oakland. Ron suspected this was all a thick smokescreen to cover up the real reason the budget was in freefall. And that lay firmly in the hands of Presiding Judge Griffin Harper.

Harper had been a court staple for three decades. Tough on crime, favored incarceration over rehabilitation; the guy should have stepped down years ago, but his ego had become a wedge between himself and reality. Retirement would mean a decent pension, one large enough to live a comfortable life, die a comfortable death even, but the hard-working folks grinding the wheels at the rumor mill had picked up on Harper's taste for the good life. He'd run a successful construction company before entering public service; he drove a Mercedes Maybach, had a thirty-foot Hunter sailboat docked at Jack London, and put four of his grandchildren through college. I couldn't imagine a state pension could finance that lifestyle for long. Or maybe Harper wasn't aiming for longevity.

There's an old saying at the courthouse: *Old judges never retire, they just stay on call.* According to Ron's documents, Harper had been calling in retired judges for years to try cases ranging from parking violations to homicides. Completely legitimate, if there was a shortage of judges in the courthouse, but the opposite was true. Alameda Superior Court had any number of judges who could have tried every case that came through the courts and still had time to take a decent lunch break.

Every time they're called in, a retired judge makes five hundred dollars a day, plus expenses. On top of that, each courtroom costs a million dollars a year to staff and manage. The more money that's spent on calling in retired judges, the less money there is to spread among the other court employees. What Ron Boone had uncovered was a sweetheart deal lining the pockets of retired judges already receiving a state pension. An arrangement I was sure Harper was hoping to continue well into his own retirement.

Ron had culled his evidence from the court administrative staff, who had access to the time sheets and had calculated the number of retired judges called in weekly, then raised their concerns to their union rep. Right off the bat, I could see the call-ins were excessive and had probably cost the court millions of dollars over the years, money that could have been spent on decent salary increases across the board.

To add to his dossier, Ron had unearthed a critical piece of evidence that I guessed most lawmakers hadn't even read; an appendix to a Judicial Council report that laid out a clear case why counties in the Bay Area with fast-growing populations desperately needed more judges. According to their best practices, California was short by more than a hundred judges in those cities. But there was a kicker — the report showed, thanks to shifting demographics and no doubt rapid gentrification, that some counties had way more judges than they needed. Alameda, I knew, was sitting on over a dozen judges with barely enough cases to keep them busy. I was impressed. Ron had done his homework and found the smoking gun he needed. He'd dug so far back in the court records it must have taken him weeks to unearth that appendix.

That splinter of injustice nicked under my skin as I reread the papers to make sure I'd got it right: the court was subsidizing retired judges at the expense of the courthouse employees. Ron knew me well enough to know that once I saw the evidence, it wasn't in my nature to let this go.

I sat back after reading the papers a third time and added this to the shit pile growing larger at my feet. The final thought I had before the Gods of Sleep granted me mercy was how far this rot was embedded in the system. Systemic or a one-off? I suspected the former. A rot doesn't set in overnight; it seeps in slowly, untraceable at first. You won't even know it's there until the whole building collapses and you're left standing in the rubble.

CHAPTER 17

The aftershock from the accident tailgated me into the following day. With my bike out of commission, I drove to work, the whole time ruminating on the seed of doubt Paco had planted in my mind. What if my cycling accident wasn't an accident? I wasn't aware of anyone hating me enough to run me over, kill me even. The thought was absurd. Then again, four days ago, I was a Superior Court lawyer cruising to a comfortable retirement, and today, I was the latest recruit to *La Sangres Norteñas*, tasked with tracking down Paco Castillo's errant wife.

I couldn't deny that the ordeal had set my nerves unraveling, yet a satisfying buzz oscillated through my bones that made me think I hadn't felt this alive in years, not since my days back in Brighton, running on adrenaline and the cheap thrill of the chase.

As a lifestyle, it wasn't the healthiest nor the most sustainable, not that the guys I worked with at Knight Arrow Security had seemed to care. They'd been attached to the private security game way too long, ex-military types whiplashed by the action they'd seen out in the Falklands decades before, or Afghanistan twenty years later, carrying themselves as if they were surviving a beat or two out of sync with the rest of the world. Hang around those types for a while, and you begin to think they're blessed with some Zen-like detachment, possessed some deep insights into the human condition the rest of us had missed. Hang around them a decent amount longer, and you realize that detachment is just collateral damage, a coping mechanism to navigate the no-man's-land between war and a civilian world. They did the only work they knew how to do, stuck together like damaged atoms binding to damaged atoms.

Walking into the courthouse that morning, a sense of detachment followed me like a shadow looking for a host. I felt my senses heightened to eleven, as if a switch in my brain had suddenly flipped, focusing everything into sharp relief. It was the most alive I'd felt in months.

After accepting with good grace the sympathies extended to my bruised face, I spent the rest of the day avoiding the three musketeers. I sensed they were itching to talk, but I needed to meet with Ron first and get his take on the Harper Griffin papers.

When I met him in the courthouse café, he was sitting by the window, the late-afternoon sunlight picking up the motes and dust mites from his crumpled black suit and tie. As usual, a yellow SEIU pin secured on his right lapel.

"What the hell happened to you?" he asked, staring at my cheek. "Get into a fight?"

"You should see the other guy," I said, throwing the tired old cliché around as casually as possible. I dragged up a chair. "What's with the suit? Management meeting?"

He slid a printed leaflet across the table. "Buried her today," he said flatly, like the words hurt to get them out.

I flipped over the leaflet. An order of service for Masie Dawn Howard, Ron's niece. The photo must have been taken while she was vacationing in Hawaii, I thought, studying the off-the-shoulder pink sundress and white plumeria resting behind her left ear; the ear of choice if you were a single woman looking for love.

Masie's smile was a thing of wonder that signaled an imagined lifetime of romance, heartbreak, and eventual true love over the sun-setting horizon.

"Christ, I'm so sorry, Ron. She looks like a really nice person."

"Yeah, yeah, she was . . . real nice, a doll."

Ron contemplated a couple of crows pecking at the small square of lawn in the courtyard and wiped a tear from his eyes. "The kids at her school made her a memorial. Photos, stuff Masie used to say to them, what they loved about her, then hung it up by the coffin for the service. Mitch, I gotta tell you, those tiny scribbles would have torn your heart out."

I handed back the leaflet and felt a lump in my throat as he spoke. I thought of Sierra and Kurt and imagined the complete devastation of losing either of them. Then I thought about Paco Castillo holding their photograph in his thick fingers last night. It sent a shiver down my spine. It hadn't occurred to me until then that Paco was maybe making some twisted metaphor of holding my family's lives in his hands. I shook away the thought. My imagination was running in overdrive. This would be over soon. I'd find Charlotte, get on with my life, debt paid, job done.

"And you know what that cocksucker Castillo did?" Ron leaned over the table, fists bunching. "Sends this cross-shaped wreath the size of two grown men; you can't take your eyes off the damned thing, like he was making some big gesture of sympathy. Let me tell you, Mitch, I wanted to tear every single carnation from that thing, stuff 'em down Castillo's throat, choke him for what he did."

"You still think he killed Masie?"

"Gun's all the evidence you need, but that got suppressed, so I guess that ain't happening."

He stared me down with red, spider-veined eyes, awaiting my comeback. I refused to take to the bait.

99

"Victor was right in his defense," I eventually said. "The search was illegal. Trust me, Castillo's not driving around shooting young women in broad daylight."

"Then he got someone else to do it."

"Was Masie involved with that gang in any way?"

"What the heck do you think?"

"Then there's your answer. Masie got caught in the crossfire, and—"

"But Castillo?" he interrupted. I could tell Ron wasn't switched to "listening mode." His emotions were still raw to the touch. "He's the head of this gang, right? Couldn't they arrest him for capital murder?"

"You've been studying up?"

"Had to do something. I felt so goddamned useless." He wiped away another tear.

"You're right. A capital murder charge applies if the accused committed a murder to benefit a street gang, but the evidence just isn't there. Masie was in the wrong place at the wrong time. Absolute tragedy, the very worst, and I know it won't bring her back or make anything right, but I see this happen way too often."

Ron looked at me with uncomprehending eyes. "So, you're telling me nobody's gonna stand trial for Masie's murder?" His gaze flipped from bewildered to angry in a flash. He slapped his palms on the table. "How the fuck is that any kind of justice?"

"It's not," I agreed. "You know how these gangs operate. They'll intimidate anyone who's even thinking of talking. You might catch a lucky break, but don't hold your breath."

Ron loosened his tie another notch and exhaled a long, drawn-out breath. I guessed he was mentally exhausted from the constant rumination, as if replaying the events might alter the outcome. Wasn't going to happen. I'd trodden that road myself and knew every turn, marker, and fork on that highway to hell. But Ron wasn't ready to hear that yet. He had his own road to travel.

Momentarily, he turned his gaze back from the distance he'd been staring into. "You got round to reading what I gave you?"

"Talk me through it. What do you think's going on?"

"It's goddamn obvious. Harper's filling the retired judges' pockets at the expense of the court employees. It's not rocket science."

"You've got the foundation of something, I'll give you that, and that appendix you uncovered was impressive, but you can't go in, guns blazing. You need a plan."

"A plan? The plan is that you help us get more evidence to confirm this."

"It's not that easy. Say you get the evidence you need, then what?"

"We take it to management, force their hand."

"And if they won't be forced?"

"We keep forcing. Go to the press if we have to, expose that corrupt fucker."

"Risky strategy. Harper's a powerful man, got a lot of friends around town."

"You taking his side?"

"No, I'm saying if you want to poke a bear, you'd better be prepared for a mauling."

"The way I look at it," Ron said, standing and hiking up his pants by his belt. "I've given you the match. Question is, Sweeney, do you have the balls to light the fire?"

PART 3:
THE VIOLET HOUR

CHAPTER 18

The series of events that concluded with me lying in a bloody mess in a piss-stained alley in downtown Palm Springs began thus.

Arrival at Palm Springs International, cab ride to downtown; retro-chic, sun-bleached buildings, jagged-boned mountain spines scarring the desert backdrop. Venture into that hinterland too long, and it feels like you've reached the end of the world; walk too far and might find yourself right back where you started.

Victor's investigator, Alma Torres, had booked me for a two-night stay at the Flamingo Inn, a four-star mid-century modern on the edge of town. She emailed me the confirmation the day before with a curt note that implied this wasn't in her job description and that she wasn't my "friggin' travel agent." I sensed Alma had issues she wasn't shy about sharing.

Checking in at the Flamingo Inn, my immediate impression was that the original Rat Pack would have looked right at home here ambling through the mahogany-lined lobby in their tuxes, finger-snapping to the piped swing jazz, ordering vodka martinis and getting up to their Rat-Packy high jinks. By the time I dumped my luggage in my third-floor suite, the sun was dipping like a giant glazed cherry behind the ice-cream-hued dunes. I ordered room service, sat at the edge of my California king snarfing a medium-rare ribeye, plugged in the flash drive, and pored over the report of Charlotte's final movements. She'd picked up a Bentley Bentayga from the airport, then checked in at the Flamingo Inn. The next day, she'd driven to the Empire Polo Fields, left around four that afternoon, and lost the Cadillac Escalade tailing after a fender bender downtown on Indian Canyon Drive.

I clicked on a folder titled "footage" and watched a video of the accident captured by the security camera from a pawnbroker across the street. The black Cadillac Escalade following Charlotte's Bentley comes to a halt at a stoplight two cars behind. As the light turns, a red, dust-shod Toyota Camry plows into the Escalade's rear fender. Two stocky guys in black suits jump out and inspect the damage. The driver of the Camry, a young woman with a scarlet-streaked mullet haircut, thick-soled boots, and tattoos on her thighs and arms, approaches them in an apologetic fashion. Their body language implies neither guy has any interest in exchanging insurance details. The interaction lasts long enough for Charlotte to burn Bentley rubber and vanish into the desert dust before the two guys figure out what's gone down. In a flash of panic, one guy flips out a wad of cash and waves it at the woman. After a moment's hesitation, she takes it, stuffs it in her pocket, and looks on as they haul ass.

A less inquisitive soul might have stopped the video there; I let it play. As the Escalade squeals a sharp left, the woman leans on her car hood, makes a call, strolls into the pawnbrokers, and never comes out again. I fast-forwarded through an hour of additional footage covering the narrow alleyway to the rear of the store: the mullet lady never left the store, as if she'd vanished into the ether. Paco's words came flooding back to me. In his orbit, maybe there were no such things as accidents, just incidents that required investigating — and, if necessary, rectifying. I read the attached digital paperwork, which was just a poorly written summary of what I'd just seen, and headed to the bar.

The background music was predictably fitting: easy crooning over a Ring-a-Ding-Ding backbeat, barely audible over the cacophony of laughter from herds of men in cheap suits positioned like hunting packs around the watering hole. I squeezed through the crowds and asked the bartender — McKay, according to her name tag — for a Glen Grant 18, which she poured into a Norlan whiskey glass. Things were already looking up.

"Here for the convention?" McKay asked, placing the caramel-colored nectar within arm's reach. I guessed McKay was in her fifties, with shoulder-length blonde hair and dazzling azure eyes that made you look twice, maybe even a third time, if you figured you could get away with it. She carried a patina of faded glamour like she might have been a hot-shit actress back in the day, but that slim window of opportunity had long passed. In Hollywood, work for women of a certain age dried up like desert cacti in a blink of an eye, and McKay found herself serving cocktails in a Palm Springs hotel. A three-hour drive, but at the same time a million miles from LA. This was all speculation, but some people you meet wear their life story on their sleeve, and if you picked at the loose thread long enough, the revelation would be worth the wait.

Taking a sip, I asked, "What convention?"

"Pool and Hot Tub Association of America," McKay said, handing me a crumpled card with a blue PHTA logo embossed in the corner.

"Sounds like a riot."

"Everyone's gotta make a living."

I flipped the card. On the back was a scribbled name and room number — some convention jockey riding on his expense account and high hopes.

I gestured at the chicken scratch. "You must get a lot of that."

"Honey, the stories I could tell. Another?" she asked, noticing I'd downed my first.

"Sure, why not?" I handed the card back with a smile. "In case you get lonely, later."

"Oh, you're the funny guy?" She threw the card in the trash. "Get at least one of your type a night. Two, if I'm real unlucky."

"That so?" I paused. "I bet these guys get into a lot of hot water at these conventions."

She arched her perfectly sculpted eyebrows, giving me a full megawatt, Hollywood billboard smile that, for a second, cast a warm spell over me. "That was pretty freakin' lame."

"Maybe, but it made you smile," I said, focusing my eyes back on my drink.

"Only because I feel sorry for you," she said, pointing at my scar, which still burned like I'd taken a cheese grater to my cheek and rubbed in lemon juice for the hell of it.

"What are you, a stand-up? Someone sucker punch you for ruining their evening?"

"Fell off my bike."

"You don't look the cycling type."

"Motorcycle. One of those Italian brands," I lied, trying to regain a modicum of dignity.

"Vespa?" she said playfully. "You got one of those cute matching pink helmets, too?"

"Now, McKay," I said, raising my glass. "Do you always fuck with your customers like this?"

"It passes the time."

"Then you need to get a hobby," I said, raising my glass.

"I'll get right on that," McKay said. Our eyes locked for a moment before she turned her attention to another customer.

Scanning the crowd, a punch of a thrill hit me. It was more than the warm glow of single malt caressing my stomach. This was Mitch Sweeney, twenty-one years old, bluffing his way through another teenage runaway case, thinking on my feet, gaining trust.

I couldn't deny it felt good being back in the groove, knowing I hadn't lost my touch. Flirting with McKay only added to the buzz. I couldn't be sure, but I was certain I sensed a spark between us. It had been so long since I'd even looked at another woman that way, the sensation took me by surprise. A few moments later, McKay flashed me another smile and tipped another shot into my glass.

"By the way, what's with the whole Ralph Lauren vibe?" I asked, gesturing at the framed polo pony photos behind the bar.

"Polo tournaments," she said, confirming my suspicions. "If you think the hot tub guys are a pain, try dealing with the rich assholes." She gestured around the bar. "At least these guys back off when you let them know they've crossed the line. Those rich fucks think they own you, haven't met a woman who says no."

"Until you," I said, gesturing for another pour. This was all on Paco's tab; I was just playing my role.

"You got that right," she said, with a proud tilt of her chin.

I took out my phone and showed her a photo of Charlotte I'd snapped from a printout. "You ever see this woman here?"

"Are you a cop?" She leaned across the bar, looked me in the eyes, and lowered her voice. "I've just got two rules in my job: I don't talk to cops, and I don't sleep with the guests."

"Rules to live by," I said. "But I'm not a cop, and I'm not about to scribble my room number on the back of my business card."

"Right, so, what are you?"

"A good friend doing a favor," I lied, figuring McKay might have a soft spot for a sob story told right. "My buddy, Frisco, that's his wife," I said, gesturing at the screen.

"Frisco?" she said, eyebrows raised. "What is he, a gunslinger?"

"Just down on his luck," I said. "Poor sucker's going out of his mind, reckons she's cheating on him. He traced her credit card to this hotel. Last transaction she made before disappearing off the face of the desert."

"Maybe he deserved it. Husbands can be real assholes. I divorced two of 'em, I should know."

"Then that's their loss," I said.

McKay shook her head. "You're a smooth one, I'll give you that," she said, winking.

"Promised Frisco I'd do him a solid, see if I can't get him some answers. Told him it was a long shot, but the guy sobs like a child. I said, one weekend, then we're out of favors. Friends, right? What you gonna do?"

McKay weighed up the story and probably figured it was plausible enough. "Give me that." As she reached for my phone, her fingertips lingered a moment too long on the side of my hand. She studied Charlotte's photo. "Maybe," she said. "We get a lot of those polo groupies here when it's tournament weekend, hoping they're gonna strike gold with some European prince or trust-fund billionaire. The men usually buy all the drinks, but they expect something in return."

"No such thing as a free lunch."

"Damn right. The girls usually end up crying in the bathroom, hating themselves, then do it all again the next time the pony show hits town."

"Definition of insanity, right? Doing the same thing over and over, hoping for a different result?"

McKay shrugged. "If you say so, but I'll tell you one thing: if your friend's wife was here, and he tracked her through her credit card, she sure as hell wasn't running up a tab at this bar."

"Sounds like the lovely Angie, all right. Always thought she was the gold-digging type," I said, conjuring up the name from a black-and-white photograph of Angie Dickinson and Dean Martin hanging behind the bar. "So, these guys buying drinks? Anyone special come to mind?"

"Special? Honey, if you let them buy you a drink, you treat them all special. Until they give you a reason not to."

"Got ya. Do you remember when you last saw Angie?"

"Didn't mention I'd seen her."

"But if you had, you'd remember?"

"Face like that? Yeah, guess I might."

"But you didn't?"

"Like I said. We were real busy last weekend. Big international tournament, couldn't move for the Range Rovers and horse trailers, gridlocked the I-10 for hours. Worked my ass off all weekend."

"Hope the boss paid you overtime."

"And then some. Now, if that's all, I've got a job to do. Can't stand around yapping with tall, handsome strangers all night."

Short of waterboarding her back in my room, I figured I'd wrung all I was going to get out of McKay. She was playing her cards close to her chest, but instinct told me she knew more than she was letting on.

"Thanks, McKay, you've been a great help," I said. "Frisco's not gonna like it, but I'll be honest with you, that guy's his own worst enemy."

CHAPTER 19

The weight of the afternoon heat creased the air like tissue paper as the cab dropped me off at the Empire Polo Fields at lunchtime the following day. Over the entrance, a colorful banner announced I'd arrived in time for the Indio Valley Annual Golf Cart Polo Championship. I paid my thirty-five-dollar admission and mixed in with the crowds, baseball cap tugged low, shirt sticking like damp rice to my armpits under my suit jacket.

The merciless noon sun hit the seventy-five-acre field like a flash from an atom bomb, the desert air holding fast around my throat. Under the sun's savage glare, the fields resembled a giant checkerboard, the alternating patches of green and brown creating an optical illusion that made me dizzy. A brilliant white stadium, which also served as the main stage for the Coachella music festival, dominated the center of the field, but the afternoon's guests hardly seemed the crowd-surfing types. This was a pageant of linen blazers, floral dresses, large-brimmed sun hats, and designer handbags that would have cost me a month's salary.

The PA announced the match was starting, and this was the last opportunity to place your bets on the team of your choice. A predictable urge tugged at my core. I kept my hands deep in my pockets as a modest cheer erupted from the crowd. "Eye of the Tiger" roared over the speakers as twenty golf carts puttered from either side of the field, driven by modern-day golf-wear warriors ready to face off in a low-stakes, slow-motion battle of no consequence. Golf Cart Polo: the sport of mattress kings and retired car dealership jesters. I looked on, bemused, as the cadre of white-haired retirees in pastel-colored polos whirred around on souped-up carts tapping a wooden ball. I spectated for five minutes before turning my back on the heart-pounding action and walked to the food court, figuring if anyone had the inside track on these events, it was the caterers.

The loaded trestle tables were an embarrassment of riches: *A Global Culinary Adventure from Australia to Zimbabwe*, according to the signage. I snagged a couple of hors d'oeuvres, Indian samosas, and looked around for a victim. It didn't take long. He was lingering at the appetizers, fussing around with the food placement. Early twenties, frayed suit hanging off his skinny bones, and face that seemed to apologize for being there. He wasn't working here because Daddy's connections had secured him the gig and intended to use his hourly pay to fuel his cocaine habit. This kid needed the money.

"Quite the spread," I said, affecting a slight accent; an East Coast English professor maybe, who'd recently hit the *New York Times* Bestseller list.

Startled, he looked up. "Erm, thank you . . . sir. Can I get you anything? Champagne? Cocktail?"

I checked his name tag. "Jason. You a regular here?"

"Kinda. I'm a student, so there's, like, the studying, but the company gives me as many shifts as I want."

"Excellent. Persevere, Jason, you'll be glad you did. Education is the cornerstone of civilized society."

I let my words sink in and leaned closer. "Look, a good friend of mine was here last week for the international match, mentioned she'd eaten the best Dungeness crab cakes she'd ever tasted. Now, this is a long shot, but I don't suppose this company you work for catered the event last week?"

"Oh, yeah, we cater all of them. We've got, like, the exclusive contract or whatever."

"That so? Seems I'm in luck, then."

A vague smile flitted across Jason's face; message not received.

"Crab cakes?" I prompted.

"Oh, yeah, sorry. North America," he said, gesturing behind my shoulder. "Way over on the right."

Brow furrowed, I said, "Isn't that the truth these days, Jason?"

He gave me a blank look, the quip scuttling past him like a carpet beetle.

I took out my phone. "Listen, this is random, but you might be able to help me out." I showed him Charlotte's screenshot. "Did you happen to see this woman here last week at the match?"

Jason looked around. "Erm, we're not really allowed, and we get like a lot of people, so . . ."

I tugged back my jacket, letting the hundred-dollar bill tucked in the inside pocket complete his sentence for him. "That's got your name on it, Jason, if you answer two questions. Was the lady here, and who was she with?"

His eyes darted as he made a stealth calculation and landed on the right solution. "Yeah, I remember her."

"Now, Jason, you wouldn't be telling me what I want to hear just because you want that hundred-dollar bill now, would you?"

He shook his head. "She had this British accent. Anyway, she kept asking for refills on her champagne, like every five minutes. She got majorly wasted, fell on one of the food tables. I had to clear that shit up."

"That would be memorable," I said, palming the hundred into his jacket pocket. "And my other question?"

He hesitated. "Two hundred. That'll cost you two hundred."

"You're shaking me down?" I stepped back in mock surprise. "Gotta hand it to you, Jason, you're a quick study. Sure, I'll give you another hundred."

He cocked his head in the "follow me" manner, weaved his way through a gap in the marquee, and led me to a shaded area under a copse of palm trees.

"I was on my break. She was with some dude over where they keep the golf carts." He gestured to a small parking lot next to a clubhouse. "They were getting into it, big time. She was screaming, couldn't hear what she was screaming about, they were too far away. The dude grabs her shoulders and starts shaking her like really violently, like he's about to hit her or something. Then he pushes her. Next thing, she's on her knees in the grass, crying. I thought the dude might apologize, you know, help her up, but he turns his back, walks away."

"And you saw all this?"

"For sure. I'm not shitting you. Do I get my other hundred now?"

I handed over the bill, flipped another hundred in my palm, and made sure he noticed the tempting crisp green. "One more question. Did you recognize the man she was with?"

A flutter of nervousness played around his eyes and cheeks.

"Jason?" I said, waving the bill like I was about to slip it inside his belt as a tip for a riveting performance.

He debated briefly, cocked his head, and walked.

I followed him for a few yards into one of the nearby restrooms. The place was like a club locker room; spotless tiled walls and framed photographs of past polo glories hung at eye level. Jason shuffled over to a urinal and nodded. I should take the one next to him. I hesitated.

"You want my help or not?" he snapped.

I stepped forward. A gallery of photographs taken last weekend, as featured in *Palm Springs Life*, hung above my urinal. The scene looked similar to today, though with more entitled youth and showy glamour.

Jason palmed his right hand on the wall in the manner of a drunk bracing himself before unzipping, crawled his finger along the tiles, and stopped at a photograph to the left of the gallery; three people, champagne flutes in hand, caught in a candid moment by the winner's enclosure. I recognized two of them, the other fading into a blur as I focused on the couple I knew. The woman, Charlotte, wasn't a surprise, but the man to her left — studious, glasses, cream linen suit, thick mop of hair — left my throat dry.

Jason zipped up, wiped his hands through several paper napkins, and looked at me in the mirror. "Dude reminded me of my stepdad," he said, spitting into the basin. "Made my mom cry all the time. Hated that fuck. Now, do I get my other hundred?"

* * *

I arrived back downtown at four that afternoon and asked to be dropped off outside the Harley Davidson dealership a block from the pawnbroker's. My mind was still wrestling with the photograph I'd seen in the restroom, trying to figure out what the hell it meant. Stepping onto the sidewalk, the heat hit me like a truck. Everything dazzled. Everything hurt as I navigated my way from shadow to shadow, shade to shade, to avoid the relentless scourge of the sun.

Inside, Hector's Pawn Emporium was the expected circus of woe. Stringless guitars and discarded musical instruments hung on the walls and on the shelves, rows of dusty old computer servers and laptops. The glass cabinets, functioning as counters, reminded me of open caskets lined with cheap trinkets and jewelry.

I walked to the counter and assumed this was the eponymous Hector: sixties, gray hair pulled into a ponytail, beard, eyes set back deep, a pinch of a roll-up cigarette hanging from his razor-thin lips. I heard voices coming from the back of the store and caught the drift of cigar smoke: the cheap liquor store variety that sticks in your throat like chalk dust. Hector raised his glazed expression from the porno he was watching on his cell phone. All credit to the man, he did lower volume so as not to cause offense.

"Hector?" I asked.

"Says so on the door," he confirmed. "It's my given name, but I never took to it. Most folks call me Hetch. Unless you're from the police, then you can call me when you've got a warrant." He smiled, revealing a lifetime of oral neglect that gave the impression of a man who cared little about his appearance, which was maybe why Hetch was watching pornography in his store at four in the afternoon.

"Enjoying the movie?"

"S'all right," he said, sniffing. "Storyline sucks."

"You watch that stuff for the storyline? Must be the intellectual type."

Hetch paused the movie. "How can I help you . . . sir?" He stubbed the butt of his cigarette in a nearby ashtray, which I noticed contained the black plastic tip of a Sobranie Black Russian, the same brand Charlotte was smoking in the photographs Paco had showed me. Something didn't sit right. If Charlotte had left it, what was a woman of her means frequenting a pawnbroker in downtown Palm Springs? She hardly needed the cash. I let the thought percolate as I took out my phone and showed Hetch the security footage taken outside his store.

"You ain't police, so you from the insurance?" he asked, stressing the "in" of insurance like he was hoisting a heavy weight.

"No, I'm just interested in the woman with the shit-kicking boots and retro hair," I said, fast-forwarding the video. "She walks into your store and leaves her car outside. A few hours later, the police tow the vehicle and discover that someone stole it from a motel in Joshua Tree National Park. Now, I've watched this footage more times than I care to remember. This young woman walks in, but never makes it back out of your store. So I've got to figure one of two things: she either found an alternative route out of here, or you've got her tied up in your basement. Which is it?"

"Sure you ain't a cop?"

"Just a concerned citizen."

"Then I got nothing to say. And unless you've got somethin' worth my time . . ."

He reached down and settled a Smith and Wesson .38 on the counter. The action sent a tremor through me, reminding me of the dangerous game I was playing. Maybe I'd been enjoying this pretense too much and had forgotten nobody else knew this was all an act. I had two options: bluff, or apologize and leave. Not one to leave matters unresolved, and my debt to Paco still heavy on my mind, I chose the former.

"No need to get our dicks out on the table here," I said, patting a non-existent gun in my jacket pocket. "I'm just trying to save you a world of pain. Why don't you hear me out?"

"Reckon you got nothin' I'm in want of hearin' today or any other day. I'll ask you one time politely to leave, then if you ain't gone, I'm gonna have to get me a little less polite." He tapped on the gun barrel and narrowed his eyes. "We got us an understanding?"

"Despite the tortured syntax of what you just said, Hetch, you're wrong." I gestured to the in-store cameras plugged into the ceiling. "Shooting a man for just asking questions? That's got to affect your foot traffic. And when the police check the cameras to confirm what went down, I don't see them letting you off with a caution and a pat on the back. So, why don't you take the foot off the gas, huh?"

He considered my words, keeping his hand on the .38. "You got two minutes."

"Right. I'm guessing you surrendered this footage under duress to the two attack dogs driving the Escalade. Now, I know those guys, they live life on a very short fuse. I keep telling them, 'Ease up, can't be good for the heart.' I'd hate to have them come back, carry out whatever threat they made that compelled you to hand over the footage. They're married to their work, these guys. You gotta admire their dedication. Work a job you love. It's a gift these days, right?"

As Hetch considered his options, he turned toward a noise from the back room.

"Card game?"

"Friendly game of Texas Hold 'Em. Ain't no law 'gainst it."

"What happened, Hetch? She give you a hundred bucks for a getaway into the alley while you turned off the cameras?"

Hetch tapped on the gun barrel. "You seem like a real smart ass. Reckon you'll figure it out."

"Right on both counts. So, did you recognize this woman? Ever see her again?"

"Nope and nope."

"Quite the conversationalist, aren't you, Hetch?"

He turned to the back room as he heard his name being called. I took the opportunity, snatched the cigarette tip from the ashtray, and pocketed it before he turned back around.

"That it?" he said.

"For now. But if I find out that woman's your stepsister, third cousin, twice removed, whatever, I'll have to inform the Doberman twins." I raised my hands. "We all gotta job to do, right?"

Hetch rubbed at his right wrist as if recalling the ghost of violence past, or else his favored porno hand had a twinge of arthritis. He scribbled on a scrap of paper and handed it over.

"Now, maybe you should get the fuck out of my store . . . sir," he said, slipping the gun back under the counter and tapping his phone.

A chorus of orgasms that could have stirred the dead from their eternal slumber serenaded my exit.

CHAPTER 20

After visiting Hetch, I was buzzing; the adrenaline flowing. I'd returned to the hotel feeling way too pleased with myself for an acting job well done and celebrated with a slug of Scotch from the minibar. I'd called Kurt and made sure the little guy was doing okay. He filled me in on his week. I sat back and listened, calibrated myself back to my real life behind the pretense. The grounding felt good; for thirty minutes, I was dad and husband again. How long the latter would remain true was a thought I couldn't linger on for long; that way lay untold despair and a pawn store of abandoned hopes.

Scrolling through my emails, I noticed Ron Boone had sent a barrage of missives. He was probably pickled, riffing on Paco Castillo and the Judge Griffin Harper papers, asking what I intended to do about them. *Right now, Ron? Not a damn thing,* I said to myself and bulk-deleted his emails.

I stood by the third-story window and looked out to the serrated spine of San Jacinto Mountains, the sky burnished in heliotrope paint strokes. This was the desert's violet hour; the sliver of time between dusk and nightfall, when the night sets the stage with its own plot twists and fresh cast of characters. It left me uneasy; the violet hour seemed laced with too many shadows and held a slippery current of treachery and unpredictability at its edges.

Hungry and in need of a proper drink, I'd checked the paper Hector had handed me and then headed over to the Desert Palm.

* * *

Decor last updated during the mid-'80s, faded posters peeling off the walls, lighting low and unobtrusive, neon sign flickering as if it were in two minds whether to reveal itself . . . the Desert Palm, located at the end of the block from Hetch's Pawn Emporium, was the kind of establishment that preferred not to draw attention to itself.

"Sweet Home Alabama" hailed my entrance. The bar was empty save for a dour old couple sipping at their beers like they intended to make them last all night. I sat at the bar and checked the menu. A long list of American bar fare, either deep-fried, slapped between bread, or slathered in cheese. I'd decided on the chicken wings chased down with a draft IPA when the bartender appeared and adjusted her scarlet-streaked mullet in the mirror. I checked her out. Her lace-up boots, soles as thick as bricks, reached the tops of her heavily inked calves, and her sleeveless T-shirt revealed a skin gallery of arm tattoos. I was sure she was the same woman I'd seen on the security footage entering Hetch's pawn store. As I debated how to approach her, I figured adding a shot of bourbon to the mix would help my thinking.

I studied the bartender as she served my beer and set down the bourbon. She was in her early thirties with a hardcore rock chick, young Joan Jett vibe, which, two decades ago, I would have found irresistible. There was no doubt she was the woman I'd seen in the security footage. Fake Joan Jett walked back into the kitchen and returned a few minutes later with a plate of steaming-hot wings.

"So, what brings you in?" she asked. I rated her interest level in my reply at a three out of ten at best.

I dove right in. "Hetch," I said. "Owns the pawn store down the block. You probably know him, what with you guys practically being neighbors."

She crossed her arms. "You two buddies?"

"I was hocking an old guitar, asked him for a bar to drown my sorrows, and here I am."

"Yep, here you are," she said, narrowing her eyes.

I downed the bourbon, the caramel finish cloying on my teeth.

"What kind of guitar?"

"Sorry?"

"The one you pawned. What kind? Electric? Acoustic?"

"Electric. Fender Stratocaster, orange burst. Not an original, just some knock-off. Don't play much anymore, since . . . well . . ." I left the sentence hanging in the air like a sustained note and took a sip of beer.

"Hey, never give up on your dreams, man. Get some dough, buy it back. Keep on rockin', yeah?" She extended me the two-horned rock salute, which I thought had died a welcome death during the decade Guns N' Roses were recording their second album. She hiked a thumb over her left shoulder. "I gotta go get another order."

I imagined she was back there busting the short-order-cook's balls. It took me a few minutes to figure out she'd made a call; after all, I was the sole patron sitting at the bar, and the glum twins didn't look like they were in a hurry to order anything except maybe another express delivery of life regrets.

Five minutes later, two guys the size of WWE wrestlers but with less comic sensibility, both sporting thick beards that ended at their chests, sat on either side of me. I knew this wasn't good and braced myself for whatever shit storm was brewing.

One man reached for his glass, turned, then spilled most of his beer over my jacket. Things rapidly turned, to quote one of my favorite British sayings, "tits up." The meathead to my left blamed me for this so-called "accident," which the meathead to my right confirmed. Keen to avoid trouble, I offered to buy them both a beer. It wasn't the peace offering I'd hoped for. They grabbed me under the armpits, led me through the back door, and threw me into the alley like the night's trash.

I scrabbled to my knees. A dull snap of a boot cuffed under my chin, sending me spilling back down. Following that, another boot in my ribs, then one in the kidneys, forcing the bourbon and hot wings back up the same path they went down.

A powerful hand grappled at my collar and yanked me up. An iron wedge of knuckles pummeled into my cheek. Blood streamed over my face and down to my neck. Another punch to my solar plexus and the world spun like an invisible hand had sped up its rotation.

I gasped for breath, spitting blood clots on the floor. As the pain seared through my teeth, an old instinct kicked in. From the corner of my eye, I noticed the meathead who'd face-punched me was flicking his punching hand like he'd damaged his knuckles in the action. I grabbed the opportunity with both feet, swung my legs at his ankles, sent him off balance, stood, and landed two snap punches to his chest as he lay on the floor before meathead number two dragged me off, cannonballing another fist into my ribs.

Groaning, I was back on the ground, knees scraping the concrete. This was nowhere close to a fair fight, but at least I'd landed a couple of punches and saved some dignity. I was out of practice, fifteen pounds overweight, hadn't been in a fight since I was dating Sierra and some punk had tried to pick her up at a bar and wouldn't take "fuck off, asshole" for an answer. That's the problem with violence: unless you're in the groove, you lose the edge, get soft. These guys were pros, lived and breathed this kind of shit daily.

Sprawled out on the cold concrete, the pain seared; skin, bones, and blood vessels all throbbed in ugly, harmonious agony. I braced myself for another onslaught. Instead, I heard a voice calling out, "Leave something for me, jerkoffs."

The meatheads backed off, snarling like chained pit bulls.

As I looked up, fake Joan Jett squatted next to me. "My pops called, warned you might pay me a visit," she said, brushing a scruff of dirt from my face. "His long-term memory's not what it was, but his short-term memory? That's still pretty sharp. He don't remember nobody pawning a Stratocaster today. He did mention some douchebag in a suit and baseball hat asking too many questions; a real cocksucker, he said."

I mumbled something. It might have been a zinger, I'll never know. I passed out for a couple of seconds.

She leaned over. The heady musk of patchouli oil almost caused me to retch a second time. As I looked closer, the familial resemblance struck me; eyes set back deep under the brow, thin lips that seemed to vibrate like piano wire as she spoke. "I don't know who you are or why you're here, but no one gets to threaten my pops at his place of work. Now, why don't you get the fuck back to wherever it was you came from? And if you need some extra motivation . . ."

She stood, drew her foot back, and shot a boot into my kidneys. I groaned and rolled into the fetal position. As she drew her foot back, ready to catapult another fourteen-eye Doc Marten missile into my ribs, a female voice, tense as if it was forced through gritted teeth, echoed from the darkness.

"For fuck's sake, Betsy. Your instructions were to question him, not put him in a bloody coma."

I heard the clink of high heels, like the tick of a loud clock, stepping across the concrete toward me. As the heels stopped inches from my face, I pulled into focus a pair of nicely shaped ankles cuffed with skin-tight black jeans.

Fake Joan Jett, Betsy, took a step back. "Asshole threatened my pops, and he owes me. For the food and shit."

"Well, hardly my problem now, is it?" A pause, accompanied by the breathy pull on a cigarette. "What is my problem is your lack of discretion. Out in the street? What were you thinking? What if someone saw you and called the police?"

I caught the hint of an accent in the exchange, though I still couldn't trust what my ears were telegraphing to my brain through the chorus of dull ringing that accompanied every rib-crushing breath.

"Go ahead, get your money, then make yourself scarce. Can you do that, Betsy?"

Betsy grunted, rummaged in my pockets, and extracted a twenty. "For the food and drinks," she snipped, then took another twenty. "This one's for my troubles. If I ever see you in my bar again, my friends are gonna get real upset. If you're not as dumb as you look, you'll make the right choice."

Make the right choice. I'd heard that a lot lately. I was thinking I had no idea what the right choice was anymore. Maybe I'd never known. Or maybe I knew all along, and I'd just chosen to ignore good advice when I offered it to myself.

"Happy now?" I caught the citrusy aroma of perfume and cigarette smoke as the woman spoke.

"They'll need paying," Betsy said, pointing at the muscle twins, who looked like a couple of dejected schoolboys who'd just had their football taken away: playtime over.

A deep sigh, followed by another long draw on a cigarette. "I'll make sure they'll get their money. Now, can you and ZZ Top toddle off back inside that shitty bar of yours before someone starts selling tickets to this sideshow?"

I heard Betsy call out, followed by heavy boots clomping off into the distance. The woman waited. After a minute, she spoke. "Can you get up?"

I eased myself to sitting and rubbed a palm across my blood-ied cheek. The copper taint of blood flooded my mouth, but at least my vision was gradually de-fogging. Above her skinny jeans, the woman wore a tight-fitting white T-shirt and a black leather jacket that looked expensive. Under the streetlights, I could detect the outline of delicate, well-crafted features partially concealed under the shadow of her baseball cap and large sunglasses. Despite my brain lagging a few beats behind its regular cadence, I wondered if this was Charlotte Castillo.

The woman squatted and looked me over like I was some hobo she was none too keen to step over. "Mind telling me who the fuck you are?"

"Mitch," I groaned. "Mitch Sweeney."

"I don't know you. Should I know you?"

"Erm, I don't know. Probably not."

"No, probably not." Uttered pensively, as if a private thought had escaped from her brain to her lips without her consent.

A moment's silence. I could almost hear the cogs in her brain churning.

"Right, you're coming with me," she said, extending her hand.

"Erm, thanks for calling off the dogs and everything, but it's been a long night. I should probably head back to my hotel, get some shut-eye."

I heard the sharp clunk of metal against metal as the woman aimed the barrel of a bronze-colored .45 caliber handgun at my forehead.

"Oh, my mistake. Did I phrase that as if it were a question? Because I really don't think I did."

CHAPTER 21

As the woman drove, the scenery blended from one anonymous strip mall to the next in a carousel of neon. Above me, the stars in the night sky continued with their celestial turnings, unconcerned with the woes of one more human under their watch. This particular human sat in the passenger seat of a Bentley Bentayga, the driver pointing a loaded .45 at his chest.

The woman's driving was erratic; bouts of redline acceleration followed by shuddering slowdowns, as if she suddenly recalled there was such a thing as a speed limit and exceeding it would draw the attention of the highway patrol. After around thirty minutes, she slowed and turned onto a narrow lane.

"You're Charlotte," I said, as we stopped by a tall iron gate with the sign *Gable Hills* written in cursive across the top, though there were no hills, just an endless, vast desert sky that seemed to touch down on every horizon.

She punched in the code at the entrance keypad. The gates swung open with a gentle hum. "Brilliant. Paco obviously hired you for your powers of deduction."

She navigated through the gated community, eventually pulling into the driveway of a one-story mid-century modern with stark white walls and black tinted windows that reminded me of some ultra-chic open prison they might send disgraced bank executives to serve their time. She ushered me from the car, gun barrel poking at my back.

Inside, the air was blessedly cool, the furniture also mid-century modern, with clean lines, and the walls dripping with abstract art. She directed me into the gleaming kitchen. I doubted anyone had ever prepped a meal on its shiny surfaces. In fact, all the appliances looked as if they were in a holding pattern. Beyond the patio door, a lap pool shimmered like ice blue fluid jewels under the garden lights.

I noticed several packed suitcases on the floor. "Going on vacation?" I asked.

"I was. Until someone started poking around asking questions."

"You could have left days ago."

"I had personal matters to attend to, not that it's any of your business. Anyway, I was curious who Paco would send looking for me." She pointed a perfectly manicured digit my way. "I have to say, you're not what I expected."

"I get that a lot," I agreed, then grabbed my side as a sharp pain coursed through me.

"You should clean yourself up," Charlotte said, gesturing to the sink and lighting another Sobranie. "And don't get any bright ideas," she added, waving the gun. "My father taught me to shoot before I was out of nappies."

I ran a cloth under warm water and watched rivulets of red blot onto the cold steel, wondering how the hell my day had spiraled into this shit show.

Charlotte paced like a caged animal, muttering and flipping her gun from one hand to the other, dragging on her Sobranie between hand exchanges. The woman was clearly agitated. My own nerves were equally jittery, humming like the distorted feedback from a stage amplifier. I kept a lid on it and focused on dissuading Charlotte from showcasing her shooting skills.

"Sit." She pulled a chair from under the table, using the sole of her shoe to push it my way. "Pockets. Empty your pockets."

I reached inside my jacket.

"Easy, tiger," she said, waving the .45 at my chest. "I'm already jumpy. Don't give me an excuse to use this."

I carefully placed my wallet and the phone Paco had given me on the table.

"Were you followed?"

"Nobody knows I'm here. I'm meant to be invisible."

"Invisible? Really? Great job on that," she said, examining the phone, noticing the lack of anything personal or applications cluttering the screen. "Paco, I assume?"

"For emergencies."

"How's that working out for you?"

I figured a reply was moot.

She pulled up a chair, sat across from me, and removed her shades and baseball cap, shaking out her thick blonde hair. If Oksana was a nine, Charlotte had to be a ten or even an eleven; huge, cornflower-blue eyes with a tall, athletic build. Her cheekbones wide and strong, her complexion flawless, with just a hint of freckles peppering her nose, no trace of makeup, her features set in perfect proportions. She had an aristocratic air, like she'd command the attention of any room she sauntered into. She placed her gun on the table and rested a hand on the grip.

"You don't look like one of Paco's usual gangbangers. What are you?"

"Just a lawyer."

"You don't look much like a lawyer, either."

"I work at the court, doing research for judges."

"Ah. So, what's Paco got on you, Mitch Sweeney, the lawyer?"

This was no time to bullshit the beautiful lady aiming a .45 at my chest. I told her about taking the stand at the suppression of evidence motion and Paco's insistence I help track her down. I left out any reference to Victor, figuring it might be ammunition I could use later if things sunk further south than they already had.

"You think I don't know why he sent you?" she said, running a hand through her hair. "It's the fucking laptop, isn't it? Wish I'd never heard about the bloody thing. It's not here, by the way, in case you thought you'd struck gold."

A laptop? This was news to me. "Paco mentioned it," I said, bluffing.

"Mentioned it?" Charlotte laughed. "You have no idea of the clusterfuck you've walked into, do you, Mitch Sweeney? No fucking idea."

She raised the gun and closed one eye. "Maybe I'll do you a favor by shooting you right now. You do understand Paco sees people as disposable. Once they're of no more use to him, he discards them like trash."

"Is that what he did with you?" I asked.

If the question burned a hole in Charlotte's psyche, she didn't show it.

"I could shoot you right now. Nobody would know." She lowered her voice. "You do know I have people to clean up stains like you?"

I shuffled, sweat pooling through my neck hairs. "Paco would just send someone else in my place," I stammered.

She pondered this for a few seconds. "Good point. But let's run this scenario to its logical conclusion. I let you go, and you'll call Paco the minute you leave. That's a nail in my coffin. Second option, you tell him you didn't find me. Eventually, he'll work it out, because he always does, and kills you for lying to him. That's a nail in your coffin. Option three, I shoot you right now, which buys me a lot of extra time to get out of Palm Springs. No nails. No coffins, at least not for me. Hmm . . . what's a girl to do?"

"You won't kill me, Charlotte," I said hurriedly. "You're not Paco."

Sitting back in the chair, she sighed. "Oh, I don't know. Maybe some years ago, that might have been true. But I'm a different person now, stronger."

"Look, this is none of my business," I pleaded. "You should let me go. This is between you and Paco."

She smiled. "Nice try, but we have the minor matters of knowledge and trust to contend with. I don't know you, and since Paco sent you, I can't trust you, which leaves us in a bit of a pickle, doesn't it?"

"A pickle?" I said, exasperated. "You call this a fucking pickle?"

"You say tomato . . ." she said, smiling, leaving the sentence hanging. I wondered if Charlotte was as equally unhinged as Paco, just operating on a different level of fucked-up-ness.

"What's on the laptop that's so important to Paco?"

"You really don't want to know. What do you Americans say? Plausible deniability? Seriously, trust me on this."

"So you're just going to keep running? Paco will find you eventually."

She thought for a moment. "Is he still fucking that bitch, the Russian?"

"Oksana?"

"Fucking Oksana," she said, spitting out the words like apple seeds. "I'll give it another year. He'll get bored. He always does." She pulled sharply on her cigarette. "I've met women like Oksana before, young, pretty, don't care whose cock they suck, so long as it's dipped in gold. They're money-grabbing whores; they catch the barest scent of money and they're opening their legs like a nutcracker at Christmas."

131

"Paco left you for Oksana?" I said, tentatively, hoping to avoid irritating the woman holding a .45, but still desperate to keep her talking.

Charlotte nodded. "I was an actor once, you know," she said. "A dancer too, but I lost the passion somewhere along the way. I picked up the dancing again when I married Paco and found I had too much time on my hands. Paco hired her; of course, he only hires the best. Oksana was a principal with the Mariinsky Ballet in St. Petersburg, until she aged out of her pointe shoes at twenty-eight. He met her when she was whoring herself out at some lap dancing club, paid her to teach me classical ballet. I had my suspicions, but what could I do? Worse thing, she didn't just steal my husband; she stole my life. She tried to become me. Colored her hair the same, styled it like I do, got Paco to pay for a nose job. She even started dressing like me, affecting a fake English accent. Quite pathetic, really." Charlotte waved her Sobranie around in wide circles. "The cow even took up smoking. Can you believe it? She was a vacant body looking for something to fill it. No breeding, you see, a lack of class."

Charlotte was on a roll. The more she talked, the less focused she was on firing a bullet at me. I kept her on topic: "If you ask me, that's Paco's loss, Charlotte."

She smiled. "Are you flirting with me, Mitch Sweeney?" she said, leaning closer. "I'll give you an A for effort. You've got some bottle, coming on to a woman pointing a loaded gun at your head. Maybe I underestimated you?"

"No, it's just that Paco—"

She interrupted. "Okay, let me tell you about Paco fucking Castillo." Charlotte stood and paced the floor. "He grew up poor as dirt, started running drugs for the local dealers when he was eight. By the time he was sixteen, he had thirty kids working for him in six different towns across the Yucatan peninsula. At twenty-one, he got promoted to head the entire operation and catches the eye of the Sinaloa Cartel. They made him an offer, and the rest, as they say, is history."

"A self-made man," I said, keeping the conversation rolling.

"Self-made monster," she snapped. "You'd think that kind of responsibility and money would fuck up a lot of young men. Not Paco. He thrived on it, got some vicarious pleasure out of other people's suffering. Of course, that poison spilled into his personal life. His idea of love is seeing how hard he can kick someone before they finally break, then make sure they never forget what that breaking felt like."

Her voice trailed off, her eyes staring off across the sparkle of the pool.

"That laptop is the only leverage I have. I'd negotiate, but I don't trust he'd honor his end of the deal. If I give him what he wants, it's game over. He'll make sure I never see my children again. He can do that, you know? He's already had me committed once; he'll do it again, given half the chance." She slapped the gun in her palm. "No. No. That will not happen. It. Will. Not. Happen."

She wiped the back of her hand across her eyes. Despite the fact she had a loaded gun pointed my way, I felt a twinge of sympathy for the woman. I'd only dealt with Paco from a safe distance, or as safe as I imagined I was. I could only imagine what the pressure of being married to the man might do to someone.

She wrestled her attention back to the moment and raised the gun an inch higher. "You know, maybe I should call in the cleaners after all. Solves a lot of my problems if you're out of the equation."

She moved forward and slid the gun barrel across my temple. Making a grab for the weapon would have been the smart move, but my thinking was sluggish, the strength beaten out of me. I couldn't gauge how serious her intentions were, but the cold metal against my skin felt serious enough. I figured this was the time to lay my only get-out-of-jail-free card on the table.

"You could," I said. "But I'd hate to be the one who tells my son's godfather that you killed his best friend. I've never seen Victor angry, but you have, right, Charlotte?"

For the first time that evening, Charlotte was visibly shaken. Her eyes clouded with concern. She dropped the gun to her hips. "How . . . I mean, I don't—"

"You probably shouldn't pose for the local press with your husband's lawyer at polo matches. Kind of negates the whole going-into-hiding thing."

Charlotte reached for another Sobranie. Her hand trembled as she lit up. Cradling the gun under the crook of her elbow, she inhaled and pointed the cigarette at me. "You certainly buried that lead, didn't you, Mitch?"

"Just making conversation."

"You know nothing about this. I'd keep it that way if I were you." She dropped her voice a notch. "Forget you ever saw whatever it was you saw. He's been a good friend; he's trying to help."

"Help how?"

"It's complicated."

"See if you can't uncomplicate it for me."

Charlotte nodded. "Are you and Victor good friends?"

"I thought we were."

"Yes, Victor can be mercurial that way."

"Paco has no idea, right? About you and Victor?"

She turned and smiled. "Again, stunning levels of deduction. You really are wasted as a court lawyer, or whatever you are."

"It's been said before," I agreed. "Look, let me go; I promise on my son's life I'll tell Paco the trip was a bust, you'd already left town, and I never found you."

"You didn't. I found you."

I ignored the slight on my investigative abilities. "And I'll forget I ever saw that photograph."

I sensed the things were gradually turning in my favor as her voice softened. "And you're sure you and Victor are good friends? Again, no time for lies."

"He was my best man, he's my son's godfather, and he's letting me use his apartment while I'm separated from my wife. Yeah, I guess you could say we're pretty close."

Charlotte mused on this for a moment. "Marriage can be hard," she said, then gestured at the table with the gun barrel. "Hand me your wallet."

I did as she requested. She removed my driver's license and a photo of Sierra and Kurt I'd taken at the beach and snapped photos of both with her cell phone. "Insurance. In case you get a change of heart between here and Northern California."

The relief was like a tidal wave surging over me and then dragging away all my adrenaline in its backwash. Depleted and exhausted, my body felt like a dead weight around my bones. I'd never know if Charlotte would have shot me, but the threat had felt genuine enough.

She tore a sheet of paper from a notebook. "You need to get yourself cleaned up properly." She wrote down an address and handed it to me. "I'll call a cab. My friend will patch you up the best she can, then send you on your merry little way."

She handed back my wallet. "Shame you'll have to report to Paco that you've had such an unfruitful visit. And my apologies for the incident with Hetch and Betsy. You just can't find the staff these days, can you? Then again, one should always have a good friend in the pawn business. You never know when they'll come in useful."

I was parsing this information when the wind chimes out by the pool jangled as if a bird wing had interrupted their nightly meditation.

We both shifted our eyes to the patio door as the motion sensor clicked on. An intense white light burst over the pool area.

"You're positive no one followed you?" Charlotte snapped. "Not the time for lies," she added, pointing the gun my way.

"No idea. I wasn't the one driving."

At the same time, Charlotte and I both noticed the blurred reflection of a figure walking toward the patio door.

Charlotte didn't hesitate, adjusted her stance, pulled the trigger.

The discharge from the .45 was nuclear. Her body jerked back with the recoil. The patio door shattered, and chips of glass, like diamonds, cascaded into the water.

She pulled again. Another Hail Mary shot blasted into the great wide nowhere.

Before she could drop to the floor, I saw something she didn't: the cool tremor of a red dot, like a blemish, wavering on her forehead.

I shouted for her to get down. My warning came a micro-second too late.

Charlotte's head snapped back, the force of the bullet lifting her off her feet, sending her spine crashing into the kitchen island. Her body ricocheted off the marble edge with a crack, like her spine had snapped in two with the impact. In an instant, she sprawled on the floor, blood leaking onto the white tile in a grotesque Rorschach pattern, with only one possible interpretation: the worst one imaginable.

I crawled over to her and heard the crunch of footsteps over glass.

Charlotte was fading fast, her cornflower-blue eyes flickering. She managed a last turn of her head, looked at me, and spoke, her words buried deep in her final breath. "Tell . . . tell Victor . . . p, phrutecther, phutect her."

"Protect who?" I asked. "Protect who, Charlotte?"

No reply. As Charlotte's light extinguished, another red laser blemish hunted the room. Whoever the shooter was, I was sure they'd have no hesitation in serving me up as collateral damage. I had to haul ass.

From my prone position, I craned my hand to the table and grabbed my wallet and cell phone. Crawling, I noticed Charlotte's car keys poking out from the top of her handbag. I snatched them and staggered from the kitchen to the front door.

At the sidewalk, I stabbed the key fob, sprinted to the Bentley, yanked open the door, revved up the V12, and rumbled off the driveway. I stepped everything I had on the gas pedal. The Bentley's engine responded with a raucous bellow, lurching forward like a jet plane about to depart the runway, pinning me back into the hand-stitched calf-leather seat.

I didn't check the rearview, just kept my focus on the road ahead. I had a moment of mild panic at the gates as they took their time to swing open: I guessed people in this neighborhood were rarely in a rush to leave. Fortunately, there were no headlights behind me and none awaited me on the other side of the gates. I figured whoever had killed Charlotte had completed their task, mission accomplished. If they suspected someone was there, I'd left no clues about my presence. I felt safe in that sliver of knowledge, at least for the moment.

CHAPTER 22

As I drove, I punched the address Charlotte gave me into the navigation, then drove for another thirty minutes under the supervision of an English female voice, which, if it hadn't sounded so similar to Charlotte, I would have found comforting.

"You've arrived. The destination, 201 Escena Ranch, is on your right."

The complex was as different from a ranch as I could imagine. A modern development of ochre-colored townhouses corralled around a community pool. Music poured out from one of the upper-floor apartments, where a group of people partied on the balcony.

I unhooked the waist-high iron gate outside number 202 and knocked on the front door. A few seconds later, a wary but calm female voice called from behind the door.

"Yeah, who is it?"

I kept my voice low. "Erm . . . Charlotte sent me?"

The door wedged open just enough for her to give me the once-over.

"Oh, it's the funny guy," the woman said, unlatching the door.

I recognized the smoky voice before I did the face.

"Come to tell me the punchline?"

McKay stood in a flowing floral dressing gown, hair tousled into a bun. A traffic jam of words and questions backed up in my throat and refused to move.

"Well? I don't have all night. Or do I need to call the police?"

Finally, my throat mimicking the sounds of words I was familiar with, I blurted, "Charlotte. Gun, someone, had to get—"

An onslaught of pins and needles stabbed my legs. I leaned on the wall for support. "I think I need to sit down."

"Jesus Christ. Figured you were bad news the moment I saw you," McKay said, opening the door and stepping aside. "You'd best come in. And don't touch my walls. Blood's a bitch to clean off."

* * *

"Ain't gonna lie, this'll hurt like a mother," McKay said, pressing a cotton ball soaked with hydrogen peroxide against my cheek. Her words were an understatement. It stung like twenty angry bees had decided I was number one on the bees' most-wanted list.

"You're a big boy; you can take it," she said, then tenderly dabbed some salve onto the side of my face and the bruises across my ribs.

It had been a long minute since I'd sat shirtless, having my skin touched by a woman who wasn't my wife. The sensation wasn't unpleasant, but I sat awkwardly, peeking now and again at the sensual white curves of McKay's cleavage as the lapels of her dressing gown drifted open. A couple of times, her breasts brushed softly against my shoulder, sending a ripple of electricity through my skin and into my stomach. I tried to avert my gaze, but couldn't help myself from looking and convinced myself it was all part of the pain management, and if McKay was in any way concerned, she'd have put on a sweatshirt.

After a few minutes, she stood back and tugged the dressing gown belt tight across her waist. "About the best I can do," she said, then pointed at my ribs. "Not much I can do about the bruising. You probably cracked a rib; not much to do about that either, except wait for it to heal. You can put your shirt back on."

I gingerly slid my arms into the sleeves. The cotton brushed against my bruises like sandpaper.

"You need a drink? I don't keep any of that top-shelf stuff. Liquor store bourbon's about as fancy as you'll get."

"I don't need it fancy. I just need it large," I said. "And thanks, you know, for . . ."

McKay smiled that dazzling smile of hers and headed to the kitchen. I took the opportunity to look around. The townhouse was nicely furnished, maybe Crate and Barrel or Pottery Barn. To the right of the fireplace, I noticed a gallery of framed photographs. I eased myself from the couch to take a closer look.

They were mostly photos of McKay in her twenties and looked like stills from a TV show. In the center of the wall was a large photograph of her surrounded by a team of people beneath the Warner Brothers logo. I'd been right about McKay: she was majorly hot in her prime; stunning figure, a face the camera couldn't ignore, eyes alive and full of promise. She still looked like an absolute knockout today, but back then, she had a barely contained hunger. Every pose to camera signaled McKay was hell-bent on taking on the world, and the world had better stand back.

Walking back in with two double pours of bourbon over ice, McKay handed one to me and kept one for herself.

I nodded toward the gallery. "You were on TV?"

"Lifetime ago," she said. "Now, sit your ass down and tell me everything, and if I think you're lying, I will call the cops. We clear?"

Threatened by three women in one night? I was wondering if this was payback for my middle-aged white man entitlement. I took it on the chin. After swallowing a mouthful of bourbon, I spilled everything from when Charlotte had picked me up outside the Desert Palm to me cradling her head in my arms as she died on the kitchen floor.

McKay said nothing, just sipped her drink as I talked. I couldn't tell if she was showing a tough front, or if she'd been expecting something like this to happen and had already prepared herself for the worst. Her tears finally welled up when I told her about Charlotte's last words.

"Protect her? Do you know what that means?" I asked.

"Protect her? You sure you heard it, right?"

"I think so. Was she talking about her daughter, maybe?"

"She doesn't have a daughter. Two sons, Jack and Harry."

"You?"

McKay smiled, leaned over and laid a hand gently on my knee. Another spark of electricity prickled my skin. "Honey, you don't know a thing about me. I figure if anyone in this room needs protecting, it's you."

I couldn't argue. "Did you know her well?"

She leaned back and shrugged. "As well as you can ever know someone like Charlotte. She had her issues, demons she was fighting." She paused and pointed her glass my way. "Then again, we've all got our demons, just gotta figure out how tight of a leash to put them on. You got demons, Mitch?"

I hesitated before answering. I barely knew McKay, and I wasn't the kind of man to spill my guts at the first pretty woman who dazzled a pretty smile my way. But there was something about her warmth and openness that knocked a few holes in my defenses. "Erm . . . yeah, gambling," I said sheepishly. "I'm wrestling with it, though, figure I got it in a headlock for the moment. And you?"

"Since we're sharing, age-inappropriate men," she said, brushing a fingertip along the rim of her glass. "Can't be dating men of my age, too damned needy. No twelve-step program for that."

"Doesn't sound too bad. I'm sure you make a lot of young men very happy."

She smiled and crossed one leg over the other, revealing a long thigh which she didn't bother to cover up. Looking me in the eye, she held my gaze and said, "I have my moments. And I've had no complaints."

I cleared my throat, eager to shift the subject. Sensing my skin warming under my shirt, I pulled my focus back to Charlotte. "How did you and Charlotte become friends?" I asked.

"You mean, how does a bartender become best friends with the wife of a multimillionaire drug dealer? We clicked, simple as that. We talked . . . a lot. Not like girlie talk, deep stuff, stuff that mattered. She had hangers-on, plenty of people willing to help spend her money, but no one she could really talk to."

"So, she must have told you about Paco?"

"I never met him, but from what she told me, he's a real piece of work."

"Does he know about you?"

She shook her head. "Hell no. She needed something in her life that was hers."

"Did you know he's had her followed since they separated?"

"Is that why you're here?" she asked, a steelier edge to her voice. "You're working for that piece of shit?"

"It's complicated, but to be honest, he didn't leave me much choice."

"I've heard he can be like that," McKay said, softening. She leaned forward and lowered her voice. "Do you think he killed her?"

"Charlotte's the mother of his children," I said, "and he sent me to find her. Why send me and have her killed if he was close to getting the divorce papers signed? It doesn't make sense."

"Unless he wanted to frame you for Charlotte's murder. She's dead now; no need to sign anything. You think that makes sense, Mitch?"

In the night's turbulence, that nuance hadn't hit me, but my mind shot back to my conversation with Victor when he swore he had no angle to play. After what Jason, the young server, had told me, and the photo of Victor and Charlotte together, I began to suspect Victor did have an angle after all. I just hadn't figured out the dimensions or the degrees yet.

"Do you know anything about a laptop?"

"Is that why Charlotte was killed? For some laptop?"

"I was only meant to locate Charlotte," I clarified. "But she thought I'd come for a laptop. I set her straight, not that it did any good."

"Sorry," McKay said, shrugging. "Charlotte never mentioned any laptop."

We sat silently for a few minutes. McKay sipped her bourbon and kept looking at me as if expecting me to make some kind of move. I hadn't felt that kind of crackle of sexual energy for some time, not since I'd started dating Sierra. But it had been months since I'd shared Sierra's bed, and in the darkest hours of the early morning, I wondered if I'd ever share that marital bed again. McKay was sending me all the right signals, but I'd already caused Sierra enough pain, and had plenty of guilt weighing me down without adding to the burden. Hoping to distract my mind, I gestured at the photographs on the wall.

"So, you were on a TV show?"

She swirled the bourbon around her glass. "Not just *a* TV show, top-rated network sitcom of 1995, *Hollywood High*."

"Is that a drug or school reference?"

"Good question. School," she confirmed. "I played the hot young teacher, snarky attitude, feminist, sticking it to the patriarchy, but with style and sex appeal."

"Sounds like the best high-school teacher I never had. What happened?"

"Our leading man was caught in a scandal with young boys. In fact, the executive producer and most of the writers' room were all implicated."

"Don't remember reading about that in the glossies."

"No shit," she said, taking a large slug. "Anyway, the network pulled the show. It was all over in a matter of weeks. I landed a few walk-on parts after that, but like they say, shit sticks. My agent dropped me; I wasn't the hot young talent anymore. Didn't bother me too much at the time; I'd already soured on the whole LA vibe by then and figured I'd get the hell out before I became one of those desperate actors who shows up to the opening of a bag of chips. It wasn't all bad, made enough money to buy this place, and the residuals keep coming in." She leaned back. "There, that's my sad-sack 'Where are they now?' story. What about you?"

"Boring in comparison. I'm a court lawyer. I research cases for judges."

"Boring? Okay, tonight you were beaten up by two thugs, hijacked at gunpoint, then barely escaped with your life, and had a woman you just met die in your arms. If that's boring, I don't want a rundown of the exciting parts of your life."

"I like to under-promise and over-deliver."

"Still, how the hell does a court lawyer get caught up in a shit storm like this?"

"Did my best friend a favor. Stood up in court and told the truth."

"They do say the road to hell is paved with good deeds," she said, raising her glass.

A heavy weariness tsunamied through me. I felt my body sink into the couch. I pointed at the stack of DVDs lined up beside the flat screen. "Is that your show?" I asked.

"Season one and two."

"Could we watch an episode?"

"Seriously?"

"After the day I've had, I could do with some comic relief."

"Don't get your hopes up."

"Don't worry, I keep the bar real low on those these days."

McKay slotted in a DVD and punched the volume. The opening titles were your typical gritty, fast-cut, MTV-style graphics set to a faux grunge track. McKay, or Charley Lomax, as she was called in the show, was good, damn good. She reminded me of a young Kaley Cuoco, with the same vibrant energy. We watched the first episode. I laughed out loud a couple of times and encouraged her to play another. We were halfway through the episode when I saw another face I recognized: the young woman playing Charley Lomax's younger English cousin, visiting her in LA. It was Charlotte. I kicked myself for not seeing it before; the resemblance was striking, uncanny even.

I looked at McKay. She was wiping her tears with the sleeve of her gown.

"Shit," I said, turning. "You and Charlotte—?"

She inhaled a tight, grounding breath. "Half-sisters. Same father. Charlotte's mom, some rich British aristocrat; I, the daughter of a horse wrangler mom living out in Ojai. I was the embarrassing pre-marriage fuck up. Charlotte tracked me down, stayed with me in LA for a while, thought she wanted to become an actor and ended up on the casting couch with an agent and got herself a one-off role on the show. She was pretty good, but didn't have the ambition and didn't need the money. We kept in touch after that. She'd visit whenever she was in town for the polo matches." McKay wiped a tear from her eye. "Charlotte helped me out when she could. She was a good person until she got mixed up with Castillo. He did a number on her. I can never forgive him for that."

I remembered what Charlotte had said when I'd asked why she hadn't left Palm Springs days ago. "She wanted to see you before she left. A last goodbye?"

McKay nodded. "I didn't figure it would be so final, you know. I keep expecting her to turn up on my doorstep with a bottle of expensive champagne and a pack of those cigarettes she loved to smoke. Always told her they'd be the death of her, but I guess . . ." McKay's words tapered into silence.

"I'm so sorry. I had no idea. Can I do anything—?"

"No, thanks . . . I'll mourn in my own time and in my own way," McKay interrupted, pressing the remote.

I watched the show for another ten minutes before ebbing into a deep, dreamless sleep, feeling no pain for eight hours until I woke the next morning, a blanket over me, shoes removed, body aching as if I'd been tumbled around a cement mixer. McKay was still asleep, and I figured I'd leave before she woke. When you come delivering bad news, it's polite not to outstay your welcome. McKay needed her time to grieve.

* * *

Outside, the morning was already hot, the sky brutally blue, the sun a thuggish orange fist. Walking past the pool, I checked for my wallet. As I flipped it open, the photo of Sierra and Kurt fell to the floor. Last night came screaming back to me. How close I'd come to leaving Kurt fatherless and Sierra a young widow. I'd been caught up in the pretense, taken a risk I had no right in taking.

It hit me, right there as I knelt on the chlorine-speckled concrete to pick up the photograph, that this had all been one big gamble, another spin of the wheel, a shake and roll of the dice, just like I'd always done. Nothing had changed, except this time, I'd gambled with something far more important than money. I'd placed a bet on my life, and against the odds, I'd survived. Maybe next time, lady luck wouldn't be so generous.

Sliding the photo back into my wallet, another thought slammed me like a hammer in the sternum. Whoever had killed

Charlotte was looking for the laptop, would have taken the house apart searching for it, and would have most definitely taken Charlotte's cell phone. The last photos she took were of my driver's license and the snapshot of Sierra and Kurt. I could have kicked my own ass for being so stupid. I should have taken Charlotte's phone when I had the chance.

Sitting on the edge of a sun lounger, I put my head between my knees. The pummeling my body received last night was nothing compared to the brutal reality that I'd now put my family in danger. I sensed this time the pain would last longer, cut deeper.

I couldn't get the hell out of Palm Springs fast enough. Hoped I never had to set foot in the place again.

PART 4:
BANG BANG! THE BITCH IS DEAD

CHAPTER 23

I took the 9:50 a.m. flight from Palm Springs and arrived in Oakland at 12:30 p.m. Thirty minutes later, I was in the shower examining the bruises that ran over my body like tire tracks, and figured, as McKay had wisely said, there was little I could do but let them heal. But time takes its own sweet time when it comes to healing; doesn't respond well to being rushed.

Calling Sierra and Kurt was number one on my to-do list. I wanted to lose myself for a few minutes into the comfort of their voices. I couldn't be one hundred percent certain Charlotte's killer had found her phone, seen the photos, and was now headed to Northern California to hunt them down. Still, even a one percent chance was enough to spike my neck hairs and elevate my anxiety levels.

Item number two on my list was Victor. I figured neither he nor Paco would have found out about Charlotte's death yet. McKay had agreed not to alert the police until after I boarded the plane, putting several hours between me and Palm Springs. I had a dossier of questions, but had no idea how Victor would react to Charlotte's murder. All I knew was that it wasn't the kind of news you broke over the phone.

We arranged to meet on the 3 p.m. ferry from Jack London to San Francisco. The afternoon was sunny and cloudless with a light breeze, the surface of the bay troubled by a few whitecaps swirling across the swell. Compared to the searing heat of Palm Springs, it was about as perfect a Bay Area Sunday afternoon as you could hope for.

Victor was already standing at the bow of the boat when I boarded, wearing an expensive casual outfit: cream cashmere and spotless suede boots.

"What the fuck happened to you? You look like shit."

"Fell down some stairs."

"Like hell you did."

The ferry bayed its horn, spat a mass of thick backwash into the dock, and headed west.

"Why meet here?" I asked. "Didn't figure you for the public transport type, or you just into big boats?"

"Got an appointment in the City. Figured I could kill two birds. Anyway, being on the water gives you a different perspective on life, good for the soul." He paused. "So, do you come bearing good news, *amigo*?"

"Erm, not exactly."

I told Victor everything from when I arrived to being abducted by Charlotte. He said nothing, just listened; that was the lawyer in him, absorbing information, mentally laying out his questions for later. It wasn't until I told him Charlotte had died in my arms that he showed any reaction. He gripped the ferry's safety barrier and looked out to the water as we motored under the shadow of the Bay Bridge. A shiver cut through me as the bridge's gray concrete blocked out the sun for the next few minutes.

"One question. Are you one hundred percent sure?"

"She died in my arms. I was covered in her blood, Vic. There's no way she's alive."

I noticed his hands trembling. Victor was about as shaken as I'd ever seen him, a rare chink in his cool armor.

"'Protect her'? Are you sure that's what she said?"

"Best I could make out . . . *protect her*. Any idea what it means?"

Victor shook his head, reached into his pocket for a cigarette, and tried to light the tip, but his hands were trembling too much to hold the lighter steady.

"Here, let me," I said, taking the lighter and cupping my hands.

He took a long inhale and stood back.

"Thought you'd quit."

"Work in progress," he muttered, then shook his head. "Fuck, this is not good news. Not the outcome Paco was hoping for."

"Well, maybe you shouldn't have sent a court lawyer to do your dirty work. I should never have listened to you."

"You were more than happy to take the money." He took another long drag. "Fuck, Paco's not going to be happy. He is not going to be happy."

"Not happy about what, exactly? Charlotte's murder or his lawyer screwing his wife? I reckon he's gonna be pretty pissed about both those things, don't you think?"

Victor's face paled. "How did—?"

"The polo match? I saw a photograph of both of you getting cozy by the winner's enclosure. Does Paco know?"

"It wasn't like that. I was trying to help her. Jesus, you really think I was sleeping with Paco's wife?"

"Then tell me what was it like, because that's exactly how it looked to me, and how it'll look to Paco if he ever sees those pictures."

He nodded. "Appreciate your concern, but locating Charlotte was your only task, Mitch."

"Well, task accomplished, Vic. Is that why Paco sent me? So he could frame me for his wife's murder?"

"No, not in his interest."

"Why? Because he still needs to find the laptop?"

Victor pointed his cigarette at me. "Gotta hand it to you, Mitch, you're a damn sight smarter than I gave you credit for."

"So, this was about this laptop all along?"

"I didn't want to get you in this deep, I promise. Your only job was to locate Charlotte, and I'd do the rest."

"So why didn't Charlotte tell you where she was hiding, if you were helping her?"

"She didn't trust me, didn't trust anyone. Things were escalating between her and Paco, even worse than usual. Oksana was putting pressure on him for the divorce; Charlotte dug in her heels. That's why I needed someone I could trust to find Charlotte before Paco did. I trusted he wouldn't do something rash—"

"Like having his wife murdered?"

Victor wiped a hand across his face. "Yeah, something like that."

I nodded. "Okay, if you weren't sleeping with her, why were you helping her?"

Victor took a breath. "Okay, we did have sex. Just twice, I swear."

"Jesus Christ!"

"What can I tell you? The heart wants what the heart wants."

"Can I not be in the room when you spin Paco that line?" I said. "When was this?"

"It was long after they split. I don't have a death wish."

"Jesus, why the fuck didn't you tell me? I thought we were friends."

"Best you didn't know. Nobody knew."

"So, what was the plan? Find this laptop, make some deal with Paco, and you and Charlotte ride off into the sunset?"

"It's more complicated than that."

"Is that why you shook Charlotte like a rag doll and left her crying on her knees in a fucking field? Because things got complicated?"

Victor winced. "Don't pass judgment on things you don't understand."

"Then explain it to me."

Victor sighed. "Charlotte had a drinking problem from way back. Didn't know when she'd had enough. I thought she had it under control, but that day at the Polo Fields, she got totally wasted; I'd never seen her like that before. Honestly, Mitch, she scared the shit out of me. She threatened to tell Paco everything, fuck the consequences. I couldn't let her do that. It would have been a death sentence for both of us. I just panicked. I wanted to make her see sense." He looked out at the deep green roll of the bay. "Do you have any idea what being Paco's wife means?"

"I can guess."

"I don't think you can. Her children, her home? He held them over her like bargaining chips. While Paco's alive, Charlotte's never free of him."

"Well, I guess she's free now."

I noticed Victor flinch at the remark, though I didn't regret my words.

"Okay, there's something else I need to tell you . . ." I told him about the photos Charlotte had taken of Kurt and Sierra and my driver's license.

He nodded. "And now you're worried whoever killed Charlotte sees the pictures, then comes after you and your family because they think you have the laptop?"

Hearing my private thoughts spoken out loud gave them some dreadful permanence. "No, I'm not worried," I said. "I'm fucking terrified. She didn't tell me where the laptop was. Did she tell you?"

"We shared a bed. She didn't share her secrets."

I stepped closer and poked Victor in the chest. "You know what I feel like doing right now, Vic? Tossing you right off this fucking boat."

"Can I buy you a drink instead?" he said, complete with a shit-eating grin. He flicked his cigarette into the wind and watched it backflip into the water. "Be a lot less messy for both of us."

He looked to his right and made the *over here* gesture. I hadn't seen her board, but I immediately recognized the tattoos and the pierced nostril: Alma Torres, Victor's private investigator, slouching on a bench, phone in her hand, white earbuds just visible to the side of the black hoodie pulled over her head. She picked up her backpack and sauntered over. The world-weary sentiment printed on the front of her hoodie read: *Disappointed . . . but Not Surprised.*

"Yeah," she said, scuffling her boots on the deck. "Need something?"

Victor handed her two twenty-dollar bills. "Couple of beers and one for yourself."

"Sure thing. You want eats too?"

"No, but knock yourself out."

"Right on," she said, shuffling over to the indoor concession stand.

"What is she, like, your bodyguard?"

"Alma's a safe pair of hands to have around, a good note-taker." Victor put his palms on my shoulders and looked me in the eye. "I'll make this up to you, promise. I'll have Alma keep an eye on Sierra and Kurt. No charge. She'll be discreet, watch the house, you can trust her."

"That's big of you. How can I ever repay you for everything you've done for me?" The sarcasm didn't go unnoticed.

"Good, now you've got that out of your system, we've still got two major problems. Finding the laptop and telling Paco his wife's been murdered."

"No, those are your problems, Vic. I'm done."

"Done? You want to tell that to Paco?"

"If I have to, yes."

Alma returned, handed over our beers, and adjusted her earbuds. "I can start tonight," she said. "Just need your address."

I looked at Victor and noticed his cell phone was live.

"Did she hear everything?"

"Like I said, Alma's a good note-taker."

"Jesus, Victor, you could have asked. What were you hoping for? Some confession you could play to Paco?"

"You've got it all wrong, *amigo*. Just covering my bases, that's all."

As Alma slunk back to her seat, Victor took a slug of beer. "Look, I'll deliver Paco the bad news, but he'll want to see you. Make sure you keep your story straight. He'll want to know everything. Don't plan on getting home early. And, Mitch, what we just discussed—"

"Yeah, between us," I snapped.

As we passed under the deep shadow of the bridge, the sun reappeared in all its warming glory, but I kept on shivering like a wet dog until we docked on the other side of the bay.

CHAPTER 24

The Port of Oakland lies east of San Francisco Bay, a city within a city constructed of corten steel shipping containers bisected by a rat run of alleyways. Long-armed cranes dominate the iron and steel skyline, while a hundred feet below, a single access road groans under the constant roll of haulage trucks.

I was to meet Paco and Victor at dock number nine, close to where the spider-shouldered Panamax cranes off-loaded goods from container ships and onto the docks. Suite 234 was at the end of the row of offices, all with a similar red and gray exterior. It was the only office with a storage area attached to the side, secured by a corrugated iron door at least ten feet high and twenty feet wide.

The sign above the office read *Celica Holdings*. Victor had told me the company was Paco's attempt at legitimacy. A construction enterprise operating as the public face of his empire, separated from his less legitimate ventures by a labyrinth of shell companies hiding within shell companies like some Russian doll of bureaucracy.

As I entered the second-floor office, Victor sat astride the arm of a leather couch next to the window, looking distracted. Paco sat behind a walnut-colored desk, a huge aerial print of the port hung behind him. He wore a pinstriped suit and a red tie, looking at every part of the successful business owner except for the bronze-colored .45 on the desk, which immediately triggered some serious PTSD from the weekend. I pushed through the trauma and greeted them both.

Paco gestured I should sit in the chair across from him, then noticed me eyeing the weapon. "You recognize the gun, *sí*?"

My stomach tightened like someone was twisting my intestines into a bowknot as I sat. I noticed the office contained no personal artifacts; Paco probably only used the space when a discreet meeting was called for; no security cameras and only a single service road granting access in and out, the ink-green bay water the only alternative exit route.

Paco picked up the gun and cradled it in his hand. "I gave Charlotte a similar one many years ago, for her own protection." He paused, considered the .45 and shrugged. "But bullets cannot control the fates. They will always have their way."

"I'm sorry for your loss," I said.

He laid the gun back on the table. "My children will feel her loss the most, of course. With no mother, life is so much harder; children lose their buffer against the world, but on the other hand, it can also make them stronger. What do you think, Mitch?"

"Erm, I guess if it's a choice between a mother or no mother, I'd have to choose the former."

"*Sí*, you are a father also. We understand each other."

"I just wanted to say I had nothing to do with Charlotte's murder," I blurted, desperate to lay that vital information on the table next to the weapon.

"I know. If I suspected otherwise, you would not be sitting here."

My bones shivered at the remark. "Do you know who killed her?"

"We will find out," he said, twirling the gun on the table, making sure the barrel faced me. "Now, tell me everything. Every detail."

Paco's face remained rock stoic as I spoke. I could have been reading him the baseball scores, but I figured this wasn't Paco's first rodeo when it came to receiving bad news. I omitted any reference to McKay; neither Victor nor Paco knew she existed, and I wanted to keep it that way.

Like some detective trying to trip me up in an interrogation, Paco had me repeat the story three times before he was satisfied, keeping my narrative exactly the same on each telling: no deviation, no added flourishes. I felt as if I was offering the Gods of Mount Paco my words as a sacrifice to prevent the earth from splitting open and the heavens from raining hellfire over me. I expected him to kick his chair back, shove the .45 down my throat, and threaten me with all manner of unspeakable tortures, but Paco kept his cool. The rumbling volcano was placated, at least for the moment.

Finally, he spoke. "And the men who did this to you?" he said, pointing at my face.

"Couple of thugs. The daughter of the guy who runs the pawnbroker's called them while I was waiting on my hot wings. Didn't stand much of a chance."

"This Hector, *sí*?"

"He prefers Hetch."

"Do you think this Hetch and his daughter are involved in Charlotte's murder?"

"I couldn't rightly say, but I found this in the ashtray in his store," I said, placing the Sobranie tip on the table.

Paco took a breath. "I think this must be so." He pushed his chair back and stood by the window, where the sun was setting in a fireball of red behind the *fuck you* middle finger of the Salesforce Tower that dominated the San Francisco skyline. "Victor, do you have thoughts?"

Victor sat to attention. "There has to be a connection. Charlotte probably paid the daughter to run into the back of the Escalade, giving her enough time to make her getaway."

"Did Charlotte tell you anything else before she died?" Paco said, lowering his voice. "And, Mitch, think carefully before you answer."

"She mentioned a laptop, that was all."

Paco's neck muscles twitched under his shirt collar. "Did she tell you the location of the laptop?"

"It all happened too fast. I didn't wait around to make conversation."

I figured informing Paco of his wife's last words served no purpose. From the corner of my eyes, I noticed Victor discreetly shaking his head. He and I were obviously on the same page.

Paco pulled his shoulders back. "Victor, that laptop cannot fall into the wrong hands. Understand?"

"Sure, I got it covered. Mitch and I will find it."

I shot Victor a look and turned to Paco. "No, I'm done. You can count me out. I've already put my life on the line here."

Paco clenched and unclenched his fists. I sensed a vat of anger roiling inside him he was struggling hard to contain. Figuring I'd crossed some invisible line, I backtracked.

"Okay, right, look, Paco, I'm not cut out for this. I'm just a court lawyer. I found Charlotte; that was the deal. I didn't expect to get beaten up and shot at for the privilege."

Paco smiled. "Your concerns are valid," he said, the setting sun behind him casting a red hue over his face, making him look like a grotesque oil painting of Lucifer's fall from grace. "But what you must understand is that your debt to Errol Capriani is paid, and now that debt is owed to me."

He reached for the gun, slipping it into his jacket pocket. "And do not forget, Mitch, you are done when Paco Castillo says you are done."

* * *

As I left the office, Paco's parting words rang like the distant toll of a bell; a threat about as thinly veiled and revealing as a stripper's thong. I expected to feel relieved he hadn't blamed me for Charlotte's death, but any relief paled compared to the sobering reality that the pact I'd made with the devil still wasn't over, not by a long shot.

An icy wind picked up on the dockside, cutting through my thin T-shirt and bomber jacket. To the west, the sun scattered red and orange specks like some vast abstract painting onto San Francisco's downtown skyscrapers. On any other occasion, I would have taken the time to enjoy the view and add it to the long list of reasons why I loved living in the Bay Area, but fear and anger flooded my blood in equal measure, stripping any joy from the moment.

In a single weekend, my life had split apart at the seams. I now realized Paco had no intention of letting me walk into the sunset with a pat on the back and a *thank you for your service*. For Paco, coincidences didn't exist, accidents were planned or scheduled, and a debt was a debt; repay or suffer the consequences. At that moment, my thoughts turned to Ron Boone's niece. However indirectly, Paco had Masie's blood on his hands. He may not have pulled the trigger, but his fingerprints were surely on the bullet. I could only wonder how many hundreds of bullets had Paco's greasy prints smeared all over them.

I was heading back to my car when, a few feet ahead of me, like a wraith emerging from the shadows, Paco's driver, Jorge, scuttled out from behind a shipping container. He threw a cigarette to the floor and ground the stub with the sole of his sneaker. As he shuffled toward me, he made sure I saw the handle of a revolver tucked into his pants belt.

"Looking good, Jorge," I said, gesturing at his dark blue two-piece suit. He kept pulling at the sleeves as if the suit was stuck to his body with duct tape, and if he tugged hard enough, he'd free himself.

Ignoring my comment, he said, "Boss asked me to take you back to your car."

"No need. I'm parked nearby."

He gave me that crooked fifty-cent smile of his. He must have noticed how tense I was. "Hey, chill out, ay, homie, it's all good," he said, spreading his arms as if exaggerating his point. "Boss wants to make sure you get back safe, is all, and I got a job to do." He gestured to my Saab a hundred feet to the right of the nearest row of containers. "Them your wheels?"

I nodded.

"Then let's go, *pendejo*," he said, chuckling.

"You see anyone else around here?" he asked, as we threaded the narrow alleyways between the containers.

"Like who?"

"Dunno. Someone looking at shit they shouldn't be looking at."

"You'd be the first I'd tell if I did."

"Good answer. Boss likes to keep shit closed down, ay, make sure no fucker's poking around his business. Trusts me to keep things tight, you know."

"Can't be too careful," I agreed.

As we stopped at my car, he looked me over as if he was sizing me up, maybe calculating the number of weights needed to secure around my waist to guarantee my body sunk to the bottom of the bay, if that became necessary.

"I've been thinking on something, homie," he said, sucking his teeth. "How come you got outta Palm Springs before the police found Charlotte's body? Gotta be what? Eight hours between Paco's wife's getting a bullet in the head, and your plane

162

takes off. I figure that's gotta be some dumb luck nobody saw you leave, what with that being a quiet neighborhood, 'n' all. Gunshots would have woken the neighbors?"

"Old folks," I said. "Probably out cold for the night after taking their Ambien."

"Yeah, I thought of that, but it don't add up. You took Charlotte's wheels, must have driven it someplace, but in the morning it's back in the driveway like it never left. Didn't drive itself back, did it?"

"How did you know about the neighborhood anyway, Jorge?"

"Boss asked me to search on Google Maps, street view. What the fuck do you think?"

I nodded. "Well, if that's the interrogation over, I'd better get home."

Jorge had other ideas. He pinned his palm on my chest. "You ain't answered my question. Who drove the Bentley back to Charlotte's crib? Sure as hell weren't you, homie, because your ass would have been on a plane back to Oakland."

I had to think fast. McKay had assured me she'd take care of getting the car back to Charlotte's, but I hadn't bothered asking how. "I drove it myself," I said. "Later that night, well, early morning, to be precise."

"To be precise?" He shook his head. "Then how d'ya get back to the hotel?"

"I walked a mile from the house and called a cab to pick me up outside a strip mall."

"What, like an Uber?"

"No, not an Uber, Jorge; that shit's traceable. Anyway, I only had the burner phone Paco gave me, no apps. I called a cab, Palm Springs Yellow, paid cash."

"And how comes you got the number of a cab company out in butt fuck nowhere with no internet."

"The same cab company that took me to the polo fields that morning. I kept the card, just in case."

Jorge pursed his lips and drew back a little.

"Swear, it's the truth. I've got nothing to gain by lying to you or Paco."

"You swear it's the truth?" He spat a glob of phlegm on the ground. "Yeah, that's good. Guess as a lawyer you're used to that, right? Standing up, swearing to tell the truth."

"I'm not that kind of lawyer."

"Sure, you are. You stood up at Paco's trial."

"That was different. I was called as an expert witness."

"Got Paco off from standing trial, *seguro*."

"For which he was very grateful."

"Sure, forty-eight grand grateful."

"How did you know?"

"There ain't much I don't know 'bout Paco's business." He leaned closer. "I make it my business. The way I figure, plenty of people got real pissed Paco got off standing trial."

"What kind of people?"

"People looking to get revenge."

"Revenge? On me?"

He laughed. "Shit, no one gives a fuck about you, *cabrón*."

"Good to know. Can I go now?"

Jorge placed a hand on my chest. "You know, you and me, we're the same, right?"

"The same how?"

"You don't see it? It's obvious."

"You'll have to elaborate."

"Elaborate? Sure," he said, stepping closer. Alcohol and stale tobacco curled from his breath. "We're both Paco's bitches. Bought, paid for, ain't no way out until Paco decides we're out, or if he ain't alive no more to make that decision."

"I don't—"

He interrupted. "Paco don't extend any credit to no one. Always gotta be payback, you know?"

"I think our situations are different. You work for Paco. I'm just clearing my debt."

Jorge's eyes narrowed; my remark had hit a nerve. "Bullshit. Just because you're some lawyer, you think you're better than me, that it?"

"No, no, I don't—"

He poked me in the chest with his finger. "Yeah, *claro*, motherfucker, you're no better." He turned his arm to show me the blood-red *Sangres Norteñas* tattoo. "Maybe we get you one of these bad boys? Means *por vida* . . . like for ever."

"Yeah, I know what for *por vida* means, Jorge."

"Good," he said. "And, just an FY fucking I, you work for Paco, I work for Paco, and until that situation changes, if he gets shit on his shoes, we all get shit on our shoes."

"Whatever you say. Can I go now?"

Jorge pondered on the request and tugged at his jacket sleeves. "One more thing. Ain't nobody lives for ever. Comes to survival, you gotta choose sides, make allegiances. Shit's always changing, you know; just be prepared. You feel me?"

I felt nothing but a wave of fatigue, too beaten down to figure out whatever tortured point Jorge was attempting to make. This was just another threat, one of many I'd faced over the past few days. I added it to the shit pile building at the bottom of my memory dumpster, knowing deep in my gut one of those threats would eventually come home to roost. The only questions were which one and when.

CHAPTER 25

I crash-landed back to reality Monday morning and tried focusing on work, but the forty-eight hours spent in Palm Springs was taking up precious rental space in my head as I kept rewinding events like a worn-out VHS tape until the memories caught in the spindles, creasing into a mess of splintered images.

As I walked in, I saw the three musketeers absorbed in their screens. I'd done my best to disguise the sorry state of my face with a thin layer of foundation I'd found in an old makeup tub at the apartment, probably left by an ex-girlfriend of Victor's; I still looked like a human Mr. Potato Head who's suffered traumatic spousal abuse at the tiny, plastic hands of Mrs. Potato Head.

Tye was the first to spot the damage. "Jesus, boss, what the heck happened? You okay? Need anything?"

"One question at a time, Tye, please."

Katie and Muriel joined in the chorus of questions. I made up some lame story about taking an ill-advised jog along the Bay Coastal Path and tripping over a shih tzu running wild off-leash, falling face-first onto the loose gravel track.

"You should sue," Katie said. "I hate small yappy dogs, pain in the ass. I mean, if you want a dog get a proper dog, not some plush toy that shits everywhere."

"Isn't that the kind of dog your boyfriend's got?"

"Exactly my fucking point, Tye."

"Thanks, but I think I'd rather just forget about the whole thing, move on."

"Sure, but if it was me—"

Sensing Katie wasn't likely to let this go, Muriel jumped in. "You've sure been in the wars lately, Mitch," she said — I could always count on Athos to create a necessary distraction when needed. "And that makeup job's not doing you any favors. What were you thinking?" She grabbed her purse from the desk. "You've applied that foundation with the finesse of a blind drag queen."

"Bang goes my backup career," I said.

Muriel shook her head and gestured I should follow her into one of the all-gender restrooms on our floor. She took out her makeup wipes and got to work on my face. I flinched as she dabbed and fussed.

"You want to tell me what the hell's going on? First, you get knocked off your bike, and then you trip over a dog? Now, the bike I can get behind, but the dog, that's a stretch. I've known you too long, so don't bullshit me."

"Just a run of bad luck."

"No shit. Is this to do with the Judge Harper thing? Did you ask someone the wrong questions, and they gave you this for an answer?" she asked, poking my cheek.

"Ouch," I complained.

"Well, did they?"

"Like I said, tripped over a dog. Could have happened to anyone."

"Sure, have it your way." She stood back and admired her handiwork. "There, that's better."

I glanced at my reflection and had to admit it was an improvement. I looked almost human now, a slightly more glamorous Mr. Potato Head.

"You want some lipstick with that?" Muriel asked.

Normally, I would have picked up on the ribbing, but my mind was tracking slow, and it took me a moment. "Yeah, hilarious. You should go into stand-up when you retire."

She gestured at my face. "So, *was* this because of the Harper thing? You didn't answer."

"That's right, I didn't. Thanks for this. I owe you one."

"Sure you do. How about a drink tonight?"

I raised my eyebrows, mind ticking back in sync. "And here's me thinking you were a happily married woman."

"Asshole," she said, whacking my arm. "I meant the team — us, Kat, and Tye. Remember, you said we'd regroup after the weekend? And by the way, I spent the past two days digging around some old court records, put together some research that might help us out. Send out an email of where and when we'll be there. Oh, and as an FYI, you're not my type."

"Right. Prefer your men with less makeup?"

"No, the makeup I could live with. It's the lying that would push me over the edge."

* * *

As the morning slipped into lunchtime, I felt the familiar nagging pangs of hunger and headed to the courthouse café, hoping I wouldn't run into Ron Boone; the café seemed his ground zero for hunting me down. He'd sent me another five emails on top of the six he sent me over the weekend, all saying the same thing but phrased differently: that Castillo should pay for what he did, that Harper was a corrupt asshole who should spend the rest of his miserable days in a federal penitentiary, and that, by having the gall to ignore his messages, I was just as big an asshole as Harper. Though he did suggest giving me a pass on the jail time if I replied in a timely manner. *Mighty big of you*, I thought as I ransacked his emails with the delete button. Ron was still raw. Better to let him stew in his anger for a while. Hopefully, he'd eventually simmer down to a slow roil.

As I picked up my food tray, I noticed Judge Harriet Croft sitting in the corner, pecking at her chicken salad, glancing at her cell phone. She was dressed the same as always: form-fitting black dress, pearl necklace, pale blue eyeshadow, hair straightened the way older African American ladies prefer because they think it makes them look younger.

I was planning on making an appointment to see Judge Croft with some invented agenda that would allow me to probe her about Harper. I had to guess, as the assistant presiding judge, she knew about Harper calling in retired judges to try cases, but how much she knew or even if she was part of the shady dealings, I was still in the dark. Figuring an accidental meet would feel less contrived, I took my Italian three-meat torpedo roll, chips, and large Coke and sauntered over.

"Judge Croft," I said. "Surprised to see you here mingling with the masses."

She looked up. "Mr. Sweeney." She gestured at the mountain of processed calories on my tray. "You do know that's a heart attack waiting to happen?"

"Bit delicate today," I said. "Got involved in an accident over the weekend. I was feeling sorry for myself, so I figured some comfort food wouldn't hurt."

"Not in the short run, maybe," she said, studying my face. "Nice job on the cover-up. Did your wife do that?"

"Em, no, my researcher, Muriel," I said, the word "wife" having momentarily snagged in my brain. "Do you mind?" I asked, gesturing to the chair across from her.

"Highly preferable to you hovering over me."

I sat and snuck a chip from the bag. "Missed you at Paco Castillo's suppression motion, your honor. I hope everything's okay."

"Are you talking generally or referring to something more specific?"

"Judge Harper mentioned you had a family emergency, which is why he adjudicated the hearing."

"You must have heard wrong. I was assigned to another trial. Judge Harper volunteered to sit in for me. The old goat wasn't too happy, but I heard you helped sway the judgment. Expert witness?"

I leaned over the table and lowered my voice. "Just between you and me, would you have made the same call and suppressed the evidence?"

"You're asking me to comment on the Superior Court's presiding judge's ruling?"

"No, not officially, of course. Just curious."

She sat back and wiped her mouth with her napkin. "I presided at the first hearing and had doubts about the body-cam narrative back then."

"Enough doubts to make the same call as Harper?"

"Judge Harper made the call which he felt was right. He's the most experienced judge on the bench. I'm not about to second-guess his rulings."

"But it's not the call you'd have made?" I pushed.

Judge Croft shoved her plate to one side. "Exactly where are you going with this? My lunch break's nearly over, and I'm due in court for what's stacking up to be a very long and tedious afternoon."

"Oh, nowhere, really," I said. "What with Harper retiring in a few months, it surprised me he even agreed to sit in on a suppression motion. He could have called in one of the retired judges to fill in. Would you? Have called in a retired judge?"

"Odd question. I feel like I'm being set up for some kind of judicial ambush."

"No ambush. Sorry if it came off that way. It's just that the courthouse rumor mill's been working overtime. You know how these things escalate."

"No. I don't hear rumors, Mr. Sweeney, I hear evidence. Maybe if I mingled with the masses more frequently, I'd be, as they say, in the loop."

Nicely played, I thought, then said, "Thing is, some of the court admin staff noticed a sharp uptick in the number of retired judges called in to try cases. Just wondered if you were aware?"

She smiled. "Old judges never retire, they're just on call. Isn't that what they say?"

"You've heard that, too?"

"I may be out of the rumor mill, but I'm not out of touch. I had my granddaughter create a meme of the saying for me and hung it on the wall of my chambers as a warning to myself."

"A warning against what?"

"A warning that when that blessed day I retire finally comes, I won't be stepping my very expensive heels back in these hallways to try anything other than whatever's new on the café menu."

I laughed. "I guess it's good to have motivation."

"So, this a pep talk?"

"No, just making conversation."

She smiled. "An unusual conversation to be having over the lunch table."

"It was just on my mind, so . . ."

"Personally, I'd imagine those kinds of conversations are best had outside the courthouse, don't you think?"

I couldn't be sure, but I was almost certain Judge Croft was offering me an opening, or at least edging the door open a millimeter or two, to let in a chink of light.

She grabbed her tray and stood.

"Oh, one more question, your honor," I said. "Who was the judge who asked you to step down from the Castillo hearing?"

"Presiding Judge Harper. If the inquisition's over, I have work to do."

She offered a parting smile. "And Mr. Sweeney, I wouldn't pay heed to rumors. They're like ear holes: everybody's got one, and often they only hear what they want to hear. And yes, that is the PG-rated version I tell my young nieces and nephews, in case you were wondering."

CHAPTER 26

Prompted by Muriel's suggestion, I invited the three musketeers for after-work drinks at O'Neils, a classic study in Celtic cliché, with shillelaghs hanging from the faux-tin ceiling, a frayed Irish flag draped over the bar, and faded posters from the seventies which I was sure were a rallying call encouraging *fine young men like you* to sign up for the Provisional IRA.

Walking to our table, we passed several off-duty OPD uniformed officers huddled in a cove to the right of the bar. Despite their having their backs turned to the incoming foot traffic, I sensed their eyes follow us as we walked by.

I'd have preferred a less *judicial* meeting place, but everyone had lives to attend to and the pub was only two blocks from the courthouse and a short walk to the BART station. As we sat, The Pogues' "Streets of Sorrow" played over the sound system while an older man in a black beret and camo jacket mumbled along with the lyrics, gazing into his whiskey as if searching for his memories shipwrecked somewhere on the ice cubes.

Muriel was the first to speak. "I can't stay long. I've got dinner to prepare, and it's book club night."

"Sweet," Tye said, sipping his Guinness. "Means we get more cookies tomorrow."

"Don't get too excited, Tye, Lori's baking."

"Hey, a cookie's a cookie. I ain't fussy."

"All I'm saying," Muriel said, lowering her voice, "Lori's no Martha Stewart. Uses way too much sugar. You know why, right?"

"Because she likes it sweet?"

"Because, if you put enough sugar in anything, it covers the taste. Any fool can throw sugar, eggs, and flour in a bowl and call it a cookie. Didn't your mom ever tell you that?"

"Nope. She told me to be grateful if someone gives me a free cookie, though."

I watched this brief exchange like a spectator neck-flicking at a tennis game. Athos and Porthos were seriously invested in this conversation, like it really mattered. But who was I to judge? I'd have welcomed to have nothing more pressing on my mind than Book Club Lori's lack of baking skills.

Katie spoke up. "Jesus, can you two stop jerking off to your cookie cum show for a second and focus?"

"Whoa! 'Cookie cum show'?" Tye said. "What's up? Got a hot game of Catan waiting for you back at home? Can't keep those settlers waiting, right? They get all restless?"

"Fuck you, Tye. And fuck that tweed you're wearing," she said, gesturing at his jacket-and-tie ensemble, finished with a polka dot pocket square. "It's seventy-five degrees. How are you not roasting in that?"

"Nah, Tye always keeps it cool," he said, brushing down his lapel.

"Third person, seriously?" Katie muttered, wiping the Guinness foam from her lips.

"Glad to see those team-building workshops paid off," I said.

"Corporate circle jerk," Katie snapped, crossing her arms.

"I don't know what a circle jerk is, but I thought the sessions were very educational," Muriel said, scrunching her brow as if untangling a challenging math puzzle. In due time, she solved it.

"There's no 'i' in team," she finally said, proudly, as if she'd conjured up the tired old maxim on the spot.

"No, Muriel, there isn't," Katie said, a glint in her eyes. "But there is an 'i' in bullshit."

Muriel chose the higher ground and refused to be drawn into Katie's mind games, of which she was a Zen master by now. We all turned as a loud roar of laughter and table slapping erupted from the cops' table to our right.

"Got to figure it's a bad day for someone if Oakland PD's got something to celebrate," Tye said, with an uncharacteristic snarl.

I turned to the group. "I met with Ron Boone—"

"And he needs our help," Muriel interrupted and extracted three manila folders from her handbag like a magician conjuring rabbits from a hat.

"I hope those aren't confidential court records," I said.

"No one will ever know. Besides, they're not confidential. Anyone with a password and access to the court intranet can access them."

"Isn't that the definition of confidential?" Katie said. "If they're behind a freakin' firewall?"

Muriel shrugged. "Well, you know, Kat, sometimes you've got to raze the village to save the community."

"What the fuck does that mean?"

"Means, Miss M's turned black hat on us," Tye said. "Way to go."

"I don't know what that means either, but thank you, Tye," Muriel said, handing each of us a folder. "Don't open them in here because, well, walls have eyes."

"Ears. It's 'walls have ears,'" Katie said, snatching a folder.

"Eyes, ears, same difference. Can't be too careful, is what I'm saying."

"Summary, Muriel?" I asked.

"Right. Question first. If what Ron Boone uncovered is true, does that mean all the judges are complicit?"

I shrugged. "Doubtful. The new incumbents are too green to know any better. Probably still taking selfies with their robes on to impress the family."

"Yeah," Katie agreed. "Easier to cover shit up when you're the patriarchy. Harper and his cronies manipulate the system for their own gain, and we get fucked over. I vote we take this to the press and put them on the defensive. Your wife's a journo, right?"

"Think it through, Kat," I said. "When Sierra writes that story, all fingers point back to me and, by association, my team. When they figure out who leaked the information, it puts all our jobs on the line."

"Mitch is right," Muriel agreed. "They might not fire us, but they could demote us, and I, for one, am not taking a pay cut five years before my retirement. That's going to impact my pension. Jim and I've got big travel plans, South Asia, Australia—"

"Oh right," Katie interrupted. "God forbid an epic corruption in the Alameda Justice system fucks up your global fucking travel adventures."

"It's a legitimate concern. You're young enough to find another job. That's not so easy at my age. If I get demoted, that's something I'm not going to recover from: thirty-five years of hard work down the toilet. If we do something, it's got to be by the book, legitimate, not leaked by any of us."

Katie gazed into her Guinness. "I was just sayin', we can't sit on our asses."

"That's not what I'm proposing," Muriel insisted. "Look, we already know we have a surplus of judges, so there's no legitimate reason to bring in the retired judges, so I did some research to find out what kind of cases these retired judges are working on."

She laid one of the manila envelopes on the table, tapping it with her finger.

"Now, you've got your regular misdemeanors and non-violent felonies. No red flags. Same story with the more serious crimes: homicides, sex crimes, crimes leading to great or serious bodily injury and such — just a slight uptick in lighter sentences, nothing too concerning. Where it gets interesting is when you look at the mid-level crimes: auto burglaries, assaults, robberies, weapons activity, pretty much the bread and butter of these street gangs, there's a statistically significant decline in sentencing."

"How significant?" I asked, my curiosity piqued.

"Very. Compared to, say, five years ago, the sentences for those crimes have gotten lighter year on year, and not just for first-time offenders. There are criminals I remember passing through the system years ago who've already served their time getting little more than their knuckles rapped for the same crimes they were sent to jail for the first time around." Muriel paused. "But here's the thing: they dismissed eighty percent of those charges before they even made it to trial. It's a pattern."

"That's no surprise," I said. "Given the new DA's push for minimal incarceration for any crime that's not a felony."

"Yeah, sent out a freakin' Tweet about it, too," Katie said. "A prosecutor who's not big on prosecuting? Only in Oakland. Go figure."

"No argument from me," Muriel agreed. "But here's something else I discovered. You know that street gang, *Sangres Norteñas?*"

My body tensed in anticipation of some discomfort heading its way.

"Sure," Tye said. "Had dealers on every street corner in my neighborhood, ran protection on all the bars and stores downtown. Friend of mine crossed them one time. Didn't end so well for him."

"Well, here's the thing," Muriel said. "Every defendant entering the court who was identified as a member of the *Sangres*

Norteñas was given disproportionally lighter sentences. Even the repeat offenders. Minimal fines, a few months' probation, community service, even dismissal before trial."

This spiked my attention. "You think the Alameda Superior Court is deliberately handing out lighter sentences to members of *Sangres Norteñas*?"

"Not just that. I cross-referenced all the cases where a gang member was implicated in a crime. All of them, bar two, were tried by one of the retired judges Harper called in."

I mulled over this information before responding.

"What the holy fuck?" Katie said, needing no such processing time. "You sure about this?"

"Read it for yourselves," Muriel gestured at the folders. "But not here, obviously."

I took mine and looked over as a bellow of laughter erupted from the cops' table.

"Wait up," Tye said, whose mouth had been in "agape" mode throughout the exchange. "If I'm hearing this right, you think the Presiding Judge at the Alameda Superior Court is calling in retired judges to try cases with a *Sangres Norteñas* connection, then none of these gang members get prosecuted? How the fuck does that happen?"

"It's pretty freakin' obvious," Katie said. "Harper's got to be in their pocket, which by default means Paco Castillo. Right, Mitch?"

"Yeah, maybe," I muttered.

"The guy you testified for at that suppression of evidence motion?" Tye asked. "For real?"

"I didn't testify, Tye, I was called as an expert witness." I said, wishing I'd ordered a double Bushmills chaser to take the edge off the conversation.

Katie lowered her voice. "So, you reckon Paco Castillo's paying off Harper so his guys don't serve jail time?"

"The more gang members incarcerated, the less money the gang makes," Tye said. "Simple economics."

"What about the retired judges, though?" Muriel asked.

"Harper's gotta be giving them a percentage of his payout. It's a double whammy, right?" Katie said, sitting back, a sparkle in her eyes. "Day rate for a call-in, then Harper sweetens the pot with a share of the money Castillo pays him."

"That's a lot of speculation, Kat," I said, aiming to dampen the enthusiasm. "There's a bunch of different ways to interpret data. This could all be a coincidence, something else entirely."

"I'm not buying it. I think Muriel's right on the money."

"If you're looking for conspiracies around every corner, then they'll be there waiting for you," I said. "We take nothing at face value, take a hard look at the evidence and then make the call, just like we do with every case that comes across our desks. This is no different. Let's all take a deep breath and figure out our next move. Nothing half-assed that's going to get any of us demoted or shifted to some broom closet down in the courthouse basement, shuffling papers. Good, Kat?"

I sensed Katie was about to parry with some sharp-assed comment my way when one of the uniformed officers from the table to our right loomed out from the shadows. The man carried himself like John Wayne, left thumb hooked inside his utility belt, right palm resting on his Glock, his huge square face and ginger Vandyke goatee glaring down on us. The last time I saw Officer Theodore Connor was at the courthouse, getting his ass handed to him by Victor Santiago.

"Well, if it ain't the courthouse judicial. You folks having yourselves a good time?"

Katie looked up. "Yep." Smirked. "We were."

Connor attempted a nonchalant smile that looked as if trying it on for size, and the fit wasn't working for him. He gestured at the folders. "Lawyer's day's never over, huh?"

"You know how it goes," I said. "Always someone trying to get away with something."

"Ain't that the truth," Connor said, then paused as if his response was an invitation to share. When no invitation was forthcoming, he persisted. "You know, me and the guys down the station were just talking 'bout you the other day, Sweeney."

"All good things, I hope."

"Nothing you'd want heard repeating."

"Really? Always had the impression I was well-liked down at OPD central."

"Might have been, one time . . . until you got a killer released without a trial. Plenty of folks real pissed you took the stand to protect a scumbag like Castillo."

"Just doing my job, Officer Connor. Like you, upholding the rule of law."

"See, that's where we're different," Connor said, tapping the handle of his Glock. "My job is to arrest criminals, make sure they get what's coming. You, on the other hand, seem to think your job is to send 'em back on the streets again."

"Oh, I figure the new DA's already got that covered," Katie said, giving Connor another trademark smirk. "She doesn't need our help putting criminals back on the streets."

"And who are you?" Connor asked.

"Just a researcher. Crossing *i*s, dotting *t*s, making sure everyone's operating within the law. You know, that kind of boring shit."

Connor looked at her through narrowed eyes; he seemed to look over all of us in the same way, as if he hoped to force some confession by the act of staring. The man's attitude burrowed like a colony of lice under my skin.

"In fact, Officer Connor," I said, with a friendly smile, "we were just discussing OPD's fine tradition of equal treatment for minorities in our community. Isn't that right, Tye?"

"Eh, sure," Tye said, sitting up. "Gotta say, I figure there's room for improvement for y'all."

Connor tilted his chin. "Improvement, huh?" he said, lacing the word "improvement" with a sneer thick enough to drip onto the table. "See, here's the problem with people like you," he continued. "You think because you got some college degree and wear fancy clothes, you got all the answers. You should ride along with me for a shift in the back of my vehicle. Reckon that'll change your perception real quick."

Katie stared hard at Connor. "Whoa, 'people like you'? Did you really just say that?"

I noticed Tye squirming. He didn't want to be within a city block of this conversation; he'd probably been at the wrong end of this kind of encounter enough times to know the best course of action was to say nothing, and it dawned on me too late that I'd forced his participation and subsequent subjugation, playing right into Connor's hand.

"Probably time you called it a night, Officer," I said. "Your colleagues are waiting." I gestured to the other three cops standing impatiently at the door.

Connor glanced over his left shoulder and pushed his tongue against his lower lip as if he were scouring for the right words. "You stay safe out there, Sweeney. Got us some real crazies out there on the roads these days, don't we?"

* * *

When, three shots of Bushmills and a ten-dollar cab ride later, I was back in my apartment, Connor's words still niggled; another seed planted and sprouting. I'd sown enough seeds recently to start a damned orchard of conspiracy theories. Maybe Connor had heard about my accident from someone at the courthouse, or maybe he hadn't, and his parting comment was a thinly veiled warning. I'd put my money on the latter.

That night, sleep was elusive. Maybe it was exhaustion, maybe it was the alcohol. Somewhere in the dark, desperate hours, I dreamed of violet desert skies, dusty bars, burning red sunsets, and a beautiful English woman lying dead on a kitchen floor.

CHAPTER 27

The phone call that tilted my world from its axis of crap came a few days later. Sierra's tone was dialed up to panic mode; I could almost hear her tearing out her gorgeous red hair on the other end of the line.

The last time I'd heard her that distraught, we were vacationing at the family lake house on one of the few weekends my father would take off during the year. He'd just finished executing a perfect hand pass behind the ski boat when the rope slacked. It took Sierra, who was piloting the Malibu Wakesetter, a minute to figure out what had gone down. What had gone down was two hundred and sixty-five pounds of husband, father, and senior management, felled like an old redwood by a massive cardiac arrest — or, to give it its medical term, "the widow maker." It lived up to its moniker. Hank Sweeney, VP of Software Sales, released the tow ropes as if letting go of life itself, then crumpled with a muted splash into the lake water.

My father was sixty-nine, had worked his entire career in sales, and spent more time on the road than he did with his family. At the time, I was forty-five years old, with a four-year-old son, and Victor was pressing me to move to the private legal sector, where he assured me my future was so bright I'd have to wear shades. That day, as the first responders dredged Hank's body. I vowed I'd wouldn't end up like my father. But for me, that's when those kinds of vows have a short half-life. That's when my gambling addiction had switched into high gear.

Granted, I hadn't succumbed to the temptation to lay down a wager for months. If I'd had the guts or motivation to attend one of those addiction programs, I'd probably get some token to mark the occasion. But I didn't need some pseudo-psychology bullshit to tell me that by agreeing to do Paco's bidding, all I'd accomplished was to satisfy that craving for excitement elsewhere. I was like a junkie switching his allegiances from heroin to cocaine and calling it a win.

Packing that thought into the overhead luggage compartment of my mind, I focused on what Sierra was telling me: "Kurt's been injured." She said a bunch of other stuff, too, but I'd tuned out everything else except the words "Kurt" and "injured."

* * *

I rushed into the emergency room waiting area. Sierra was sitting, wringing a tissue through her hands. She stood and called my name as she saw me.

I took her hands in mine. "What happened?" I asked, looking around the room for any clues. "Is Kurt all right? Tell me he's all right. Sierra?"

Sierra nodded and calmly said. "I think he's going to be fine, Mitch. He'll be out of surgery soon."

"Surgery? What the hell happened?"

She gestured we should sit. I was shell-shocked, body numb, mind racing. I didn't ask, but I was sure Sierra felt the same. I could see it in her eyes, that glazed look that telegraphed disbelief. She took my hand in hers, squeezing it tight. A warm sensation passed through me like a light passing over my body.

"Okay, tell me what happened?" I said, tamping down my panic.

She took a breath. "Kurt was in the yard with his phone taking photos; you know he loves to do that when there's a full moon. I was watching him the whole time, Mitch. I was there, not ten feet away. I must have looked away for a second, I swear, like a second."

"Hey," I said. "This is not your fault."

She nodded. "I heard a truck go past the house really fast, then a gunshot. All I could think of was Kurt . . . I had this awful, I mean this fucking awful feeling that something really bad was about to happen. I ran out; I think there was another gunshot, then Kurt . . ."

She paused and held back the tears. "Then Kurt just fell. I ran to him. The truck drove off. I didn't see their faces." Sierra looked up at me. "They shot a little boy and drove off. I mean, what kind of monster does that, Mitch?"

I had no answer. Not that she was looking for one.

I was about to ask Sierra if she'd noticed anything else when I felt someone standing over us. I immediately recognized the piercings, tattoos, and the black hoodie with *Disappointed . . . but Not Surprised* written on the chest: Alma Torres.

Before I could stop her from blurting out anything I didn't want Sierra hearing, she said, "Dude! What the fuck! I am so fucking sorry. I was right there, watching the house, like I promised. It all happened so fucking fast. Like, one second I'm looking down playing Wordle, then bam, it's like, gunshots. By the time I get out of my car, it's all over. I tried to chase the fuckers, but they were already gone." She caught her breath. "He's going to be okay, though, right, your kid?"

Sierra let go of my hand and stood. "Mitch, who is this? Do we know you? Why were you watching our house?"

The lightbulb suddenly flashed on in Alma's brain. "Stupid!" she said, slapping her forehead with her palm. "Stupid," she repeated, then looked at me. "Oh, man, I'm sorry. This is your wife, right?" She held out her hand to Sierra. "Alma Torres, private investigator."

Sierra limply shook her hand.

"Me and my big fucking mouth. It's a thing, I just blurt out any old crap that comes into my head. Victor says I need to work on my people filter, be more aware."

I felt Sierra tense. "Again, why were you watching our house?"

Alma looked at me and raised her hands in the *this one's on you* manner.

Sierra caught the gesture and turned to me. "Our child is in intensive care with a bullet wound, and if that has anything to do with why this woman was watching our house, then you need to tell me right now, Mitch."

"Right on," Alma said, backing away from the mess she'd just created like it was a bad smell. "I'll go get some coffee. You two got stuff to discuss, obviously."

As Alma scuttled to the vending machine, Sierra turned her attention to me. "Mitch, what was that woman doing watching our house? What aren't you telling me?"

That was the $64,000 question, the elephant taking up all the air in the room. Even if I wanted to tell Sierra everything, I wouldn't know where to start. My mind shot through a litany of lies before settling on the half-lie that I hoped she would buy.

"The Paco Castillo case. Remember, I was the expert witness? Victor thought it would be smart to have someone watch the house, just in case."

"In case of what? Didn't you help get the evidence dismissed?"

"Yeah, yeah, I did." That day seemed like a lifetime ago.

"So, why would he threaten you?"

"He didn't. Paco Castillo has a lot of enemies. Victor heard they were pretty pissed his case got dismissed."

Sierra pointed at the scars peppering my face. "Is that what all this is about? Someone got to you?"

"Fell off my bike." The first true thing I'd said all evening.

"You fell off your bike? I didn't even know you had a bike."

"Yeah, I just got one, figured I needed the exercise."

Sierra ran a hand through her hair. "Honestly, Mitch, I don't know if you're lying or not, I just know you're very good at it. You lied to me for years about your gambling. Why should this be any different?"

"Because it is," I said lamely.

"Is it?"

I let the question linger, hoping the air conditioning might suck it deep into its ducts.

Sierra took a breath. "If you're lying to me, and our son was shot because of something you did or didn't do, then this is over. All of it. I love you, I do, but I didn't sign up for this. Any of it."

"It's a shitty, fucked-up coincidence, that's all," I pleaded. "A stray bullet, gangbangers? You write about this stuff all the time. It was just an accident, an awful accident. I'd take Kurt's place in a heartbeat, if I could."

As Sierra contemplated this, one of the emergency room doctors walked over to us and removed his glasses. Sierra grabbed my hand, squeezed it tight.

"Good news," the doctor said. "A superficial flesh wound. Your son's going to be fine. A few more inches to the left, though, we'd be having a very different discussion. Kurt was one of the lucky ones. We'll keep him in overnight. You can see him now."

We both shook his hand and spilled our communal thanks at the feet of the doctor. He took it with good grace — I guess he'd treated plenty of kids where the bullet had landed a few inches further left, and was glad to be delivering a rare sliver of good news. In my job, I'd pored over dozens of cases where parents hadn't been so lucky.

"The bullet," I said. "Do you know what caliber it was?"

The doctor narrowed his eyes. "Does it matter? Your son's alive. Be thankful."

"I'd like to know," I persisted.

The doctor sighed. "I'm no ballistics expert, but I'd say it was possibly a nine-millimeter, judging by the size of the wound."

"Not a .45?"

"Not in my opinion. Now, if you'll excuse me."

As the doctor headed off, I noticed Special Agent Eric Landry leaning against the vending machine and chatting to Alma Torres like they were best buddies. My gut tightened: who knew if Alma had her people filter switched on or not? I made an excuse to Sierra that I needed the restroom and headed over.

"Mitch," Landry said. "I heard about your kid. Is he going to make it?"

"Yeah, yeah, he is. How did you—?"

"I make it my job to know."

Alma slurped on her coffee. "You two know each other?"

"Special Agent Landry and I go way back," I said, sure Landry hadn't let slip about his FBI credentials to Alma. I was right.

Landry showed his badge and smiled that disagreeable smile of his, which distorted his entire face into something entirely more disagreeable, the opposite effect he was aiming for.

Alma spat into her coffee dregs. "Fuckin' Feds. I didn't say nothing," she said, looking over at me, then turned on her heel and stormed off.

"You always have that effect on women, Landry?"

"Only the guilty ones. They get all edgy as soon as I mention FBI, for some reason."

"Or it could just be your charming disposition."

"Had crossed my mind," he said, smirking.

"What are you doing here?"

"In the area. Thought I'd check in." He pointed at my scarred face. "Looks nasty."

"Perils of cycling in the city. Anything else?"

"Yeah, there is. We heard that Paco Castillo's wife was killed in Palm Springs two days ago. He mention anything about that to you?"

I shook my head. "Why would he? I haven't seen him since the night your goons picked me up."

"That right?"

I'd backed myself into a corner with a lie I couldn't sweet talk my way out of. "Yeah, that's right," I confirmed.

He nodded and reached into his pocket and took out a photograph from the collection he'd shown me at the field office. "See that guy's reflection in the window? You know who that is?"

Another lie I was compelled to continue. "I told you already, not my kind of people."

"See, that seems odd to me, you not recognizing Alameda's Presiding Judge, seeing as you probably see Griffin Harper most days."

I shrugged. "Could be I was tired that night. You sure it's him? Looks pretty blurry to me. Could be any old, fat white guy grazing on free food and booze."

"Oh, it's him," Landry confirmed. "You and Judge Harper at Castillo's place on the same night. Gotta admit that could look suspicious to some folk."

"Only if you're of a suspicious mind. Now, if you're done asking questions, I've got problems of my own to deal with," I said, nodding toward the hallway.

"Then best not keep you, Mitch. A lot of bad people out there these days wouldn't think twice about shooting a kid. Just wanted to make sure you and your family's all good."

"Your concern is noted. I'll be sure to leave you a five-star review on the FBI website. Now, I need to go see my son."

"Go do that," Landry said and popped mint into his mouth. "But remember what I said back at the field office?"

"You said a lot of shit."

Landry leaned in. "If Paco Castillo's not your friend, he's your enemy, and if he's your enemy, there isn't a place you can hide he won't find you."

I tried to shake off the implication, but Landry's words were like pouring a gallon bag of ice on my chest. He must have caught my reaction.

"Shoot, didn't mean to shake you up, Mitch." He put his hand on my shoulder. "But like you said, you haven't seen him since we last spoke, so I doubt you've got anything to worry about. Now, go take care of your son."

CHAPTER 28

Nothing in life prepares you for the sight of your ten-year-old son laid out on a hospital bed, plugged into a web of machinery.

After the initial shock, you obsess about the fortress of paraphernalia, become finely attuned to every bleep and pulse. It brought home to me how little control we have over anything in our lives. No amount of profound, put-your-life-on-the-line love could have protected Kurt from that bullet. You worry, protect, nurture, but one random act of violence makes a mockery of all that love. The only option you have is to love your children, love them like a force of nature, love them with every ounce of love you have in you, and hope to God, or whichever higher being you believe in, that it's enough.

When I walked into the room, Sierra had just hung up on a call. I sat close and tried to take her hand, but she shook me away. Something had changed in those few minutes since I'd been out of her sphere talking with Landry, or maybe now the doctor had assured us Kurt was okay, I was surplus to requirements. She probably still suspected I had something to do with Kurt's shooting, and the truth was, I didn't know if my actions had led to Kurt lying in a hospital bed or not. I'd half-convinced Sierra the shooting was an accident, but I was much further from convincing myself. I made myself a promise to find out, just not tonight.

I looked at Sierra. "Who were you calling?"

She sat up and cleared her throat. I recognized the gesture: the big news posture that telegraphed, *you need to sit and listen, Mitch, and listen good.*

"Okay," I said, taking the chair across the bed. "Lay it on me."

"My mom, I was speaking to my mom," she said, gently patting Kurt's hand. "She said Kurt and I should come stay with her for a while."

Sierra's mom, Clara, lived on the west coast of Mexico in a small surf town called Sayulita. We'd vacationed there a bunch of times. Kurt loved the place.

"And what does that really mean?"

"It means, Mitch, that I need some time from all this, some space. I warned you something like this might happen, but you kept insisting it wouldn't, or you just ignored the facts staring you in the face, which, let's be honest, is a talent of yours. I don't know if this is your fault or not, but the fact that I can't rule that out, and I'm even thinking that you might have something to do with this, has to tell you something."

I took the bruising with the love it was given. "How long for?"

"A couple of weeks. I can work remotely. This will be good for Kurt."

"But do you have to leave the country? You could use my parents' lake house. It's no Mexico, but at least I could come to see you both at the weekends."

After I'd said the words, I realized that maybe Sierra and Kurt would be safer in Mexico, at least until I'd fulfilled my obligations to Paco.

Sierra stiffened and rested her hands on her lap. "I've made my mind up; you won't talk me out of it. Whatever's going on with you right now, whatever it is, you're not telling me, I know

192

it can't be good. Kurt and I can't . . . *won't* be a part of it. I won't put him through any more trauma."

I nodded. Sierra was right on the money as usual. She could read me like a trashy local newspaper horoscope.

"If I object, you'll need my permission to take Kurt out of the country, you know that."

Sierra smiled; damn, I'd have done anything to keep that smile close to me for a lifetime. "You're his father; he looks up to you. I'd never do anything to jeopardize that. You need to do this one thing for me. Do you think you can do that, Mitch?"

CHAPTER 29

Two days after they discharged Kurt from the hospital, I said an emotional goodbye to my family at Oakland Airport. I kept the *bon voyage* as light and breezy for Kurt's sake. I told him this was all a big adventure, and I'd see him soon. As I watched them both walk through security, it felt as if someone had dragged out my insides across the floor, pounded them against the wall, and then handed them back to me, dazed, bruised, and beaten.

I consoled myself with the thought that they were safely out of the country for a while, which gave me some breathing time to bring things to a head with Paco, which was why, the following day, I found myself outside his house, the afternoon balmy, the sky cloud-starved, the aroma of eucalyptus lingering like liquid on the ether.

Despite my nervousness at confronting Paco, I needed to hear something directly from him. I figured I could spot his tell in an instant, look into those black, soulless eyes, and know if he was lying. But as I stood shuffling my shoes across the welcome mat, I wondered if I'd overestimated my powers of observation, especially when pitted against a man like Paco Castillo, whose stoic demeanor never betrayed a flicker of emotion.

I rang the doorbell and heard the chimes of the "Dance of the Little Swans" from *The Nutcracker* echo inside the house. Victor

194

had assured me Paco would be there; he spent his afternoons working from his home office. He'd also tried to dissuade me from making the journey. But Victor didn't have a kid, and couldn't begin to understand that the shockwaves of Kurt's shooting still reverberated like razor wire.

All respect to Victor, though, he'd driven to the hospital as soon as he'd heard the news. He'd even returned the following morning with an armful of *National Geographic* magazines and a McDonald's breakfast muffin stashed inside the pile. I still harbored a stomach full of anger toward Vic, but he took his duties as Kurt's godfather seriously. His thoughtfulness shaved some of the edges off my anger, but it still lingered, poking me like a sharp rock every few hours.

The oak door swung open, pulled by a short, gray-haired woman wearing a black dress and a white apron. I figured this must be the housekeeper; hard face, her features squished into the flesh, as if she'd spent a life with her nose pressed against a window.

"You sit here," she said, gesturing at the club chair with clawed feet and blood-red upholstery. Classical music filtered from the room across the foyer as I waited. A few minutes later, she returned and escorted me to Paco.

His office resembled a dusty old library, the walls lined with bookshelves groaning under the weight of ancient hardbacks, the decor positively muted compared to the rest of the house. Paintings of pastoral hunting scenes decorated the walls, and the lingering but not unpleasant funk of cigar smoke added to the English squire vibe. I sensed this to be Paco's sanctuary, the one room in the house where Oksana didn't get to exercise her Tsarist design aesthetic.

Paco gestured to the housekeeper that she was no longer needed. She scooted off, pulling the door behind her.

"You've come to give me good news?" he asked, lifting a smoldering Churchill from the ashtray on his desk and bringing the butt to his lips. This time, he didn't offer me a cigar, pre-embargo Cuban or otherwise. Not that I would have partaken; I was sure it would have turned my stomach.

"Erm, not exactly," I said, taking a seat and noticing through Tudor-style windows two security guards patrolling the grounds. By the thick bulges under their jackets, I figured they were carrying heavy weaponry.

Paco adjusted a button on the Prince of Wales checkered vest. "So, why are you here?"

Suddenly, the courage that had invigorated me on the drive seemed to have dissipated. I decided I needed to ease into it, softshoe around my question like I was stalking prey.

"A few days back, someone shot my son outside my family's home."

Paco sat back, his leather chair creaking like bones yielding under pressure. "Violence in this city has taken a very bad turn. Too many weapons in the hands of those who should not have them. I sent your wife flowers. I hope she liked them."

"Nice gesture, but she'd already left."

"Unfortunate, but maybe you'll take them to your apartment?"

"Sure, better than letting them rot."

Paco nodded. "It is important to acknowledge these events when they happen and not accept them as how things are or should be. Incidents like this, unsettling as they are, help us appreciate what we have. I'm sure you must be feeling that now, Mitch. Grateful, no?"

"Sure. But all the appreciation in the world doesn't change the fact someone shot my son."

"Of course. And they are now in Mexico, your wife and your son?"

"How did you know?"

"Victor told me. Sayulita, yes? I have business interests there." He twisted his cigar between his index finger and thumb as if testing its rigidity. "Mexico can be dangerous, especially for a young woman traveling alone."

"She's not alone; my son's with her, and she's staying with her mother."

"Even so, if we are to believe the news reports, violence in my country has taken an ugly turn lately." He nodded, as if agreeing with himself. "I will make sure your family is safe. My people are very discreet."

"No need. I'm sure they'll be fine."

Paco waved his cigar like he was writing an edict in the air. "It is done. We will speak no more about it."

He slid a printed leaflet toward me. Another Order of Service, the second one I'd seen in a matter of days, this one in honor of Charlotte Esme Fitzroy-Castillo. Cigar smoke curled from his fist as he spoke. "A suitable photograph for the funeral service, yes?"

A tremor flitted around my throat as I looked at the photograph of Charlotte taken a few years back, standing in a paddock, a white thoroughbred horse nudging her shoulder. Charlotte's smile was as wide as the horizon, as if there were no other place she'd rather be.

"Good choice," I agreed.

"Charlotte was always more comfortable with animals than with people," Paco mused as he pulled back the leaflet. "I travel to London next week to attend the service. My children will need me there. It would be a comfort to me if you located the laptop before I leave. There is something unsettling about traveling and leaving important matters unresolved."

"When do you leave?"

"Next week, Friday. It will take them some time to fly Charlotte's body back to England."

"I'm . . . I can't—" I stammered.

"I'm sure this won't be a problem for you, Mitch. The sooner you find the laptop, the sooner you get to see Sierra and Kurt again. Maybe you could all take a small vacation after all this . . . activity."

I didn't fail to notice the threat lurking in the shadow of his words. Instead of challenging him, I raised the question I'd been hankering to ask since I'd arrived.

"Did you have anything to do with my son's shooting?"

Paco's face was unreadable; an emotionless stone carving sat upon a muscular plinth of a neck. "I understand why you would ask. No. The answer is no, I had no hand in your son's shooting."

The casualness of his reply irritated me. "Seriously? Just a 'no' and we leave it at that?"

"I give you my word; that should be enough."

"What if it isn't enough?"

Paco considered his cigar. "As we are having an honest exchange, let me also ask you a question."

"Sure. I've nothing to hide."

"Before she died, did Charlotte tell you where she had hidden the laptop?"

"No. I already told you. I gave you my word."

"And she said nothing else that maybe you remembered since we last met? Something that could be important?"

"Like I said, I was running for my life, no time to chat."

"Okay, Mitch, it is so. You do not lie to me, and I do not lie to you. And as a sign of good faith, I would like to give you this."

He pushed a small, sealed envelope toward me. "As I have said before, you work for Paco Castillo. If something happens to you, it happens to me also. No coincidences, no accidents." He brushed the cigar flakes off his vest. "Now, if there is nothing else," he said, gesturing to the doorway.

As if someone had invisibly summoned her, the housekeeper appeared and opened the door.

I wanted to press Paco further, but his dark look indicated our business was done. Well, that was fine. I'd asked what I'd come here to ask. If I didn't like the answer, that was on me. Maybe I had some harebrained notion Paco would hold up his hands, confess he'd orchestrated Kurt's shooting as some cruel act of motivation. I realized later I'd only gone there to make myself feel better. Rather than surrendering to the powerlessness of my situation, I'd tried to wrestle control, and control was something a man like Paco Castillo wouldn't cede without a fight. There was no gain in him lying to me about Kurt's shooting, and anyway, I had all the motivation I needed to help him retrieve the laptop. He'd made it clear the debt I owed Errol Capriani was now owed to Paco Castillo. And that debt unsettled me more than any financial debt ever could.

As he rose from behind his desk and walked me to the doorway, a photograph next to the walnut liquor bureau caught my attention. It was taken at a golf tournament, a row of ten older white men holding an oversized check for $50,000. In the center, the only brown man, Paco Castillo, shaking hands with Judge Griffin Harper.

"Didn't know you played."

"I don't. Knocking a small ball into a hole is such a silly pastime. I sponsor the event every year for charity."

"Very noble." I gestured at the image. "Judge Harper, right?"

Paco nodded. "Your boss?"

"Kind of."

Paco rested his hand on my shoulder. "A businessman like myself makes many friends. Lawyers, judges, police officers, council members. Few meaningful deals are made in the boardroom."

"Who you know, not what you know?"

Paco shook his head. "A flawed cliché. That is just half of the equation. Success requires both knowledge and connections. Like truth and lies, one cannot exist without the other."

I nodded. "One last question. If you hadn't seen Charlotte for years, how did she get hold of this laptop?"

"A good question. There was a break-in at my office some weeks ago. At the time, I didn't suspect Charlotte. Why would I? As you said, I had not seen her for eight years. She called and told me she had my Apple laptop, and then several weeks later, she vanished."

"Which is when you asked me to help?"

"After the break-in and Charlotte's threat, you can understand my reluctance to trust anyone within my organization."

"So you thought a gambler with a heavy debt was easy prey?"

"We all have our price, and Victor spoke highly of you."

I took a breath. "What's on that laptop that's so important?"

Paco guided me, his hand on my shoulder, from the room. "Thank you for coming, Mitch. I hope for better news next time we meet."

He shoved the envelope in my pocket and shook my hand, his grip a torque wrench around my bones. Just Paco's way of keeping the pressure on.

* * *

As I emerged from his den and into the foyer, the spaghetti strap-thin figure of Oksana, like some dated advertisement for heroin chic, stood by the staircase, one leg poised on the banister, her body bent at an angle I don't think mine had ever been supple enough to execute. She wore a bright blue leotard, her hair pulled back in a ponytail, and a glaze of sweat covering her ivory-white skin. The thick leg warmers bunched at her ankles made me think she'd been practicing at the barre, and the classical music I'd heard as I came in was her soundtrack. She looked up and unhooked her ballet-slippered foot from the railing.

"Ah," she said, wiping her brow with a towel. "Mitch Sweeney. The man who does not listen." She chuckled. "How was your visit to Palm Springs?"

"How did you know?"

Oksana reached into the fold in one of her leg warmers, pulled out a pack of Sobranie Black Russians, flicked open a lighter, drew deeply, then exhaled a plume of smoke up to the teardrop chandelier. The light, woody aroma took me right back to the night of Charlotte's murder. It wired a tremor through me like an aftershock long after the quake's damage had been done.

She glided toward me, her feet barely making a sound on the marble floor. As her features caught the dapple of sunlight streaming through the skylight, her uncanny resemblance to Charlotte was undeniable. The pale skin, the finely etched features, the way she held herself, like she owned the air around her, the way she drew on her cigarette, as if each draw was a *fuck you* to the world. She stopped a couple of feet away from me and rested a palm on the nub of her bony hip.

"I asked you to not do what Paco requested. Now Charlotte is dead, and Paco must travel to London for the funeral."

"Have *you* tried saying no to your husband?"

The question seemed to momentarily rattle her cool facade, but she quickly regained her composure. "Charlotte was never good for Paco. Her life of privilege made her weak. Without struggle, how can a person become strong? Maybe it is better this way for all of us, don't you think?"

"Be sure to include that in your eulogy."

"Oh, I only fly to London for the shopping. No one will want me there, and I don't wish to be there."

"Figures. All that gossiping behind my back would irritate the heck out of me, too."

She scrunched her brow. "Gossip?"

"It's how it goes, right? First wife dies in suspicious circumstances, the second wife in waiting's always going to be number one on the suspect list."

She narrowed her eyes. "Suspicious?" She made the sign of a gun with her fingers. "Bang bang, the bitch is dead. A home invasion. Not so suspicious. I think maybe you've been watching too many true crime shows."

"I figure my life's already a true crime show. I don't need the added entertainment."

Oksana walked closer and rested a hand on my shoulder. She smelled of fresh sweat and the remnants of a flowery perfume, which I was sure was the same as Charlotte had worn. "You must not take it too hard," she said, her lips arcing into a pitying smile. "I'm sure there was nothing you could have done to save poor Charlotte."

I tried to look past those cold, gunmetal-gray eyes and wondered what Siberian-level cold calculations were going on behind them. I wondered if I'd gone there and asked the wrong question of the wrong member of the Castillo family. I wondered, given the right circumstances, what the hell Oksana was capable of.

202

CHAPTER 30

Victor pushed a sequence of buttons on his espresso machine and slid my caffeine jolt across the kitchen island. "Seriously? Oksana?"

It was early morning, the day following my visit to Paco's. I'd driven from Jack London Square to Victor's house, two miles north in the city of Piedmont. Nestled like an unattainable fairy-tale oasis amidst Oakland's urban sprawl, Piedmont was the kind of city Sierra and I could only have dreamed of living in. I hadn't seen a single-family home for sale in Piedmont for less than $3m since the great financial bust of 2008. Victor had bought in just as the real estate market plummeted, picked up a deal on what the realtors called an "entertainer's delight" — a kitchen you could park several SUVs in, vaulted ceilings, and a redwood deck bigger than my entire apartment.

"Just a theory," I said, taking a sip.

"How's the coffee?"

"Not bad."

"Not bad? That stuff's premium roast. Seventy-five bucks a pound from a roaster I know in Honolulu. The guy's an artist."

"You know your problem, Vic? Way too much disposable income."

"Fuck you. I'm surprised your tastebuds haven't called it a day already, considering all the crap you put in your body."

"Want me to tell you it's the best damn cup of coffee I've ever tasted?"

It pretty much did taste like it, but I wasn't about to give Victor the satisfaction.

"Would it kill you?"

"Stroke your ego any more, and you'll be walking around with a hard-on all day."

"My ego doesn't need stroking, from you or anyone else." He downed his shot. "And, by the way, that image is going to haunt me the rest of the day."

I laughed. It felt good shooting the shit with Victor just like the old days; the days before he'd set me up as a stooge for his client and almost got me killed. It's what we did, what we'd always done. What most men did, I guessed: avoid talking about anything real, gloss over those slippery fucks called feelings with lame jokes and a light to medium roasting.

God knew I had enough to spill my guts about: Sierra and Kurt leaving for Mexico, Paco's demands, the whole judicial shit show with Judge Harper, not to mention Ron Boone, who was still sending me several emails a day, each one notching up a degree on the vitriol. *One fresh, freakin' pickle at a time*, I'd told myself. *Set your priorities, Mitch, figure all the shit out with Paco first, then focus on the next crisis nipping at your heels.*

"Oksana's got to be involved in Charlotte's murder," I insisted.

Victor pulled up a stool. "Really? You think Oksana murdered Charlotte because she was taking too long to sign the divorce papers?"

"You weren't there. She had this coldness. I can't describe. It sent a chill through me, Vic."

"Did she tell you outright? Confess?"

"It's what she didn't say. No empathy, zero, like she was glad Charlotte was dead."

"That figures, but it's still a long shot. How did she murder Charlotte? Walk me through it."

"I don't know. Maybe she hired someone? A hitman? Assassin?"

"Of course she did. Probably has John Wick on speed dial."

"He's a fictional character, asshole."

"Like all of this," Victor said, waving his hand. "Fiction. Some story you've made up because you feel guilty. Let it go. We've both got enough guilt to work through, and you're making me late for my acupuncture appointment."

I was about to fire another zinger Victor's way when I heard a voice coming from the doorway leading to the lower-level bedrooms.

"I buy it," the voice said.

Alma Torres leaned on the doorframe, wearing sweatpants paired with an oversized T-shirt with the words, *Shhh. No One Cares* printed in large letters.

"I'd kill for a friggin' coffee if you're making one, boss," she said, slouching toward the island, her flip-flops slapping on the hardwood floor like a slow hand clap. "Double espresso, if you got it."

I gestured at them both. "Erm. What? Hold on. Are you two—?"

"Ew, that is so beyond gross," Alma interrupted, sounding like a petulant teenager.

"Alma's staying with me for a few days," Victor explained, resuming his coffee-brewing duties. "Until she finds a new place."

"My landlord was being a total ass. Said I had a shitty attitude, and he didn't need the hassle, so he kicked me out. Fucking millennials. Over-fucking-sensitive, if you ask me."

"Aren't you a millennial?"

"I don't do labels," she said, grabbing her coffee.

"Didn't you just? . . . Never mind."

Alma continued. "Reckon this theory of yours might not be as crazy as the boss here thinks."

"The floor is yours," Victor said, checking his Breitling. "You've got five minutes."

"Okay. So, Oksana puts the pressure on you to refuse Paco Castillo's ask, but she's not stupid. She knows you'll have to say yes to whatever he wants."

"An offer I can't refuse?"

"I'm kind of over the whole *Godfather* references, TBH. But, yeah, she could have been covering her own ass."

"How?"

"She knows you're gonna have to accept. Nobody says no to that dude, right? Oh, and there's your massive gambling debt, if she knew about that—"

"Thanks for the reminder."

Alma continued. "She's got the money and the connections to hire a pro. The guy follows you to Palm Springs, then to Charlotte's digs, where things turn to all shades of shittery. Wife's dead, Castillo's a widower . . ."

"And we all get an invitation to the wedding of the year," Victor said with a sarcastic flourish.

"Not too crazy," I said.

Victor shook his head. "There's got to be more. Oksana's a piece of work, but she's smart enough to know Paco would figure out that ruse in a second."

"Then it has to be about the laptop," I said. "Charlotte shot first. The shooter returned fire. The killer was after the laptop; Charlotte's murder wasn't planned; it was an accident. Oksana wanted the laptop before Paco. Any idea why, Victor?"

He shrugged.

"And, about that," I added. "Are you sure you don't know what's on that laptop that's so important to Paco?"

"Paco doesn't tell me everything. I just handle his legal problems. And if I did know, I couldn't tell you; he's a client. Anything he tells me is confidential."

"So, you might know what's on there, and you're just not telling us?"

"Good point, bro," Alma agreed.

"No, bad point," Victor said. "Very wrong, and very off base."

Another thought hit me. "Maybe it's something to do with the paintings the FBI were tracking down when they raided Paco's house."

"Is that why that FBI dude was hanging around the hospital when your kid got shot?" Alma asked. "Still feel like total shit about that, by the way."

"Wait," Victor snapped. "Can you two just spool back a few seconds here? FBI?"

"Fuck! Did it again, didn't I? God damn people filter. Keep forgetting I shouldn't do caffeine before I eat, start running my mouth off like Kanye fucking West."

"Who's this FBI agent?" Victor asked.

Alma, for the second time in a matter of days, had backed me into a corner. I'd deliberately skirted around the whole FBI interview and passed it off as no big deal, but now here it was, breaking the surface like a fat, breaching whale. "Special Agent Eric Landry. You know him?"

Victor nodded. "Yeah, I know Landry. Hard-ass, big chip on his shoulder."

"Ugly fuck, too," Alma added. "Even gave me the creeps, and I know some pretty fucking scary dudes."

"Why did he come to the hospital to see you?"

I hesitated. "Erm . . . he was the agent who questioned me the night after the raid."

"I thought you said that was no big deal. Why is the FBI visiting you at the hospital the night Kurt gets shot?"

"Honestly, Vic, I have no idea. I told him to go to hell."

Victor didn't seem convinced, but rolled with it anyway. "Well, all this Nancy Drew shit has been a fucking great start to my morning. So glad you dropped in, Mitch."

"You're welcome," I said, with a sarcastic flourish of my own.

Victor grabbed his suit jacket. "I gotta go. Put the cups in the dishwasher before you leave."

"All good if I raid your refrigerator for some eats?" Alma asked. "I'm starving."

Victor grabbed his briefcase. "Knock yourself out."

"Right on. You got a meet or something?"

No reply. Victor was already out of the door. A second later, he shot back into the kitchen. "And Mitch. The laptop? You're still on the hook for finding that. Any progress?"

"Working on it," I confirmed.

Victor spoke through his teeth. "Not the news I wanted to hear. Paco's patience is wearing thin." He headed out again, this time slamming the door as he left.

"Acupuncture appointment," I clarified. "Stress relief."

"Acupuncture? What the fuck?" Alma said, rummaging through the fridge. "Gotta say, if some hippie with a man bun was poking me with needles, that would stress the hell out of me, for real."

"Listen, Alma," I said, lowering my voice. "I was wondering if you could do me a favor?"

She turned, her arms cradling a smorgasbord of cured meats, cheese wedges, and a pack of fresh bagels. "Legal or illegal?"

"Borderline."

"Sweet," she said, spilling her treasures onto the kitchen island. "Borderline's my specialty. What you got?"

I handed her the envelope Paco gave me yesterday. "License plate number. Can you trace it?"

Showing little mercy, Alma launched into the doughy round of a sesame bagel. "Sure, but want to tell me what this is all about? I work better with some context."

"I was knocked off my bike last week. Probably just an accident—"

"Yeah, sure, an accident. Like Charlotte's murder was an accident," she said, her cheeks masticating like they had been out of commission for days. "Don't worry, dude, I got you. Figure I owe you one. I'll be in touch."

CHAPTER 31

Protect her . . .
Protect her . . .
Protect her . . .

I'd scribbled Charlotte's words multiple times on my notepad, hoping some bolt of inspiration would hit me. It didn't. Maybe they meant nothing, just the garbled last words of a woman suffering a violent death. I guess death doesn't always extend the luxury of allowing you to go gently into that good night. Sometimes, the grim reaper leaps from the shadows, takes you by surprise, rifles through your pockets for your loose change, and leaves you for dead on the sidewalk. I was sure that, given the opportunity, Charlotte would have raved and burned with all her soul, fought death with all she had. But death, the ultimate savage, that night had other plans.

Running those thoughts around my mind on repeat had led to an unproductive morning, so I headed out of the office to grab an early lunch.

Lake Merritt had returned to its usual rush of foot traffic as the downtown office workers congregated at the food trucks on 13th Street. The algae bloom had bloomed and died, the stench of rotting marine life now usurped by the much-improved aroma of grilled meats and warm maize. As I expected, there was a line, ten people deep waiting, outside the Taco Sinaloa truck.

Twenty minutes later, I was just about to scarf the last of my three carnitas street tacos, when I saw Katie leaning against the stone wall at the south of the lake. She was chatting with a guy wearing khakis and a plaid shirt. From the thick-rimmed black spectacles and the on-trend fade haircut, I figured he was either a tech-bro or a real estate agent. I was mistaken on both counts.

As I looked closer, I recognized the face. We'd been introduced at one of Sierra's work parties. Scavenging around my memory dumpster, I exhumed from the junk the name Javier Madrigal, a junior reporter working on the *Oakland Tribune*'s online edition. I recalled he was the eager type, chatty, keen to make friends and influence people.

I observed the conversation for a few minutes. Javier was being his extroverted self, with exaggerated body language and sympathetic head nods. Katie was his mirror opposite, arms tight across her chest, head cocked at a slight angle as if she were waiting to be impressed. If I'd been closer, I'd have told Javier to take a seat; he'd be in for a long wait. The conversation ended with Javier handing over his business card. As he sauntered toward downtown, I wiped my greasy hands through some napkins and walked toward Katie, hoping to orchestrate a casual run-in.

"Hey, Kat," I called out. "Heading back to the office?"

I caught a flick of concern, as if some invisible length of wire pulled at the corner of her eyes.

"Erm, I suppose." She gestured to the Day-Glo orange food truck to our right. "You get the tacos?"

"Triple order."

"They're the bomb, right?"

"I'm beginning to think Sinaloa's had a bad rap all these years."

"Yeah, like the place needs a PR campaign or a new slogan."

"Sinaloa . . . come for the drugs, stay for the tacos," I offered.

She smiled. "Welcome to Sinaloa, where tacos are the only thing getting baked."

"Bit clunky, but I'll buy it."

We walked silently for a minute, passing a homeless man washing his bare chest in the lake water, his worldly belongings bungled into an overstuffed shopping cart.

"Jesus, it's like the banks of the freakin' Ganges," Katie said, shaking her head.

"Hard to believe Oakland's made the top ten list of the most expensive cities in California when you see this kind of thing."

"Not really," she said, shrugging. "It's how gentrification works, right? Rich people move in, house prices go through the roof, and the poor get left behind. You'd think with all those tax dollars, they'd have figured this shit out by now."

"Been reading the editorials in the locals again?"

"Nah, Nextdoor dot com. It gets a bit white and shouty out there, but it's the real deal. Citizen power, you know, get the facts as they happen, no filter."

"Turned the notifications off on mine. Stressed me out too much."

"Yeah, it can do that, you gotta be selective. But I reckon I'd rather know than not know."

"Information is power?"

"Kind of a cliché, but I guess so."

"Is that why you were talking to that reporter?" I asked. "Providing him information?"

Katie stopped. That same etch of worry back around the edges of her eyes.

"I know Javier. He works with Sierra."

She continued walking and picked up her pace. I did the same.

"Kat, there's only one reason you're talking to a journo, and I'll bet you tacos every lunch break for the next month it's to do with the retired judges."

"I didn't tell him shit," Katie muttered, her focus on the sidewalk ahead.

Her pace quickened again. My lunch complained as I struggled to match her gait. "One question. Did you make first contact, or did he?"

She slowed down. "He did, I guess."

"You guess?"

To my relief, she stopped and crossed her arms over her chest, Katie's go-to defensive strategy. "I met the dude at a party. He got all up in my face about my job, like he was really interested. I didn't say shit. I'm not stupid . . . If you wanna talk stupid, how about Muriel breaching the freakin' court firewall?"

"This isn't about Muriel. Did you arrange to meet here?"

"No. The asshole stalked me, obviously, followed me from the courthouse."

"Was he fishing, or did he have specific questions?"

"Kind of specific, I guess, mostly about Judge Griffin."

"What did he want to know?"

"Did I know him? Had I heard any rumors? The usual shit reporters ask when they're fishing for something."

"Did you—?"

"You really wanna know?" Katie looked around and lowered her voice. "I told him to go fuck himself."

"That's good. You did the right thing."

"Like you think I wouldn't?"

"No, but I wouldn't be doing my job if I didn't ask."

"Well, maybe you're just asking the wrong person."

"What does that mean?"

"If I didn't tell him, and I'm sure as hell Muriel didn't go shooting her mouth off, what with her global travel plans, that leaves one person."

"Tye? No. He's green, but he's not dumb."

"Whatever you say, but you gotta figure you've got someone at the courthouse is leaking confidential information like they're Julian freakin' Assange."

CHAPTER 32

Alma had called that afternoon and suggested we meet at a microbrewery in Oakland's Temescal neighborhood. I arrived early at Rosa's Taproom and waited outside in the parklet built over three parking spaces. Parklets had sprung up like wildflowers in Oakland during the pandemic, and I guessed were now here to stay; I took it as social progress of sorts. The parklet outside Rosa's had a cross-stitch of yellow Edison lights and loops of colored paper triangles hung around the eaves. For a moment, I could almost imagine I was sitting in a bustling piazza in some cool European city, if it wasn't for the choke of traffic fumes, the butt-ugly strip mall directly in my line of sight, and the homeless dude across the road venting his holy rage against the world. *Right there with you, brother,* I thought, *but do you have to stick it to the man in the middle of the sidewalk with your pants dropped around your ankles?*

The server took my order. My three-taco lunch was already a distant memory, though my conversation with Katie still niggled at the back of my mind. I was certain she wasn't lying, and equally sure she was correct that Muriel wouldn't leak anything if it meant putting her retirement in jeopardy. But Tye? Neither my head nor my heart could find their way there.

As I waited for Alma, I grabbed my notebook and wrote Charlotte's last words again, as if a change of location might help unlock the mystery. No such luck. I was still staring at the notebook, as if hoping that through sheer willpower, the answer would manifest, fully formed and undeniable, when Alma plonked herself in the chair across from me. Her T-shirt read, *Apparently, I Have an Attitude.*

"I'd never have guessed," I said.

"What's that, like, lawyer humor?" She gestured to the server and glanced at my notebook. "You studying or something?"

"Feels like studying. Trying to solve the puzzle of a dying woman's last words."

She ordered a hazy IPA and spun my notebook around. "I rock puzzles, top of the league in my Wordle group," she said. "Charlotte?"

"Can't make any sense of it, no matter how many times I look."

She scrunched her brow. "Yeah, not much to go on. You think she was referring to a person, like someone she wanted you to protect?"

"No one comes to mind. She doesn't have a daughter. Victor wasn't much help, either."

"Even though he was screwing her?"

"Lay it out there on the table, why don't you, Alma?"

"Yeah, think I just did," she said, taking her beer. "And you can't ask Castillo, because you already told him she told you bupkes before she died?"

"Not only that. Maybe Paco's the one this person needs protection from."

"Yeah, fucking conundrum time, for sure."

I allowed her the luxury of savoring the first sips of her beer without interruption. I figured it was the gentlemanly thing to do.

"So, do you have a name for me?" I finally asked.

Before answering, she launched into her warning, which, if Alma had the social skills to read the room, would have realized only ramped up my curiosity as to the identity of the culprit who'd knocked me flying.

She leaned her elbows on the table. "Look, I like you, Mitch . . . well, as much as I can like any dumb fuck who gets himself involved in Paco Castillo's business."

"Easy, Alma. That almost sounded like a compliment."

"Yeah? My mistake." She continued. "You're Victor's buddy. I don't want anything happening to you because of me. I don't handle guilt too well, tend to spiral, you know, then there's—"

"Alma," I interrupted. "Can you just tell me the damn name? I'm not about to do anything stupid. Promise."

"You agreed to work for Castillo to pay off your debt. Gotta say that's pretty high on the stupid scale."

"Thanks for the reminder."

"Just keeping it real."

"Maybe just keep working on that people filter of yours. Not everyone wants you to keep it real 24/7. Now, that name . . . please."

With a resigned sigh, she placed a scrap of paper between us. As I reached for it, she stabbed a finger on the paper. "Are you sure this is what you want?"

I nodded.

"Okay, your funeral, dude."

I unfolded the paper, read the name and address, and sat back.

"Make you feel any better?"

"Not really."

"You're welcome, by the way."

"Yeah, thanks, really appreciate it," I said flatly.

"Hey, don't blame me if you ask the question and don't like the answer."

I needed another drink. Something harder, more resilient than beer.

She gestured at my notebook. "Charlotte was dying when she said that, right? Just been shot? Blood in her mouth?"

I nodded, my stomach churning as I recalled that night. "Lots of it."

"So, you sure you heard it right? Someone who's just been shot and speaking through a mouthful of blood might just choke on their words. Just sayin'."

"You know this from experience?"

"Not personally, but I've seen it happen."

"Jesus, where the hell did Victor find you?"

Alma, true to form, failed to register the question as rhetorical. "He was my lawyer way back before he got all fancy with the downtown office and the big house in Piedmont. Got me off an assault charge. I was guilty, but the asshole had it coming. I couldn't afford Victor's hourly, so I started working for him to pay off what I owed. Figured it was a good gig, never left."

"Thanks for the diversion, but you were saying?"

"Oh, sure." She took a long sip of beer. "Here's my take. You've been obsessing about this person you think Charlotte asked you to protect. What if she was trying to say something different, but it just sounded like those words? You were in shock, and your mind went to the first thing you thought she was saying. Could be it just sounded like 'protect her', but she was saying something kinda like it?"

"You think so?"

"I dunno. Try one of those rhyming apps or something, see what comes up."

"Seems like a long shot."

"Beats writing the same thing a hundred times, like you're punishing yourself."

Alma wasn't the most tactful tool in the box, but she was one of the sharpest; the subtlety of a hammer with the precision of a utility knife. Maybe she was right, and this was my way of punishing myself for what happened to Charlotte.

Alma stood, grabbed the remainder of my pretzel, dipped it in the cold, coagulated cheese, and shoved it in her mouth. "And remember, don't do anything stupid, got me? I don't know what you did to piss them off, but I don't figure escalation's your next move in this situation."

I nodded. Problem was, doing stupid shit seemed to be my MO these days.

* * *

Hector.
Hector.
Hector.

The word bounced around my mind like a pinball, lighting up my synapses until I could almost see the orange neon flashes dancing in front of my eyes. I got up from the couch and walked to the window.

Eight fifteen in the evening, and Jack London Square buzzed and crackled with crowds strolling to the bars and restaurants fronting the dock. Beyond the yawning stanchions of the yachts and powerboats, the Port of Oakland cranes stood still and silent, like sleeping iron giants, and beyond the cranes, the tule fog belt had stretched its ample girth from the central coast, wrapping itself tight around the downtown San Francisco skyline. It wouldn't ease up a notch or two until dawn.

Between episodes of some South Korean gladiator-style reality show, I'd taken Alma's advice and typed "protect her" into an online rhyming dictionary. The results yielded a dead end of words, setting me back to square one. As I waited for the next episode of *Goryeo Gauntlet*, I re-entered my prompt, this time asking the engine to search for near rhymes. Around a hundred words appeared on my screen. As I scanned the two-syllable list, about halfway down, one word seemed to leap out of the screen:

Hector.

I stared at the word — the verb, *hector*. It wasn't a common word, but I'd heard trial lawyers use it when they accused their opponents of 'hectoring' their witnesses. A shadow of irony crept over me; Charlotte's words had done the same to me over the past week, hectored and bullied me until I'd unscrambled their code.

Protect her . . . Hector.

It must have been what Charlotte was trying to say with her dying breath. *Hector.*

The pieces fell into place like the reels of a slot machine lining up in a perfect matching line of symbols, the whole casino turning to look as the jackpot light ignited and the coins flowed out in a river mouth of silver and gold.

Charlotte wasn't asking me to protect anyone. She was saying *Hector . . . Tell Victor . . . Hector.*

Once I figured that out, everything else she'd said became clear, as if she were feeding me clues, just in case.

You just can't find the staff these days, can you? Then again, one should always have a good friend in the pawn business, don't you think? You never know when they'll come in useful.

My mind flashed back to my encounter with Hector, his miserable pawn store, the rows of old dusty computers, and the carcasses of hard drives. I was sure Charlotte's laptop was somewhere amongst the debris of Hetch's electronic graveyard. The laptop was hiding in plain sight; it had just taken me this long to figure it out.

As I looked through the window, Jack London Square night-life scurrying below, two thoughts struck me: if I was ever to free myself from Paco Castillo's grip, I had to return to Palm Springs, retrieve the laptop, and pay off my debt.

My other thought landed closer to home. I'd promised Alma I wouldn't do anything stupid, but where was the harm in just checking out the address?

Like I said. I'd recently graduated at the top of my class in executing dumbass moves.

PART 5:
BULLET NUMBER FOUR

CHAPTER 33

When the moon manifests somewhere between a waxing crescent and first quarter, it looks like a tiny rip in the velvet fabric of the night sky, one I could imagine slipping a fingernail under and peeling away to reveal another layer of the cosmos, one that existed before the universe came into being, like an art restorer methodically exposing the layers of an old master painting to uncover the original sketches beneath. Sitting in my car across from 1419 Ansel Court, it struck me I was itching toward something similar, slowly flaking off the layers as I dug closer to the truth.

Alma had asked me earlier that evening if knowing the name of the person who'd run into me had made me feel better. It hadn't. What it had done was confirm what I suspected was true, and when that truth comes into the light, there's no shade for it to hide under. It's the elephant on your back, the itch under the sweaty cast around a broken leg, the crazed chimp running around the room throwing shit at the walls for attention.

My mind trapezed through these high-wire musings as I studied the house across from me: another two-story, anonymous home fallen victim to a personality bypass at the stilted imagination of the corporate architects. Cookie-cutter housing developments were common enough around the East Bay suburbs, and I figured OPD officers, even banking all the overtime hours they could work, still struggled to afford a home in Oakland. Pleasant Hill, some eighteen miles east of Oakland, was the closest option if you wanted to ensure you were far enough away from the city where you patrolled, and unlikely to run into some thug you'd help send to jail and who had a good memory for faces and a grudge against the arresting officer.

I glanced at the truck parked in the driveway and checked the license plate against the number Paco had given me. Part of me hoped Alma was wrong, and I could have driven away and avoided the whole shit storm that rained down that night. But Alma was good at her job. I shouldn't have doubted her. I should have also listened to her advice about not doing anything stupid. However, that slim window of time for inaction had passed, and I was already in the driveway checking out the front passenger side of the burgundy Ford Maverick.

My eyes took a minute to adjust to the darkness: the nights fall blacker out in the suburbs while the stars seem to shine brighter, free from the halo of light pollution spilling from the city. The front window of the house was cracked open, canned laughter from a TV show filtered through the gap, and a pale light washed over the front lawn.

I switched on my phone's video function and squatted at the truck's front fender. A scratch, around three inches long and a pencil width across, manifested on my screen. Judging by the position of the scrape, it would have been the correct height to hit my bike's rear seat stay. Moving closer, I was sure the flake of neon green paint etched into the scratch was the same color as my bike. Hardly damning evidence, and impossible to prove in a court of law, but it proved Paco's theory that my accident was likely no accident.

That ignited another thought, one which sparked a fresh flash of anger: maybe Kurt's shooting wasn't an accident, either.

As my anger simmered to a slow roil, my ringtone, the guitar opening of the Clash's "Should I Stay or Should I Go," fractured the quiet neighborhood at full volume.

I checked the caller ID: *Ron Boone.*

In my panic to silence the three-chord battle cry, I dropped the phone under the truck. As I clawed around, a burst of light from the porch illuminated the driveway. When I stood again, Officer Darlene Mason was at the opposite side of the truck, Glock 19 in both hands, face wired into a tight scowl.

She spoke, controlled and practiced. "I'll tell you this one time only. I'm a police officer, and you're trespassing on my property. I'm within my rights to shoot you. If you do anything that's gonna piss me off, that's exactly what I'm gonna do."

I took a beat. Darlene was bluffing. California had the Castle Doctrine; if a person breaks into your home, unless your life is in imminent danger, you're prohibited from using deadly force. I doubted a cell phone loaded with apps and six thousand songs would qualify as a lethal weapon. Still, I wasn't about to explain the intricacies of Penal Code Section 198.5 to a police officer aiming a gun at me. Besides, I was sure Darlene was well-versed in this aspect of the law and was just intent on making a point.

"Come on, Darlene," I said, slipping the phone into my jacket pocket. "This isn't Florida. You can put the gun down. I'm no danger to you or your property."

Darlene squinted as she studied my face. She wore purple sweats, a scruffy purple fleece dressing gown, and matching purple slippers. Her hair looked as if she hadn't run a brush through it for days, and even from fifteen feet away, I caught a strong tide of alcohol, accompanied by the smoky backwash of nicotine.

"You're that asshole lawyer," she said. "What you doing on my property?" I noticed her arms were shaking, a subtle quiver that brought to mind an alcoholic's tremor when a glass of something stronger was beyond easy reach.

"Nasty scratch you got there." I gestured at the fender. "You should get it seen to."

"What are you, my insurance agent?"

"My bike got pretty beat up by that truck of yours."

"If you're looking for reparation, you're shit out of luck."

"I didn't come here for money. I was looking for proof that you or Connor were the assholes who knocked me off my bike."

She sniffed loudly and tipped her head back as if she were testing the air for the scent of fear. "Well, if you found what you're looking for, you'd best fuck off, and I won't need to discharge my weapon."

"Why, Darlene? Why do it?"

The question gave her pause. She swayed, as if a stiff wind had picked up around her; whatever she'd been drinking had messed with her equilibrium. Figuring that drunks with a few drinks already inside them are partial to letting their tongues run off-leash — they like to prove a point — I decided to push Darlene's buttons and see what triggered.

"It was Connor, right, who put you up to this? His idea? What was the plan? Teach me a lesson? Scare me off?"

Darlene shrugged. "Guess if you're gonna help criminals like Castillo walk free, then you get what's coming."

"And my son? Did he get what was coming to him, too?"

That was the trigger moment. Darlene's arms shook as if the weapon weighed heavily in her hands. The look in her eyes reminded me of a squirrel paralyzed in the middle of the road as the traffic thundered onward. Releasing one hand from the gun, she reached the other into her pocket, slipped out a medium-sized bourbon bottle, and slugged.

"So, you coming in or what?" she said, gesturing at the doorway. "I don't have all night."

I debated walking away, leaving Darlene to the remainder of the bottle and a brutal hangover in the making, but it seemed her tongue was loosening, and that crazed chimp inside my head was curious as hell as to what she had to say.

* * *

Darlene still had the gun aimed at my chest as I took the chair across from her in the living room. Inside, the house was as bland as the exterior: white walls and beige-colored furniture, the only color thrown on the walls by the flickering images from the flat-screen above the fireplace. She stabbed the remote, muting the show she was watching, took a cigarette from the table beside her La-Z-Boy, and from somewhere, conjured up a lighter.

"I'd offer you one, but I only got two left," she said, smoke billowing from her nostrils. "And I ain't hauling ass to the 7-Eleven this time of night."

This time of night being only eight fifteen; out in suburbia, people march to the beat of a different clock.

"Why invite me in, Darlene? Got something you want to get off your chest?"

She gave me a wire-tight smile. "Like a confession? You don't look much like a priest."

"No, but I'm a good listener. Put the gun down, and we can talk."

Darlene laid the Glock beside her cigarettes on the table. The silent images cast by the TV spilled over her face like dancing ghosts. I could tell she was itching to say something; I just needed the right questions to get her to turn on that faucet, start spilling.

On the mantel above the fireplace, I noticed a row of unframed photographs propped up against the wall: Darlene and Office Theodore Connor smiling, cradling semi-automatic weapons, a shooting range serving as the romantic backdrop. In another, Darlene and Connor sat on the deck of a sailboat on the bay, arms wrapped around each other, the Golden Gate Bridge looming majestically over the horizon.

I gestured at the photos and said, "So, you and Connor—"

"Fuck him," she snapped, then took a deep swig, wiping her mouth with the sleeve of her dressing gown.

"You're together?"

Another swig, followed by a chuckle. "Yeah, until his wife found out. Said he was going to leave her; like a fucking idiot I believed him."

"Oldest story in the book. Sorry to hear that. Must be hard."

"Hard?" Darlene rested her forearms on her thighs, her cigarette pointing at me like a red-tipped finger. "I'll tell you what's fucking hard. I get suspended without pay until Internal Affairs finishes their investigation on the whole body-cam incident. Thanks for that, by the way; real fucking helpful, you taking the stand."

"I was under oath. I wasn't going to lie for you or Connor."

"Connor? That sack of shit." She let out a snort-like laugh. "You know what he told those jerkoffs at IA to save his ass? Told them it was all my idea. The illegal search, switching off the body cams. Spun some cockamamie story about how he'd suspected I was corrupt for months, and just went along with it because he was gathering evidence against me. It's bullshit, all of it. But Connor gets his story out there first, so I'm on the back foot, having to defend myself. If shit goes south, I could lose my job, my house . . ."

"Did you tell Internal Affairs all this?"

"Of course I fucking did. They didn't seem too interested in listening. Connor's got seniority, been on the force a lot longer, and he's a guy, which kinda gives him the dick advantage over at OPD." She paused and took another hit of bourbon. "You're a lawyer. What do you think?"

"Is that why you asked me in? You wanted my legal advice?"

"Figured a second option couldn't hurt."

"I'm not that kind of lawyer. Your union rep should have advised you to hire a lawyer specializing in Internal Affairs investigations."

"Yeah, and what's that gonna cost me? Just bought this house and the truck. Don't have the money for a fancy lawyer."

"If I were you, I'd find that money, quick. You get fired, odds are you'll lose the house, anyway."

Darlene picked up the bourbon bottle and shook it at me as if she were expecting me to drop some loose coinage down its neck.

"No thanks, I'm driving. Wouldn't want to get pulled over."

"Smart," she said, nursing the bottle in the crook of her arm. "Now, if you're done being no fucking help whatsoever, you can leave."

I should have taken Darlene's cue and left, but that crazed chimp in my head was in major shit-hurling mode.

"One more question. Did you and Connor have anything to do with my son getting shot?"

Another Darlene trigger moment. Her hands trembled as she brushed a stray strand of hair from her cheek. "Don't know what you're talking about."

"Let me spell it out for you, Darlene. After knocking me off my bike, did you and Connor decide to escalate the situation with some fucked-up plan to shoot my son?" I was keeping a lid on my anger, but the image of Kurt lying in his hospital bed kept nudging at me like an elbow to the gut. "You know how close he came to dying?" I made a small space between my thumb and index finger. "This close. I came this close to losing my son because you and Connor were pissed that I stood up and told the truth. He's just a boy." I took a photo from my wallet. "Kurt, ten years old. Ten, Darlene, how's that make you feel?"

Her eyes moistened. Her shoulders shook. "I swear, it was Connor's idea. You know, just drive there, shoot above the house, no big deal, we weren't gonna hit anything. It was dark. How the hell did we know your kid would be out in the yard that time of night? Bullet must have ricocheted. I didn't mean to hurt him, swear to God. A big mistake, that's all. But your son, he's okay now, right?"

"He'll live, no thanks to you."

She sighed and nodded her head. "Good, yeah, that's good."

"What the fuck were you thinking?" I asked, raising my voice. "You're a police officer; you nearly killed my son, and for what? Some fucked-up vendetta you and your boyfriend cooked up to fuck me over? How the hell did they ever give you a badge, let alone let you carry a weapon?"

"Connor—"

"Bullshit. This is on you, Darlene. You *and* Connor." I stood, my head spinning. The truth was out there now, and like I said, when it's out in the light, the truth demands to be dealt with, insists on it. "I'll make sure you and Connor both pay for this."

Darlene wiped her eyes. "Go ahead. It's not like you've got any proof. I'll deny it. Connor, too — your word against two cops. As far as I know, this conversation never happened. Now, you can get the fuck out of my house."

Reaching into my jacket pocket, I pulled out my cell phone. I'd taken a leaf out of Paco Castillo's book and kept my video function on my phone recording the whole time. I wouldn't need moving pictures to prove her and Connor's guilt; the audio was plenty, and I'd recorded every breath of her confession.

She stared at the phone, her face turning as pale as the living room walls as I replayed the last few moments of our conversation. She mouthed something incoherent. Whatever it was, I had no interest in hearing.

Slipping the phone back into my pocket, I marched out of the house. I was halfway down the front path when I heard three gunshots rip open the silence.

I ran back inside, expecting the worst.

Darlene was still nesting in her La-Z-Boy, gun in one hand, bourbon in the other, bringing to mind some grotesque, purple-clad, female Las Vegas-era Elvis, having shot a king-sized, belt-buckle-shaped hole in the flat-screen.

That was the first bullet.

The other two bullets had landed in the center of the photos of her and Connor, which had now toppled from the fireplace like she'd been shooting ducks at the county fair.

I looked at Darlene. The nub of her Glock scraped at the hard bone just behind her right ear. Her face was composed, telegraphing to anyone in the room that her decision was made.

Before I got my words out, she pulled the trigger.

Bullet number four. Embedded deep in Darlene Mason's brain stem. An instant death guaranteed; no do-overs, no gimmes, no get-out-of-jail-free card.

I watched, helpless, as her body bent at the waist and slumped forward, the gun slipping to the floor, the white walls behind her a Jackson Pollock of thick, bloody brushstrokes and etchings of gray matter.

CHAPTER 34

The Stork Club, on the fringes of downtown and uptown Oakland, was an institution around these parts. During the pandemic, the Stork Club had shuttered its doors, with few people ever imagining them opening again. By some minor miracle, the Stork Club recovered and was now thriving more than it had before the pandemic almost shuttered the place for good.

Grungy, and as gritty as a boot full of gravel, the Stork Club looked like a gone-to-seed Mexican taqueria. Bright yellow and pink paint peeled off the walls like dried tears. A rogues' gallery of battered piñatas hanging from the ceiling gave the impression of a retired sanctuary, where their flimsy bones would never again have to face the cruel swing of the bat.

Tattoos with surly attitudes, wearing black, cap-sleeved T-shirts, staffed the bar. Beer was served in cans and the liquor poured neat; no cocktails, no wine. That suited me fine; the fewer complications my life had, the better. The stage was to the rear of the main bar, the mosh pit humming with sweat and spilled beer. At one time, I would have dived on in there with reckless abandon, but I'd brushed too close to death recently, and the thought of catching some infection to satisfy my lust for a good old-fashioned pogo didn't sit well with me, so I let the youngsters have at it and stood at the bar nursing my beer.

The band was a scruffy outfit called Ratchet Carnage. They lived up to their name; vocals barely audible, a distorted fuzz of the standard suite of chords (three, I think), violent drumming, and a bass guitar that wandered around the tracks with the wanton abandon of a freight-train-hopping hobo. I loved the feral energy, the recklessness, the couldn't-give-a-fuckness of it all, and that wrecking ball of noise was exactly what I needed to detonate last night's memory of Darlene Mason's brain splattered on the canvas of her living room wall.

I was to meet Victor at the Stork later, and I knew the Prince of Lawyerly Cool well enough to know he'd hate the music. That was fine. Punk gigs are meant to be short. It's built into the unspoken punk manifesto: stagger on stage, play fast and loose, get the hell off stage, job done. Ratchet Carnage's set was about forty-five minutes, a veritable Bruce Springsteen-length gig where punk was concerned. They left the stage with a drum smash and a middle finger *fuck you* to the crowd from the lead singer, channeling the spirit of Sid Vicious drunkenly crooning through "My Way" at the end of *The Great Rock 'n' Roll Swindle*.

My ears ringing, I shoved through the crowd to the beer garden, found a seat at one of the plastic tables, and waited for Victor. He arrived ten minutes later, dressed, as expected, in gear totally inappropriate for the venue: designer sweats, a cream-colored hoodie, and pristine white high-tops.

He sat with a scowl. "Where the hell do you find these places?"

"Keep my ear to the ground."

"Fucked if I'm putting anything on the ground here except my shoes." He looked down and noticed a fresh beer stain running down his high-tops. "Jesus, these are brand new."

"Should have worn boots. Big black ones with steel toe caps."

"My mistake. Let me call 1983 and see if they've still got my Doc Martens in storage."

"You never owned a pair of Doc Martens in your life."

"Not the point, but seeing as you invited me to this cesspit, you can go get me a beer. Mexican lager if they've got it, or do they just serve PBR with a side of an STD of your choice?"

"I think they've got Red Stripe."

"Whatever, so long as it's cold."

"Now, you start being demanding, you're going to piss off the bar staff."

"Just get me a damn beer."

I did as he requested and returned with a plastic cup full to the brim with Red Stripe. Victor took a tentative sip, grimaced, and placed the beer on the table an arm's length away, then spoke.

"I heard you were in the same room when Darlene Mason shot herself last night. What the hell were you even doing at her place?"

I ran down the events, omitting the fact I'd recorded her confession; I still couldn't one hundred percent trust Victor. After Darlene had pulled the trigger and redecorated her walls, I'd called the cops. Pleasant Hill PD was at the house within minutes, along with most of the neighborhood standing and gawping on their doorsteps. The cops questioned me for a few hours before releasing me. I conveniently forgot to mention I'd recorded my conversation with Darlene; they'd have seized that as evidence, and I wasn't about to let the recording end up in anyone's hands. Cops stick together, and Connor just needed one friend in the Pleasant Hill Police Department and that recording would never see the light of day, and who knows what retribution he'd send my way to teach me another one of Connor's lessons.

I told the officers I suspected Darlene and her partner had conspired to cause me bodily harm, and one of them had also fired the gun that injured my son. I also mentioned Darlene had been drinking heavily and was likely to lose both her job and her home. After making a few calls, they had me sign a statement then released me.

Victor let a few seconds pass before speaking. "How did you track the license plate?"

"Erm . . . Paco."

"And how did he obtain it?"

"I don't know, but he was probably having me followed at the time."

"Seems like his style. But how did you get Darlene's name without breaking into the police ANPR database?"

"Someone owed me a favor."

"Was that someone Alma?"

"Possibly."

"Jesus, you're like a walking advertisement for dumbass moves."

"Yeah, that's pretty much what Alma said."

"Good, now we've got that cleared up. Why am I here at your shithole away from home?"

Lowering my voice, I said, "I think I figured out what Charlotte was trying to tell me."

"Okay, shoot."

I ran down the evidence as if I were presenting a case.

Victor sat back. "If what you're saying is right, you know what that means?"

"Yep, back to Palm fucking Springs, but this time you're coming with me."

Victor shook his head. "Would love the time away, *amigo*, but I'm in court for the next two weeks. No way I can swing a trip to Palm Springs."

"Swing a trip? You're making it sound like a vacation, which, trust me, it wasn't. I need you there, Victor. What am I meant to do? Walk into the store, ask politely for the dead woman's computer, and hope Porno Hand Hetch lets me walk out of there with the laptop under my arm?"

"You'll just have to figure out another way to get it."

"*We.* We need to figure out a way."

"Happy to brainstorm, run some ideas up the flagpole, but there's no way I can make it down there, not with my caseload." He leaned forward, put his forearms on the table, then quickly raised them when he realized the sleeves of his cashmere hoodie were sticking to whatever syrupy residue had settled on the surface. "Paco's anxious. I'm keeping him off your back, but I can't do that much longer. I'll speak to him, tell him you've got a lead, he'll pay for your ticket, hotel, whatever you need."

"Are you serious?"

"Best I can do. Look, you'll figure this out. I'll speak to Paco, but remember he leaves for London at the end of next week. If he doesn't have it by then . . . well—"

"Yeah, you don't need to paint me a picture. Do you know what this laptop even looks like? There was a shelf full of old computers back in the store."

"I have no idea. But if it's Charlotte's, it's probably going to be expensive, top-of-the-line. That's assuming you're right."

I ran a hand over my face. "Guess I don't have the luxury of being wrong."

"No, I guess you don't." Victor stood and brushed himself down. "I'd ask you where the restrooms are in this place, but I figure I'd need a hazmat suit."

"Or you could just hold your breath."

He shook his head. "You know, most people grow up as they get older. I think you're regressing. Not a good look, *amigo*. I'll be in touch."

But Victor was wrong. To regress, you had to move on in the first place. From where I sat, that moving on had been glacial in its progress. Maybe that's why I was still behaving like a rebellious teenager, frequenting seedy bars for their "Trunk of Punk" nights, still itching for the thrill of a quick gamble, still pogoing headlong into situations that I should know better than to pogo into.

I figured there was nothing I could do about it right then, downed the remainder of Victor's beer, and headed out to the evening's next meeting.

CHAPTER 35

At night, looking from above, the old cliché that describes freeways as the arteries that connect us rings strikingly true. From my vantage point, some hundred feet above Highway 24, the San Francisco skyline glimmered and hummed silently. Across the Bay Bridge, the flow of red corpuscles was a relentless river, dumping cars and trucks into the city's heart. I stood at the corner of a gazebo-like structure constructed as a memorial to the Oakland Firestorm of 1991. A bunch of educational blurbs concerning wildfire protection were stuck behind what I assumed was fire-retardant clear plastic.

In Northern California, we'd struck an uneasy truce with nature, each natural disaster an escalation on the next, as if nature was dishing out minor warnings of more consequential disasters to come if we didn't get our shit together. But that's the problem with hope built on a fault line: it's not hope, it's wishful thinking.

As a graze of headlights scuttled over the nearby oaks and ferns, I heard a car pull up in the parking lot. A car door slammed shut, followed by heels clicking across paving stones. I leaned on the steel barrier and watched her draw closer.

"Strange place to meet up, Mr. Sweeney. Couldn't we have arranged a wine bar? Somewhere a little . . . warmer?"

"Got to admit the view's worth the drive up here."

"Down here," Judge Harriet Croft corrected me and gestured to the black, serrated outline of the hills behind us. "I live on Grizzly Peak. My view's a hundred feet above this and a lot less chilly from my living room window."

I nodded. "Thanks for coming. I appreciate you making the drive down here."

"Didn't sound like I had much choice."

"Yeah, sorry, but it's important, and . . ." I hesitated, wondering how to best to say what I'd come to say.

"Go on. I don't intend to be up here all night admiring the view. If I do, I'll have to start charging you by the hour."

"Doubt I could afford those prices."

"Damn right, you couldn't. Now get to the point."

"Okay, you probably heard Officer Darlene Mason committed suicide last night."

"It's always a tragedy when one of our law enforcement officers takes their own lives. Makes me think that maybe someone wasn't paying enough attention, the guardrails taken away when she needed them."

"You do know she was corrupt. Both her and Connor?"

"She was still a fellow human being. We can still have some respect in death, no matter the wrongs she may have committed in life."

This is why I liked working for Judge Croft, liked her as a person. She drew a hard line when the situation demanded but hadn't lost her humanity. A tough achievement given her position, but that's why I felt I could trust her with what I had to say.

"I was with Darlene Mason last night when she shot herself."

"My, you are a dark horse," she said, shoving her hands in her coat pockets. "Why on earth were you making a house call on Officer Mason?"

I took a breath. "Look, before I tell you anything, I need to ask you something important. Remember when we sat in the courthouse café a few days back?"

"When you questioned me about Judge Harper's ruling?"

"I thought you'd maybe left the door open, that you couldn't or wouldn't discuss it in the courthouse . . ."

"And you thought a cloak-and-dagger clandestine meeting would be more appropriate?"

"If I stepped over the line, I'm—"

Judge Croft interrupted. "How much do you know?"

"Know or suspect?"

"You wouldn't have called me if you just had suspicions. You must know something."

I took a beat and told her about Muriel's findings, including the preferential treatment given to the *Sangres Norteñas* members, how their hearings were mostly officiated by retired judges with a link to Judge Harper, and how the charges were more often than not dismissed.

She turned to look at the snake of red lights moving below us. "I guessed this would get out sooner or later. Still, I'm glad it landed on your desk, Mitch," she said, switching to the informal. "But, and this is a very important 'but,' keep this between us. Make sure your team's not a leaky vessel. I assume they already know?"

"They're loyal," I assured her.

"Good, keep it that way. I can't reveal details, but plans are already in motion. Make no mistake, I intend to clean up that office the moment I take up the Presiding Judgeship. Cancer or no cancer, Judge Harper will get what's coming to him. Is anybody else aware of this?"

I hesitated. "Em . . . a journalist's been sniffing around. Javier Madrigal."

She stiffened. "Sniffing? Did he pick up a scent?"

"Maybe. But I doubt he has enough to print a story."

"These days, you don't need a story. One Tweet goes viral, and that *is* the story."

She was right. Nuance seemed to be a relic of smarter times. People had gotten used to shaping their opinions on inflammatory clickbait and a trending hashtag.

"Anyone else?"

"Ron Boone. He's the one who brought it to my attention. He's got a vested interest, obviously."

"Ron's a good man, but he's a loudmouth, likes to agitate. Will he agitate?"

"I've asked him to stand down, wait until we get more evidence."

"Did he listen?"

"He trusts me. That's about as much as I can say."

"Good, keep him on a tight leash. We don't need a barking dog waking up the whole damned neighborhood."

"Understood. But there is one more thing," I said, reaching into my jacket pocket for a flash drive. I'd transferred Darlene's confession from my phone onto the device earlier that day.

Judge Croft raised her hands and stepped back. "If that's any evidence you want me to look at, then I'll have to decline. Plausible deniability. It could compromise the case."

"It's nothing to do with Harper," I said, then explained the episode with Connor and Mason, the manufactured bike accident, Kurt's shooting, and Darlene's confession.

"My, you have been a busy bee," Judge Croft said. "You know I can't listen to that. It could prejudice any case we bring against Officer Connor."

"I don't want you to listen to it. I just want you to keep it safe. It's a copy, in case something happens to me."

"Are you expecting something to happen?"

I shrugged. "Just leave it behind a locked door, forget about it. I'll come and get it in a few days."

"Why a few days? If you already have a confession, why not strike while the iron's hot?"

"I need to go away, taking some vacation time with the family."

She eyed me suspiciously. "I'll secure the flash drive, but don't bullshit me. I know you're separated from your wife, and she and your son are in Mexico right now, recovering."

"How—?"

"Everyone at the courthouse knows. I said I don't listen to gossip, but sometimes it arrives unsolicited with a loud thud in my inbox. This was one of those times. I figured you must have a good reason for not telling anyone, so I wasn't going to push. We all have our right to privacy."

"Thanks, I appreciate that," I said.

She slipped the flash drive into her pocket, looked at the steady pulse of traffic, said wistfully, "Everybody's got someplace to leave and someplace to be. Which is it for you, Mr. Sweeney?"

"Sorry?"

"This vacation of yours? Start of the journey, or end of the road?"

I paused. "Guess I'll figure it out when I get there."

CHAPTER 36

Ignore a problem long enough, and it'll come back and bite a chunk out of your ass when you least expect it. The problem in question was Ron Boone. The ass in question, mine.

Since returning from Palm Springs, I'd given his emails the cold shoulder. I had baggage enough weighing me down, and Ron was just another load adding to the burden. But Ron was determined, hadn't made it twenty-five years as a union negotiator without developing a crustacean-like thick skin and the tenacity of a bone-digging terrier.

Between the memory of Darlene Mason's gray matter sprayed over her living room wall and witnessing Charlotte's murder, I was sure the trauma would leave a lesion somewhere on my psyche. But I'd become an expert at shoving that stuff down to the bottom of my memory dumpster, along with a bunch of other debris that I was sure at some point would combust, ignited by some reaction of heat, oxygen, fuel, and guilt. But for the time being, I was spared that dumpster fire.

At least Kurt and Sierra were two thousand miles away, but Paco's insistence on "keeping an eye" on my family had disturbed me. I imagined a bunch of goons decked out in faded beachwear and flip-flops, hanging out in open-top jeeps as they staked out my mother-in-law's house: Jorge 2.0 types, hungrier, more ruthless.

This sobering thought rattled through me as I pulled up in the underground courthouse parking lot. Stepping out of my car, I heard my name being called from ten spaces away. The booming voice was instantly recognizable. Ron's voice carried like a fart from a brass trombone.

He marched over and stood a few feet from me, looking more disheveled than usual: hair uncombed, tie askew and stained, jacket fastened at the top button, giving the impression of someone who'd gotten dressed in the dark while still asleep.

"Sweeney," he said. "You're a sight for sore eyes."

From the swell of alcohol rising from his breath, I guessed Ron was still drunk or hungover. At eight in the morning, I hoped it was the latter, but the lazy slur of his words made me wonder if he hadn't washed down his morning toast with a side of Scotch and a mug of beer.

"Ron," I said, fixing my bag across my shoulder. "Good to see you."

"Is that right? Been thinking it would be a damn sight easier to get an audience with the Pope than schedule a meeting with you these days."

"Just been really busy, you know . . . and the whole thing with Kurt."

"Yeah, we all heard. How's the kid doing?"

"He's fine. My wife's taken him to her mom's for a couple of weeks."

"Yeah, good plan," Ron agreed, gesturing to the city above us. "This city's turning into a goddam war zone."

"It's not getting any better, that's for sure."

Ron looked furtively around the parking lot, probably checking if some spook from upper management had followed him down. He spoke in hushed tones, or at least he imagined he'd done so; his voice still bounced off the concrete walls with the ferocity of a marching band. "We gotta pull the trigger on this Judge Harper shit show. Clock's ticking, buddy."

"I keep telling you, Ron, don't be the bull in the china shop here. Hang tight."

He ignored my sage advice and kept talking. "And there's Masie. It's damn well tearing me up what happened to that kid. Keep thinking on that asshole, Castillo . . ." He rubbed at his temple with the side of his palm as if trying to remove a stubborn spot of dirt. "My sleep's gone to hell. Keep turning over all kinds of bad stuff in my head."

At that moment, Ron looked the most vulnerable I'd ever seen him, all the bravado yanked out of him, his stuffing removed and flung to the floor. He reminded me of a discarded teddy bear on a charity store shelf.

"Listen to me. Castillo's not connected to Masie's death. I told you that. Let it go."

Ron wasn't in the platitude-purchasing mood. "Not directly, but that murdering asshole's got his fingerprints all over it. I'd bet my last dime on that."

"Bad call," I insisted. "Don't go betting a thing on that outcome."

Ron shook his head, lips quivering. "Just because they've got money and connections, men like Castillo think they can get away with anything, destroy people's lives without a second thought. If it wasn't for him, Masie would still be alive. I'm damned sure about that, too, and you want me to let it go?"

"That's exactly what you should do. Believe me, that road doesn't end up anyplace good." I paused. "Look, you should get some help, talk to someone."

"I'm talking to you."

"I meant a professional."

"What, like a shrink?" He shook his head. "Never been, not starting now."

"You're going to have to do something. You're a hot mess."

He looked down at his scuffed shoes. "Yeah, my wife keeps telling me the same thing."

"Maybe you should listen to her. Seriously."

He wiped a hand across his face, which looked a few shades grayer than usual, as if someone had taken paint stripper to that ruddy Irish complexion and reduced it to ash. "So, you got any further with the Judge Harper papers or not? We gotta get a move on; negotiations are coming up fast."

I could understand his eagerness, but it wasn't the right time to tell him about Muriel's findings nor my meeting with Judge Croft. Spilling that information would have rocked an already unstable boat, or sunk it completely. I didn't want the responsibility of instigating that wreck.

"Like I said, we can't go in half-assed on this. We need more evidence."

"You got more evidence?"

"Working on it."

It wasn't the answer Ron hoped for. "What's that mean?"

"It means we're working on it. Look, sit tight for a while longer, okay?"

He leaned in and poked my shoulder, the stale waft of whatever booze he'd been drinking hitting me square in the nose. "Maybe you're sitting on it because you're in on this whole fucking scam too, Sweeney?" he said, wagging an index finger in my face. "Getting some nice backhanders for yourself from the judges to keep your mouth shut?"

"Jesus, come on, Ron, you know me, I'd never—"

He huffed. "Thought I knew you, but turns out you're just like the rest of 'em, eh? Looking out for number one, like you did when you took the stand for Castillo? Got that son of a bitch off from standing trial."

His words didn't land without some sprig of guilt forming from the impact, but Ron's knowledge gap was as wide and deep as the San Francisco Bay.

"You're over the line, Ron. Go home, sober up, and we'll forget this ever happened. Good?"

Something in my words must have triggered him. If he were a cartoon character, steam would be whistling out of both his ears. Glancing down, I noticed his fists clenching, his upper body rocking forward as if building momentum. I knew what came next, but his punch was a slow train coming. I easily side-stepped the lazy right hook. Ron lost his footing, stumbled forward, and fell to his knees with a grunt.

"Jesus," I said, reaching to help him back to his feet. "You're too old and out of shape to be playing fisticuffs in the playground."

He pushed me away and reached for my Saab's rear wheel to lever himself to standing. He was wheezing, and I worried that the man was heading for a heart attack right there in the parking lot.

To my relief, he got his breathing under control, but his anger still had the upper hand. "Get the hell off of me. I don't need your help."

"I thought that's exactly what you wanted," I said. "Listen, trust me. Let this play out."

He wiped a sleeve across his sweaty brow. "Trust? Nah, don't think so," he said, adjusting his tie. "Reckon you've had that match long enough, and if you ain't gonna strike it, someone else will."

He hiked up his pants, turned his back, and shuffled toward the elevators.

"Ron!" I shouted. "Call me, all right? If you need someone to talk to." Then, echoing the same words someone had said to me not two days ago, I added, "Promise me you won't do anything stupid. Can you promise me that?"

I doubted my words had any impact. They seemed to bounce like wood chips off Ron's stiff shoulders.

CHAPTER 37

Working an office job, you're almost obliged to indulge in the fine art of people-watching. My office had a wall-sized pane of glass separating me from the rest of the world, the rest of this small world comprising the three musketeers. In idle moments, I'd catch myself observing the trio the same way a birdwatcher might observe a flock of rare birds, staying far enough away so as not to ruffle feathers, yet close enough that I could study their rituals.

I couldn't deny they were an odd bunch, but what office isn't complete without its collection of eccentrics and misfits? And besides, they were my bunch of eccentrics and misfits, and by some strange twist of Human Resources fate, they fitted together like pieces of a puzzle. The alternatives of trios could have been far bleaker: The Three Stooges? Three Blind Mice? The Jonas Brothers?

These musings were a distraction from the morning's encounter with Ron Boone. The man was in no shape to be throwing punches in the parking lot like some extra from *The Fast and the Furious*; at least he had the "furious" part down pat. Frustration and anger can lead you to dark places. But I hoped my words had been enough to discourage him from shooting his mouth off and derailing whatever stack of dominoes Judge Croft had set in motion, but I wasn't holding my breath.

As loath as I was to return to Palm Springs, I was eager to put this whole episode behind me, retrieve the laptop, and deliver it, like the head of John the Baptist, on a silver platter to Paco. Debt paid. Life resumed to normal. Well, that's what all those self-help gurus teach, right? Visualize your dreams, and they'll come true. Tell the universe your deepest desires, and all its abundance will be yours. Yeah, that's about as helpful as rubbing your Ikea bedside lamp and making three wishes.

I mentioned none of this to the waiting and patient universe nor to the three musketeers later that evening as we settled in our usual cove at O'Neil's. I'd have rather been at my apartment planning some genius scheme for retrieving the laptop. I'd been focused on little else all day and had come up with nothing. Victor had been no help whatsoever in brainstorming nor running any ideas up any kind of flagpoles, but had agreed to ask Paco how much he'd be willing to pay for the laptop's safe return. Promising he'd get back to me, he followed up with a curt text, *Good luck, amigo*, as if I was heading off for a colonoscopy.

As I suspected, the three musketeers had heard it through the courthouse grapevine that I was at Officer Darlene Mason's house the night she shot herself, and were thirsty as lions at the watering hole for the meaty details.

Katie spoke first. "Let me get this straight," she said, eyes widening. "Mason and Connor drove a freakin' truck into your bike while you were riding it? What the actual fuck?"

"Damn," Tye said, shaking his head. "If you got proof, you could sue that corrupt mother's ass. You got proof?"

"Not exactly," I lied. "Darlene's dead, and Connor doesn't strike me as the type to come clean, if it means putting his career on the line."

Muriel looked wistfully into her white wine spritz. "What if they'd killed you, Mitch?" she said, looking up.

"They were just trying to scare me," I assured her. "Now, anyone need a refill?"

Nods all around, except for Muriel, who hovered a palm over her drink in the *that's plenty for me* fashion.

When I returned, the table fell silent. "Please, don't stop sharing on my account," I said, handing out the drinks.

Katie broke the awkward silence in the only way she knew how, with an elbow nudge of snark. "Hey, Mitch, didn't you have something you wanted to ask Tye?"

"Don't know what you mean, Kat," I said, glaring at her over my foamy head of Guinness.

She gave a wry smile. "About the Griffin Harper papers?"

"Sure," Tye said. "Anything I can do to help, boss."

"You can all relax," I said, settling my drink down. "I think I figured out who leaked the information to that journalist you met with, Kat."

"Whoa," Tye said. "You met with a journalist? Seriously?"

"No . . . well, yeah, maybe," Katie said, settling a loose strand of dyed pink hair behind her left ear. "Not 'met with' exactly, more like he followed me . . . stalked me, you know."

Tye nodded and pursed his lips. "Yeah? So that's how it goes down?" Tye was sharper on the uptake than Katie gave him credit for; that was her Achilles heel, always thinking she was the smartest person around the table. "You figured Muriel wouldn't talk to some journalist, but I would? Good to know you've got my back when the shit hits the fan."

"Oh, Katie, that's pretty low," Muriel said. "Even for you."

"What the fuck is that supposed to mean?" Katie snapped. "'Even for you'?"

"Nothing . . ." Muriel paused. "Well, you can be very, em, combative. It's not one of your more endearing traits."

"Well, at least someone thought I was worth approaching. Didn't hear about any journos tracking you down for a story."

"And you're proud about that?" Tye said. "Damn, girl, you got some twisted sense of logic."

Katie stiffened. "Girl?"

Figuring she might just launch a fist into Tye's groin, I stepped in. "Before this turns into a *Real Housewives of New Jersey* season finale, none of you leaked the information, and if it makes a difference, I never suspected any of you."

"Then who did?" Katie asked, glaring at Tye. "Because it was as sure as fuck wasn't me."

"Me neither," Tye confirmed, then looked directly at Katie. "Straight up."

I took a breath. "I'm still not sure, but—"

"Ron Boone, right?" Muriel interrupted. "He gave you the papers to begin with. I mean, it stands to reason he was the only other person who knew."

"That we know of," I said. "Look, what's important is that nobody from our team leaked the information; let's leave it there. And while I'm gone, you guys keep your heads down and focus on your caseloads. Good?"

"Gone?" Tye asked. "Like away, gone?"

"Short break, that's all."

"Are you sure this is a good time to take a vacation?" Muriel asked. "What with everything that's going on?"

"Just visiting Kurt and Sierra for a few days. I'll be back Monday." Another lie, this one coming out as smooth as the Guinness was going down. "My family takes priority. All this can wait a couple more days."

As I spoke, my phone vibrated in my pocket. "I gotta get this," I said, scooting out of O'Neil's and onto the sidewalk.

* * *

Kurt's face was like a ray of sunshine bursting out of my phone.

"Hey, kiddo, how's it going?"

"It's so cool here, Dad. Check this out," he said, swinging his phone one eighty.

He was standing in the garden of my mother-in-law's beach house. Behind the trees marking the garden borders, the sun was descending over the Pacific, brushing the sky a vibrant red with the odd palette splash of blood orange and purple. The ocean seemed to have soaked in the encroaching twilight, transforming the waters into a dark, menacing swell.

"That's some sunset," I said.

Another kid, around Kurt's age, darker-skinned, edged into frame and pulled a face as kids are prone to do when within ten feet of a camera.

"Who's that?" I asked.

"Andres. He's a new friend."

Andres began jumping up and down. The kid was annoying in the way only other people's kids can be annoying; I could barely hear Kurt. I was about to ask the kid to shut the fuck up, though more politely, when who I assumed was the kid's father walked into the picture. Late forties, I guessed, hair slicked back, face heavily weathered and pock-marked, dark, deep-set eyes, and what I imagined was the remnant of a scar dragging down his left cheek. There was something disingenuous about the way his smile settled on his face, like it struggled to make a home there.

"I am sorry," he said. "Andres can be very boisterous." He took a beat. "You must be Mitch, no?"

"Em, yeah . . ."

"Your son and your wife, Sierra, told me about you," he said, gesturing at the camera. "You are a lawyer, right, in California? I make a lot of business in California myself. Fantastic place, no?"

"What kind of business?"

"The leisure industry. Boats, luxury yachts. My company operates from the Marina in La Cruz. Maybe you heard of it?"

I had. La Cruz was one of the largest marinas on the West Coast, about a thirty-minute drive from Sayulita. We'd take a day trip out of there to the Marieta Islands every time we visited Clara. It was one of Kurt's favorite outings.

"Sorry, I didn't get your name," I said, feeling uneasy about this character.

"Oh, sure," he said, smiling. "Everyone calls me Captain."

"Captain?"

"Sure, just Captain. I will hand you back to your son now. Maybe we bump into each other in California one day, yes?"

A prickle settled like a yellowjacket preparing to sting the back of my neck as the Captain handed the phone back to Kurt.

"Guess what, Dad?"

"Hit me."

"Andres's dad owns a boat. He took me and Mom out yesterday to see the sunset. Here, I'll send you some pictures."

I checked out the photos as they pinged into my text thread. Sunset, pink skies, a boat moored at the dockside. I zoomed into the vessel, a sleek, white catamaran, and took a mental note of the name, *Gordo Loco*.

"Great photos, kiddo," I said, hoping my unease didn't translate down the line. "Listen, can you get your mom? I need to speak to her."

"Okay."

Sierra walked over and took the phone. She looked the most relaxed I'd seen her in months, radiant under the shadow of twilight.

"The sea air must be agreeing with you," I said.

She smiled and tucked a lock of hair behind her ear. She looked so damn beautiful I could have hopped on the next flight out to Puerto Vallarta to be at her side.

"Kurt's made a new friend."

"Andres? Yeah, he seems like a good kid. Little older, but they're inseparable."

"After a few days?"

"You know how kids get."

"And this Captain guy? Who even calls themselves Captain?"

"I don't know, Mitch, a captain, maybe? He came over with his wife to pick up Andres."

"How did they meet?"

Sierra furrowed her brow. "I have no idea. I only just met them."

"No, Andres and Kurt. How did they meet?"

She shrugged. "Like how most kids meet around here, on the beach. What is this, an interrogation?"

"No, I just worry, that's all."

"Mitch, we're staying at a beach house in Mexico. It's peaceful here. There's nothing to worry about other than where we're going to eat out tonight. Kurt's doing fine. This has been good for him."

"Just like you said."

"Just like I said."

I heard Clara's voice calling Sierra from off-camera.

"I've got to go."

"Say good night to Kurt from me."

"Of course. Look after yourself, Mitch."

After Sierra hung up, I paced the sidewalk. For some reason, I suddenly craved a cigarette. I'd never taken to smoking and was probably just looking for something to distract me from the one thought hijacking my brain: Paco's insistence on keeping my family safe.

The guy calling himself Captain? Was he there to "look after" my family, another henchman willing to do Paco's bidding? I shoved the thought into the recess of my mind, but I'd learned enough over the past few weeks never to underestimate what Paco was capable of.

256

PART 6
TRUCE OR DARE

CHAPTER 38

When I arrived just after midday the following afternoon, the bullying yellow fist of the sun beat down on Palm Springs as if intent on robbing the city of its dinner money and sending it home with a bloody nose and a wedgie.

The drive from the airport to the hotel passed in a blur of desert beige while above me, Mr. Blue Skies played the only number he knew by heart: a wide, one-note, open chord of blazing cobalt. The air conditioning in the Ford Focus I'd rented competed with a country music radio station playing Hank Williams on repeat: I considered myself lucky it wasn't that "bro country" manufactured country pop fodder. Poor lonesome Hank was probably two-stepping in his grave back in Montgomery, Alabama, glad he didn't get out of this world alive if he'd had to listen to what passed for country music these days.

I'd booked a room at the Flamingo Inn, hoping I'd run into McKay again and thank her profusely for helping me out, but I wasn't going to push my luck. The last thing she needed was a reminder of me arriving at her house and delivering bad news. I'd tried to shove the trauma of Charlotte's murder to the back of my mind, but like a belligerent drunk at a house party, it kept nudging my ribs, sharing stories of his glory days, insisting I should try the canapes.

My mind was a five-ton truck stuck in overdrive and careering downhill since I'd spoken to Sierra and Kurt the night before. I couldn't stop thinking about the guy who called himself Captain as if the self-anointed moniker gave him some air of unearned respect. His smile made me think something rotten lurked behind the glossy surface, a shitty paint job covering up the decay. I guessed he was one of Paco's henchmen, a none-too-subtle reminder that despite my protests, he'd delivered on his promise of "watching over" my family.

After checking in, I headed to my room to focus on my mission: pay Hetch for the safe return of the laptop, skip town as soon as the deal was done, gather my family in my arms once again, and put everything that had happened in the past two weeks in the rearview. If Hetch was reluctant to hand over the laptop, I was to offer him enough money to make him think otherwise, set him on the road to an early retirement and all the illegal card games he could run. It should have been easy street all the way; a swift exchange of bank details, Victor wires the funds into Hetch's account, he hands over the laptop, deal sealed with a handshake and a *nice doing business with you*.

But Palm Springs, never one to let a good plan ruin its day, had other things in mind.

* * *

I parked across the street from Hetch's store, air conditioning set to max. Downtown Palm Springs seemed like some vast architectural solar battery, trapping the day's heat in its tarmac, concrete, and glass, then releasing it in drabs as the night trundled on before the whole cycle kicked off again the following morning, the unrepentant sun rising to replenish the city's barely extinguished heat coffers.

The cursive neon sign, *Hector's Pawn Emporium*, twitched anxiously above the entrance. The window shutters were rolled down, a single light shining inside the store. I hadn't seen Hetch leave; I figured he was still inside, counting his day's takings, salivating like some modern-day Fagin from *Oliver Twist* as he fingered his dollar bills.

Crossing the street, the air was both syrupy, the macadam warm under my sneakers. The store door was locked, but the faded sign still declared *open*. Maybe Hetch, in his eagerness to count his cash, had forgotten to flip the sign. Above the door, the red light on the security camera had gone dark. The two electrical wires protruding from the wall cut and fraying like short silver hairs from the connectors.

I squinted through the narrow gap between the window shades, seeing nothing but dark corners and sprays of dirt over the glass. I knocked on the door. After the fifth attempt, I gave up and remembered the rear entrance, the one Hetch used to slip in his buddies for his Texas Hold 'Em games. I took a gamble of my own.

A few minutes later, I stood in the narrow alley behind the store. The doorway was ajar and above it, a pale orange light was home to a whisper of moths flitting wingtip to bulb. My better instincts told me to step away, head back to the hotel, return tomorrow morning, and make the exchange in the stark light of day. But here's the problem with gamblers and their better instincts: you learn to override them, they become Beta to your Alpha. That night, the Alpha had the upper hand, and practically shoved me through the door and into the back room of Hector's Pawn Emporium.

The flooring creaked as I stepped in and took inventory: circular table in the center, empty beer bottle labels peeled, and two decks of cards, one still uncut, scattered across its surface. To my right, a sink and countertop supporting a bubble-shaped TV with rabbit ears, which looked like a relic from an episode of *The Twilight Zone*. Another doorway made of beads, the kind fortune tellers might use as a portal their inner sanctum, separated the main store from the back room. The beads rustled like brushes over cymbals as I parted them.

I called out and waited. No response other than the slow clanking of the ceiling fan.

My eyes adapted to the dim light. Someone had ransacked the store. Debris littered the floor, cabinets smashed, glass crunching under my feet as I ventured in. It was as if a mini tornado had torn through, scattering all kinds of reproduction gemstones, plastic ornaments, and metallic knick-knacks to the four corners. The only organic matter in the store, other than me, was Hetch, and by the looks of him, his next port of call was the back of a coroner's van.

He was laid out in the middle of the floor, a pool of scarlet spread out behind his neck. Red spray speckled the walls, and what I'd thought was dirt on the glass door was, in fact, flecks of Hetch's blood. Looking up at the ceiling fan, I noticed drops of blood drip from the blades as it continued its chug-chug rhythm. As I steadied myself on the cabinet and took a moment, my fingers grazed something metallic and cold: Hetch's Smith and Wesson. Whatever had gone down, the gruff old pawnbroker didn't get the opportunity to fight back.

I took a deep breath before clambering over the detritus to check the corpse. From my vantage point — three feet away and looking down — the only injury I could discern was a single, clean bullet hole to the forehead, similar to the shot that had killed Charlotte. Hetch's ponytail splayed from the back of his neck like a gray and scarlet scarf, his beard peppered with the same multi-patterned coloring, his eyes wide open in surprise, as if in the moments before he died, he couldn't believe this was happening to him. Six feet above him, someone had removed everything from the computer shelf except a tangle of wires and adapters.

The good news was that I'd been right about the laptop's location, which suddenly felt like snatching defeat from the jaws of victory. How the hell would I explain this to Paco? I'd arrived at Hetch's too late; the laptop was gone, and I had no idea where to start looking.

The crunch of boots over the broken glass behind me pulled me out of another mental tailspin. I turned and found myself facing the barrel of a shotgun. My throat chalked. From this distance, a single slug would be enough to blast a hubcap-sized hole in my chest. I raised my arms in surrender mode and took a step back, almost tripping over Hetch's feet as I backed toward the front door.

"Don't you fucking move, asshole, or you're a dead man. We clear?"

I recognized the voice, and the Joan Jett mullet framed behind the barrel.

The gun trembled in Betsy's hands. A mere trace of a quiver, certainly not enough to force her into missing her target from this close angle. As she checked her father's body, her cheek twitched, the shotgun wavering some more as she tried to keep composed.

"Betsy, I had nothing to do with this, I swear," I said, predicting where her mind was headed.

"Turn around!" She gestured with the shotgun that I should turn to face the doorway, my back to her. Reluctantly, I complied, the weapon now aimed at the back of my head. In the reflection of the glass door, I saw her circle toward Hetch and check her father's neck vein with her fingertips. A futile act, but I couldn't blame her. Hetch was her father, and maybe they had a close relationship. I'd never know.

"Look, I don't even have a gun. I couldn't have done this. I just got here. He was like this when I found him. Swear to God."

But Betsy wasn't in listening mode. "Thought I told you never to come back here. What's your deal? You deaf or just a fucking dumbass?"

I was about to answer negatively on both counts when I felt the cold press of a gun barrel at the back of my neck. "Don't bother answering that." Urging the shotgun deeper into my nape, she sneered, "Shoulda had my guys finish you when I had the chance. I guess if you want a job done right, you gotta do it yourself."

"No, this is a mistake, Betsy," I said, watching her reflection behind my shoulders. "You don't need any more bodies piling up in here."

"Just one more. I can live with that."

I was about to plead my case again when I heard a voice, female, coming from the back room, followed by the swish of beads.

"Drop your weapon right now, and nobody gets hurt."

The voice sounded muffled, as if coming from behind a wedge of cloth.

The curtains fell back into place with a rustle as the voice drew closer. "One twitch on that trigger finger, and you'll end up like that guy on the floor. So, let's agree you don't kill the lawyer, and I don't shoot you in the face. Think we can agree to that, Betsy?"

"He's not some guy. He's my pops," Betsy said, her voice cracking.

"Well, then, I'm sorry for your loss, but we had nothing to do with that, so let's all just cool our jets, all right?"

Betsy stayed mute, no doubt weighing up her limited options: shoot and die, or don't shoot and live.

I heard a revolver barrel spin, followed by the mechanism clicking back into place; whoever was back there had picked up Hetch's Smith and Wesson.

"Now, I figure you got maybe one shell in the chamber of that shotgun," the voice said. "Use it to kill him and I shoot your face off. Turn it on me; the lawyer grabs the Smith and Wesson, which is fully loaded — just checked — and shoots you. Either way, you join your pops wherever he's headed."

Betsy sniffed, said, "How do you know I don't have two in the chamber?"

"I don't, but I'll take the gamble."

The dull clank of the ceiling fan cut through the silence as Betsy's eyes darted from me and then settled on Hetch as if she was holding out for some miracle that the old man would rise like Lazarus from the dead and offer some fatherly advice as to her next move.

"I don't have all night, Betsy. What we thinking here? Truce or dare? And like I keep telling this dumb lawyer, don't do anything stupid that's gonna get you killed."

CHAPTER 39

As Betsy wrestled with her dilemma, the sweat slid from my brow like rainwater off a slate roof. I had a dilemma of my own. I doubted I had the guts to grab Hetch's gun and shoot Betsy. I'd never handled a gun before, let alone shot someone in cold blood. Finally, after what seemed like a long, hot eternity, Betsy set her weapon on the shattered glass cabinet. I almost laughed with the relief.

"You made the right choice," Alma Torres said, stepping over Hetch's body and ejecting the single shell from Betsy's shotgun. She tugged the red bandana wrapped around her face and gestured to the bare shelf. "They take it?"

"Take what?" Betsy asked.

"The laptop. Did they take it?"

"Who's this 'they'? Do you know who killed my pops? Were they working for you?" Betsy stepped closer with each question, as if hoping to take Alma by surprise.

"Hey, ease up there, Betsy Boop," Alma said, scoping her gun toward Betsy's chest. "Anyone told you you've got a real inability to focus in stressful situations? Personally, I'm the opposite; my instincts get real sharp when shit's going down. Reverse stress management, my therapist calls it. Now, again: the laptop?"

"Don't know about any laptop."

265

Alma peeked through the blinds and into the street. "Is this town always like a friggin' oven, or did I just arrive on a bad day?" She mopped the sweat from her brow with the bandana. "For sure, you couldn't pay me enough to live in this heat."

"You get used to it."

"What, like grief? Time heals, that kind of thing?" Alma said, gesturing at Hetch's body. "You know, Betsy, if I lived here, think I'd buy myself a dive bar down the block with kick-ass air conditioning and a jukebox that doesn't play any music released after 1985. Mind you, with my mental conditions, I'd probably set off a kitchen fire, burn the place down, or some such disaster."

Betsy's eyes darted between Alma and me. "Who the fuck are you people?"

"We're not here to hurt you, Betsy," I said. "We just want the laptop."

"Keep telling you, dipshits, I don't know anything about a laptop. Now, take whatever the fuck you want and leave. I've got to call emergency services."

Alma shrugged and looked at Hetch's body. "Bit late for that, Betsy."

"Seriously? What the fuck is wrong with you?"

Alma, always prone to missing the rhetorical question when it slapped her in the face, replied, "Impulse control issues, ADHD, and social anxiety disorder. Therapist reckons I'm a triple threat."

Betsy looked over at me. I shrugged in the *you're asking the wrong man* manner.

Alma gestured to the cabinet. "Hey, Mitch, go grab that Smith and Wesson. Odds are, Kinky Boots is hiding a knife down the side of those Docs."

I stepped around Hetch's body and reached for the gun. It felt all shapes of wrong in my hands. I handed it to Alma, who casually shoved it into the back of her jeans.

"Okay, let's try again," Alma said. "Charlotte's laptop? Mitch and I got a theory on that. Want to hear it?"

"Do I have a choice?"

Alma waved her gun. "Would you like a choice?"

Betsy scowled.

"Didn't think so." Alma lowered her weapon. "Charlotte paid you to run into the back of the SUV tailing her, making it look like an accident. You kept the two goons busy long enough for Charlotte to make her getaway. We also figured she paid this guy — sorry, your pops — to keep the laptop safe until someone came to pick it up. That someone is me and the lawyer. You following so far?"

"Sure. Nice story. Don't mean it's true."

"Fair point. But what we don't know is the exact location of that laptop, and judging by the mess, I'm guessing neither did the amateurs who broke in here and shot your pops. Me, because I have this whole crazy OCD crap going on, I'd have approached things differently. Something as valuable as Charlotte's laptop? That's not going on display with all this other sad-sack crap. Your old man was a pawnbroker; he's gotta have a safe for the valuable stuff, gold, diamond jewelry, expensive laptops he's been paid to look after. Am I getting warm, Betsy?"

Betsy kept her gaze fixed on the floor.

"Play dumb if you like, but if you don't take us to the safe, I'll shoot a bullet through those boots of yours, and you spend the rest of your life with a hole in your foot as a reminder of your shitty attitude. What do you think? We got ourselves a deal?"

Reluctantly, Betsy stepped away from her father's body and pushed on a shelving unit to the right of the register. It opened with a loud creak.

"No shit," Alma said, stepping back.

"My pops had it fitted for emergencies," Betsy explained, before leading us down a narrow flight of creaking stairs to a space which was little more than a glorified cellar with a desk and a chair, and a metallic green safe tucked in the corner.

"That it?" Alma asked, gesturing at the safe.

Betsy nodded and ran a finger over the desk, lost momentarily in her thoughts.

"I assume you know the combination?" Alma said. "Now would be a good time to use it, then we'll be out of your hair, and you can begin the grieving process."

Betsy shook her head. "You are seriously fucked up, you know that?"

"Appreciate the medical diagnosis, Doc Marten. Now the safe, *rapido*."

Betsy squatted and clicked the dial lock until the safe door tumbled open.

Alma reached, knees on the floor, into the safe. My heart pumped hard as she extracted folders, envelopes, an antique gun still in its case, and several clear bags full of jewelry. It felt like the longest thirty seconds of my life. If Betsy was lying to us, or if the laptop was already gone, I was back to square one, throwing myself on the slim mercy of Paco Castillo.

Eventually, Alma slid out a silver laptop and laid it on the table. I exhaled the breath I'd been holding and ran my fingers over the computer's surface.

"Good job, Betsy," Alma said. "It's been a blast, but we gotta bounce, and—"

Alma didn't get to finish her sentence. We all hit the mute button as we heard footsteps creaking along the floorboards above us, echoing like the ominous march of bad news telegraphing itself down into the basement.

"Shit," Betsy whispered. "That's not good."

"You pulled that false door shut, right?" Alma asked, also lowering her voice.

Betsy looked at me. "You were the last one down the stairs."

She was right. I was the last, and I didn't remember pulling any door closed behind me.

"Is there another way out?" I asked.

Betsy pointed to a door at the end of the basement, some ten feet to our right. "Takes us under the road. Back in the prohibition days, they dug tunnels to smuggle liquor from one place to the next, keep one step ahead of the Feds."

"Where does it lead?"

"Like I said, end of the block."

"The Desert Palm," I said, a chunk of the puzzle tumbling into place. "That's why the security cameras never picked you up leaving the store after the crash?"

"Not as dumb as you act," Betsy said. Directly above us, footsteps creaked toward the stairs. "We gotta hustle," she added and led the way.

The space through the door was dark, fortified with bricks, the ceiling low, forcing me to duck as we walked across the uneven stone floor. The aroma of hops and stale liquor grew stronger the further we slogged. After a few minutes, we stopped at another doorway. As Betsy slid a key into the lock, a gunshot echoed like a hand grenade thrown into the narrow space. Instinctively, we crouched down as the bullet ricocheted off the wall, scuffing up a blast of gray dust.

"Hurry the fuck up," Alma said.

Betsy pushed, but the door refused to yield. "Some help here?"

We shoved our shoulders against the door until it fell open and we stumbled into another basement, this one under the Desert Palm and filled with beer kegs and shelves full of liquor bottles — a lush's paradise.

Betsy gestured to a wooden door facing the alley above us. "Can't go through the kitchen, too many eyes. We load the kegs from the delivery trucks here. We can climb out to the alley, but hurry the fuck up."

She unhooked the iron brackets, threw the doors wide open, and peeked her head up like some curious meerkat. "Clear."

She clambered up the ramp to daylight. Alma followed, with me close behind. When we were all gathered in the alley, Betsy let the cellar door fall back into place.

"Where to now?" Alma asked.

"Got my rental; it's just across the road," I said.

Betsy shook her head. "Fuck that. You guys are on your own."

I was about to agree that splitting up was probably a smart move when I saw someone step under the glow of light from the rear of Hector's Pawn Emporium. The figure, cast in shadow, stood for a moment, then raised an arm.

We turned and bolted, Alma to my left, Betsy a few feet behind. As we sprinted to the next block, Betsy split from the pack. The gunman seized the opportunity and fired. Betsy stumbled and fell to the concrete with a groan. Alma turned and fired the Smith and Wesson down the alleyway, which bought us a few precious seconds as the shooter crouched behind a dumpster.

I ran to Betsy, helped her to her feet, and almost dragged her across the road and into my rental car. I jumped in. Alma assumed shotgun. Betsy threw herself across the back seat, palm pressed to her bleeding shoulder. Just as I fired up the engine and notched the car into gear, the figure stepped from the alley and aimed at the windshield.

"Reverse!" Alma shouted.

I whipped the gear stick back and reversed down the street, the world whooshing past like my life in rewind. The bullet sparked off a metal signpost at the intersection. At the end of the block, I hit the brakes hard and spun the car around.

"I need the emergency room," Betsy said, gripping her shoulder.

"No can do," Alma said. "Cameras, too many questions."

"What? You gonna just let me bleed out in the back seat?"

"Let me take a look." Alma reached back to check the wound. "It's just a graze." She handed Betsy her bandana. "Take this, keep the pressure on, you'll survive."

"Easy for you to say. Hurts like hell."

"Usually how it goes down with gunshot wounds. You got any liquor to numb the pain?"

"Yeah, picked up a six-pack on the way out. What the fuck do you think?"

"I think you've got a real bad freakin' attitude, considering I just saved your life."

I slammed on the brakes.

"Hey, what's the deal?" Alma snapped. "I rented an airstream. We can hide out there, patch her up. I'll text you the directions."

"Better plan," I said, entering an address I remembered into the car's navigation system.

Pulling a sharp left, tires squealing, I headed west from downtown Palm Springs toward the vast, inhospitable desert.

CHAPTER 40

The desert is an abyss that exists because that's all its arid, sun-bleached bones have ever known to do. A place that needs no water to survive barely needs anything, and come the apocalypse, when everything else is reduced to rubble, the human race a blip on earth's time scale, the desert will always endure, the indestructible cockroach of landscapes.

These thoughts sparked through my brain as I drove. The dim glow of Palm Springs dwindled behind us, leaving us alone in the inky expanse. The radio kept cutting in and out, the signal dropping somewhere over the San Jacinto Mountains, sending out nothing but static, like the lost transmission from the edges of the universe fading into the desert rocks.

I had the driver's window wide open. The road stretched ahead of us, a ribbon of asphalt bisected by silver strips. The headlights picked up snatches of a Georgia O'Keeffe canvas of sand, rock, and lone trees humbled by the vast beauty of the night sky and half-wink of the moon, which seemed to be less watching over us than amused by our presence.

Betsy was curled in the back seat, complaining, Alma telling her not to act like "a basic bitch about some superficial flesh wound."

I turned to Alma. "I guess Victor sent you."

272

"Figured if he couldn't be here himself . . ."

"Generous of him."

"Hey, I saved your ass back there," she said, then addressed Betsy. "And yours, too. A little gratitude would be nice."

Betsy mumbled something incoherent.

"Yeah, sorry, it's all just been, you know, a . . ." I began.

"A shit show?"

"I was going to say clusterfuck."

"That too. Still, you got what you came for," she said, patting the backpack resting on her lap. "Hand it over to Paco and the whole shit show, clusterfuck, whatever's over, right?"

I nodded. But I was still twenty-four hours away from returning to the Bay Area, and I'd learned things had a nasty habit of heading south faster than cacti prick piercing skin out in Palm Springs.

As Alma turned to look through the window, I wondered if she was imagining, like I was, all the silent ghosts that had passed over this land, leaving no footprints, only flurries of dirt scattered across the unforgiving plains.

Alma wasn't thinking of ghosts of the desert. She was thinking of things far closer to home: "Still don't know how the hell a guy like you gets involved with Paco Castillo."

"Thought I was doing Victor a favor."

"I avoid favors. They always come back and bite you on the ass."

"You did me a favor."

"No, I did it for your kid. Felt like shit after he got shot, like it was my fault. You know, I was meant to be watching the house."

"Don't blame yourself. That was all Mason and Connor."

"Still, should have been more vigilant, seen it coming."

"Don't beat yourself up over stuff you have no control over. Never does you any good in the long run."

"That what you tell yourself?"

"Yeah, well, I'm not too good at listening to good advice these days, my own or anyone else's."

"No shit."

Alma glanced out of the window as we passed a series of illuminated billboards promoting a new housing development. Random phrases like *find your happiness here, your desert dream home awaits, luxury living every day*, were stuck across the billboards, as if the developers had thrown a stack of words at the billboards in the hope something would stick.

"Where we headed? It's like the middle of butt fuck nowhere out here," Alma said.

"Going to a friend's," I said and left it at that.

* * *

I was about to peel off Highway 62 when the shimmer of headlights cut through the darkness a mile behind us; just another traveler traversing the desert plains, I figured. Some thirty seconds later, the headlights began riding my tail, beaming like searchlights from a high-wheelbase truck, flooding the car with a glaring white phosphorescence.

Through the glare, I focused on the road ahead, squinting through the bleached-out windshield. I stepped on the gas and lurched forward; the truck did the same. As I slowed, the truck fell back, then pitched forward again. I stuck my arm through the window and gestured for the driver to pass, though I had a nasty suspicion that wasn't the reason the truck was tailgating me with the intensity of Charlie Daniels chasing the devil out of Georgia. There was plenty of passing space. I hadn't seen a car driving in the opposite direction since we'd turned onto the highway.

Alma squirmed. "What the fuck is his problem?" She stuck her arm out of the window and flipped the bird. "Just fucking pass, asshole!"

Betsy stirred. "Is that the same dude who shot at us back at the store?"

"Probably just some asshole in a hurry to get home."

Even as I said the words, an uneasy feeling seeped into my bones. If the truck was in any kind of rush, it would be two miles ahead of us by now. I gripped my hands around the wheel, the blood draining from my knuckles.

As I pressed harder on the gas, the Ford Focus whined and complained, showing little interest in picking up the pace, while the truck easily kept up, engine rumbling like some relentless roll of thunder tailgating us at seventy-five miles per hour. I pushed the reluctant rental to eight-five.

The first contact came seconds later: a violent shunt to the rear fender. I struggled to right the car. We swerved off the road, kicking up a curtain of desert dust before I wrestled all four wheels back onto the asphalt.

"Fuck this." Alma reached for the Smith and Wesson, leaned her upper body through the window, turned, and fired into the spray of headlights.

"Jesus, Alma!" I shouted.

"What?" She threw herself back in her seat. "You think this is the Palm Springs Highway Patrol asking us to politely to pull the fuck over?"

I didn't get the opportunity to reply. A metal-on-metal shunt, like the grinding of industrial-strength gears, sent my world reeling. The steering wheel became air in my hands, and the desert spun around me like a carousel ride in slow motion. Alma and Betsy were both shouting something, but it was all white noise, drowned out by the screeching of tires as I urged all the strength of my right foot down on the brake pedal.

It took the front wheels a few seconds to go into lockdown. When they finally did, the forward velocity of half a ton of fast-moving metal quickly transferred to the rear end, spinning us a full one eighty until we pirouetted across the road and plowed into a narrow ditch separating the road from the desert. A loud crunch of metal on dirt as the chassis scraped the gravel and rebounded off the lip of the ditch. We hit air before landing on the rocky terrain with a harsh jolt, which sent Betsy smacking into the back of my seat and bounced Alma's head off the dashboard.

It took me a moment to reset my brain functions and check out the damage. Betsy was groaning in the fetal position in the rear footwell. Alma was out for the count, blood trailing from her forehead and down her cheek. My seatbelt had saved me from any serious damage, though it cut into my shoulder like someone was digging around in there with a knife.

A minute later, the truck rumbled into view, its brights searing through the windshield, the thirsty V8 thumping like a relentless mechanical heartbeat.

The driver's door swung open, followed by heavy boots crushing gravel. The silhouette of a tall man dressed in black and wearing a cowboy hat walked casually toward me. He had a slow, arrogant gait, as if the world owed him, and he was here to make good on that promise. In my confusion, I wondered for a moment if he was one of those desert ghosts that I imagined haunted the landscape; maybe a malevolent spirit come to claim three fresh souls.

The man looked around and then marched to the car's passenger side. His arm reached through the open window and fumbled for Alma's gun resting on her lap. He took the weapon, paced around the car until he was a few yards away from the driver's side, checked the Smith and Wesson, then aimed it in my direction.

"Okay, Mitch, if you have a gun, throw it to the ground. I don't want to shoot you, but if I have to, I will have no problem in doing that."

The voice had a strong Spanish lilt, and I was sure I recognized it from somewhere, but my brain was lagging.

I raised my hands. "No gun," I shouted. "Unarmed."

"Good. And the laptop? I will need the laptop."

"Erm, there's no—" I began.

A bullet bounced off a rock close to me, sending up a plume of brown dust and cracking open the desert stillness. "No games or the next one don't land so safely."

I got the message and reached over for the backpack that had fallen in the footwell and held it aloft.

"Okay, this is how we will do this. You step out of the car, holding the bag above your head. When you are ten feet away from the car, you put the backpack on the floor. Then you step away another ten feet, arms raised. Is that clear to you?"

I nodded.

"Be real nice to hear the words, Mitch."

"Yes, clear!" I shouted, then slid out of the car.

When I'd stepped back the requisite ten feet, he called out, "Turn around."

I complied, the man's face gradually falling into focus as I turned. His features became clear, his smile as slippery and insincere as it had been two days ago when he insisted I call him Captain. I swallowed hard and asked the first dumb question that came to mind. "How did you know where we were?"

"You are a very easy target, Mitch. I watched you outside that pawn store. When you went inside, I attached a tracking device to your car." He pointed to the rear fender. "It is good to have a backup plan, no?" The Captain smiled a glossy mask, hiding what I imagined was a multitude of sins. "I told you we would meet in California someday. Sooner than we both expected, but fate is not a mistress to be tamed, yes?"

"Kurt and Sierra," I said, finally finding some words, the only words that really mattered. "Are they safe?"

"Kurt? Sure, he's a nice kid. Your wife is a smart lady. We had some good conversations. I like her. You know, when she divorces you, I might consider dating her myself. Given a respectable amount of time, of course."

"You fucking leave my family alone. Or I swear I'll hunt you down myself and kill you."

I sensed how hollow and pathetic my words sounded as soon as they left my lips, like I was repeating lame dialogue from some shitty B-movie. But I guess it's what happens when you're facing a situation far beyond your everyday reality. You reach for the first words that come to mind, tired old phrases you've heard a thousand times before in TV shows and movies, clichés you imagine make you sound tough, the kind of man people would think twice before messing with. But without the weight and authority to carry them off, they're as weak as raindrops in the desert, and just like raindrops, they're quickly swallowed into the dirt.

The Captain shrugged like this was all business as usual for him. "I think you have things — how you Americans say, ass-backward? I am the one holding the gun, so I am the one who makes the demands. Unfair, but life is like that. Power always wins, no?"

"What the fuck do you want?"

"My demands?" He tapped the backpack. "If what is on this computer is not what I am looking for, then your wife and child will suffer the error of your judgment. And you can also tell Paco his way of doing business is ending. Time to make way for fresh blood."

The reality of the situation suddenly hit me. This Captain character wasn't working for Paco, he was out for himself, working against Paco, and whatever was on that laptop was a means to an end.

"You're the knife in the heart," I said, remembering Paco's words.

"I have no idea what that means. But you do understand what I'm telling you, correct?"

"I don't know what's on that laptop. Wish I'd never heard about it."

"I understand," he said, voice softening, which only gave his words a more sinister resonance. "You made a bad choice, working with Paco Castillo. But a man should always face up to his choices, good or bad, and see his obligations through to the end." He slipped the gun into his jacket pocket. "I will give your regards to Sierra and Kurt when I see them. *Adios*, Mitch."

With that, he strode back to the truck and slammed the door, the rear wheels kicking up a bucketful of dust as he roared off in the same direction he'd come: back to Palm Springs, back to Mexico, back to my family.

As the truck dissolved into the desert darkness, leaving behind the smell of ignited gas and dust, a lone coyote howled in the distance. The tension and stress I'd been storing rose like floodwater. I bent over and retched over the desert floor. Coming up for air, I heard a sound from the car. Alma was crawling out.

"What the fuck just happened?" She wiped the back of her hand over her bloodied brow. "Head hurts like a mother," she said, then looked around the car. "Where's the backpack?"

"It's gone," I said, sensing my legs were about to let my body fall onto the grit and scrubland.

"Gone? Who took it?"

"A ghost," I said, walking back to the car. "Just some fucking ghost."

Alma looked confused but said nothing. There was nothing much to say.

Kneeling down in the dirt, I stretched my arm under the rear fender until my fingers scraped against a small metallic box. I pulled hard and ripped the tracker from its mounting, threw it to the ground, then stamped my heel on the device until its electronic guts spilled onto the sand and gravel.

Alma shrugged. "That figures."

"Let's get the fuck out of here," I said, leaning on the car roof to catch my breath.

"Where to? This friend of yours?"

I wiped my mouth and nodded.

"Good friend? The kind that won't complain when you turn up in the middle of the night with a car full of casualties?"

"Guess we'll find out," I said, throwing myself into the driver's seat.

The ignition button took a couple of presses before spinning the puny four-cylinder engine to life. I maneuvered off the dirt and onto the shoulder. Betsy looked up, predictably moaned, and asked what the fuck was going on.

Palm Springs had lived up to its reputation and had let no one's plans spoil its day. But as the road opened up before us in a rolling carpet of black, I had the unsettling feeling the desert wasn't done with me yet.

CHAPTER 41

"I'm not your personal emergency room, Mitch. Keep this up, and I'm going to have to start charging you medical rates."

McKay and I sat across from each other over her breakfast bar. She was dressed in a tight-fitting, two-tone tracksuit that reminded me of Uma Thurman in *Kill Bill*. Behind us, Alma and Betsy were splayed out on the couch. Alma was dabbing at the cut on her forehead, while Betsy had her arms folded across her chest, scowling at the walls as if they had offended her in some way. When we arrived thirty minutes ago, we must have resembled a caravan of refugees. To McKay's credit, she barely raised an eyebrow and asked only one question: "Were you followed?"

When I answered, "Not since I was shot at in the desert," she ushered us inside and locked the door.

Betsy's wound was nowhere close to needing an emergency room, a minor graze. McKay cleaned the wound and bandaged it up like a pro. After wiping the blood, Alma's forehead looked less serious than I had first thought, a shallow cut that had drawn blood but didn't look in need of stitches. McKay handed her a pack of Band-Aids.

"Dora the freakin' Explorer?" Alma said, examining the packaging.

Dylan H. Jones

"Take it or leave it, honey." McKay headed to the kitchen and poured us all a generous measure of bourbon and one for herself.

"Nah, that's cool," Alma said, ripping the packing open. "Dora's badass."

My injuries amounted to little more than a bruised shoulder and a searing headache. I lowered my voice a couple of notches. "Listen, I know this is an imposition; we just need a couple of hours, and we'll be out of your hair. It won't happen again, promise."

She pointed her glass at me. "Don't make promises you can't keep. Don't they teach you that at Gamblers Anonymous, or whatever meetings you go to?"

I shook my head. "Like Groucho Marx said, I wouldn't want to be part of a club that'll have me as a member."

"Great. You arrive here with two injured women, and you're quoting Groucho Marx? You sure you're not trying out for a second career in stand-up?"

I shrugged. "Coping mechanism."

"Here's a better one." McKay slid a bottle of Advil across the counter. "Now, want to tell me what the hell this is all about?"

I necked four pills and told her everything; Alma and Betsy interjected, adding their own color to the narration. By the end, I was exhausted, and all I could focus on was throwing myself under the seven-hundred-thread-count sheets at the Flamingo Inn and pretending none of this had happened.

McKay considered the information. "Okay, just so I'm clear, this guy, who calls himself Captain, killed Charlotte, killed Betsy's father, and would have probably killed the three of you if you didn't have the laptop? And now this guy's taken the laptop to Mexico and intends to use whatever's on there against Paco Castillo?"

"That's about the sum of it," I said, gulping down the last of my bourbon. Ever the attentive bar professional, McKay refilled my glass.

"Who the fuck is this dude, anyway?" Alma asked. "Does he work for Paco?"

"Don't think so, or maybe he used to," I said. "More like working against him, from what I could tell. Looking to take over the throne, maybe?"

"What, like a coup?" Alma said. "And whatever's on that laptop is gonna make this coup possible?"

"No idea."

She let out a long exhale. "Man, wish I knew what the hell was on that thing. Must be some pretty gnarly shit."

A few moments of silence passed before Betsy spoke. "Yeah, there is," she said, her voice flat and emotionless. "Some real gnarly shit."

We all snapped our attention in Betsy's direction.

"Hold up," I said. "You saw what was on the laptop and waited until now to tell us?"

"Yeah, well, didn't know if I could trust you, all right," she muttered. "Not my fault. Y'all just come down here threatening my pops, then getting him killed. Don't inspire confidence in sharing information, you know."

"What did you see, Betsy?" McKay asked softly.

Betsy twisted her fingers into themselves like fleshy worry beads. "Bad shit. The kind of shit you don't ever want to see again . . . the kind of shit you can't unsee."

"Like what?" I asked.

"Videos mostly, and a list of names in a file with numbers next to them, like the profit-and-loss sheets I use for the business, but in some kind of code, like it's encrypted or some such shit."

I took another swig. "What kind of videos did you see, Betsy?"

She slipped a pack of cigarettes from under the sleeve of her T-shirt and looked at McKay, whose glare telegraphed, *Don't even think about it*. Betsy laid the pack down. "The kind of videos that get men locked away in a high-security prison, separated from the other inmates for their own safety. Those kinds of videos."

"Jesus," Alma said. "You mean like young girls?"

"Yeah, like really young. Dark-skinned, like Mexican or South American, maybe. I stopped watching after the first few minutes, felt I was gonna throw up. I've got a daughter, just kept imagining . . . well, I don't need to spell it the fuck out, do I?"

"And the men with them?" I asked.

"Older, obviously, didn't know they were being filmed."

"Could you tell where this was? Hotel room? Someone's house?" I pushed.

"All I could make out was a bed against a wall. The light was pretty shitty."

"Did you recognize any of the faces?"

"They all looked the same to me, monsters in designer suits. There was always a woman, though, at the start, like she was getting the girls all comfortable, giving out drinks. Drugs too, pills and shit. She'd leave when the men came in. I mean, what kind of woman does that?"

"Did you recognize her?"

Betsy shook her head. "Tall, thin, baseball cap, wearing black, never got to see her face, like she knew the cameras were there and where to stand so her face wouldn't be on screen."

"Jesus," Alma said. "A child sex ring? This is what this has been about the whole time?"

A vein of ice crystallized my bones. My first thought was of Victor. Had he known all along? Had he and Paco set me up to retrieve the laptop because they knew I'd fetch it like a good dog, no questions asked, and return it without ever knowing what was on there? The bourbon soured to vinegar in my stomach.

We were all quiet for a few minutes, absorbing the information as if we couldn't believe what Betsy was telling us.

"Well, I am now completely fucked," I said, gulping down the last of my drink. The liquid crashed over my stomach like a waterfall of acid.

"Erm, not necessarily," Betsy said. She set the heel of her boot onto the edge of the coffee table, reached down the back of her Doc Martens, and pulled out a small thumb drive in the shape of a guitar machine head.

"The fuck you didn't?" Alma said, sitting upright.

"Charlotte knew Paco would send someone for the laptop, so she made sure I made a copy."

"A copy?" I said, sensing a glimmer of pale light at the far end of a very dark tunnel. "On that drive?"

"Kind of," Betsy said. "Only it's not a copy. After Charlotte was killed, I figured someone would come and try to take it, so I wiped the laptop clean. Nothing on there but a few apps and a screen saver." She waved the thumb drive around like she'd just won the device in a raffle. "It's all on here."

"How do you know the laptop was wiped clean?" Alma asked. "You can't just hit the delete button and hope it's gone. All this guy needs is a tech kid with half a brain, and they'll retrieve the data."

Betsy shook her head. "My pops had this magnetic degausser. After about six months, he wiped every computer clean so he could resell them."

My head spun as I considered Betsy's words.

McKay reached out and placed her hands gently over mine. "Mitch, are you okay?" she asked. She must have seen what I felt: the blood draining cold from my face.

"Erm, sure, yeah," I mumbled.

"You don't look okay."

I stood. "No, you're right, I'm not okay. When this Captain guy realizes the laptop's wiped clean, then it's done, game over."

"Not following. This is a good thing, right?" Betsy said, setting the drive on the coffee table. "You got what you wanted. Now you can fuck off back to NorCal, and I can take care of my pops. Win fucking win."

Alma shuffled to the edge of the couch and looked at me. "This guy's gonna come after you, isn't he, when he realizes there's jack shit on the laptop?"

"Worse. He'll go after my family."

"Christ," McKay said. "When things fuck up, they go all out with you, huh?"

"Yep, the whole nine fucking yards," I agreed, reaching for another drink, which McKay had already poured in anticipation.

"Shit, I need to let Victor know," Alma said, reaching for her phone.

"Don't do that," I snapped.

"Dude, he's my boss."

"And what if Victor's right in the sticky fucking middle of all this, Alma, did you think about that?"

"What's that mean?"

"Think about it. If he knows what's on that flash drive and he's helping Paco, what does that tell you?"

"Nah, not Victor. He can be a douchebag, too much money, but covering up something like this for Paco? I don't see it."

"Well, I do. I see it pretty fucking clearly. Until we know how deep in this shit Victor's involved, we keep it between us. Can we agree on that? A day is all I'm asking."

Alma shrugged. "Sure, a day. Still think you're way off base, just sayin'."

"Message received." I reached for my phone. "I need some air."

I marched out and sat on the edge of a lounger by the poolside. My call to Sierra went to voicemail, as did my other ten attempts. I felt like dunking my head in the deep end, screaming through the blue pool water until my lungs pleaded for mercy. I stayed out there for an hour, pacing, mumbling to myself like a crazy person. When I returned to McKay's, the house had a calmness at odds with the carnival parade marching through my mind. Betsy and Alma were fast asleep on the couch after watching one of McKay's shows.

"They insisted," McKay said, clearing the glasses.

Betsy's head leaned to the side and fell on Alma's shoulder; she didn't stir.

McKay handed me my drink. "So, got your head together now?"

"Not even close," I said, throwing myself into a chair and taking a generous mouthful.

"A plan, then? You got one of those, at least?"

I shook my head.

"You can stay the night if you want. The two sleeping beauties can make do with the couch. I don't have a spare room, but I'll make space for you on my bed. Looks like you could do with a good night's sleep,"

Her invitation was as tempting as they came, and the thought of curling up under the sheets with McKay sent a tremor of excitement through me. But my headache still carved at my skull with the intensity of a buzz saw, and I couldn't get the thought of Sierra and Kurt at the mercy of the Captain out of my mind. At the same time, the prospect of driving thirty minutes through the desert back to the hotel filled me with a damp weariness. But I knew the Gods of Sleep wouldn't be making a house call tonight, at least not in my neighborhood, and any step I made toward McKay's bedroom would have been another wrong decision I'd come to regret.

I walked toward McKay and hugged her. "You've been a lifesaver," I said. "I won't forget this. Paco won't hear about you from me; I promise you that."

As I pulled away, she leaned forward and kissed me lightly on the cheek. "Take care of yourself, Mitch."

I reached down and took the thumb drive from the table. It felt as light as a snowflake in my hand.

"You got a plan for that?" McKay asked.

"Just got a delivery to make that's long overdue," I said, and headed back into the desert.

PART 7:
ORIGINAL SIN

CHAPTER 42

Sunshine pooled through the windows, casting a harsh spotlight over the scuffed walls and carpet in the Oakland FBI field office. It reminded me of a nightclub in the cold light of morning: makeup smudged, hungover, and in need of a hot shower. After spending a few minutes on the nineteenth floor, Agents Landry and Finley had escorted me into an interrogation room furnished with a table, four metal chairs, and a rectangular mirror stretching the length of the wall. I wondered who the fourth chair might be for. It would be another hour before I got an answer to that question.

"Okay, if I'm getting this story straight, Landry said. "Paco Castillo paid off your gambling debt in return for you finding his wife and locating this laptop?"

"I wasn't aware of the laptop at the time. My job was to locate Charlotte. Nothing illegal," I stressed, eager to make the point.

To Landry's left, Finley took notes, clicking her pen as if keeping the beat of the interview on track. "Judge and jury might think otherwise," she said. "That's a lot of affiliating with a known criminal for a state-employed lawyer."

Landry continued. "While in Palm Springs, you witnessed the murder of Castillo's wife, and then, on your return to Oakland, you were also present when Officer Darlene Mason committed suicide because of an unrelated case involving a truck driving into your bike and the accidental shooting of your son."

"It's not unrelated," I insisted. "All these events are connected. I don't know why or how yet, but this whole shit show started when I took the stand as an expert witness in Paco Castillo's case."

"No good deed goes unpunished, right?"

"They teach you that at Quantico?"

"First day," Landry said.

Finley checked her notes. "And this pawnbroker, Hector DeWitt? You were also present at his murder?"

"He was dead before I arrived."

"Shot by this man you say calls himself Captain?"

I nodded.

"But you have no evidence. This is all speculation?"

I pulled out my cell phone and scrolled through the photos Kurt had sent me. "His boat," I said, stabbing the screen. "It's moored at La Cruz Marina in Mexico, one of those charter boats. You can see the name, *Gordo Loco*. I looked it up; it's owned by a company called Vallarta Sea Tours."

"Proves nothing," Finley said, clicking her pen like it was punctuation.

"I'm aware. But with the FBI's vast resources, I'm sure you could track the owner of the boat and locate this Captain?"

"Why would we do that?" Landry asked.

"Because he killed an American citizen."

"Allegedly," Finley interrupted.

"He also killed Charlotte Castillo."

"Another speculation," Landry said.

"Look," I said, my anger and impatience rising. "Are you going to help my family or not?"

"This evidence you insist will help put Castillo away. Do you have it with you?" Landry asked.

"I'm happy to hand it over when we've made a deal."

Landry grinned; the action didn't improve with practice. "A deal? Now you've got me curious. What kind of deal were you hoping for?"

"One that protects my family . . . and myself."

Finley spoke. "You're aware the US government has no jurisdiction in Mexico? We're not the CIA."

I gave her the *of course I fucking do* eye roll. "But the FBI must have some quid pro quo with the Mexican Federal Police?"

"I could make some calls, but from what you've told me, I don't see a compelling reason to pull that very complicated diplomatic trigger."

"Listen," I said, my voice rising. "Two Americans are in danger—"

"Based on what evidence?" Landry interrupted. "Some character we've never heard of calling himself Captain making a vague threat? We only have your word, and I'm sure as hell not inclined to call in diplomatic favors based on the confession of someone who's already told us he's in the employ of a wanted criminal."

"I have no reason to lie. I just want protection for my family."

Finley clicked her pen and checked her notes. "Right, but your family's safe. You spoke to them this morning?"

She was correct. I'd spoken to Sierra and Kurt the morning I left Palm Springs. As desperate as I was to pour my heart out to Sierra, it wasn't the kind of conversation to be had over the phone; too many nuances, too many questions that would remain unanswered, too many lies. After hanging up, my thoughts shot back to the Captain's words:

If what is on this computer is not what I am looking for, then your wife and child, they will suffer the error of your judgment.

He hadn't made good on that threat, but I figured it was just a matter of time, which is why I'd thrown myself on the mercy of the FBI. I didn't know if I could trust Victor. Maybe he knew all along what was on the laptop and was protecting Paco. If that was the case, I'd severely misjudged my friend of twenty years. Victor had already lied about locating Charlotte and their relationship. His get-out-of-jail-free card — *Even if I knew what was on there, I couldn't tell you because of client confidentiality* — seemed too convenient, something he could shelter behind when the bullets started flying. I had no such cover.

Handing the thumb drive to Paco and walking away went against everything I believed in when it came to justice. If Paco was running an underground child sex trafficking ring and was keeping the videos as insurance to blackmail the men concerned, then what choice did I have? I took some solace that maybe the Captain hadn't yet returned to Mexico and was biding his time. Maybe he'd travel to the Bay Area first, find me, take care of business. But then again, the Captain seemed the kind of psychopath that likes to keep you guessing. Either way, I figured seeking protection from the FBI was my only choice.

Landry sat back. "Have you seen the contents of this drive?"

"I watched the first few minutes. Didn't seem like a watch party kind of event."

"So how do you know the footage implicates Paco Castillo?"

"Isn't that your job?"

"And the person who told you this footage came from Paco Castillo's laptop is reliable?"

"She had no reason to lie. Charlotte — Paco's ex-wife, or wife, whatever — paid Betsy and her father to look after the laptop. Betsy was only in it for the money."

Finley clicked her pen and smirked. "We know who Charlotte Castillo is, but thanks for the clarification."

I decided Finley's incessant pen-clicking and snarky attitude was rubbing me the wrong way. I returned the smirk and said, "I don't see the FBI presenting any fresh evidence to put Castillo away, so you're very fucking welcome."

She brushed off my barb like a dust mote. "And you were also the last person to see Charlotte alive, which, of course, would make you a prime suspect in her murder, or at least complicit."

"Really? You're going there?"

"We'll need to examine the contents of that drive before we agree to anything," Landry said. "That's the only way it's going to work."

I figured this addendum to the negotiation was coming. "On one condition."

"Conditions?"

"I need to hand a copy of the footage to Paco. If I don't, he'll probably kill me, then my family, if this Captain guy doesn't beat him to it. You guys need to make up some story about how you got the drive. It can't lead back to me."

"We need—?"

"Look," I interrupted. "I'm running out of options here. Make up some story that doesn't have my name attached. I want to put this guy away as much as you do, but I can't risk my family's life to do it. That's non-negotiable."

A heavy silence opened up in the room. For the first time since confessing, I doubted my decision. It felt like I'd free-jumped from the door of an airplane, my parachute failing to deploy, and I was hurtling to a messy and limb-shattering landing. Confession may be good for the soul, but as I looked at Landry and Finley's stern faces, I doubted it would do my health much good.

Finally, after a few clicks of Finley's pen, Landry spoke. "You've lied to the FBI already, right? Told me you had no affiliation with Paco Castillo after the party."

"If I'd told you and Paco had found out, he'd have had his goons beat the crap out of me, or worse. So yes, I withheld information to protect myself and my family."

Landry nodded. "Okay, so let's forget for a minute your deliberate omission of the facts. You've also admitted you're in possession of evidence that suggests serious criminal activity. I don't need to remind you, but I will. You're legally obliged to hand that evidence over to the FBI, unless you want to be charged with accessory to commit a crime and obstruction of a criminal investigation."

"I told you I'd hand it over. I just need reassurance that my family's protected."

"Okay, Mitch, we're circling here; why don't we take a minute to recalibrate? You claim to have a flash drive containing very disturbing footage and what might be encrypted account information or might not; either way, you can't be sure. Is there anything on this footage or in that account information that links directly back to Paco Castillo?"

I shuffled, sensing more discomfort ahead. "Paco told me that someone broke into his office a couple of months ago and stole his laptop."

After another click of her pen, Finley spoke. "But all you have is a flash drive, which anyone could have copied from anywhere, using any device. Unless Castillo himself is on that footage, this is all conjecture. We wouldn't get a warrant to search his golf bag, let alone his home."

"He doesn't play golf. And anyway, I figure Paco's way smarter than putting his face on camera, don't you, Agent Finley?"

Shuffling forward, Landry said, "If this footage contains evidence of child abuse, sex trafficking, or some underground pedophile ring, then you've got a moral and legal obligation to turn that footage over. No conditions. No demands."

295

I knew Landry was right, but that knowledge didn't help me one bit. "If I hand it over, what protection can you give my family?"

"Let our tech forensics comb through the footage, then we'll discuss it."

"How long will that take?"

"A few days, a week at the most."

"I don't have a few days," I countered, the frustration boiling inside me. "Neither does my family. We need protection now."

Finley spoke. "Maybe if you'd agreed to work with us when we asked, you could have avoided all this, huh, Mitch?"

"What? So this is payback for not helping you out when you asked? Gotta say that's petty, even for a government agency."

Landry spoke. "Like I said, we need that footage, Mitch. I'd rather avoid all the paperwork of issuing a warrant for your arrest and the seizure of the evidence, but if that's what it takes, then that's exactly what I'll do."

As I took in the information, Landry reached inside his jacket pocket for a mint. He chewed, then spoke: "Let me tell you a story, Mitch, one that might help you reframe your decision here."

"Sure, if it helps protect my family, read me the fucking phone book."

He grinned. "Back in September 2001 I was living in New York working at one of those fancy Wall Street investment banks, heading for a nice annual bonus. I was on vacation, visiting my mom in Florida, when I saw the news. I worked for Cantor Fitzgerald in the North Tower, the first one to fall. Just blind luck I wasn't in the office that day."

He lowered his voice. "That day changed my life, Mitch. Everyone who worked in that office, friends of mine, just gone, lost in the rubble and dust."

He tapped his FBI badge clipped to his belt. "I decided to join up the next day. Figured I could do a lot more good serving my country than making some hedge fund manager more money than he could ever spend in a lifetime. Which brings us to this moment and the decision you're going to have to make, Mitch. Are you following me?"

"I'm sorry for your loss, Landry, but how's this relevant?"

He took a moment and looked me in the eye. "Right now, you're me the day after 9/11 changed everything." He softened his tone. "Look, I get it. You want to be on the side of the good guys. Why else are you working at the courts? I'm sure as hell it's not for the pay. But you can't be on the side of the good guys if your ass is on the fence and you're sitting there hoping it's all going to go away. Let me tell you something: it never goes away. Choose a side. You'll feel a lot better about yourself. That's a promise."

Landry gestured at the mirror as if beckoning someone to enter the room. He and Finley gathered up their possessions.

"We'll give you some time," Finley said. "Talk it over with someone. We're sure you'll make the smart decision."

My throat tightened. I imagined some burly FBI enforcer type was on his way to show me the error of my ways. But as the interrogation room door creaked open and the well-dressed man walked in, my assumption couldn't have been more wrong.

"Mind if I take that seat, *amigo*?" Victor said, gesturing at the empty chair next to mine. He shuffled around the table, sat, and gave a tight smile. It wasn't returned. I was too numb to react.

"You two probably got a lot to talk about," Landry said. "Take your time. Agent Finley and myself got no place else we need to be other than behind that mirror over there. Have a productive chat. See if we can't wrap this damned mess in a nice tidy bow and give it to my boss as an early Christmas present."

CHAPTER 43

By the time I left the field office, the glimmer of late-afternoon sunlight was surrendering to early evening, casting a warm sheen over downtown Oakland. I took some time to reflect on what had gone down and found myself lumbering south down Broadway's wide sidewalks, past several shiny new cannabis dispensaries designed for the high-end seekers of the perfect high — a stark contrast to Paco's drug trade, which I imagined had a grubbier patina, dealt in deadlier substances, left dead bodies and broken people in its wake.

The cannabis trade may have gained the gloss of acceptance, but the hard stuff, the stuff that poisons your blood, eats at your ambition, gets you dead in a piss-stained alleyway with a dirty needle hanging from your vein or a crust of contaminated dust under your nose, that stuff? This was Paco Castillo's dominion.

I'd convinced myself I'd constructed an intellectual distance from Paco's business, and what I'd done was honorable because I was doing it for my family. But the truth was, no matter how I sliced it, I was part of that same empire of filth and death.

It took me too long to realize I couldn't separate the man from his actions, the thug from his fine cigars and expensive tequila; the monster from the monstrosities he perpetrated or had others perpetrate for him. I'd lied to myself for the convenience of paying my debts, and that was the worst kind of lie. Lie to other people and you can always apologize, heal the hurt, and hope for forgiveness. Forgiving yourself? That's doesn't go down so easy. You live with that guilt every day. The only way forward is to make amends, try to fix the errors you've made, and hope in some small way you can make the world a better place. As I'd always said, make enough beats, at some point, the rhythm's gotta start changing. I'd lost sight of that path in the past few weeks. The time had come to make things right, change up the beat.

As much as I disliked Landry and his pen-clicking sidekick, what he'd told me back in the interrogation room had struck a chord and opened a tentative doorway back to redemption. After weeks of doing Paco's bidding, it was time to remove my ass from off the fence, face up to the choices I'd made, and help in any way I could to ensure he never got to hurt another child.

As I'd listened to Landry, the murder of Ron Boone's niece, Masie, came back to me. Like Ron, I imagined Paco's fingerprints were on the bullet that killed her, but maybe I was being too generous. Paco may as well have chambered that bullet, pulled the trigger, and left a young woman to die in agony in her car. They say capitalism has a long tail, but so does organized crime, a cascading ripple of cause and effect. Everyone up the chain of command, from the trigger puller to the gun seller, the ammunition supplier to the street-corner dealer, the shady accountants obfuscating money trails, to the overpaid lawyers digging at legal loopholes, exploiting them in the hope of making them even wider and deeper . . . they were all complicit. And, at the top of that greedy, convoluted, and poisoned food chain was Paco Castillo, the commander-in-chief who barked orders, shaped the company culture, and led from the top down with an iron fist that crushed anyone who got in his way.

* * *

Negotiating with Landry and Finley for three hours left me with a head full of pop rocks and a grumbling stomach. I stepped into the first restaurant I saw, a hole-in-the-wall ramen establishment where the staff were surly and the windows soaked with a thick veil of condensation. The faded certificate from two decades earlier, *Best ramen in the East Bay*, framed over the bar seemed like a sad relic of past glories, but the soup was all kinds of hot and comforting as I parsed everything that had just gone down with Victor and the FBI. I needed time to get matters straight in mind, figure out exactly what they were asking of me, and how I could execute a clean exit without putting myself or my family in any more danger.

I was slurping my noodles like an Olympic sport when I sensed someone standing across from me, blocking out the wan light. Despite the warm soup doing its job, I felt a cold rush pucker my skin. I thought for sure this was the Captain come to take his cruel revenge, and a half-eaten ramen would be my last supper.

I resisted the temptation to acknowledge his presence until the man pulled out a chair and sat. Silently, I sighed with relief; relief which quickly soured to irritation as I recognized the fade-and-taper haircut and the meticulously groomed beard smiling at me like we were old buddies.

"What, are you following me now, Madrigal? Got nothing better to do on a Sunday?"

The young journalist smiled. "Just passing, saw you in the window."

"You can't see your own damned reflection in that window," I said, gesturing at the fogged glass. "Cut the crap."

He removed his shades. "I just live a few blocks away."

"Coincidence, then?"

"Must be," he said, ordering a Tsing Tao beer. "Saw you leaving the FBI field office over on thirteenth. Meeting with the FBI on a Sunday afternoon? Must be important."

I set my chopsticks in the bowl and sat back. "What do you want, Madrigal? I'm beat. I just want to finish my food in peace. Think you can extend me that courtesy? Or do I have to be more direct, like telling you to leave me the fuck alone?"

"Just enjoying my beer," he said, taking the bottle and sipping it as if it were hot tea.

"How about you enjoy it someplace else, like your apartment? Oh, and if you come near my staff again asking questions, I will make an official complaint to your editor. Understood?"

"No problem. It's you I need to talk to, anyway."

"I'm done talking. If you're feeling lonely, go find yourself a chat room."

"You're a funny guy . . . for a lawyer."

"It's been said before. Now, why are you still here?"

"I'm confused," Madrigal said. "Why didn't Sierra write the story? You must have told her. She's the senior features writer, and with you being a court lawyer, I thought for sure she'd have called dibs on the inside track."

A familiar weariness fell over me. My plate was full enough already, and after all the shit that had gone down in Palm Springs and the FBI, I'd relegated the Griffin Harper papers to the bottom of my dumpster.

"What story?"

Madrigal smiled. "Don't act like you don't know shit. That's just insulting."

"Then consider yourself insulted. Now, if you got what you came for . . ." I said, making the *skedaddle* gesture.

Madrigal wasn't moving anywhere. "Here, let me remind you," he said, scooting forward. "Alameda County calling in retired judges and paying them a buttload of money to try cases. Now, according to my research, the Superior Court has plenty of staff judges who can do the work. Must be costing the state millions, right? Staffing all those additional courtrooms for no good reason, wiring them with all that new tech you need these days, not to mention all the admin staff, cleaners, maintenance."

"You been sitting in one of our courthouse budget committee hearings, Madrigal? That's a lot of insider information."

"I do my research."

"You mean someone gave you the research?"

"Either way, it's a major scandal if it's true. Is it true, Mitch?"

"Sounds like some half-assed rumor you'd publish in the digital edition to me. A couple of trending hashtags and a tweet and it's job done, right? Maybe Sierra didn't want to touch the story because she could smell bullshit from the other side of the block and didn't think it was worth crossing the road for a closer sniff. Still, nice of her to leave some scraps for you. Beats scrolling around Nextdoor and Citizen for your stories."

"I see what you did there," he said, grinning. "If I had thinner skin, maybe I'd be triggered."

"Triggered?" I shook my head. "Sure, okay. Now, let me ask you a question. Who gave you this misinformation?"

"That's the $64,000 question, right? But then again, the courthouse rumor mill's a 24/7 operation these days."

"You know what they say about rumors."

"Yep. They're like assholes. Everyone's got one, and odds are, they're all full of shit."

"If you know that, why are you still bugging me?"

"Because, Mitch, a good journalist doesn't give up when he gets a bloody nose from the first door slammed in his face."

"Good journalist? They tell you in your last performance review, or do you make that shit up to impress young women?"

He ignored the quip. "A good journalist keeps digging until he finds a shiny golden nugget buried somewhere in the middle of all that shit."

"You've got a shit-coated nugget of a news story? Congratulations, I'm sure your editor's doing cartwheels around the office."

Madrigal sighed. "What do you know about Judge Harper Griffin, Mitch?"

"I know he's a dead man walking."

"Yeah, I heard about the cancer," Madrigal said, with a tight frown. "But Harper's an interesting character."

"Must be a slow news season if you're interested in a dying man. Or are you hoping for a shot at writing his obituary?"

"Did you know Harper was a big player in the construction business back in the day? Sells his company for a shit load just before the 2008 bust, then lands himself a cushy board seat on the city planning authority before making judge."

"Why are you telling me this?"

"Because, Mitch, I like to share, bring the truth out of the dark and into the light. Truths some people would rather remain buried."

"So, what, you're a moral crusader now?"

In the manner his cheek twitched, I could tell that remark hit a nerve. "Here's the deal, Mitch. Harper awarded a bunch of lucrative contracts to a company called Celica Holdings when he was on the planning committee. You ever heard of them?"

My stomach corkscrewed. Celica Holdings was Paco's semi-legitimate construction company. "Never heard of them," I lied.

Madrigal twirled his bottle on the table. "I dug around, eventually found a bunch of offshore shell companies, then dug some more and found out Celica Holdings is owned by one Francisco Castillo. Also known as Paco Magic. You're aware of him, right?"

"If you say so."

"Don't take me for a fool. We both know Harper was the judge on the suppression of evidence hearing, and you took the stand as the expert witness, and Castillo walks away, no trial, all charges dropped."

"Just doing my job."

"Yeah, like I am. Look, you've gotta figure those two go way back."

"How?"

"Oh, now you want answers?"

"Fuck off, Madrigal."

"Here's how I see it. As head of the planning committee, Harper secures a bunch of contracts for Castillo's construction company and gets a nice fat paycheck for his efforts. I'm just spitballing here, but I'd wager there's a line as straight as a steel rail that leads back to the retired judges. It's all connected. These kinds of criminal activity don't happen in isolation."

"That's a lot of speculation."

"Not just speculation, evidence. Lucky for democracy, there are some brave souls at the courthouse a lot more generous with their time and information than you."

"And you won't name your sources."

"Bingo. But there's one thing I haven't figured out yet . . ." He paused, raised his bottle to eye level. "How you're connected to all this? Care to enlighten me?"

"Time you left, Madrigal." I felt myself rise from my seat, my fists clenching on the table.

Madrigal noticed the whites of my knuckles and scooted back. "Oh, you want to hit me?" he said, raising his arms. "Go right ahead. That headline pretty much writes itself."

Finally, realizing he was circling around a cul-de-sac, he stood. "I'll get to the truth eventually, Mitch. I always do. Who knows, this kind of scandal could go national with the right push."

"National? I wouldn't go polishing your Pulitzer just yet," I said, relaxing back into my chair.

I was sure his chest puffed out an extra few inches as if the word "Pulitzer" had inflated his ego. But Madrigal had already left before I could give him shit about it.

CHAPTER 44

Ghosts linger like bored teenagers on a street corner, waiting for something to kick off. The personal ghosts waiting for me back at the family home were stuck to the refrigerator door, fingerprinted into the stainless-steel kitchen appliances, and scratched across the hardwood floors and baseboards.

In the semi-darkness of the kitchen, I sat and sipped my Scotch, waited for the spirits to make some noise. But ghosts are reluctant companions, refuse to give the living the satisfaction of having dominion over them. I sensed their presence, though, specters of happier times. Maybe that's why I'd come back: to punish myself and remind myself what my bad decisions had cost me. Not that I needed the reminder. Agents Landry and Finley had made my position clear earlier that day when they insisted I surrender the flash drive, and Victor walking into the interrogation room was when the tide turned in the FBI's favor.

"I am so fucking sorry you and the family got caught in the middle of this," Victor had said after the agents left. He looked exhausted and pale. I imagined he'd spent the last few hours being interrogated under the heat of a glaring spotlight. "Trust me, I would never put Sierra and Kurt in danger. You know that."

I knew nothing of the kind. All I was sure of was the anger swelling in my chest like a bad infection. But Landry and Finley were listening on the other side of the glass, and I wasn't about to blurt out something incriminating in a fit of rage. I tamped down my impulse to grab Victor by his suit lapels and shove him up against the wall until he confessed everything. Luckily, Victor was in a talkative mood.

"How long have you been working with the FBI? And no lies. I'm done being lied to."

"Alma called me after the shit show in Palm Springs."

That didn't surprise me. Alma had saved my ass, but her allegiances lay with Victor; he paid her salary. "So, it took me being shot at twice for you to act? That's reassuring."

"Look, I'm taking a huge gamble," he said, lowering his voice. "If Paco knew I was talking to the Feds, I'm a dead man. I don't need to tell you that."

"Then tell me everything. You owe me."

He glanced at the two-way mirror as if expecting some sign would magically appear, giving him permission to answer. When none was forthcoming, he continued. "Charlotte told me about the laptop a few months ago."

"After you'd started seeing her?"

"I was flying to meet her two weekends a month, drafting papers, trying to smooth out the waters as best I could. We didn't plan any of it. It just happened."

"Did you love her? Did she love you?"

Victor shrugged. "It was an impossible situation. Another lifetime? No Paco? Maybe things would have turned out differently."

"Did Charlotte tell you what she found on the laptop?"

"It took her a while to trust me. When she told me, I felt sick to my stomach. I told her to hand it over to the FBI right away. We had the mother of all arguments, but she dug her heels in, figured using it as leverage was the only way to get Paco out of her life for good."

"How did she find out about the laptop? She hasn't seen Paco for years."

"My guess? Someone from Paco's inner circle."

"Right. Someone grew a conscience all of a sudden?"

"If you're hoping for Kumbayas around the campfire, you're looking at the wrong organization. Probably someone setting the groundwork to take Paco down. They threaten to hand the laptop to the authorities unless Paco surrenders the throne."

"What about Charlotte? She must have known about the laptop."

"She wouldn't have had the access, more likely someone high in Paco's inner circle."

"The Captain?"

"Like I told the Feds, I'm not aware of anyone in Paco's organization who goes by that name. But if this Captain guy's based in Mexico, he's got limited access to Paco's affairs. It had to be someone close to Paco who made the call to the Captain, then he contacted Charlotte."

"Why go through Charlotte? Why not just take the laptop?"

"Risk mitigation. If Paco gets a whiff of what's going down, the guy's history. Roping in Charlotte keeps him in the shadows, lessens the chance of exposure."

"And having the laptop gave Charlotte leverage against Paco?"

"She'd been followed for years. It didn't bother her at first, but eventually, it wore her down. She was ready to give Paco the divorce, but with two conditions: stop having her followed and sign over full custody of the children."

"Did you steal the laptop for Charlotte?"

Victor's eyes shot wide open. "Me? Are you fucking kidding?"

"You're in his so-called inner circle. Wouldn't have been that hard."

Victor laughed. "You have no fucking idea, do you, Mitch? I'm just a cog in the machinery of lawyers working for him, and honestly, that's more than fine with me." He leaned in. "Look, I'm under no illusions about the kind of man Paco is, but I was happy to take his money, make sure he got a fair trial, but that's about as far as it went. I had no insights into his business dealings, and he never offered. Plausible deniability worked best for both of us."

"I don't understand why Charlotte didn't take the laptop to the FBI once she saw what was on there."

"At first, she thought it was just a digital ledger, records of bribes paid, debts due, that kind of thing. When she saw the footage, the game changed."

"Right. She was okay with the drugs, weapons, and prostitution, but the child trafficking pushed her over the edge?"

"People compartmentalize, you know that, set boundaries they swear never to cross. Charlotte did the same. When you're married to Paco Castillo, you learn pretty quickly not to ask too many questions."

"So, she turned a blind eye?" As soon as the words left my lips, they came out leaden and thick with irony. Hadn't I done the same and ignored the grim reality of Paco's business for my own gain?

"Like I said, people compartmentalize," Victor repeated, casting his eyes to the table. I was sure he felt the same pangs of guilt. Despite our better judgment, we'd both been dragged into the heavy gravitation of Paco Castillo's orbit. Victor for the glory and the money; me to clear my debts and put back together the broken bits of my family.

"You knew what was on the laptop when you sent me to Palm Springs?"

"Your task was to locate Charlotte, nothing more. Easy money."

"No such thing."

"Noted. But understand that everything that followed was out of my control. Betsy got word to Charlotte you were at the pawnbroker's asking questions, and instead of skipping town like she'd planned, Charlotte stuck around to check out who Paco had sent. She probably would have shot you, too, just to send him a message."

"Until I mentioned your name."

"Our relationship was over by then."

"Who ended it?"

"I did."

"The polo field?"

"Not my proudest moment. Women like Charlotte never get used to being told 'no.' She had this fantasy we'd sail into the sunset together. For a smart woman, she could be pretty naïve. I couldn't do it. I'd spent too long building my practice; everything I had was here. What was I going to do? Spend the rest of my life under a beach cabana sipping pina coladas, looking over my shoulder?"

"If you loved her enough, it wouldn't have mattered."

He shrugged. "Guess I didn't love her enough, then."

"Why didn't you get me out of this after Charlotte's murder?"

"I tried, but Paco trusted you. You'd located Charlotte, proved your worth, and he'd paid off your debt to Cipriani. Remember, you owed him."

"Like I need the reminder."

"We all need reminders now and again, Mitch, to keep us honest." Victor slumped a little in his chair. "I've lost sight of that myself over the past few years, forgot to remind myself why the hell I became a lawyer in the first place."

"And now you're making amends," I said, gesturing at the two-way mirror. "By talking to the FBI?"

Victor rubbed a hand over his face. "Remember when we were in law school? We were going to stand up for the little guy, fight injustice every chance we got? We lost sight of that somewhere along the way."

"I didn't."

"I know. That's why I've always envied you. You always did the right thing, even when it cost you. Agreeing to Paco's demands to pay your debt? You did that to fix your family. My intentions weren't nearly as noble. I wanted the fancy uptown office and the big house — which, by the way, when you've got five thousand square feet to rattle around in by yourself, gets pretty fucking lonely."

"Sure, let me get out my tiny violin, serenade your tragic fucking soliloquy, Vic."

"Look, I get you're angry, but the point is, working for Paco, I forgot why I started practicing law in the first place." He smiled. "Remember that shitty office I rented on Grand Lake above the hot yoga studio?"

"Sure, smelled like stale sweat and piss."

"Figured I'd spend the rest of my career with the window wedged open and a handful of low-rent clients. Five years ago, Paco came knocking after watching me argue down a murder charge handed to one of his lieutenants to involuntary manslaughter. After that, things changed. He sent referrals and hired me for the trickier criminal cases. I was like a kid in a candy shop. More clients than I knew what to do with, hourly billings through the roof, but none of it means anything, nothing solid anyway. Nothing you can feel proud of, look back and say you made a damned bit of difference."

"You made your choice."

"Yeah, I did . . . and so did you." He raised a wan smile. "Remember when you first introduced me to Sierra? You'd only been seeing her for a week. You pulled me aside and told me you were going to marry her? I envied the hell out of you that night. Not that you had Sierra, but that you could be so sure about someone that you'd want to spend the rest of your life with them. The older I get, the further away all that seems. I guess that's why I threw myself into my work, figuring money and respect would make up for that gaping hole. Believe me, it doesn't. It just makes things worse, like a huge exclamation point emphasizing everything that's missing in my life."

I shook my head. "You want me to feel sorry for you? Three-million-dollar house, shipping coffee beans from Hawaii at seventy-five bucks a pound? Yeah, poor you, Victor, poor fucking you."

"I'm not looking for pity, just laying it out on the table. I can't make you feel a certain way. I'm just trying to explain why I'm doing this now."

"Maybe it's too fucking late for gestures, Vic. I've got some lunatic calling himself Captain looking to kill both me and my family, and I'm in debt to the head of a criminal organization, so forgive me if your sob story's running hollow for me."

Victor shook his head. "Mitch, have you been listening to anything I've said? The reason I wanted you to agree to Paco's offer wasn't because of the money.

"I knew if Sierra had found out about your debt to Capriani, it would have pushed her over the edge. She told me as much, said if anything else about your gambling came to light, it was all over . . . for good. Deep down, you knew that too, which is why you agreed to Paco's deal."

He was right, I knew that. Not that I would have given Victor the satisfaction of agreeing with him. "So, you persuaded me to take Paco's money to help save my marriage? Why did it matter that much to you? I was figuring out a way back to Sierra and Kurt. I didn't need your help."

"And what if you couldn't figure out a way back? What then?"

I had no reply. I'd always imagined Sierra and I would work things out and somehow find our way back to what we had before. As Victor's words sunk in, the interrogation room door opened. Agents Landry and Finley stepped in.

Dylan H. Jones

"Thoroughly enjoyed your chat," Finley said, sitting across from us. "Almost had me in tears at the end there, Mr. Santiago."

Landry pulled out a chair and sat. "Good. Now, seeing as we've all got our cards on the table and we're all working together like one happy family, let's figure out how to nail this mother-fucker, Castillo, and finally send his ass to jail."

312

CHAPTER 45

As the elevator pinged to a stop, a twitch of anxiety rose in my gut. I stood in the no-man's-land between the elevator and the hallway, hesitating to step out. Something smelled off, like the stench of last week's fish supper rotting in the garbage.

Loud music leaked down the hallway. That was unusual. None of the Jack London Waterfront Apartments residents played their music that loud, except me. It took me a few seconds to recognize the choppy guitar riffs of "Helicopter" from XTC's *Drums and Wire* (an example of the finest early literary punk experimentation, in my not-so-humble opinion).

A reflection in the mirror across the hallway caught my attention. I had no time to react. Something hard came down with enormous force at the back of my skull.

Confusion. Darkness. They fell on me in a hailstone of pain.

I recovered consciousness a few minutes later, gasping for air out on my apartment balcony, my throat pressed into the railings, a foot pushing into my spine. I was knee-bound, neck raw with pain, ears whistling like a tornado was whipping through them. At the dockside, a flock of seagulls was all aflutter, probably some dispute over territory or food; it was always one or the other with those feathered fucks. I was sure their cackles were cruel, avian laughs at my expense: *the joke's on you buddy; the joke's on you.*

Five stories below, Jack London's nightlife trundled on, oblivious in the early evening gray.

I was seconds from passing out again when a voice from inside called out: "*Enough!*"

My torturer stepped back. "You sure, boss? Don't know if he got the message."

The voice I placed immediately: Jorge, Paco's driver, henchman, enforcer, or whatever he claimed to be; his role changed with the wind.

"I think he got it, Jorge."

The other voice had to be Paco. Jorge always called him boss.

I turned. Jorge stood in the balcony doorway holding a gun, flashing his gold tooth. The XTC album had segued into "Making Plans for Nigel," which meant only a few minutes had passed since Jorge had pistol-whipped me out in the hallway. The ordeal had seemed a lot longer.

"You're a lucky bastard," he said, shoving his weapon in his pant belt.

I responded with a feeble grunt.

"What? You got nothing to say? Be good for your health if you started talking, or else the boss here's gonna get real pissed, and I'm gonna have to hang you off that balcony, may drop your ass down there, too. Your choice, homie."

I pulled myself up. My vision was gradually returning to normal, at least well enough to make out a figure, whom I assumed was Paco, hunched over my turntable. He grabbed the stylus and dragged it across the surface of the record. The vinyl responded with a loud screech of pain. I also felt its pain, like a needle had been scratched across my own gut; I'd spent a hundred bucks for the 1979 original from a collector in Swindon, England.

The man flipped through my vinyl collection with a sigh, then turned, that sly, disingenuous smile of his, making my stomach lurch.

"You like analog?" the Captain asked. "Sure you do," he said, answering his own question, which I'd realized was how he liked to play things. "But I have never heard of any of these bands. You need to get yourself some real music, some *narcocorridos*. Ever heard of that?"

I shook my head. The action hurt like someone was clanging a bell in there.

"Means 'drug ballads' in English. You know Los Huracanes del Norte? The Hurricanes of the North. Better than this *gringo* shit."

"Or some *corridos tumbados*," Jorge interjected. "You listen to Natanael Cano? Mexican hip-hop? Bad Bunny remixed, like, a bunch of his tracks."

Another dumb, painful shake of my head.

"They take traditional shit, make it modern, right, *patrón*?" he said, looking to the Captain for confirmation.

"Yes, Jorge, though I would argue *narcocorrido*, as a sub-genre of *corrido*, speaks more to someone in our line of business."

Jorge bit his lower lip, considering the point. "Ay, I guess."

Despite being lost in the miasma of this ridiculous discourse, one thought rang clear: Jorge and the Captain were working together.

My mind shot back to that day outside the courtroom, Paco insisting that Jorge was a new hire, came highly recommended, and Jorge's barely contained irritation at being bullied into wearing a suit. Then, our conversation at the Port of Oakland, when Jorge implied Paco wouldn't be around for ever. I was now sure Jorge was the knife in Paco's heart, and the Captain was the one who'd sharpened the blade.

"You," I said, gesturing at Jorge. "You stole Paco's laptop."

He shook his head. "Not me, homie. Some other fucker."

I turned to the Captain. "And you're the one who got Charlotte involved."

The Captain reached for a bottle of Calo Isla on my kitchen island and poured himself a shot. "Your taste in Scotch is much better than your taste in music," he said, then helped himself to another. "I learned of the laptop through an intermediary who insisted on staying anonymous."

"What was the plan?" I asked. "Depose Paco, kill him?"

"Kill Paco? You do not just kill a man like Paco Castillo. Imagine the instability and bloodshed that would cause. My plan was much simpler. While in prison, Paco would announce his retirement and name me as his successor. I am anointed, no blood spilled, a seamless transition."

"You were going to threaten Paco with the footage on the laptop if he didn't step down?"

"A good plan."

"Was killing Charlotte part of that plan?"

He shrugged. "We had a deal. Charlotte chose not to honor that deal. She wanted to use it as leverage against Paco for her own gain. She betrayed me."

"And Hector?"

"The man should have shown me more respect. But that is ancient history. What is done cannot be undone. But what happens next? That is your call, Mitch."

He reached into a backpack at his feet, took out the silver laptop he'd taken from me in the desert, and flung it across the floor. "What you gave me was an empty coffin. I considered flying back to Sayulita and making good on my threat to harm your family, but I reevaluated my position, because I understand the human condition well enough to know that a man with nothing left to lose will never cooperate. Do you know why?"

"Because he's already lost everything?"

"*Sí*," he said, pointing at me. "I can see what Paco saw in you. Why would a man cooperate if the people he loves the most are taken from him? Except to save his own life, of course. But what kind of life would that be without the people that make his life worth living? Often there are worse things than death. Living but not really alive, yes?"

He paused and stepped closer. "I am here, Mitch, to ask you some very important questions, which you will answer without hesitation."

"Look," I pleaded. "My job was just to locate Charlotte. I didn't know about the laptop until later. I had no idea what was on there."

"But now you do."

"Not anything I want to see again anytime soon."

"Then you still have it? In this apartment?" he said, looking around as if hoping it might miraculously leap into his hands.

"I don't have it."

"Then someone must have it. Not Paco, I am sure. The FBI, maybe?" He raised his hand as I was about to speak. "Jorge has followed you since you returned. Why were you talking to the FBI? Confessing? Negotiating a deal?"

I looked to the floor, neither confirming nor denying the fact.

"So, a deal. What is the nature of this deal?"

"There is no deal. I was there because of another case."

That earned me a sharp blow in the solar plexus from Jorge. The pain ricocheted through me like the slug of a sledgehammer.

Frowning, the Captain reached for his cell phone, poked the screen, muttered something in Spanish, then turned the screen to face me. "Would you like to speak to your family? I am sure they would appreciate the gesture, considering the circumstances."

As I focused on the screen, a crater-sized pit imploded in my stomach. Sierra and Kurt were inside what looked like the cabin of a boat, with porthole windows behind them, wooden-clad walls studded with chrome hooks, and recessed lighting with a dim violet hue. They were sitting on a bunk bed, moving with the rocking motion of the water, hands tied at the wrists, black tape wrapped around their mouths. They looked terrified.

"Sierra! Kurt!" I shouted. I lunged at the phone as if I imagined I could dive through the screen and rescue them. Jorge grabbed the back of my shirt and pulled me back.

"Easy," the Captain said, "or else I will have to terminate the connection." He handed me the phone. "Your family can see and hear you, but they won't be able to speak . . . for obvious reasons."

I took the phone. Sierra's eyes had some steel in them, as if she'd put up the fight of her life and wasn't giving up. Kurt's big blue eyes told a different story. They were red and milky, that wide-eyed innocence drained out of them. It broke my heart as he struggled to wipe his tears with his jacket sleeve. I searched for words that might bring them comfort or hope, but like the threats I'd made to the Captain out in the desert, the words came out hollow and meaningless. "I'm sorry. It'll be all right. Don't worry, this will all be over soon. I'll get you out of there, promise."

Kurt nodded. He trusted his dad to save him and get him safely back home. I would have given my right arm for that kind of trust in myself right then.

Sierra, her chin thrust forward, made sure I knew where her feelings stood. I'd been the victim of that look plenty of times; the look that said she didn't believe me didn't buy a word of the bullshit I was peddling. Just like the times I'd insisted I'd stopped gambling, pleaded with her to trust me, that I'd crawled out of the wreckage scarred but changed, changed for the better. But whatever splinter of trust that remained had, by now, been dug out. I could almost hear the voice in her head: *what the hell have you done, Mitch? What the hell have you done to us?*

Jorge snatched the phone from my hands. "Time's up, *pendejo*."

My anger swelled like air in my chest. "Fuck you, Jorge," I snapped, stepping closer. "My family's got nothing to do with this."

"What, you mister tough guy all of a sudden?" He swiped the gun from his belt and pressed the cold metal under my chin. "You gotta death wish? One shot, motherfucker. You want me to grant your fucking wish?"

I raised my hands. "I'm just saying, let them go, and I'll answer any questions. Just let my family go, please. They're innocent."

The Captain, gesturing for Jorge to stand down, looked my way. "Innocent? I'm curious: do you think people can be truly innocent? I am not so sure. All of us bear the burden of past sins within ourselves. The question is, are you aware of your sins, Mitch?"

"Too fucking aware. Look, please, Captain," I said, using his preferred name for the first time. It sounded leaden in my mouth. "Let Kurt and Sierra go, please." I harbored some vague hope that saying their names would sway his decision, but I may as well have whistled Dixie, hoping to halt a tornado in its tracks. "I'll do whatever you want, just let them go. They shouldn't have to pay for my mistakes."

"But still, here we are," the Captain responded with a shrug. "Now, do you know the sin you committed that resulted in your family being held captive?"

"Honestly, I wouldn't know where to fucking start."

"Standing as a witness in Paco Castillo's hearing, that was the sin . . . your original sin, maybe?" He chuckled as if he were proud of the biblical reference. "Your testimony swung the verdict in Paco's favor. Do you see now, Mitch?"

A penny dropped with a loud, undeniable clang in the recess of my memory dumpster. "This whole thing was a setup to depose Paco?"

"A bloodless coup, until you took the stand and gave your expert opinion."

I turned to Jorge. "You killed Masie Howard and planted the gun in Paco's car?"

"If you say so, *amigo*."

I sensed a creep of pride in Jorge's tone, and the reality of what had happened hit me hard in the chest. "Officers Connor and Mason knew the weapon was in the glove compartment before they pulled him over for that bullshit traffic violation. It was all a setup."

"Officer Connor was aware. Officer Mason, may her soul rest in peace, was not, but she was in love with Connor, so she did as instructed. The heart is never rational, is it, Mitch?"

"So, you paid Connor off? Bribed him, whatever?"

"Connor has expensive tastes, and his wife is filing for divorce — which, in California, I've heard, can be very expensive. Officer Connor was open to a substantial financial arrangement to help him through his struggles."

"How could you be sure the verdict would go against Paco?"

"We could never be sure. That is why we had a backup plan."

Another loud clang against the dumpster walls. "The laptop. If Paco didn't stand trial, then you'd use the laptop to blackmail him?"

"After the suppression of evidence hearing ended unfavorably, we switched to Plan B."

As I processed the information, the Captain took a deep breath. "But that is the past. The question is, how will you atone for your sins? I recommend confession. They say it is very good for the soul. As a devout Catholic, I believe it is so. I visit my priest every week to confess my sins, and my burdens are lifted."

"Yeah, good for you. I'm sure that's reserved you a front-row seat next to the big guy when the time comes."

"I have faith, Mitch. Faith that God sees all and forgives all."

He stepped closer; close enough that my nostrils twitched at the smell of his cheap cologne. "I expect you handed over the footage to the FBI, hoping they would protect you and your family. A noble gesture, but ultimately worthless. Cooperating with me is the only way to protect your family."

"Wait," I said. "This makes no sense. When the FBI gets the footage, they'll figure out how to tie it back to Paco. You don't need to threaten my family. Let the FBI do what you couldn't."

"And leave my fate in the hands of the American justice system? Didn't work out so well for me the last time," he said with a shake of his head. "My concern, and the organization's concern, is that Paco will take the coward's way and sell out his colleagues for his freedom. That would be a very big problem. I cannot allow that kind of deal to happen. Do we understand each other?"

The Captain looked over at Jorge, who tapped the handle of his Glock.

"You want to kill Paco before he's arrested? Didn't you just say—"

"A smart businessman must always be prepared to pivot. Of course, it is not so easy to get close enough to Paco, and his home is very well protected."

"You're serious?"

"Deadly serious," he said, a menacing smile blooming. "I expect you have made a deal of your own and intend to deliver Paco the footage, after which point he will be arrested? Correct?"

He was half right. Handing the footage over was one thing; proving it belonged to Paco was another entirely. As I protested, the Captain held out his palm.

"No, please, do not insult me. Now is the time you tell me when and where you intend to hand over the footage to Paco. Do that, and I set your family free. A generous deal, no?"

"Generous?"

"I am not an unreasonable man. Tell me what I need to know, and Jorge and I will take care of the rest. And before you decide to lie or tell me this is a story invented for my own entertainment, know that I have instructed my crew that your family should not be harmed for the next forty-eight hours. If the crew fails to hear from me after that time, then . . . well, I don't need to paint you a picture, do I?"

He paused and tapped my temple. "I am sure in here you are painting enough pictures of your own, huh?"

I nodded dumbly.

"Good," he said, stepping back. "Now, tell me about this deal you made with the FBI. Time you made amends to your family, don't you think, Mitch?"

CHAPTER 46

I talked. Spilled my guts like a child caught with his sweaty hand stuck in the cookie jar. The Captain analyzed every word as I outlined the plan we'd negotiated with Landry and Finley earlier that day.

We were to hand over the flash drive at Paco's office in the Port of Oakland the following night at 7 p.m. Victor had insisted we go alone, no FBI agents lurking in the shadows. He'd also nixed the idea of us wearing any kind of recording device. Victor had noticed Paco seemed more paranoid than usual as he prepared to fly to London for Charlotte's funeral, and he suspected a thorough pat-down at the port.

While we'd hashed out the deal, the FBI had made a copy of the footage. Their tech nerds would spend the next few days passing a fine-tooth comb through the contents for any clues that tied back to Paco. They'd also smuggled a software program into the original flash drive that would log Paco's every keystroke and track his location the second he inserted the drive into a computer. In return, Landry had agreed to have his contact in Sayulita send out an alert for two American citizens who were possibly in danger. I gave him my mother-in-law's address and a photo of Sierra and Kurt to send on, but with no actual crime to report, he doubted the Municipal *Policia* would move with any speed or urgency.

"Remember, they're under no obligation to do a damn thing," he'd said. "But I did inform them it was in their best interests to cooperate and promised them a share of the glory if we put this fucker away. I can't rule out the possibility Paco's paid off a bunch of law enforcement officers over there, so I'd guess their motivation levels are close to zero. On the flip side, you spoke to your family this morning, and they seemed fine; take that as good news. Just don't get your hopes up."

But my hopes had been up, elevated more than they had been in weeks. The plan had given me some relief, but after having my throat crushed at my apartment, Landry's words had carried about as much weight and authority as a three-dollar bill.

The night after Jorge and the Captain had left, I'd reached for the closest comfort to hand, a single malt Scotch, and threw back a couple of shots while weighing up my limited options. I was in major panic mode, pacing the apartment like some sweat-soaked addict who was sure he'd hidden the last of his stash down the back of the couch. That old itch to flip open my laptop and roll the dice on an online wager came on thick and fast. I chased the demon away with more Scotch and maxed the volume on the Beastie Boys' "Paul's Boutique" until the dense breakbeats and drum loops were all I could hear; all I wanted to hear. Anything was better than listening to the incessant voice whispering in my ear, assigning blame, telling me I should have never agreed to Paco's offer, should have walked away, should have taken the beating from Errol Capriani for the money I owed him; it couldn't have hurt any more than the pain I was feeling right then. Several times, I reached for my cell phone, intending to call someone — Victor, the FBI, maybe even warn Paco, but I knew by calling any of them, I'd have signed my family's death sentence.

* * *

The following day, I turned up for work a pale shadow of my usual self, throat aching, eyes bloodshot from another sleepless night. I'd spent most of the morning gazing off into the vast, untamed wilderness of my imagination, playing out terrifying scenarios about how things might go down at the handover. Would the Captain turn up and kill Paco? Then kill Victor and me? Had Paco suspected a mutiny was brewing in his organization? My thoughts were spiraling into a soupy maelstrom when I received a call from Judge Harper Griffin's office requesting my presence.

"When? Now; now would be a good time, Mr. Sweeney," the judge's secretary said, hanging up before I could respond.

Five minutes later, I stood at the Judge's door, shifting from foot to foot like a naughty schoolboy awaiting his punishment. The judge looked up from his desk and gestured I should sit.

"Mr. Sweeney," he said, a thin smile puckering his face. "Tell me, do you make a habit of talking to reporters about matters of the court?"

Confused, I said, "Erm, I'm not sure what—"

"Cut the bullshit. I've no time for it," he said, turning that rictus smile upside down. "You know what else I don't have the time for? Third-division local journalists poking a finger up my ass like I'm a ventriloquist's dummy, hoping I'll talk."

"Doesn't sound too pleasant, your honor."

"Pleasant?" He coughed, his chest rattling like bones across an iron cage — I guessed that was the cancer talking. "Damned intrusive is what it is. A violation," he said, wrestling his coughing fit under control. "And since you seem to have set this damned rectal probe in motion, now would be a good time to explain yourself. Javier Madrigal, you know him, correct?"

"I met him once at a party."

"Really. He informed me you two were firm friends."

My fists clenched. Madrigal was going all out to push my buttons, shake the justice tree to see what fell out. "You know what reporters are like, your honor; they'll pretend they're best friends with the devil if it gets them a byline. Can I ask what this is about?"

The judge humphed, a shine of sweat forming on his forehead. "The obnoxious turd seems to be under the delusion I'm covering up for some scandal at the Superior Court. Wanted a comment."

"Did you . . . comment?"

"Of course I damn well didn't. What do you take me for?"

"Apologies. I was just—"

The judge sprang to his feet with a nimbleness I'd have expected from a man half his size, stood by the window, and took in a lungful of air. "Madrigal insists someone in the Superior Court provided him with, what did he call it, a hand grenade? And he was extending me the courtesy of commenting before he pulled the pin."

"Sounds like the kind of melodramatic bullshit he'd say. Did he tell you who gave him this misinformation?"

"He implied he'd spoken to a senior member of the Superior Court, and what with your wife being a reporter on the same paper as this bottom feeder, I—"

"You thought I'd said something to Sierra, and she told Madrigal? Didn't happen, your honor."

"And your research team? Any of them caught loose lip syndrome?"

"They're loyal. They wouldn't put their jobs on the line for some half-assed rumor."

"Well, someone's been singing like a canary down a coal mine. Doesn't bode well for the court's reputation."

"Depends."

"On what?"

"If Madrigal even has a story. Could be he's trying to rattle your cage. This might all be one big non-event, a fishing expedition."

The judge shrugged. "Makes no difference if it's true or not, optics are what count these days. We're already under scrutiny from the bean counters in Sacramento. A story, even if it's half-assed, is only going to get them all hot and bothered for an investigation."

"If there's no substance and someone's handed Madrigal a bunch of BS, then I'd say you've got nothing to worry about."

The judge's right eye twitched like a fly had landed in the cornea. "I'm not worried, Sweeney; damned irritated is what I am."

"That's what Madrigal does best: irritate people. I wouldn't take it personally." I stood, eager to leave. "Anything else, your honor?"

The judge's face turned a darker shade of purple as he tried to speak; whatever brand of cancer was ravaging his body had taken another stab. He stood and leaned a hand against the window, coughing for a solid minute, his whole body rattling with the force. I reached to his desk and handed him a glass of water. He gulped it down, the liquid spilling onto his shirtfront.

Steadying himself against the window, he recoiled like a vampire who'd stayed up well past his bedtime, the harsh sunlight seeming to wash away his strength. I figured at this late stage, the cancer had nothing much left to feast on, quickening its own demise as it ravaged what remained of Judge Harper's insides.

I felt a pang of sympathy for the man; you wouldn't wish that kind of death for your worst enemy. But, if what Javier Madrigal had said was true, and the judge had been in Paco Castillo's pocket from the start, I hoped the cancer would hold back its final assault long enough to allow me the pleasure of witnessing Griffin Harper standing on the wrong side of the bench and answering for his crimes.

PART 8:
ONE GOOD DEED

CHAPTER 47

Guilt is lazy. Fear is an overachiever.

Guilt is the noose around your neck, the knot in your chest, the sour, sick feeling leaking through your stomach wall. Guilt kicks you when you're down, extends you the liberty to get to your feet long enough so it can inflict another beating. Guilt settles in for the duration, like an unwelcome house guest who refuses to leave.

Fear is the opposite; keeps you guessing, leaps out of the shadows like a mechanical monster in the ghost train ride. Fear is always on the make, a snake oil salesman looking to fleece you of your wits and sanity. Fear won't rest until it reduces you to a quivering wreck on the kitchen floor; then, as a reminder its work here is still not done, shoves its big fat boot in your face just for the hell of it.

When I woke up on the morning of the handover, both fear and guilt lingered at the foot of my bed like concerned relatives waiting for me to open my eyes. They'd chased me through the dark, lonely hours until, exhausted, I'd managed to steal from them a couple of hours of sleep.

I walked from my apartment toward uptown and sat inside one of those sterile, six-bucks-a-cappuccino coffee shops where I'd arranged to meet Judge Croft and retrieve the copy of the flash drive containing Darlene Mason's confession.

"So, you're finally ready to lay all this to rest?" the judge said, placing the thumb drive onto the table.

"Figured it was about time." I turned the device over in my palm and stared at the small yellow-and-chrome object. It weighed barely an ounce, but the gravity of its contents had consequences that stretched far beyond the binary of ones and zeros held inside.

"Having second thoughts?" she asked, noticing my attention drifting.

"Just sensing things are coming to a head."

"Well, that's a good feeling, isn't it, closure? You'll be helping get one more corrupt officer off the streets. You should be proud of that."

Proud? The judge's words were salt rubbed into a fresh paper cut. "Closure if things go the way I hope they will."

"Are we still talking about Officer Connor here, or something else?"

I shuffled. "Yes, of course, Connor. What else would there be?"

She paused and sipped her coffee. "How was your trip to Mexico?"

Her question confused me for a moment.

"To visit your family?"

I quickly remembered this was another one of my lies. I'd begun to lose track. "Erm . . . it was good to see them," I muttered. "They're staying a while longer. Kurt's having a ball; I don't want to drag him back just yet."

Setting her cup on the table, the judge's voice softened. "You know, when you've been a judge as long as I have, you get a sixth sense about people. When they might be lying, if they're itching to confess something . . ."

"Nothing to confess," I said, more cheerfully than I intended. "Just, you know, the usual life stuff."

The judge narrowed her eyes. "There, the way you overcompensated just then? That tells me you're covering something up, something you'd rather not tell me, so you mask it with a smile, hoping I'll let it go." She lowered her voice. "Look, I'm not one to pry. We're all entitled to our secrets, but if you sent your family to Mexico to protect them until all this is over, then that's commendable. Is that why you sent them? You were afraid Officer Connor would retaliate if he knew you had Officer Mason's confession?"

My chest tightened as if someone had lassoed a wire noose around it. I had a burning urge to leave, get some air, and avoid Judge Croft's questions, which poked too close to an open nerve. "I'm sorry." I stood up abruptly. "I've taken up too much of your time."

"Wait . . . just a moment, please," she said, gesturing I should sit my ass back down. "I heard Judge Harper summoned you to his office yesterday."

I eased back into my seat. "How—?"

"Buy the judge's secretaries a nice lunch, and they're more than happy to divulge. Did he quiz you about that journalist, Javier Madrigal?"

"How do you know Madrigal?"

Judge Croft settled her forearms on the table and wove her fingers together. "I approached Madrigal some weeks ago."

"Don't you mean he approached you?"

"No, Mr. Sweeney, I most certainly approached him."

She let the words linger long enough for me to absorb their full implications. I lowered my voice. "You're the senior court official—?"

"I'm only telling you this because you're the one who came to me with information that confirmed what I'd suspected for some time. It goes without saying that this conversation travels no further than this table."

"Understood. So, when I met you that night, you'd already leaked the story to Madrigal?"

"What you told me encouraged me to dig deeper, but my hands were tied. I couldn't research any further without Harper becoming suspicious or someone tipping him off."

"So, you had Madrigal do the legwork?"

"Much cleaner that way. I couldn't trust any of the senior staff at the paper, and Madrigal fitted the bill. He'd only worked there a few months. Getting the exclusive on a potential scandal at the Alameda Superior Court was too tempting to refuse. I have to give him credit; he's the one who uncovered the connection between Paco Castillo and Judge Harper."

Leaning back, I wiped a clammy hand across my face.

"I know it's a lot to take in, but you understand why I couldn't tell you sooner."

"Did you encourage Madrigal to reach out to Harper?"

A smidge of a smile crossed her face. "I'd liked to have been a fly on the wall when he got that call."

"But why alert him to the story?"

"To put Harper on the defensive, of course. Guilty people get sloppy when they think the net's closing in, and try to cover their tracks. I expect Harper to do the same. When he does, we'll be ready for him."

"Who's we?"

"That's one piece of information I'm afraid I can't disclose. All I can say is this goes deeper than Judge Harper."

"How much deeper?"

"You can trust me; nothing's getting swept under the carpet here."

Judge Croft finished her coffee and slipped on her sunglasses. "I've always admired the work you and your team do for the courts, Mr. Sweeney. We could do with more principled lawyers like yourself in the judicial system."

Admirable? Principled? The specter of guilt rose again, this time standing behind me, twisting the noose so tight around my throat that all I could offer the judge in return was a weak grunt.

"So, what's next for you, Mr. Sweeney?"

I took a large breath of air. "A delivery," I said, slipping the flash drive into my pocket. "One I'm not much looking forward to."

CHAPTER 48

Max Hale ushered me from the reception at the Alameda District Attorney's Office and gestured I should follow him. As he walked, he shook a plastic container full of salad like he was playing the maracas. He opened a conference room door and instructed me to sit.

"This going to take long?" he said, ripping the lid off his salad. "This is my lunch break, and I've got caseloads coming out of my ass." I couldn't argue with the man's stress levels: dark circles bloomed like coffee stains under his eyes, and his right leg bounced like a piston under the table.

I gestured at the mountain of green he was poking at with little enthusiasm. "So much for the glamorous life of public prosecution."

"Glamorous? Sure," he said, shoving a forkful of lettuce into his mouth. "Now, why are you here? More expert witness testimony that gets another murdering asshole off from facing trial?"

"Suspected murderer. As far as I know, Paco Castillo's only ever been in front of a judge for a bogus traffic infraction."

Hale smirked, a wedge of bright greenery stuck in his front teeth. "No thanks to you and Santiago."

I was about to shoot my mouth off with a glib comment about the DA's own aversion to prosecuting, but I needed Hale on my side. I set the flash drive on the table.

"What's this? We swapping music downloads? Very early 2000s, Sweeney. You got a box set of DVDs to go with that?"

"Funny, but trust me, you'll want to hear this."

He dug the errant shred of lettuce from his teeth. "Sure. Why the fuck not." He shoved his salad to the side of the desk. "This tastes like shit in a box, anyway."

I settled into my chair and explained about Connor and Mason playing bumper cars with my bike and using my home as a shooting gallery. For maximum effect, I left out Darlene Mason's confession until the end.

After a moment's consideration, Hale picked up the flash drive. "Are you sure Mason's confession implicates Officer Connor?"

"Slam dunk for a prosecution, I'd say . . . once you decide which hearsay exception you want to use."

He laid the drive on the table. "This is an OPD disciplinary matter. Shouldn't you be bugging them about this?"

"Let's just say I'd prefer the anonymity."

"But I presume your voice is all over that recording?"

I nodded. "Which is why I'm asking you to hand it into the OPD for me."

"And why would I do that?"

"Because, Hale, if I take it to the OPD, there's every chance it ends up lost in the evidence room or used as target practice at the shooting range. If the DA's office hands it in, there's an official record. Less chance it accidentally gets mislaid on its journey to where it's meant to be."

"You really don't trust the police, do you, Sweeney?"

"I trust some. At the moment, I'm just not sure which ones."

"I'll see what I can do. Not that this makes up for what happened in the courtroom." Hale pointed the flash drive in my face. "Between you and Santiago, you made me look like a fucking amateur in there."

"You were outplayed. Take it as a learning experience. This is a chance for you to redeem yourself."

He huffed. "What? You want a big fat thank you and a pat on the back?"

"Just looking for justice and put a corrupt cop behind bars. Figured you'd want the same."

* * *

Later that afternoon, I met up with Victor at a Cuban coffee shop overlooking Lake Merritt. I was early and grabbed a table on the patio. The sunlight was glorious, reflecting off the lake water in bright sparkles, and thin wisps of clouds drifted nowhere in the endless blue. I closed my eyes. The sun fell warm on my face, and for a few precious seconds, everything felt normal, like I'd open my eyes and Sierra and Kurt would be sitting across from me like the past three weeks had never happened.

"Not disturbing your siesta are we, *amigo*?"

We? Rudely shaken from my fantasy, I opened my eyes. Victor stood before me dressed in cream chinos and an expensive-looking white polo shirt. Next to him stood Alma Torres, decked out in black cargo pants and a black, cap-sleeved Motörhead T-shirt; I had to assume this was an ironic statement, but with Alma, I could never be sure. They looked like opposing pieces on a chessboard. They both sat. Victor ordered three Cuban coffees from the server.

"Glad you made it out of Palm Springs okay," I said, gesturing at the scratch on Alma's forehead. I couldn't believe that it had only been three days since we were chased like wolves through the desert.

Alma shrugged. "Yeah, like, obviously."

"And Betsy?"

Alma diverted her gaze to a couple of kids riding their BMX bikes at the cross street. "Yeah, she's good," she mumbled, blushing. "Gonna come up to the Bay Area to visit, you know, after her pop's funeral and all."

I raised my eyebrows.

"She needs a change of scenery after all that happened. Friends is all," she said, nodding, as if convincing herself.

"Sure," I said, looking over at Victor, who shrugged. "Friends."

"The fam all good?" Alma asked, eager to shift the spotlight.

"Yeah. Spoke to them both yesterday," I mumbled. Another half-lie that made me despise myself even more and turned the screws tighter on the guilt.

Our coffees arrived, and we waited for the server to leave before resuming our conversation.

Victor raised his cup. "To finally putting shit to rest."

"Fuckin' A," Alma agreed. She took a sip of coffee and spat it back into the cup. "What the—?"

"Finest Cuban coffee in town," Victor said.

Alma set down the tiny cup and wiped her mouth with her sleeve. "Boss, I love working for you and all, but what the fuck is this?"

"Takes a refined palate to appreciate its flavor."

"Yeah? Gotta tell you, my palate's never getting used to the taste of ass."

"Look," I said, my impatience getting the better of me. "Hate to interrupt your coffee chat, but we've got serious shit to discuss."

"Yeah, sorry," Victor said. "You're probably anxious."

"And you're not?"

"Yeah, of course. But look, we hand over the drive, and if the FBI does its job, we both get out from under Paco's thumb.

He'll be arrested and ask me to defend him in court, which I'll do, but with the weight of all that evidence, he's going away for a long time, even if he cuts a deal. Either way, he's done running the organization."

"Then someone else takes over. Carries on the work."

"That, *amigo*, is the kind of shit we have no control over. You can't go there."

I shook my head. "You think it'll be that easy, we just walk away? What if Paco suspects we sold him out to the Feds?"

"He can suspect all he wants, but he won't find any proof. Plus, he'll be in custody; not much he can do."

Alma took another sip of coffee, winced, and slid the cup an arm's-length away. "He doesn't sound like the kind of dude who needs proof before acting."

"Thanks for the reassurance, Alma, glad you're here."

"Yeah, me too, bro," she said, patting my shoulder. "For real."

I turned to Victor. "Have you thought through all the shit that could go wrong tonight?"

"That's what I pay Alma for. Extra set of eyes in case shit goes south."

I shot Alma a look. "Are you expecting shit to go south?"

She leaned back. "If you want my opinion, there's a lot of risk here. Get the Feds in as backup."

"Not going to happen," Victor said. "If Paco finds out—"

"Boss, you know I wouldn't usually give those fucks the time of day, but Paco's unpredictable; you gotta have backup."

"Victor's right." I said. "Paco can never know we sold him out to the FBI."

"Just sayin' you're compounding the risk, is all. But if you don't want to hear it, then your funeral."

"No FBI," Victor insisted. "Look, this time tomorrow, this mess will be behind us and we all get on with our lives."

This time tomorrow, my family could be dead, I thought, but kept it to myself. If there was any hope of saving Sierra and Kurt, I owed it to them to do exactly as the Captain had said: follow through with the plan to meet Paco like everything was situation normal.

Victor looked at the lake and shook his head. "I'll never forgive myself for getting you involved, Mitch. It wasn't meant to end this way."

Whatever guilt Victor was feeling, I felt its weight ten times heavier. "Look, Vic, maybe you should sit this out. Let me hand over the drive, you don't need to be there."

That was the guilt talking. Now that the Captain knew the time and location of the handover, my gut told me something terrible would go down, and despite Victor having got me involved in this whole shit show to begin with, he didn't deserve to be caught in the crossfire of whatever the Captain had planned.

"Are you shitting me?"

"I can handle this."

Victor leaned forward. "Paco's expecting me. It'll look suspicious if I don't turn up. He'll know something's off."

"I just figure the fewer people, the better."

"Then I'll come with," Alma said.

"Not going to happen," Victor said. "Paco gets spooked with new people."

"I'll observe from a distance, get the Feds on speed dial, just in case."

"Too risky."

Alma crossed her arms across her chest and nudged her chin at me. "I saved his sorry lawyer ass once already. If you ask me, the dude's a liability. He should be the one sitting this out."

"You do know I'm sitting here, right?"

"Yeah, like, of course," she said, missing my point. "But if you don't need me, I got enough other shit to do." She shoved her coffee cup toward Victor. "All yours, I need some real java. I passed a Dunkin' on the way. And just for the record, I think this is all bullshit. Just sayin'."

As Alma sprinted across the road to her truck, Victor turned to me. "When were you going to tell me about McKay?"

"Alma?"

He nodded.

"I didn't tell you or Paco because I didn't want her dragged into all this. She's good people, helped me out twice, no questions asked."

"How did Charlotte know her?"

I debated how to pitch my answer, then figured Victor had a right to know. I told him what McKay had told me.

"Half-sister? Charlotte never said."

"She was protecting McKay, that's all."

"Well, thanks for telling me, I guess," he said, downing the rest of his coffee. "Not holding out on anything else, are you? Because if you are, now would be the right time to spill."

I sensed that vicious duo of fear and guilt rearing their ugly heads, wringing their hands and grinning at me with a twinkle in their callous eyes.

"Nothing more to tell, Vic. You know everything I know."

CHAPTER 49

Six p.m. on the evening of the handover, I stood on my apartment balcony watching the good people of the world go about their business as the sunlight faded like a long-forgiven lie behind the San Francisco skyline.

My phone buzzed in my back pocket. I didn't recognize the number. A faint hope lingered that it was the Captain calling to allow me the privilege of speaking to my family. That fantasy was quickly kicked to the curb. This was a woman's voice, older, smoker's rasp. Rock music and the clanking of pool balls rumbled in the background as she spoke in an irritable tone that insinuated I was the one who had called and disturbed her evening.

"This Mitch Sweeney?"

"Who is this?"

"Name's Marge, I own McNally's on 40th, you know it?"

"Erm, no."

"You don't?" She sounded surprised. "Well, guess you better take down the address and haul ass down here before I call the police."

"The police? Are you sure you've got the right number?"

"I'm sure. Unless you got another Mitch Sweeney who's a giant asshole — not my words — and works at the Alameda courthouse?"

"Sorry, how did you get my number?"

Marge sighed, suggesting she'd endured several decades of making similar calls. "Got a barfly who keeps shouting his mouth off, says he's gonna kill some guy. Don't know if that's just the booze talking, but I'm not taking any chances. Gave me your number."

"Did he give a name?" Though, in the back of my mind, I suspected the identity of this barfly.

Marge hollered across the noise. "Hey, bozo, what's your name again?" She paused. "Right, got it . . . says his name's Ron." Another pause. "And I'm to tell you, you're still a giant asshole."

I mouthed a silent *fuck*. *Not tonight, Ron, of all nights.*

"Hey, you still there?"

"Yeah, yeah, I'm here. Look, can't you call him a cab? I'll pay."

"A cab? Now, you're mistaking me for one of those heart-of-gold bartenders you see in the movies. I'm too jaded and way too busy for that good Samaritan shit."

"Fine, my mistake. I'll call him an Uber."

Marge cackled her laugh a brittle snap of dried twigs. "Let me tell you, hon, no driver this side of the Bay is picking up this hot mess. The guy's already turned my restrooms into a biohazard, which I'm now gonna have to clean up, like I don't have enough to deal with."

I mouthed another silent *fuck*. "I can call his wife," I said, then realized I had no idea of Ron's home number. "Actually, I don't have her number."

"Well, looks like it's your lucky night."

"Marge, I can't do this right now. Can you look after him for a couple more hours, give him some coffee, let him sleep it off?"

"Coffee and a bed? What am I, his wife, now?"

"No, I—"

"Listen, hon," Marge interrupted. "I don't know you from Adam, but if you don't come pick up this sad sack, I'm gonna have to call the police. Don't think he means any harm, but he needs to get the hell out of my bar. I hate calling the cops on old guys tearing one up. We all gotta let off some steam once in a while, but if you're not here in twenty, OPD gets an emergency call. Now, do you need the address, or can you find it all on your lonesome?"

* * *

McNally's Pub, 6:17 p.m. The bar had seen better days; bashed up Seeburg jukebox in the corner, torn red upholstery, and the clientele, mostly older men, hunched over the wooden bar like they were deep in prayer.

"Marge?" I asked, walking over to the woman pouring a bourbon.

She looked up. "Over there," she said, nodding to her left.

Ron sat in the corner, chin slumped on his chest, drool trickling from his mouth. He looked like he'd been dragged through a blackberry bush by his ankles, hair plastered flat on his forehead, damp patches on his shirt, suit jacket folded onto his lap.

I headed over and shook him by the shoulder. "Ron, hey, buddy."

He opened his eyes and scrunched his face, as if trying to make out who I was. Smiling, he raised the middle finger of his right hand as if reaching out to make sure I wasn't some drunken illusion, then turned his finger around and stuck it proudly in my face. "Fuck you, Sweeney, fuck you!"

"Good to see you too, Ron."

"What you doin' here?"

"Come to take you home."

He looked at his shirt and mumbled. "Nah. Don't wanna go home."

I checked my watch. I needed Ron out of there fast, but the man wasn't in a rush to go anywhere. Figuring the situation required some finesse and patience, I sat. "Look, what's going on here, Ron? Is this about Masie? I already told you that's a bad road to travel. It doesn't end anyplace good."

He shook his head. "Masie . . . sweetest kid you ever met, swear to God, Mitch, the sweetest. Whole life ahead of her." A darkness filled his eyes like a storm cloud had settled over them. "Then that asshole, Castillo, puts an end to all that, even sends flowers to her funeral. You know why he did that? I'll tell you why, because he's guilty as sin, that's why." He clenched his fist and rapped it hard on the table. The whole bar turned. "Guilty as fucking sin."

Marge glared at me, phone in her hand. I got the message.

"We've been over this, Ron. Now, let's get you home, huh?" I said, wrapping an arm around his bulky shoulders, hoping to shift him toward the door.

He shrugged me off and lowered his voice the way drunks do when they imagine they have some important insight to share. "I know where Castillo lives, you know that? Went over there this afternoon, see if I could get some answers."

"Jesus, Ron. Why the hell did you do that?"

He brought an index finger to his lips. "Shhh . . . between us boys," he said, slowly lifting the jacket on his lap. The neon lights from the jukebox reflected off the cold steel of the handgun like a mirror ball.

I reached down and flipped Ron's jacket back over what looked like a .22 mini revolver. "What the hell were you thinking? The man's got armed guards all over the place. You could have been killed."

His eyes gazed off someplace else. "Yeah, I know. Noticed some nasty types patrolling around the house. Don't think they saw me."

"You're pretty hard to miss, Ron."

He shrugged and leaned in close. "I'll tell you this, Sweeney, this is America. Folk shouldn't get away with murdering innocent people. Castillo's gotta pay for what he did. It's the law. I mean, there's gotta be justice. You see that, right?"

"Not with a gun, there doesn't have to be," I said. "Paco Castillo will pay for his crimes, I promise you. Now, let's get out of here, get you back home."

* * *

I'd finally, by 6:35 p.m., coaxed Ron out of the bar with a promise of hot food and a couch to sleep on before dropping him home. I think I got through to him, but that's the problem with drunks: they forget what they told you from one minute to the next, their minds distracted by the next shiny object that catches their attention.

He'd surrendered his weapon without a struggle. I was sure he'd never have used it, but I understood his logic. He felt powerless and desperate to wrestle back some control, do something other than waiting for the slow grind of the courts to bring Castillo to justice.

Easing Ron into the rear of my Saab, I shoved the revolver in the glove compartment while he folded his jacket into a pillow and laid across the back seat.

I ran some quick calculations. We were on 40th Street, a ten-minute drive from my apartment, then another ten-minute drive to the Port of Oakland for the handover. Adding an extra few minutes to get Ron settled, I figured the timing would be tight, and that was without accounting for the evening commuter traffic. Arriving late wasn't an option. The Captain needed to see everything was going to plan.

Ron groaned as I drove, asking me to slow the hell down. We were five minutes out from McNally's when Ron abruptly sat up.

"Think I'm gonna throw up."

"Jesus, can't you hold it for ten?"

He shook his head. "No. Gonna puke up all over your back seat."

I pulled into an empty parking space close to a trash can and dragged Ron onto the sidewalk in the nick of time. He set his palms on the edge of the trash can, did what he'd threatened to do all over my back seat, then, after he'd finished, sat himself down on the sidewalk, wiping his mouth with his shirtsleeve.

"We've got no time for this, Ron. We gotta go," I urged.

"Give me a minute here, buddy, okay?"

I checked my watch. "I don't have a minute,"

"What? You gotta hot date?"

"No, Ron, no date. Now, can we go?"

Ron observed his hands as if they were alien appendages he had just noticed were connected to his body.

"Ron, please," I pleaded.

He looked up, his eyes moist and bloodshot. "Five minutes. Would it kill ya?"

Yeah, it just might.

I took a breath and sat next to him on the curb. "Okay, five minutes."

"I'm getting too old for this," he said, shaking his head.

"You and me both."

"That's what they say, right? Getting old's gonna kill ya?"

"Yeah, a lot faster if you keep drinking like that."

"You sound like my wife."

"She's obviously a smart woman. You should listen to her."

He coughed and looked down at the sidewalk. "What you said earlier about Castillo getting what's coming? That true, or just a lie to get me out of there? No bullshit."

"True. I can't tell you how I know, but you've got to trust me on this."

"And Judge Harper? You got some secret inside information on that, too? Because that's not going away any time soon. I'll go to the press; don't think I won't."

"Like I told you before, let this play out. You running around with a loaded weapon and causing a scene in dive bars isn't solving a damn thing."

He patted my knee. "I've always liked you, Sweeney. You're one of the decent ones. Most people? Can't trust a damn thing they tell you these days, always got some hidden agenda. Not like the old days. You could trust a man's word when he gave it to you. Can't trust those management cocksuckers as far as I could spit 'em."

"Maybe it's time you retired, get out while you've still got a few good years ahead of you."

"Don't think I haven't been thinking on it. Jenny's on my case about it."

"Your wife?"

He nodded.

"She's got a point."

"Yeah, she's usually right about that stuff . . . I hate that." He paused. "What I said in the parking lot the other day when I took a swing at you, I didn't mean any of it, just the bile talking."

"I know."

He bunched his fists. "I had this anger, you know, it just kept boiling inside me. That wasn't me, and I gotta apologize for that. Weren't about you, either."

"No apology needed."

"No, hear me out. I know why you took the stand and told the truth. It was your job. I shouldn't have questioned that. You stood up for what was right. Wasn't my place to doubt you."

A knot wove around my throat as he spoke — guilt, that ever-present specter reminding me of its presence. If Ron had known what I'd put my family through in the last three weeks, I was sure his judgment wouldn't have been so generous.

"Five minutes is up, buddy." I stood and held out my arm. "We've got to go, and I've got someplace I need to be."

CHAPTER 50

The traffic backed up to the 12th Street exit on Highway 980. I confirmed the situation on my maps app. A thick, arterial line of red blocked the highway ahead and didn't resolve until five miles south of Oakland Airport. A choke of panic caught in my throat. I'd be lucky to make it to my apartment by seven, then another twenty-minute drive to the Celica Holdings office.

Short on options, I pulled left into a narrow gap in the traffic and cut over to 11th street to hit the surface streets. Ron was passed out, snoring like a warthog. I checked my arrival time. There was no time to drop him off at my apartment. By the state of him, I figured he'd be out for a few hours. Whether he liked it or not, Ron was coming with me.

I leadfooted the Saab, the wide streets and old buildings of West Oakland passing by me in a blur of gray and brown. When I finally arrived at the port two minutes after seven, I pulled up next to the shipping container closest to Paco's office. Victor had parked his SUV close by. He was leaning against the side panel, tapping his wristwatch, mouthing something which looked like *hurry the fuck up*.

Taking a moment to check my reflection in the rearview mirror, I was greeted by a ghost staring back at me; my eyes milky, cheeks drawn of color. I gripped the steering wheel to stop my hands from trembling and told myself to get my shit together. My one job, delivering the footage to Paco, was almost done. Whatever else the Captain had planned was beyond my control.

I checked on Ron, he was still passed out in the back seat. *Good, let's keep it that way, buddy, and we'll both be home before nightfall.*

* * *

As I stepped out, a chilly breeze billowed in from the Bay. The air felt tense, as if bracing for a coming storm, though the sky was cloudless and turning a similar violet color to the one I'd seen back in Palm Springs; I didn't take it as a good omen.

Walking toward Victor, it struck me how isolated we were out on this jut of land hovering above the water, just a few feet of concrete separating us from the inky black water of the Bay. No passing foot traffic, no witness to confirm or deny a damn thing that happened out here. I scanned the tops of the shipping containers in case the Captain had positioned himself close by. There was no sign of him, but that meant nothing; there were plenty of dark alleyways and blind corners where he could be lying in wait.

"Cutting it fine," Victor said, looking up from his watch. "Got the drive?"

"Of course, I've got the fucking drive. What kind of question is that?"

He put a hand on my shoulder. "Hey, relax, we got this, okay?"

I gestured to Paco's office. "Can we just go in and get this over with?"

Victor shook his head. "Paco wants us to wait here. He'll come to us."

That sparked an alarm in my gut. "Why not the office?"

"He didn't say. Maybe he's got some business meeting going on, or he likes the fresh air. Who cares? We're this close to getting all this over with."

I looked over to my car, checking Ron hadn't woken from his bourbon slumbers, and scanned the containers and dockside for any sign of the Captain. Other than the dull hum of traffic rolling over the Bay Bridge and the loud whomp of my heart beating, there were no other sounds: no screams of car engines, no burning of tire rubber, no rumble of FBI helicopter blades over the horizon.

"You expecting someone?" Victor asked, noticing my agitation.

"Anxious is all. Just want this over with and get the hell out of here."

"Amen to that, *amigo*."

A minute later, the door of Celica Holdings swung open, and Paco emerged wearing a suit and a large camel-colored overcoat, the hem lifting as the breeze picked up around him. I stiffened, clenched my fists tight, and noticed Victor had done the same. He was as anxious as I was; he'd just done a better job of hiding it.

Behind Paco followed the scrawny figure of Jorge shuffling in his downdraft, shoulders hunched, pulling hard on a cigarette before flicking it to the ground.

Jorge and Paco, together? My brain took a moment to calibrate the scene. For a second, I wondered if Jorge's allegiance with the Captain was some double cross, but then figured Jorge lacked the necessary smarts for that kind of deception: he was a follower, an opportunist who shuffled his allegiances like pieces around a checkerboard, depending who paid him the most or offered him the best protection.

Jorge stood to Paco's right and looked at me. He tapped his left hip, where I knew he kept his weapon tucked into his pant belt. The coded message was clear: *shoot your mouth off, and you don't make it out of here alive, and your family gets the same.* I nodded back, silently assuring him I understood.

"You want me to search these *pendejos*, boss?"

Paco glared at Jorge as if scolding a disobedient dog. "Search them? This is my lawyer, Jorge, and the man who has come to deliver good news."

"A precaution is all, boss. You know, after today . . ."

Paco took a moment. "Maybe you are right," he said. "These are unstable times." He turned to Victor and me. "Don't take it personally. My guards noticed someone watching my house earlier today. Probably nothing, but vigilance is a small price for peace of mind, correct, Victor?"

I was sure that someone was Ron Boone. I stole a quick glance over to my car to make sure he was still passed out in the backseat. There was no movement. I took that as a good sign.

"Sure," Victor agreed. "Can't be too careful."

Jorge stepped forward. He searched Victor first, then me, taking his time as he patted down my legs and under my jacket. He leaned close, his breath sour, and whispered, "Not a fucking word. Remember what you gotta lose, *amigo*."

The reminder was unnecessary. That loss was all I'd thought about for the past two days.

"All clear," Jorge said, stepping back.

"I would have us meet in my office, but the air is good out here, no? And the view?" Paco said, extending his arms and smiling. "Now, I assume you have the laptop?"

"Erm, not exactly." I reached into my jacket pocket.

Jorge's hand hovered over his right hip.

"The laptop was useless," I said, taking out the flash drive. "The pawnbroker's daughter wiped it clean before we got there."

Paco narrowed his eyes. "So, what do you have for me, Mitch?"

"Everything you need is on here."

Jorge stepped forward, snatched the drive, and handed it to Paco, who held it up to the light, studying the machine head design.

"Victor, can I be sure this is the only copy?"

"Mitch almost got himself killed getting this," Victor said. "We can show you the laptop, but it's wiped clean, like Mitch said. Charlotte paid the pawnbrokers to keep it safe."

"And what if they decide they want more money?"

Victor smiled and held out his upturned palms. "Paco, you really think some low-life hustlers out of Palm Springs are going to try to blackmail you? Trust me, this is the only copy."

Paco turned his attention to me. "How did you acquire the drive?"

"Betsy, the pawnbroker's daughter. She came into the store just after I found her father's body. She thought I'd shot him, then she threatened to kill me. After I talked her down, she told me Hetch had the laptop locked in a safe in the basement. I figured they both panicked when they found out about Charlotte's murder, and Betsy took the initiative to copy the drive and wipe the laptop clean."

"And she just handed it to you?"

"I explained to her the danger she was in, that she might be next on the hit list if she didn't get rid of it. She was happy to hand it over. Didn't want to end up like her father."

Paco slipped the drive into his jacket pocket. "Has this Betsy seen the contents of the drive?"

"She didn't mention," I lied.

He considered this, then spoke to Jorge. "If she copied the footage, then most likely she has seen it. We should make sure Betsy does not get the urge to . . . talk. Jorge?"

"I'll take care of it, boss."

Paco turned to Victor. "Have you seen the contents of this drive?"

"No," Victor said. "Plausible deniability, like we always agreed."

"And you?"

"I brought it straight back here," I said, my throat feeling as if it was filled with gravel as I coughed up another lie at Paco's feet. "Whatever's on there is your business. Honestly, I don't want to know. I just want this whole thing over and get on with my life."

Paco smiled and walked toward me. "Of course you do, Mitch," he said, placing his huge, cold palm against my cheek. It reminded me of the day I'd first met him outside the courtroom when he'd done the same, and it felt as if he could have crushed my skull with one hand.

"I think you are a good man, Mitch, but a terrible liar."

He reached into his jacket, slipped out the bronze .45 I'd last seen on his desk, and cradled it in his hands, studying the weapon as if debating how best to deploy it.

My body tensed like tripwire. I looked over at Victor, who was about to say something. Paco raised his hand and shook his head. He stepped closer, those dark, soulless eyes of his boring into me, his body seeming to take up all the space and air around me, a black hole sucking all life into its core.

"You know, I have never used this weapon in anger," he said, grazing the tip of the weapon under my chin. "But there is a first time for everything, no?"

CHAPTER 51

I held my breath, felt sure it would be my last, and prepared myself for the shot that never came. At least not in my direction.

Paco kept his eyes laser-fixed on mine, swung his arm like a mechanical crane, and aimed the gun one hundred and eighty degrees away from me.

Realizing he was Paco's target, Jorge whipped his hand down to his hip. The gesture was a finger length too slow and a micro-second too late.

Without looking at Jorge, Paco pulled the trigger.

The vibration from the shot echoed over the port's iron and steel with a dull clang before sinking deep into the bay. Spittle sprayed from Jorge's mouth as his neck snapped back, the right side of his head ripped open by the ballistic force of the .45, flesh torn from his skull in red-and-black clumps. A stream of blood arced upward and spat onto the ground in a shower of red.

For a moment, Jorge stayed motionless, his body reacting a couple of beats behind the trauma. A second later, his legs buckled. He fell back, his head smacking the cold concrete with a loud crack.

Victor and I looked at each other. I was sure he was having the same panicked thoughts as I was. *Did Paco know about the FBI? Were we the next to be executed? Is that why he wanted to meet out here and not in his office — less mess to clean up?* And, the one question I was wrestling to figure out: *How the hell had Paco found out about Jorge's betrayal?*

There was no time to dwell on this. Paco had lowered his weapon and, without looking back at Jorge's body, whistled toward the maze of shipping containers to our right.

Another of Paco's henchmen, one of the muscle brothers I'd seen at his trial, all shoulders and no neck, had a gun pressed into the small of a man's back as he urged him from the shadows into the light.

It took me a few seconds to recognize the pathetic figure staggering toward us.

The Captain was badly beaten, eyes swollen, fresh cuts bleeding onto his shirt collar, head bowed. Looking over at me, he threw me one of his trademark smiles, as calculated as ever, but marred by the crimson stains across his teeth and the blood seeping from a deep gash in his bottom lip.

Puffing out his chest and reaching for whatever meager reserves of bravado he had left, he eyeballed Paco, spat a glob of red phlegm at his feet, and then turned to me, his voice laden with grit. "You gonna tell him, *cabrón*, or you want me to?"

Paco grunted. "Enough talk. We settle this now, like men, eye to eye."

The henchman kicked the Captain in the small of his back, and he fell to his knees. Paco raised his gun and aimed it at the Captain's head.

A bolt of panic surged through me. Running on instinct, I stepped forward, blocking Paco's line of sight.

"Mitch!" Victor called out. "What the hell? Step the fuck away!"

"Paco!" I pleaded. "You don't need to do this. Talk it out, please. Just don't kill him."

The Captain laughed. "This gringo's more scared than me. Wanna tell the big boss why, Mitch?"

Paco ignored the remark and braced the .45 in his hand, his pitiless black eyes narrowing. "Mitch, I will give you one chance to move, then I will shoot. Understand?"

"No!" I snapped. I looked back and forth at both of them and raised my hands. "Don't do this. Think about it, Paco. Let him live, and he's in debt to you for the rest of his life. You can't buy that kind of loyalty. You see that, right?"

"Yeah," the Captain said, coughing. "The gringo's a fool, but he makes a good point."

I could tell Paco's patience was straining, that roiling volcano of anger reaching critical mass. He wasn't the type of man to back down when he had the upper hand, but I was playing for time, spouting anything that came to mind to stop him from killing the Captain and signing a death warrant for my family; twenty-four hours was about all the time I had left to make sure things didn't end in the worst way possible.

But Paco wasn't buying what I was selling. His arm stiffened, ready to take the shot. He was about to pull the trigger when a commotion close to where I'd parked my car distracted him. Craning my neck, I saw the disheveled figure of Ron Boone stumbling toward Paco, the .22 I'd shoved in the glove compartment trembling in his hands.

"Hey, Castillo!" Ron hollered. "You killed my niece. I'll be damned if I'm gonna stand by and watch you get away with murder. Ain't the way we do things here in America."

Paco adjusted his aim and leveled the .45 at Ron.

I stepped to my right, putting myself in the firing line of Paco's gun for the second time in a matter of seconds. It dawned on me this was nothing new. I'd put myself in the path of that bullet the second I agreed to his deal to pay my debt. It had just taken three weeks to fully manifest in flesh, blood, and steel.

I shouted, "Ron! Get back in the car. Now!"

He ignored my advice and staggered onwards, his shirt hanging like dirty laundry from his pants. His eyes held the same black cloud of anger I'd witnessed at the bar less than an hour before. Ron was still drunk, still hell-bent on some futile revenge.

"Who the fuck is this?" Paco said, then nodded at no-neck, who snatched his weapon around, aimed at Ron, looking at Paco for permission to shoot.

Seizing the thin moment of indecision, the Captain lunged forward, rolled across the concrete, grabbed the gun tucked in Jorge's belt, twisted around, and snapped the trigger. The force of the bullet ruptured the back of the henchman's head. He crumpled like tissue paper and face-planted in the dirt, blood pooling around his shoulders.

Paco was stuck in no-man's-land, Ron lurching toward him and waving the gun in a manner that suggested any bullet he fired would find its target anywhere within a hundred-foot radius, the Captain steadying his hands to fire another round.

Figuring Ron was the lesser threat, Paco spun around.

At the same time, the Captain leaned back and pulled the trigger.

The bullet plowed deep into Paco's shoulder.

Staggering, Paco returned fire. As he hit the ground, the gun slipped from his hand and scraped along the concrete, landing at the Captain's feet.

The Captain's body jerked back as the force of the .45 caliber bullet ripped his stomach open, sending his gun spinning out of his hands and landing several feet behind him. He looked down at the monsoon of blood flowing from his wound and muttered to himself something; maybe a prayer or some old Spanish curse. Summoning all the strength he had left, he picked up Paco's gun and fired a Hail Mary shot.

But Paco was already stumbling to the ground, clutching his shoulder, close to passing out from the pain.

The bullet whistled past him.

Behind me, I heard the dull thud of lead ripping through soft flesh. A sickening feeling infected my gut as I turned. Ron had taken the force of the Captain's bullet. He dropped to his knees like he'd been caught in a sniper's line of fire, then toppled forward onto the hard concrete.

My feet refused to move. Victor shouted something at me, but the voices competing for attention in my head drowned his words. *Do I tend to Ron or try to save the Captain?*

It was no contest. The Captain couldn't die. He needed to live long enough to make the call and release my family. But watching him press down on the wound that had ripped apart his stomach, that hope was fading as quickly as the life was fading from his eyes.

I shouted. "Vic, make sure Ron's okay."

Victor looked confused, but did as he was told and headed to Ron.

Paco had passed out from the pain and lay motionless on the ground, his thick chest rising and falling.

I had one last chance to save the Captain. I ran and knelt at his side. It didn't look good. His breathing was shallow and hurried, as if he imagined he could outpace death if he breathed fast enough. His wound was wider than I thought, and deeper, blood welling in thick red pools where the bullet had cleaved his guts. I removed my jacket and used as much downforce as I could to stop the bleeding, but I was losing the fight.

So was the Captain.

He looked up at me, bloodied and grotesque, like a carnival clown whose makeup was peeling from his face to reveal the true nature of the man underneath.

"Hey, I do you a last favor, huh, *cabrón*?" he said, his voice straining.

"No favors," I said, pressing harder on the wound. "Just stay alive. That's all you've got to do. Stay alive for me. You got that? Stay alive."

He shook his head. "I do not fear death. I made my peace with God a long time ago."

I grabbed his collar and shook him. "Don't you fucking say that! You'll make it. Come on now, don't fucking die on me! Don't you dare fucking die on me!"

He waved his hand dismissively. "Maybe I can do one last good deed for you, huh, *cabrón*?"

I stopped pressing down, a faint glitch of hope stirring in the darkness. "You'll call your men?" I said, almost choking on my words. "Do you have a phone?" In desperation, I rummaged around in his pockets, searching for his phone. "Where is it? Come on, where's your fucking phone?"

He coughed, blood spooling from the side of his mouth. "No phone," he said, his voice softening like a long fade out of a song. "Remember I told you when a man loses everything that matters the most in his life, then he is dead, too? Alive but not living?"

Before the implications of his words hit me, I heard the dull blast of a gunshot and felt the searing heat of the bullet rip through my left side, radiating pain through every nerve in my body.

I looked down at the torrent of blood flowing from my right side.

Darkness overcame me. I felt the concrete melt beneath me, and my bones turned to ice, as if the Bay itself was welcoming me in its cold embrace.

CHAPTER 52

A whoosh of sound, like a whisper lost in the wind.

Voices speaking low, anxious.

I peeled away the black curtain that had settled over me.

I was in the rear of a car, with another body pressed against mine. The body wasn't moving, but I could feel its warmth. My eyes flickered open and shut as if presenting the world to me through a zoetrope, giving the illusion of motion as I focused on what I imagined was a plane traversing the violet sky. Looking closer, I realized it was the body of an insect flattened to a window — wrong place, wrong time, and along for the ride.

The pain dug deep as I tried to sit up.

A voice called from the front seat. "Don't move. We'll get you to a hospital. Ten minutes, *amigo*, stay down, hang on, all right?"

That was Victor, but it didn't sound like him. He sounded hesitant, as if he was trying hard to convince himself as he spoke.

Another voice, this one closer, female. "You awake, dude?"

I nodded.

"Good. You know, if you'd listened to me in the first place and not done stupid shit like you did back there, I wouldn't have to save your ass . . . again."

Alma. She was leaning over from the front seat, both hands pressing hard on my side. I groaned.

"I know it hurts like a mother, but I gotta keep the pressure on," she said, then turned to Victor. "Can you step on the fucking gas there, boss?"

"The car's electric."

"Like it matters. Just speed the fuck up."

Another whir of sound as the car picked up speed.

I looked at the body to my right. "Ron?" I whispered, the words struggling to travel to my throat.

"That the dude's name? Yeah, doesn't look like he's going to make it. Friend of yours?"

"Why are you—?"

"Victor had me hide in the back seat in case shit went south. Which obviously it did, big time. You should have listened to me and told the Feds. I don't like those fucks, but they'd have stopped that bloodbath back there."

My mind spooled back the last few minutes at the dockside. "The Captain?" I muttered, trying to raise myself, but the strength was beaten out of me.

"Had to leave him behind. Figured he was done for. There's no coming back from a .45 in the stomach from that close."

"No! You don't understand," I said, a spurt of adrenaline kicking in. "He can't die, he can't!"

"Yeah, hate to tell you, but no such thing as 'can't die'," Alma said, leaning down hard on my wound.

I felt tired again, like a wave had hit me and dragged me into its undertow.

"No, you don't understand. Sierra, Kurt . . ."

"They weren't there, just you and Victor. Your family's safe."

"They're not safe, they're not safe. The Captain, the boat, he's got to call his crew . . . fuck!" I felt the adrenaline subside, leaving me drained.

"Just shut the fuck up and lie back down. And don't go to sleep, you got that? Do not go the fuck asleep."

"No, no, you don't get it," I insisted, my voice seeming to come from deep underwater. "Mexico. I've got to get to Mexico now, the next plane. We have to go to the airport . . . now. Twenty-four hours. Twenty-four hours . . ." I sensed my voice weakening, fading into the distance like an echo.

"Mexico, sure, Mitch, we'll get you to Mexico," Alma said. "A vacation with the fam sounds good. You hold on to that thought, all right? Hold on to it. But first, we gotta get you to the emergency room, get you fixed up. Got that?"

I wanted to protest and tell Alma how much she didn't understand, how much she didn't know about the Captain and how desperate I was to take the next flight to Mexico. But I couldn't find the words. They'd lodged themselves deep in my memory dumpster along with all the other detritus of my life.

As my world gradually collapsed into blackness again, I watched the insect flattened to the window somehow unfurl itself from the glass, extend its silver wings, flutter off, and lose itself in the fading light of the evening.

PART 9:
BE DONE OR BE A MASTER

CHAPTER 53

The car alarm persisted with its one-note serenade, signaling the same indecipherable message in sharp blips. It grew louder as if it were right next to me, its tone matching my heart's pulse, beat for beat.

Forcing my mind to rewind, I retraced my steps from downtown La Cruz to the marina and tried to arrange the shards of memory into a coherent narrative. Two men laying wagers outside a bar. An anxious white horse scraping its hoof along the dirt. The smell of diesel and brine as I clambered down the harbor ladder onto the jetty. Creeping across the deck of the *Gordo Loco* and checking my weapon before entering the Captain's stateroom. Two bodies, throats slit, lying on the bed, the walls covered in wet vermilion, the nauseating rise of bile clogging my throat. Falling knee-bound on the deck, a bright white light, the cocking of a gun — cold metal striking cold metal — the overwhelming smell of menthol, a familiar voice urging me to talk, tell him everything.

My eyes fluttered open like the hesitant whirl of a projector, the film looping through the sprockets.

Clearly, I was no longer in La Cruz. Maybe I'd never been to La Cruz. But that logic didn't track. I'd traveled there after the bloodbath at the dockside. Victor had dropped me off at the airport, where I'd boarded the next flight to Puerto Vallarta. Then again, part of my brain knew that was impossible, or maybe some memories were real and others figments of my imagination. But the car alarm? That had to be real. I could still hear the same monotonous tone that had followed me like a shadow.

The gruff voice I'd heard on the deck of *Gordo Loco* spoke. "Mitch, can you hear me?"

As my world reconstructed itself, I made a quick mental checklist of what I knew to be true.

I was still alive. True.

My body hurt like all hell. True.

I was no longer in Mexico. True.

The car alarm wasn't a car alarm. Probably true.

My family was still in danger. Definitely true.

The voice wanted to help me and had my best interests at heart. Most definitely false.

Turning, I focused on the blinking lights at my beside. The machine's incessant beeping filled the air around me, just like it had when I first heard it as I trudged the dusty streets of La Cruz.

I shifted my gaze to the front of the room. Bright morning sunshine streamed through the large window in swathes of white.

To my right, another cocking of a gun. I tensed. My instincts told me to run, but I lacked the strength and the will to move.

That voice again. "Never one for taking good advice when it's given, were you, Sweeney?"

A pinch of recognition puckered my brain. Landor? Landry? An FBI agent? That made sense: broken nose, bad attitude, suspicious eyes. I felt his breath on me, the menthol smell of the mints he constantly chewed on, turning my stomach.

"Best you take it easy, Mitch. Tell me everything . . . that is, if you want to see your wife and son again."

Another cocking of a gun. Panic shuddered through me. I grabbed at the arteries of tubes extending from my body. Landry took my wrists.

"Easy there, buddy. You're not going anywhere. If you're strong enough, we can talk, nice and easy. Finley will take notes, so everything's on the record."

Another cock of the gun. I looked at the woman stood behind Landry. I remembered her too; Finley, short, intelligent eyes, annoying habit of clicking her pen like she was keeping the beat. The clicking timed perfectly with the sound of the gun's cocking.

The realization hit me.

I was never in La Cruz. There was no car alarm, no gun. Just me in a hospital room, hooked to a myriad of blinking beeping machines, two anxious-looking FBI agents at my side, the residue of a terrible nightmare lingering in the shadows.

"Kurt? Sierra?" I said, the words burning my throat.

"I know you're concerned about your family, Mitch, but you need to answer some questions," Landry insisted.

I protested. "No, you don't get it . . . the Captain . . . he's—"

"Listen." Landry softened his tone. "Chances are we can locate your family. The Sayulita police are cooperating, but they need more information, which means you have to talk, and you have to trust me. Do you trust me?"

I didn't have an answer. I couldn't even trust what my own mind was telling me.

Landry leaned back. "Truth is, Mitch, it doesn't make a lick of difference if you trust me or not, but you need to tell me why we ended up with a quadruple homicide at the Port of Oakland last night."

"Quadruple? Did Paco—?"

"Castillo got away," Agent Finley interrupted. "But you gave him the flash drive, right?"

I nodded.

"Good," Landry said. "If the keystroke tracking program works like the tech geeks promised, it won't take us long to locate him."

"Can you tell us who shot the other victims?" Finley asked.

If I remembered, I would have told her, but my mind still struggled to make sense of what my memory was feeding me and coming up empty.

"Okay, this is how this is going to go down," Landry said. "You talk, I listen. I already spoke to your lawyer friend, who's claiming attorney client privilege, and his investigator's giving us bupkes and insists she was hunkered down in the back of the car when she heard the shots. Not that she'd tell us a damn thing if she did see what went down. Which leaves you, Mitch, as my only witness. Now, if I were in your shoes, I'd start talking. Tell me what happened last night."

The words "last night" struck me like a sledgehammer to the head.

"I can't be here . . . Sierra, Kurt!" I said, panic cutting through me like a knife as I fought with the tangle of tubes protruding from my body.

"Hey!" Landry snapped, grabbing my wrist. "I promise this will go far better for you if you talk. I don't like cuffing gunshot victims to the bed, but if you leave me no choice, I won't hesitate. That getting through to you?"

I relaxed, took a deep breath.

"Good. Now, maybe you can tell me why a simple handover ended with four dead bodies at the Port of Oakland. And talk fast, Sweeney, no lies, no omissions, no bullshit."

* * *

My narrative faltered as I reconstructed events and laid them out in some logical order: Jorge crushing my windpipe at the apartment, the Captain's threat to kill my family, Paco somehow finding out about the Captain's betrayal and shooting Jorge, Ron's white-hot anger at Paco for the death his niece, the Captain shooting me in the stomach out of some twisted sense of mercy . . . his last "good deed."

"You should have come to us," Landry said. "We could have helped you."

"I couldn't take the risk."

"And look where that led. Four dead bodies and your family still in danger."

"Can you help me now? Find Sierra and Kurt?"

Landry nodded. "Keep talking, Mitch; you're doing good. One more time."

I ran through the events again, adding more details as my memory solidified. I told them about the Captain's plan to over-throw Paco, first through the courts and then, after that had failed, through less official channels. After I'd finished, Landry and Finley confirmed Jorge had died at the scene, the Captain in the ambulance en route to the hospital.

"Ron . . . Ron Boone?" I asked, dreading what in my heart I already knew.

"Sorry, he didn't make it, Mitch. Friend of yours?"

"A good man," I said, a lump festering in my throat as I recalled the conversation we'd had sitting on the curbside when I'd counseled Ron to make the most of the time he had left, like I had some power over the matter. "He didn't deserve to die."

"Most good people don't, but shit happens."

"His wife?"

"She's been informed. As you'd expect, she has a lot of ques-tions. Thanks to you, we can give her some answers."

If the remark was intended to help me feel better, it didn't. I should have taken the time and dropped Ron off at my apartment before heading to the port. Another Mitch Sweeney miscalcula-tion that led to someone's death: it seemed to be a specialty of mine these days.

"Can we talk about my family?" I said, my agitation growing like an itch under my skin. "The Captain was meant to call his crew, and if he didn't, then—"

Landry raised his palm. "Let us worry about that, Mitch."

Those weren't the words I wanted to hear. "Well, you're not worrying hard enough, Landry," I said, the same panic that had gripped me for days making another tour of duty. "My family could be lying at the bottom of the Pacific Ocean by the time you decide to do something. I've told you everything. You've got the photos of the boat, the *Gordo Loco* . . . Sierra and Kurt have to be there. If you'd done your job in the first place, when I told you they were in danger, then we wouldn't be having this conversation."

Landry turned and nodded at Finley, who scuttled out, muttering, "On it, sir."

"You did well, Mitch," Landry said, patting my arm. "Now get some rest. You look like shit."

"Ever consider going into diplomacy, Landry?"

"Not exactly the diplomatic type, Sweeney. Look, if your family is where you think they are, I'll personally fly out to Mexico and make sure they come home safely. You have my word."

The man meant well, but it didn't stop the terrible thoughts from building. "What if it's too late? What then?"

He took a beat. "If it comes to that, we'll deal with it. But for now, we stay positive until we have evidence to the contrary. I'll tell the Sayulita police everything you've told me. It's in their interest to help us. The last thing the local authorities need is a major international incident in their backyard."

"Great. So, they'll help because they're worried about the tourist dollars?"

"Does the reason matter, if it gets your family back home?"

I thought for a moment. "I guess not. But if you're flying out there, I'm coming with you."

Dylan H. Jones

Landry smiled. Crooked and unappealing as always, though I was strangely warming to it. I sensed the man was trying his best to express some depth of human emotions, but it was still a struggle. "You're not going anywhere for a while. Let the FBI handle this, rest up, recover. You're alive. Be thankful for that."

After Landry left, a doctor, whom I vaguely remembered attending to my wounds when I was first admitted, stood at my bed and muttered something about having removed a bullet from my intestines and stressed how lucky I'd been to survive. He had a nurse administer a powerful sedative, and before they both left the room, I was already floating away someplace else.

I fell into a wild and fevered dream: Kurt and Sierra shivering in a rowboat out on the ocean, me swimming toward them, my arms growing weaker at every stroke as the rowboat drifted further away into the horizon's haze.

CHAPTER 54

Lying in a hospital bed, time drags its heels, leaving you to stew on your thoughts and ponder the aftershocks of your actions. Your body fills every spare space in the room until it becomes a world you imagine never leaving.

Maybe this was what I deserved. But then again, what punishment befits putting your family's life in danger? Tucked into a hospital bed with a hundred TV channels to keep me company seemed a mild penance, though the pain that shot like a hot laser through my right side when I reached for a glass of water seemed a fitting enough punishment; one I'd have gladly suffered for a lifetime if it meant I could hold Sierra and Kurt in my arms again.

Frustration and fear nicked at every pore as I waited for news from Landry. With every passing hour, my optimism was like a sunset, fading deeper into the mire of the horizon as darkness crept through the cracks. What if Landry failed? Were Sierra and Kurt already dead? Would I leave the hospital and return to a home I'd be sharing with only memories and reluctant ghosts?

In my most fevered dreams, I was back at the office or in O'Neil's pub with the three musketeers as they switched on the spotlight and interrogated me. I guessed the FBI had told them little to nothing about what had happened, which probably meant their imaginations were kicking into overdrive, figuring out why

I wasn't in the office and stuck in a hospital with an armed guard posted outside my door.

Victor and Alma were the only visitors allowed to see me, but only with Agent Finley present. I couldn't recall what we talked about, though I remember Victor apologizing profusely while Alma sat brooding in the corner, adamant she wouldn't open her mouth with a Fed standing in the same room.

A few days before the doctor discharged me, Victor shared the news that Paco was in police custody at the San Bruno Complex at San Francisco County Jail, waiting to be transported to a secure wing of the Santa Rita Jail, a maximum-security facility thirty-eight miles southeast of the city. He'd retained Victor as his defense attorney, which was good news: it meant he didn't suspect Victor or myself for instigating his arrest.

Victor explained the FBI had raided Celica Holdings' offices and found the high-value paintings Paco had been trying to shield from the IRS in the storage attached to the dock offices. That was evidence enough to obtain a warrant to search Paco's properties. They apprehended Paco the same day by using the location tracking code embedded in the flash drive and arrested him at a safe house he owned in the China Beach neighborhood of San Francisco.

I had plenty of questions, though nobody seemed willing to raise their arms with the answers, especially Agent Finley, whose stock response to any inquiry was a shrug and a "Sorry, privileged information. I can't tell you that." I was still in the dark as to how Paco had discovered Jorge's and the Captain's betrayal and how he'd made it out of the Port of Oakland with what looked like a severe gunshot wound.

Another missing part of the puzzle still niggled at the back of my mind: who had called the Captain and told him about the laptop and its contents? Jorge wasn't working for Paco when it was taken, and the Captain would have been two thousand miles away in Mexico, and Charlotte wouldn't have known about it until he roped her into his plan. I was sure there had to be someone else in the organization, someone close to Paco, who knew about the laptop, understood its value, and understood that exposing it meant Paco's grip on his empire would crumble to dust.

All this thinking was draining, and the more I ruminated, the closer I got to the point of not giving a shit about any of it. I'd already wasted too much time thinking about Paco Castillo. I hoped the old Paco Magic had worn off by now, he'd be denied bail, stand trial, and spend the rest of his life in a maximum-security prison. But, like I'd always said, the wheels of justice turn slowly, and the scales don't always tip in the direction they're meant to.

It must have been my third day in the hospital, the pain medication wearing off, when Agent Finley entered my room. She knocked first, which wasn't her usual style; typically, she'd barge without warning, as if she hoped to catch me in the middle of something nefarious. It immediately put me on guard, as did the more-serious-than-usual look on her face. She held a cell phone close to her ear and talked in hushed tones. I felt the needle on my anxiety nudge into the red as she stood at my bedside.

"Sierra? Kurt?" I said, propping myself up, barely registering the pain searing through my left side.

Finley gave a mild nod and continued mumbling into the phone.

"Is that Landry? Has he found them? Are Kurt and Sierra okay? Are they?"

Finley stopped talking. "Yeah, it's Landry," she said, handing me the phone. "Best you hear this directly from him."

CHAPTER 55

It rained the morning of the funeral, while patches of blue punched through the low, gray skies as if testing the seriousness of the clouds' intentions. But this was early fall in Northern California, and the threat level was mild; just the approaching winter poking its nose up to test the air. By late morning, the sun had dealt with the threat, wiped its hands clean, and reigned majestically again over its kingdom of blue.

Arriving thirty minutes early, I'd sat in a pew at the back. The doctors had only discharged me two days previously, and the thought of standing in a drafty church for an hour felt like the worst kind of pain imaginable. Still, I fidgeted like a bored child, trying to find a position that I could hold for more than a minute without bolts of pain shooting through my ribs.

The funeral procession veered toward the graveside where the priest was waiting. As the mourners gathered at the graveside, we turned our heads toward the sun and smiled, all of us, I imagined, grateful we were alive in this moment and not lying in a wooden box about to be lowered into the earth. The priest waited for everyone to settle, then nodded to this right. A low-pitched note drifted over the cemetery as lone bagpiper dressed in full tartan regalia stepped from behind a thick copse of trees and began his slow march, the discordant bellow maturing into a stirring rendition of "Amazing Grace". The irony wasn't lost on me: I was that wretch, but I didn't feel saved, nor was I found. But I was far from blind. My eyes were wide open to the wrongs I'd committed.

The long, piped notes ushered me back to my days at Edinburgh University, drunk on cheap Scotch, cheering from the sidelines as another Saturday afternoon rugby match descended into a mud bath of comradery and barely contained violence, followed by a procession through Edinburgh's Rose Street, trailing behind a bagpiper like children enchanted out of the walls of Hamelin by the Pied Piper, pub-crawling our way through dusk and into the wee hours. That seemed another lifetime ago, a time when maybe I could have altered the trajectory of my life — a different flap of the butterfly's wing that might have led to different decisions, better decisions.

But the grass is rarely greener. It only looks like it from a distance. On closer inspection, it's as patchy, worm-ridden, and weed-infested as the one you're standing in. As the old saying goes, better to tend to the lawn you have than seek greener pastures. I'd neglected that advice, and it had led me here, standing at a graveside, surrounded by mourners but alone in my thoughts, berating myself for not doing the one thing I should have taken the time to do: drop Ron Boone at my apartment that night before everything went south at the Port of Oakland.

The priest gestured that Ron's family should sit. His two sons helped their mother to her seat, where she sat straight-backed, looking blankly ahead like this was all a terrible dream she would eventually wake from.

As the bagpiper's lament faded, the priest cleared his throat and read a lengthy bible passage that I wasn't familiar with, though one sentence stuck with me:

I have fought the good fight to the end; I have run the race to the finish; I have kept the faith.

It was a fitting coda for Ron's life. He'd made a career out of fighting for others. He was old-school, decent, honorable. His biggest fault was believing those around him were as decent and honorable as he was. I wondered who'd go into battle for the courthouse staff now, who'd fight the good fight and keep the faith. Whoever it was, I doubted I'd see Ron's kind again in my lifetime.

* * *

"So, you're not dead, then."

Katie was the first of the three musketeers to approach me at the wake at O'Neil's pub. The music playing over the speakers was a mix of traditional Irish folk and 80s rock standards, but the choices seemed fitting. Ron's musical tastes, like his dress sense and his opinions on 'the man,' probably hadn't shifted an inch in forty years. The TV mounted over the bar played a slide show of Ron's life on repeat. I looked away, sensing my tears prickling at the back of my eyes.

In the corner of the bar, I noticed a large bouquet of white carnations shaped like a cross. A wave of nausea caught me off-guard. I was sure it was the same kind of bouquet Ron had told me Paco had sent to Masie's funeral. I wondered if Paco had the gall to send the flowers after all that had happened. It was his style, some opulent gesture that he imagined absolved him of his sins.

Before my anger swelled, I turned to a poster-sized photograph of a much younger Ron Boone resting on a stand. His hair was still full and dark, and his smile creased the skin around his eyes, reminding me of the night he'd sat on the sidewalk after I'd hauled him out of McNally's. Maybe if I hadn't been so wrapped up in my own problems, I'd have noticed how close to the edge Ron was that night and called him a cab back home.

"Hey, Mitch. I said, at least you're not dead."

I shook myself from my thoughts and pulled my focus back to Katie. She'd ditched her Settlers of Catan T-shirts for a white shirt and black blazer, which hung loosely off her shoulders.

"Good to see you too, Kat. Nice outfit."

"Muriel let me borrow one of her mom jackets," she said, looking down at the sleeves, which she'd turned up at the cuff. "Not my style, but you know . . ." She let the rest of the sentence drift off into the murmur of mourners, then gestured at my side. "They get you bad?"

"Two broken ribs and a punctured lung. Hurts like a mother, but at least I'm alive."

"We all reckoned for sure you were dead, you know, what with the FBI not telling us shit."

"They question you and the team?"

"Every day for like a week. Assholes. Kept asking the same questions over and over like they were trying to catch us out or something."

"What questions?"

"About Paco Castillo, mostly. How long you'd known him, did we ever see you and him together? We all told them the same thing: the only time we ever heard about you and Castillo was when you stood up in court for that prick and got him off standing trial." Katie looked deep into her Guinness, then looked back at me. "We got that right, yeah? You didn't know the guy from before, had no dealings with him?"

"Did the FBI imply I did?"

She shook her head. "Nah, they were smarter than that, tried to push us to confess or some such shit. But none of us knew anything, so they finally gave up, went to piss all over someone else's leg."

"Nice visual," I said, scanning the bar. "Tye and Muriel not here?"

"They're finishing up some casework. They'll come later."

"Good. I owe you all an explanation . . . a long one."

"No shit."

I was about to agree with her when I felt someone's hand on my arm. I turned. Ron's widow stood to my right, wringing a worn tissue through her fingers. Jenny was taller than I imagined; she had a couple of inches on Ron. Her face was rounded and soft, her lipstick cracked and faded: the woman probably didn't have the strength or energy to care. The red circles around her eyes were undoubtedly the aftershocks of too many sleepless nights. I imagined grief had been her constant companion lately and wasn't likely to release its grip anytime soon.

"You must be Mitch," Jenny said, her tone measured.

I nodded.

She looked around and lowered her voice. "Do you think we could talk . . . in private?"

Katie took it as her cue to leave. "Erm, I'll go get another drink . . . I'm sorry for your loss," she added, before scuttling off to the bar.

I turned to look at Jenny. "Look, I'm so—"

She held her hand up. "Please, if one more person says 'I'm sorry for your loss,' I seriously think I might lose it. I know people mean well, but it's too much."

I noticed the red-and-white pin secured to the left lapel of her jacket. "SEIU Union pin?" I asked.

She offered a wan smile. "Ron insisted I wear it to official union events. It's not exactly Tiffany's, but I figured this is probably the last time I'll get to wear it, so . . ." Her voice trailed off as she looked over to Ron's photo.

"You said you wanted to talk."

She let out a current of air. "Ron hadn't been himself for weeks, but you probably knew that already."

"His niece?"

"I kept telling him to let it go, but he was a stubborn old coot."

"Were they close?"

"Practically brought her up. Ron's sister had her problems, drugs and booze, mostly. The father ran off before Masie was born, so Ron took her under his wing. He took it hard when Masie was killed. We all did, but Ron most of all." She paused. "But I guess they're together now."

"That must be some comfort."

Jenny shook her head. "Not really. Two of the people I loved most in this world were killed for no good reason. I can't really find any comfort in that, could you?"

I had no answer. "Comfort" and "blessing" were just tired old clichés we roll out because we imagined they helped temper the grief. Truth is, grief is a titanium blade. It never responds well to being tempered.

"I wanted to ask you about that night," Jenny said. "I don't think Agent Landry told me the full story, and I was too upset to push. Why was Ron even there? How did he get mixed up with a criminal like Paco Castillo? Ron barely had a speeding ticket his whole life."

I hesitated, peering into the dark depths of my Guinness.

"Please, Mitch, you were the last person to see Ron alive, and whatever you say won't make me feel any worse than I do right now. Trust me, I'm a lot stronger than I look."

I took a breath. The woman had a right to know.

A clot set in my throat as I told Jenny about the call I got from McNally's, and I'd found Ron drunk in the corner with a gun under his jacket. I explained I had to make it to the port by seven and had no time to drop Ron off at my apartment, and not taking the time to do that was something I'd regret for the rest of my life.

Jenny placed a hand on mine. "This is not your fault. I just want to know why it happened the way it did."

I went on to tell her about the Captain and his holding my family hostage if I didn't do exactly as he demanded.

"And this Captain is the one who killed my Ron?"

I nodded. "I should have taken the gun with me, made sure Ron couldn't get hold of it."

"I don't blame you for what happened," Jenny said. "Ron was the love of my life. I was married to him for over forty years, and I'm beyond grateful I got to spend most of my life with the man I loved. Not everybody gets to have that. But when Ron got an idea in his head, there was no shaking it out of that dumb skull of his. You did what you needed to do for your family. I'll have to live with the fact that my husband made the choices he made, just like you have to live with your choices."

"I just wish—"

"We all wish, but it won't bring Ron or Masie back. I've got to get on with my life now, somehow pick up the pieces. But what about you? Is your family home safe?"

"I'm heading out in a few days to fly them home," I said. "Sierra wanted some time alone to think things over."

"Well, it's good that she's thinking. I've always been told never to make any rash decisions after a traumatic event. You need time to adjust. I'm sure you'll work it out. Love's like that. It comes and goes in waves sometimes, but it never goes away, not really."

I smiled. "I thought I was meant to be the one comforting you."

"Take comfort where you can find it, Mitch. That's the secret, right?" She gestured to the crowd. "I'd best be going."

"Before you go," I said, pointing at the bouquet of carnations. "Do you know who sent those?"

"No idea. I thought maybe his colleagues at the courthouse?" She turned and shook my hand. "Thank you for being so honest, Mitch. It means a lot."

I hadn't the heart to tell Jenny who I suspected had sent the carnations. She had insisted she was strong, but I expected that news would have tipped her over the edge. The bouquet was a reminder of what taking Paco's offer had cost me — a cross that was mine to bear.

After Jenny left, I scanned the mourners, hoping Judge Croft would have attended the wake, but more selfishly, I was hoping for an update on the Judge Harper situation. Maybe she'd been stuck in court all day and couldn't get away. I was sure she'd make a personal call on Jenny Boone when the time was right. Judge Croft didn't miss paying her respects to a colleague.

An hour later, as people drifted out, the funeral organizers respectfully removed Ron's photograph and wrapped it in stiff paper. A shower of white carnation petals fell to the floor as they separated the cross from its stand. As they passed by me, several more petals floated to the floor, like a snake shedding its skin. I had the sickening feeling the long shadow of Paco Castillo wasn't quite done with me yet.

CHAPTER 56

By 5 p.m. that evening, all the mourners, save a few of Ron's loyal bourbon-drinking union buddies had headed home, the TV now switched to the local ABC affiliate; Ron's life discarded in favor of the day's news and the latest sports scores.

I was sitting next to Katie at our usual table. Muriel and Tye sat across from us. The three musketeers were unusually subdued, probably waiting for me to address the big fat elephant in the room. I sipped my whiskey and steeled myself.

"Right, I guess there's no time like the present."

"Finally," Katie said. "We gonna get some answers?"

"Let Mitch speak, Kat," Muriel said. "He's had a tough time these past few weeks."

"Look, erm, I really don't know where to start. I—"

"The beginning, Mitch," Muriel said, squeezing my arm. "Start at the beginning,"

I girded myself and spoke. Told them how I accepted Paco's offer to pay off my gambling debt in return for locating his wife, talked them through the bloody shit show that went down in Palm Springs. I choked up telling them about Sierra and Kurt being held hostage and how Ron lost his life at the port. As I spoke, it felt as if I was treading over old ground, but with new shoes that still pinched as I walked.

"But Sierra and Kurt? They're safe, now?" Muriel asked.

"They're still with Sierra's mother, but they're safe."

"How the heck did the authorities even find them?" Tye asked. "A boat somewhere off the coast of Mexico? Gotta be some dumbassed luck for sure."

I explained what Landry had told me. What I suspected was correct. Kurt and Sierra were held hostage on the *Gordo Loco*, but by the time Landry arrived in Puerto Vallarta, the boat had already docked in San Blas, a smaller marina tucked in a hidden cove a hundred miles north of La Cruz. When the *Gordo Loco*, a commercial trimaran, dropped anchor, someone had put in an anonymous call to the Mexican State Police. The Federales were there within the hour. According to Landry, the ambush was mercifully short on drama and violence.

When a force of fully armed Federales surrounded the boat, the crew surrendered without a single shot fired. The Mexican State Police recovered Sierra and Kurt, shaken but unhurt, and spent the following day being questioned by the police under the supervision of Landry. Nobody knew who'd alerted the police. They didn't leave a name or number, but whoever had made that call, I'd be forever in their debt.

Despite my opinion of Landry, the man had made good on his promise to find my family. I wish I could have been there at the dockside, that I could have gathered Kurt and Sierra in my arms and tell them how sorry I was, how I'd make it up to them, wouldn't ever stop trying to make it up to them.

A couple of days later, I spoke to them from my hospital bed. Sierra told me they were staying in Mexico a while longer. Her mom was taking good care of them and Kurt needed the rest. I figured Sierra still harbored a burning anger she had no place to put. I didn't argue. They'd be home soon enough, and I could start to rebuild my family. I suspected that journey wouldn't be a quick or easy one. The most important journeys in life never are.

After I finished, a few moments of silence passed before anyone spoke. Katie, of course, was the first to comment.

"Jesus fucking Christ. Taking Paco Castillo's money? What the fuck were you thinking?"

"Pardon my French, but that's very, very effed up, Mitch," Muriel said. "Why didn't you tell us? We'd have understood."

"I couldn't. Things snowballed, and then there were lies on top of the lies. I wouldn't have even known where to start. And besides, I didn't want any of you involved, for your own safety."

"So, you lied," Muriel said. "To me, all of us, your family . . . to the FBI?"

I nodded. "I lied. No excuses, but at least now you know why I lied."

"To protect your family," Tye said.

"And protect his own ass," Katie sniffed.

"Yep, that too," I agreed.

"But you're all right," Muriel said. "Managing?"

I took a breath. "Getting there, slowly."

"And your gambling?" Katie asked. "You kicked that shit to the curb, too?"

"If it were that easy, I would have done it years ago, Kat. I'm signed up for my first Gamblers Anonymous meeting next week. So, yeah, making progress."

"Right, can we all take bets you'll actually turn up for that meeting?"

"Like a pool?" Tye said.

"That's not funny, Katie," Muriel said. "If Mitch says he's committed—"

"I dunno," Tye said, offering his puppy-dog smile. "Depends on what odds you're offering. I might be up for laying a few greenbacks down. Got vacation time coming up. I could do with some extra walking-around money."

A moment of silence followed, none of us sure how to react. Muriel broke the awkwardness with a giggle, which was followed by a laugh from Tye and a snort from Katie. I held up my arms in surrender and laughed, too. The release felt good; felt like things were, millimeter by millimeter, returning to normal.

As we talked, a news story on the TV caught our attention. The reporter was interviewing Javier Madrigal, who stood outside the Alameda Superior Court, all smug smiles and perfectly coiffured hair. I called out to the bartender to turn up the volume. We all sat up as the studio anchor cleared her throat and turned to the camera, adopting that familiar, trained manner anchors have that makes viewers feel complicit in the story.

"The FBI, today, raided the homes of several prominent Superior Court Judges in the Bay Area. Most significantly, the home of Griffin Harper, Presiding Judge at the Alameda Superior Court. The judge was arrested earlier this evening, along with three other judges from the Alameda Superior Court. An FBI spokesperson confirmed the arrests were part of an ongoing investigation. We also understand the FBI has made a series of similar raids in the counties of Contra Costa and Santa Clara. More details as they come in."

We all watched, slack-jawed, the shaky camera footage of Judge Harper handcuffed and bundled into the rear of a police cruiser. That was followed by three other similar scenes, all with judges I knew and had worked for being hauled off to jail.

"Holy shit," Katie said. "It finally happened."

"Did I hear that right?" Tye said. "Did she say another two counties? Contra Costa and Santa Clara?"

Katie shook her head. "We underestimated the scale. Freakin' failure of imagination on our side."

"I wouldn't be surprised if a scandal like this makes the national news," Muriel said.

"No shit," Katie agreed. "Probably call it JudgeGate or something lame like that."

Muriel adjusted her blouse and gestured at the TV. "Well, it just goes to show nobody's above the law."

A faint stirring of pride and satisfaction swelled in my chest. The odds were looking good that I'd get to see Judge Harper standing on the wrong side of the bench and standing trial.

I raised my glass. "It's a good day, but let's not forget the pain in the ass who started all this, Ron Boone."

As we clinked glasses, Muriel said, "He'd have loved this, wouldn't he? Proving everybody else wrong."

A voice just to my right spoke. "Yes, there's no doubt Ron would be celebrating with the best of them."

I turned. Judge Harriet Croft stood next to me, handbag slung over her forearm and wearing her usual black dress. "Mind if I join?"

I shuffled up and made space. Judge Croft sat and gestured at the TV. "You can understand why I couldn't pay my respects to Ron today. But I'm sure he wouldn't have minded, given the result."

"No shit," Katie blurted, then quickly added. "Your honor . . . no shit, your honor."

"No shit, indeed, Katie. So, what does a girl need to do to get a drink around here?"

I pushed my chair back. "I'll get it. It's my round anyway,"

"It's your round all night, boss," Tye said, shaking his empty beer glass. "Just in case you'd forgot."

"Top of mind, Tye. What can I get you, Judge?"

"I'll come with you and check out what's on offer."

At the bar, Judge Croft settled on a single Irish whiskey with ice.

"So, looks like you'll be sworn in as Presiding Judge?"

"As soon as the ink's dry on the paperwork."

"You'll have your work cut out, cleaning up the mess Harper left."

"I've never shirked from hard work, Mitch. What's a life without purpose and service to something other than yourself?"

I raised my glass.

As our glasses clinked, Judge Croft lowered her voice, her smile fading. "Mitch, we need to talk."

I knew this conversation was coming. "About my job?" I asked nervously. "Staying on at the court?"

"Tomorrow, 9 a.m., Judge Harper's old chambers. I have a proposition for you, so don't be late. Now, go enjoy the rest of your evening. Make your team feel appreciated. Pay it forward; they'll appreciate the gesture."

After Judge Croft left, I sat back with the three musketeers, who were discussing Tye's clothing budget, arguing about the best taco spot in town, and debating the merits of IPAs over hazy IPAs. Business as usual, I thought as I sat and listened, all the time my mind wondering what the hell kind of proposition Judge Croft had in mind and whether that proposition included a generous severance package.

CHAPTER 57

I walked into Judge Harper's old chambers the following morning just as two FBI agents were carrying out plastic bags containing his belongings. Judge Croft stood looking out of the south-facing window, the morning sun catching the dust motes circling the room.

"They're not wasting much time," I said as the FBI officer left.

"Most of it was bagged and tagged before I arrived this morning." The judge settled behind the desk and gestured that I should sit. As I took the chair across from her, I noticed a thick folder to her right. I recognized the handwriting; the stack of research papers I'd collated on Officer Connor and handed to Judge Harper weeks ago.

The Judge smoothed her palms over the knots and scratches bedded deep into the mahogany desk and said, "I think I need a new desk, something less . . ."

"Ostentatious?"

"I was going to say 'sullied,' but I get your point. A fresh start." She looked up at me. "How are you holding up?"

"Okay. Maybe ask me again at the end of this meeting?"

Judge Croft offered a thin smile. "I thought you'd like to know Officer Theodore Connor was arrested last night. With all the noise around the judges, his arrest missed the news cycle. I expect that will change today."

With everything that had happened in the last week, I'd shoved Connor to the back of my mind, though the news gave me a warm glow of satisfaction. "How's it looking?"

"For Connor? Not good. What with Officer Mason's confession and his less-than-exemplary record." She tapped the stack of folders. "Partly thanks to you, he's facing a long list of charges, including accessory to commit fraud and attempted murder. He'll be arraigned tomorrow. I don't expect he'll make bail."

"That's good to hear. And Castillo?"

"The FBI told me he's ready to talk."

I shook my head. "In exchange for a deal?"

"He'll take a plea, but I don't expect the DA's willing to accept anything less than a minor reduction in prison time for whatever information he's offering. Either way, Paco Castillo will be a very old man before he sees the outside of a prison cell . . . if he makes it out at all."

"That's good news, but you could have told me this over the phone. Why call me into your chambers?"

Judge Croft took a sharp breath. "I think you know why, Mitch."

I nodded. "You're firing me."

The judge slipped a sheet of paper from the briefcase at her feet. "I'm not going to sugarcoat this, Mitch." She read from the paper. "You've admitted to affiliating with a known criminal and taking his money in exchange for locating his wife. That in itself is enough to haul you in front of the bar and get you suspended at the very least. Not to mention the multiple lies you told to cover up your actions."

"In my defense, I only lied to protect my family."

"Lies that you wouldn't have needed to fabricate if you hadn't affiliated yourself with Paco Castillo in the first place."

"I'm aware of that." I straightened my back. "Your honor, if you're going to fire me, can we please make it quick?"

"Fair enough." She laid down the paper. "As you're aware, terminating a state employee is rarely a simple matter, lots of hoops to jump through and red tape to navigate. Also, Agent Landry provided a lengthy debrief of your involvement in the shooting at the Port of Oakland. He confirmed your fears for the safety of your family were justified and that you risked your life to help the FBI arrest Paco Castillo and put a sizable dent in his criminal organization. They also informed me they have proof Castillo has been trafficking children, mostly young girls, across the border for the best part of three decades. He'd sell them like souvenirs to the highest bidder. Thanks to you, the FBI now has a detailed list of names and dates."

"The code on the flash drive?"

"They're still trawling through the names, but from what I hear, it should be the final nail in Harper's coffin."

My brain clicked into high alert. "Harper was involved in the trafficking?"

"Along with a long list of prominent figures in the Bay Area. I have no doubt there'll be a lot of political blood spilled once the names are released."

I looked out at the wisps of clouds scuttling through the blue and thought back to the morning Judge Harper called me into his chambers. He was angry, looking for someone to blame, but in hindsight, that was the fear talking — fear of the reckoning thundering toward him like a freight train. I hoped the cancer would hold off long enough that I'd not only see him stand trial, but I'd be sitting in the courtroom when the jury pronounced him guilty, and I'd witness him being hauled off to prison for the rest of whatever short life was left in him.

"So, what now?" I asked. "The 'thanks for your service' speech?"

"What now?" Judge Croft leaned back. "Now, I administer my verbal reprimand, and have you sign a document verifying you agree to a two-month suspension without pay."

I sat up. "So, you're not firing me?"

"Would you like me to fire you?" She didn't wait for a reply. "Mitch, if I didn't believe you to be an asset to the court, I would have started the termination paperwork the moment you stepped out of that hospital room."

Unable to disguise my relief, I smiled. "So, that's the proposition? I agree to a two-month suspension?"

"That's the reprimand. The proposition is this." She leaned her forearms on the desk. "This won't come as a surprise, but Alameda Superior Court is currently short four judges, and I expect things to get a lot busier as the case builds against Castillo."

"You could always call in some retired judges," I said.

Judge Croft cocked her head. "A little too soon, don't you think?"

"Apologies, out of line," I said, raising my hands. "Just the relief, you know—"

"As I was saying, in light of this, the court is expediting the hiring of a new commissioner." She paused. "I'd like you to consider applying for that position."

I was speechless for what might have been the first time in my life.

"The commissioner's job is a significant step up from a staff attorney. You've been in the courts over two decades, you've served the County of Alameda, you're well-liked and respected by all the judges. If you decide to apply, you'll have my full support. That's not in question. It's not glamorous work, you'd be in the trenches, presiding over small claims and traffic court, and occasionally misdemeanors, but it's the best pathway to a judgeship . . . if that's something you want."

"Erm, your honor, I don't know what to say."

"A 'thank you' would be a start. Then, think about my proposal for forty-eight hours, and come back to me with an answer that makes us both happy."

* * *

"A commissioner?" Victor said. "Are you going to take it?" He took a sip of espresso. "Scrub that. Of course you're going to take it. You'd be a fool not to."

We sat across from each other at Victor's breakfast bar, the late-morning sun streaming in through the skylights and a chorus of birds out tweeting on the deck. Probably morning jays. They had a more civilized demeanor than the thuggish gulls that hung around Jack London Square, looking for trouble.

"Still deciding. Judge Croft just dropped it on me a couple of hours ago."

"What's there to think about?" Victor slid my coffee across the marble surface. "You'd make a great commissioner."

I smiled and had to admit the word "commissioner" sounded pretty good. I took another sip of coffee. "Vic," I said, setting my face to serious mode, "I need to confess something."

Victor braced himself. "Does the drama never end with you?"

"This coffee . . . best damn coffee I ever tasted, straight up."

Victor took a moment, then shook his head. "You're an asshole, you know that, right? A grade-A asshole."

I raised my cup in his direction. "I learn from the best."

As Victor mumbled something incoherent, Alma Torres came from around the hallway corner. She'd ditched her usual "T-shirts with attitude" attire for a blue floral dress and heavy black boots topped with white socks. She was also wearing makeup. A first.

"Oh hey, Mitch. You good?"

"Getting better every day," I confirmed.

Alma studied me for a moment. "You don't look so good. Kinda pale, if I'm honest. You probs need a long vacation or something."

"Keeping it real, Alma?"

"You know it." Grabbing her car keys, she turned to Victor. "You still cool with me taking off, boss?"

"Apartment hunting?" Victor asked.

"You still got bagels in the fridge?"

"I think so."

"Then no," Alma confirmed.

Victor shrugged.

"Look, Alma," I said. "Before you go, I just wanted to thank you properly, for, you know—"

"Saving you sorry ass twice?"

"Guess I owe you one."

"Yeah, and the rest. The family good?"

"Seeing them in a couple of days."

"Good. Don't fuck it up," she said, pointing at me. "If you haven't already."

"Thanks for the pep talk."

"That more lawyer humor?"

"Best I got."

"When will you be back?" Victor asked.

"Tomorrow, maybe the day after, depends. Picking a friend up at the airport."

"Betsy?" both Victor and I said at the same time.

I noticed Alma's cheeks flushing under her makeup. "I booked a place up in Point Reyes for a couple of nights. Separate rooms," she quickly added as she noticed my eyebrows rising.

"Just friends," I said and smiled at Victor.

"Friends," he said. "Nothing to say two grown women can't be friends."

"Happens all the time," I agreed.

Alma scurried around, her blushes popping up like cherry blossoms. She slung her backpack over her shoulder. "I gotta jet. You gonna be okay while I'm gone?"

"I'm sure I'll manage," Victor said. "Go have fun with your new . . . friend."

Alma's response was a high lift of the middle finger of her left hand as she turned and headed out.

As Alma pulled the door shut, Victor turned to me. "I was at Santa Rita with Paco yesterday, helping him work out a plea bargain."

I felt a prickle on the back of my neck. "Does he suspect anything?"

"He still thinks the Captain sold him out to the FBI and got you to do his bidding. He's just grateful, at least as grateful a man like Paco can ever be, that he's getting good counsel. The DA's pushing back hard, but Paco sees I'm doing my job, and that's all he needs to see."

"I'm just grateful he's behind bars, putting this whole damn nightmare behind me."

"Yeah, about that," Victor said, clearing his throat. "Paco wants to see you."

I set my coffee down. "Not going to happen."

"He was insistent. Says he has something important to tell you, in person."

"Hell no. You're not dragging me back into all that. I've moved on, Vic. That man nearly cost me my family. Paco Castillo can go fuck himself. I'm putting Kurt and Sierra first. They're my priority."

"As it should be, *amigo*. But Paco really wants to talk. He's got information you need to hear; so he told me. Your choice. But look at it this way, seeing him locked up might help you get closure on all of this. And if he's got something to get off his chest, if I were you, I'd want to hear it."

We were both silent for a moment, but that shit-hurling, one-man band chimp inside my head was banging his tambourine, pressing my curiosity buttons like he was playing the piano and stamping, demanding I throw some loose change in the hat at his feet.

CHAPTER 58

The fluorescent lights inside the visiting area hummed anxiously as two guards buzzed me into the Special Management Unit at Santa Rita Jail. Unlike the low-security visitor area — open plan with rows of glass partitions — the Special Management Unit had six individual booths, none of which were occupied that day. To my right, another guard, built like a Hummer truck, gestured I should sit at the booth furthest from my left.

They'd housed Paco in the Administrative Segregation Unit. "Ad Seg" was where the high-profile inmates were held in individual cells rather than dormitory-style housing. As I waited, I imagined Paco pacing his cell all day, anger roiling, the great white finally in captivity.

A few minutes later, two guards escorted Paco into the booth. Placing their hands on his shoulders, they pushed him into the chair. He scowled at them as he sat. One guard glanced my way, as if to confirm I was all good with the situation. I nodded. The guards swaggered back into the prison's bowels.

As I expected, Paco wore a regulation red jumpsuit, the color reserved for the most dangerous or high-risk individuals in Ad Seg, his arm cradled in a shoulder sling. What I didn't expect was the power he still exuded. I imagined prison might have diminished him, stripped away the layer of menace he carried around like a weapon. But that wasn't the case. His presence was as unsettling and intimidating as I remembered that first day I met him, maybe more so, as if he understood the key to survival in captivity was to amplify that undercurrent of violence, sending an unspoken message to the other inmates that one wrong look or wrong word would unleash a world of hurt.

We both picked up the telephone receivers. I could hear his breathing, slow and controlled, as he put the receiver to his mouth. His soulless eyes were darker than I recalled, reflecting nothing and giving away nothing.

"Thank you for coming, Mitch." His voice was deep, like a dog's first warning growl. "I know you were under no obligation to do so."

A chill spiraled up my spine. Despite being separated by three inches of impenetrable glass, I could sense him like a powerful, malignant force sitting across from me. Ignoring the creeping sense of unease as his eyes met mine, I asked, "How's the shoulder?"

He glanced at the sling. "I have suffered worse. And you?"

"I'm alive," I said, subconsciously reaching for my ribs. "I was lucky."

He grinned. "We were both lucky, no?"

I thought for a moment. "Paco Magic?"

He craned his neck to the steel door behind him. "Lucky to be alive; not so lucky to be here."

I wanted to tell him that this was where he belonged, that he deserved to spend the rest of his life rotting in a jail cell. The moment I'd walked in and felt the oppressive prison air, I regretted giving that shit-hurling chimp the satisfaction of agreeing to Paco's request. I wanted the meeting over and done with, shove everything that had happened in the past few weeks into the murky depths of my memory dumpster. But the chimp had other ideas.

"Victor said you had something to tell me."

Paco took a large intake of air, which ballooned his chest like an over-inflated red beach ball. "Your family is safe?"

"I'll see them in a few days."

"You understand, Mitch, I had nothing to do with their kidnapping,"

"Is that what you wanted to tell me? I already knew that."

"I see you are impatient."

"I don't intend to be here any longer than I have to. Say what you have to say."

"I requested you to come here because I believe you owe me a favor."

A nick of irritation knotted behind my brow. "Sorry, but I have no idea what you're talking about, and I'm all out of favors. If that's why I'm here, then—"

Paco held out his baseball glove-sized palm. "Do you know how big the Pacific Ocean is, Mitch?" he interrupted, sensing I was about to hang up and march out.

"What is this, Santa Rita Jail trivia night?"

He smiled, tight, like chicken wire. "Sixty million square miles. A lot of ocean, no? Now, imagine searching for a fifty-five-foot trimaran in an ocean of that size. An impossible task. Unless, of course, you know the approximate location of the boat."

The penny dropped with a loud clatter that made me sit up. "You alerted the Federales?" I said, the wind taken out of my compulsion to leave. "You helped locate Kurt and Sierra?"

He studied his nails. "The Captain was not so smart, but he served his purpose, transporting goods, souvenirs mostly, along the west coast of Mexico."

"Souvenirs?" I said, shaking my head.

"For the tourists," he clarified. "The Captain's route was very predictable. Nuevo Vallarta, La Cruz, and, of course, Marina

San Blas, where he spent much of his time. He had a woman there, I think." He paused, as if considering the word "woman," then continued. "After Charlotte's death, I knew the Captain was responsible."

"But you never thought to mention that? You told me Hetch and his daughter were involved. You're the one who insisted I return to Palm Springs and hold up my end of the deal."

"I suspected they were involved, but they were not the killers. It was important the Captain believe I was not looking in his direction."

"And what about Jorge?"

He exhaled a long, drawn-out breath. "Much ambition, but no intelligence; a dangerous combination. Jorge was a dumb puppy with no house training. If he was smarter, he would have been more suspicious and checked to make sure the phone I had given him was not bugged. I recorded all his conversations with the Captain. When the opportunity presented itself at the port that night, the stars aligned: two birds, one stone. My only regret is that your friend was caught in the crossfire." He paused. "I did send my condolences."

"Yeah, I saw," I said, barely hiding my contempt. "You think that absolves you?"

"I don't seek forgiveness. The Captain killed your friend, not me."

"And what about the other things you've done? The footage? The kids . . . children, fuck's sake."

"Innocent until proven guilty, a tenet of the American judicial system, yes?"

"How did you make it out of the port that night?"

He lifted a hand to his heart. "Oksana. She is my rock, my confidant, and, of course, my business partner. She would do anything to protect me."

My mind shot back to the sickening footage I'd seen on the flash drive and the woman standing in the camera's shadow, her face hidden, handing out pills and drinks to the petrified young girls. Another piece of the Paco Castillo horror show unspooled before my eyes. I should have figured it out sooner. The way the woman stood, straight-backed, poised almost, and the long blonde ponytail poking from the back of her baseball hat, exactly the way Charlotte had worn hers the night she was killed. My gut clenched as a slick of acid rose in my throat.

Paco nodded as if he'd twigged where my mind had gone but fell short of confirming my suspicions. "We are to be married, soon, before the trial. I have faith in the American judicial system that I will be acquitted on all charges."

I was dumbfounded. The man was either deluded or living on a different planet. There was not one glitch in his self-belief, not a single dent in his armor-like ego. He honestly believed he'd be out of prison in a few months and skip off into the sunset with his new bride.

"Hate to burst your bubble, but I wouldn't order the wedding cake just yet."

He let out a roar of laughter and pointed a thick finger at me. "You will be invited, of course. Bring your wife. I would like to meet her."

I shook my head. "This is a joke, right?" I leaned close to the partition, my breath steaming the glass, a slow burn of anger kindling in my chest. "If it wasn't for you—"

"If it wasn't for me," he interrupted, his tone dropping a few growls deeper on the threat scale. "Your family would be lying at the bottom of the ocean where no one would ever find them. Now, I do not expect your thanks for what I did, but I would appreciate an acknowledgment in public, at my trial, that Paco Castillo was the person, the only person, who helped save your family. A small ask, considering the size of the favor I extended."

I blinked, struggling to process what I'd just heard. "What, like a character witness? Are you serious?"

He scuttled forward, his eyes still and quiet. "Very serious, Mitch. I have helped many people: politicians, businessmen, judges. Like you, they are all in my debt, and I'm certain they will also testify as to my good moral character when asked."

"Really? You think that when the rubber hits the road, these people will take the stand and defend your 'good moral character'?"

"Of course. And you, most of all, Mitch. You have a very compelling story to tell a jury. How Paco Castillo saved your family from certain death."

My fingernails dug into my palms. I should've known better than to come. Curiosity had got the better of me. Maybe I had some crazy notion Paco would show some contrition, offer a sliver of regret. But there was nothing.

Despite being condemned to spend the rest of his life behind prison walls, Paco had convinced himself that this was all a big misunderstanding, believed he would walk away a free man. I knew it wouldn't happen. But no matter how many ways I'd spin it, Paco wouldn't listen. He'd spent decades ruling his kingdom with unchallenged power, surrounded by minions who did his dirty work so he could stay unblemished, several steps removed from the squalor and filth he perpetrated. Paco would stand trial and be found guilty on all charges, but I doubted even that would dampen his belief that he was innocent. Paco Castillo was the kind of man who would never accept his fate unless that fate was completely in his control, guided by his own hand.

In that airless, depressing room, the overhead lights flickering, I felt the anger I'd been holding onto for so long gradually fade. My body relaxed like a heavy burden had been lifted off my shoulders. At that moment, I realized that my anger was just another weapon Paco had held at my throat. It was time I shook it loose. Taking a deep breath, I said the words I should have said that night in his garden when he asked for my help to find Charlotte.

"I'm sorry, Paco, I can't help you."

Slamming the receiver back in its place, I gestured to the guard that I was done.

CHAPTER 59

In the parking lot, the air held a chill that hinted at the coming fall. Looking west to the steep hills of Dublin National Park, I felt a sense of relief that things were as they should be, the natural order of the seasons rolling onwards.

That would be the last I saw of Paco Castillo, other than his photo pasted across the papers and the TV news over the coming months. My pact with the devil was finally laid to rest. A pact that had almost cost me my life and that of my family. I was bruised, scarred but alive, and standing outside the prison that day, I couldn't have been more grateful.

Heading toward my car, I noticed a black Range Rover parked next to my Saab. The rear door opened. A woman stepped out, dressed in black jeans, a white T-shirt, a black leather jacket, and sunglasses the size of wine coasters. Her long blonde hair fell in a ponytail from the back of her baseball cap. She lit a cigarette and leaned against the tailgate, the subtle, woodsy aroma of the Sobranie wafting my way.

"Paco's popular today," I said, walking toward her, and noting the figure of a thick-faced man reflected in the Range Rover's side mirror. "Organizing another party?"

Oksana tilted her chin, blowing a trail of light smoke into the blue. "Party? No. Paco's party days are finished. Do you not think?"

"Really? He just told me the happy news. Congratulations, you'll make a lovely prison bride."

She pointed her cigarette at my chest. "You think you are a very smart man, yes, Mitch?"

I shrugged. "Smart enough to know Paco won't be cutting up the dance floor at your wedding reception anytime soon."

Her cheek twitched as if what I'd said had stung. She cocked her head and looked me up and down with a contemptuous sneer. "You are just like every other man I know. You underestimate me." She waved her arm theatrically, like she was swatting a fly. "Some pretty ballerina with nothing between her ears," she said, tapping a finger on her temple.

"If the pointe shoe fits," I said with a wry smile.

I could see that comment riled her, but I didn't care. She was as evil as Paco; both as rotten as each other.

"So, what's next? More shopping trips to London?"

She shook her head. "No, I will marry Paco, just like we agreed. As a lawyer, you know a wife in California has many rights."

"So, it's financial? A marriage of convenience? More convenient for you, though, what with Paco set to spend the rest of his life in prison. You know the government will seize all his assets if they haven't done so already. That'll just leave you the scraps to feed off."

"I am not so fucking stupid," she snapped. "We made plans for the organization in Paco's absence."

"Then it's the businesses. You'll be taking over from Paco?"

"I am more than qualified."

"To traffic young girls? I don't doubt it. But you'll need new customers, what with most of your client base heading for prison alongside your fiancé."

She took a drag, forcing the smoke through her nose. "There is an old Russian saying my mother liked to tell me." She paused as if silently translating. "Be done or be a master. I chose to be a master. There was an opportunity, and I took it. Any man would have done the same."

"Got it. Trafficking young girls for sex was too tempting a career move to pass up?"

"Understand, Mitch, these young girls are from very bad places, brutal regimes, abusive families, no future. We give them a path, a chance to improve themselves. But opportunities all come at a price."

"Really, that's your argument? You're giving them opportunities in return for ruining their lives? Good luck with that in court."

"Oh, it won't come to that. As Paco's wife, I won't be able to testify against him, and he will not testify against me."

I was about to point out how wrong Oksana was, but held back. She'd find out soon enough that spousal privilege didn't extent to crimes committed before the marriage. I'd let the authorities deliver that surprise when the time was right. Still, her arrogant attitude burrowed under my skin. The anger I thought I'd tamped down back in the visiting area rose back to the surface with a vengeance.

"You think you'll be immune from all of this, from what you and Paco did?"

I noticed the hand holding her cigarette tremble as she tried to stay composed. But she was no Paco in that regard. Oksana's anger and frustration broke through her cool facade like cracks in a wall. After a moment, she wrestled back control, but the damage was already done. I knew I'd touched a raw nerve, and the more I dug around, the more she was likely to reveal something she'd regret.

"I will not go to jail. Not for this; not for any of it."

"Then you're as dumb as you think you're smart, Oksana."

She removed her sunglasses, her gunmetal Slavic eyes as soulless and vacant as Paco's. "Dumb? No, not me." She paused. "You have no idea, do you, Mitch?"

"Evil, then? Can we settle on 'evil' and call it a day?"

Her lip twitched as if I'd poked it with a pin. She walked closer, the skin around her neck straining. I could tell she was out to make a point, prove me wrong, prove she was as smart as she insisted she was. "Let me ask you a question."

"Shoot."

"Do you know how the Captain found out about Paco's laptop?"

I shrugged. "Someone close to him . . ."

I stopped, realizing in an instant what Oksana couldn't resist telling me, to prove how smart she was.

"Nobody ever suspects the dumb ballerina with no brains. As I have said, men have always underestimated me, even Paco." She paused. "Be a master. You see, Mitch, I am not so dumb. Paco will never get out of prison, I know this, but we will marry, and I will run his business. He will never accept this to be a permanent situation, but so what? There is nothing he can do. Nothing you can do."

She straightened her back and stood proudly, like she expected me to pin a medal on her chest. "I could see the long game, Paco could not. I already knew Paco suspected the Captain, so I made a call. What I didn't expect was for him to include Charlotte in the plan, a misstep on his behalf. Even so, he took care of the bitch for me. Eventually, I would have had to dispose of the Captain, too, but thanks to my Paco—"

"You orchestrated this whole thing?" I interrupted, my words barely making it from my throat.

"I prefer to think of it as choreography."

Her smug expression and self-satisfied grin stoked the slow-building rage in my chest. But I kept quiet. She was on a roll, and I wasn't about to put up a roadblock.

Oksana continued. "The Captain thought he would take over when Paco was gone. He probably told you this was all his plan." She shook her head and exhaled a sharp current of air.

"Another man who underestimated me and paid the price. Just like you, Mitch. And you will pay the price, also."

She ground her cigarette into the Range Rover's fender and reached a hand into her back pocket. I took a step back.

"Oh, you think I have a gun, a knife, maybe? If I wanted you dead, I would not dirty my hands," she said, nodding to the goon in the driver's seat.

I looked at the cell phone she'd taken from her pocket and was coolly scrolling through, as if checking her Instagram posts.

"If you want my number," I snarled, fishing for my car keys, "you can go fuck yourself." My fingers trembled as they closed around the cold metal. Every second in Oksana's presence felt like I was drowning in toxic waste. "Enjoy your freedom while you can. When the truth gets out, you'll end up like your fiancé."

"Oh, I already have your number, Mitch," she snipped, then brushed a strand of hair from her shoulder as she turned the screen toward me.

My world tilted as I took in the images. The official photo of my driving license. The sun-drenched portrait of Sierra and Kurt at the beach a few years back. Minutes before her death, Charlotte had taken the photos. The bile rose like hot mercury in my throat.

"Cute family," she said, slipping the phone back into her pocket. "I am sure I don't need to tell you, but I will anyway, just in case you misunderstand me." She gave me a paper-thin smile, her lipstick like a bloodied scratch across her face. "If Paco, or anyone, were to hear what I just told you . . . well, you are a smart man. I think we can both agree to part on that understanding, yes, Mitch?"

I held firm as she brushed past me. Her heels struck a funeral march on the asphalt while her lingering fragrance whispered a final *fuck you*. Head held high, Oksana marched toward the prison entrance, her sleek form a pinprick of black swallowed into the looming gray of the prison walls.

CHAPTER 60

Twilight at Sayulita Beach paints in colors of burned orange and deep scarlet. Long shadows creep across the shore while the ocean beats a steady retreat, revealing a ribbing of sand stretching to the water's edge. Surfers on short boards catch the last of the day's waves, cutting and frothing through the breakers, while the familiar calls from the beach vendor selling cheap souvenirs take on a tone of desperation; one last circuit of the tourists before scuttling to the downtown bars to try their luck.

As they recede into the noise and color of the town, the food vendors appear, as if materializing out of the waves, ice chests packed with freshly caught oysters, spiced mango slices, and warm tamales wrapped in foil. The locals, their workday done, roll out blankets on the soft sand and listen to the local Mexican radio stations as the sun fades to a pale ghost over the horizon.

This is my favorite part of the day at Sayulita Beach, the brutal sun weakening as night sneaks in, soft-shoed, to take its natural place. It's a stark contrast to how I remember Palm Springs, where the night seemed to ambush the day, snatching the light away like a pickpocket. Here, the light is mellower, more forgiving, holds a faint promise of something better tomorrow.

Sierra and I walk toward the parking lot. Ahead of us, Kurt runs with the enthusiasm of a ten-year-old boy caught in the excitement of a long day at the beach. Later, he'll crash. Sleep the kind of sleep that's eluded me for months.

I'd arrived in Sayulita two days ago, a heart full of hope and a backpack full of apologies and promises; heavy baggage of my own making. I'd rented a small apartment downtown, determined to give Sierra the space she needed. The past two days had been intense: tears, recriminations, shouting, anger, regrets. All of it justified. I didn't challenge Sierra on any of it, just let her say what she needed to say, however much it stung.

After Sierra had vented her anger, I told her everything, every final detail. She wasn't in the forgiving mood; I couldn't blame her. All I could offer was honesty and hope it was enough to repair the damage. I stopped short of asking if she was intending to leave me. That kind of finality would have been too much to bear; some questions are best left unasked until an answer is urgent. I could wait.

* * *

Taking the steady rise of the hill, the three of us walk along the pathway that curves like a crescent moon around the beachhead. We take a moment and take in the ochre-tinged sun as it touches the dark shimmer of the ocean. I have a strong urge to take Sierra's hands in mine, but resist the temptation. She'd reach out in her own time, when she was good and ready.

At the end of the path, we climb over the rough ground leading to *Playa de Los Muertos* — the beach of the dead — a sheltered cove next to a graveyard strewn with colorful banners, necklaces of chained gardenias, and loops of multicolored ribbons.

We head to the edge of the graveyard, passing the simple stone markers, then walk to the more elaborate glass mausoleums in the center. They remind me of tiny, colorful homes for the deceased, with pitched roofs, small windows, and intricate paintwork. Inside, they're adorned with hanging crosses, faded drawings of the Virgin

Mary, and photographs of happier times. The Mexican Day of the Dead is only a few weeks away, and already candles are lit, flickering in the evening breeze, giving off the sweet scent of jasmine mingled with the saltiness of the ocean breeze.

As Kurt plays in the ocean, Sierra and I walk respectfully around the graves. I expect to feel sadness, but instead, I sense a rush of optimism. The tenderness and care offered to the dead feels like comfort. It reminds me that if you're lucky enough to be loved, you'll always be remembered, long after your passing.

At an altar of candles set in a copper holder, I kneel, take a match from a nearby box, and strike the head, bringing the flame to the wick.

"Who's that for?" Sierra asks.

I shrug. "Anybody who needs it."

She looks over the graveyard. "I know it's kind of weird, but I really love this place; it's so peaceful. It's like we've stumbled across somewhere special no one else knows about."

"Like the passage between one world and the next," I say, standing. "One foot in this world and the other in the next one."

She looks at me, her eyes reflecting the dusk light in tiny green specks. "Is that how you feel?"

I look out at the vast, untamed roll of the ocean. "Hard not to."

She gestures at Kurt as he splashes through the break of waves hitting the shore. "He's happy you're here. It's been good for him."

"You were right."

"I'm always right," Sierra says, smiling. It fills me with a faint stirring of unearned hope.

Sierra looks down. "I think we're going to stay here a while longer."

I stop. "I thought I was here to take you both home."

"I never said that, Mitch. I just said you could visit. No promises, remember?"

"How long?"

"As long as it takes. We've been through a lot."

"You know I never meant any of this to happen, don't you?"

"But it doesn't change the fact that it did happen, and I'm having a hard time forgiving you for that. I need time." She takes a breath. "I'm not ready to go back. Neither is Kurt. He's hiding it well, but what happened affected him more than he's letting on. Staying on will be good for him."

"He's got his mother's strength."

Sierra smiles.

"And us? Is that why you wanted to bring me here?" I ask, gesturing across the graveyard. "Fitting place to end a marriage?"

"Let's not go there, Mitch," she says, stiffening.

My name on her lips sends a flutter through my stomach. "I won't stop trying to make amends for everything. Whatever it takes; you know that."

"I know. I'm not asking you to stop."

We both turn as we hear Kurt call our names.

"One last swim before sunset?" she asks.

We head to the water. I grab Kurt and swing him around. For a moment, nothing else matters. The world could stop turning, and in that moment, I wouldn't notice or care. Sierra had told me to not stop trying. I would hold on to those words like gold dust for the months to come.

The odds were slim, but I took them, hauled them back to California with me, and promised myself to undo the damage as best I could. Sometimes it's all we can do. Move forward inch by inch, try to make the next day better than the one before.

Like I'd always said . . . small beats. Make enough of them and at some point, the rhythm's gonna start to change.

THE END

THE LUME & JOFFE BOOKS STORY

Lume Books was founded by Matthew Lynn, one of the true pioneers of independent publishing. In 2023 Lume Books was acquired by Joffe Books and now its story continues as part of the Joffe Books family of companies.

Joffe Books began in 2014 when Jasper agreed to publish his mum's much-rejected romance novel and it became a bestseller.

Since then we've grown into the largest independent publisher in the UK. We're extremely proud to publish some of the very best writers in the world, including Joy Ellis, Faith Martin, Caro Ramsay, Helen Forrester, Simon Brett and Robert Goddard. Everyone at Joffe Books loves reading and we never forget that it all begins with the magic of an author telling a story.

We are proud to publish talented first-time authors, as well as established writers whose books we love introducing to a new generation of readers.

We won Trade Publisher of the Year at the Independent Publishing Awards in 2023 and Best Publisher Award in 2024 at the People's Book Prize. We have been shortlisted for Independent Publisher of the Year at the British Book Awards for the last five years, and were shortlisted for the Diversity and Inclusivity Award at the 2022 Independent Publishing Awards. In 2023 we were shortlisted for Publisher of the Year at the RNA Industry Awards, and in 2024 we were shortlisted at the CWA Daggers for the Best Crime and Mystery Publisher.

We built this company with your help, and we love to hear from you, so please email us about absolutely anything bookish at feedback@joffebooks.com.

If you want to receive free books every Friday and hear about all our new releases, join our mailing list here: www.joffebooks.com/freebooks.

And when you tell your friends about us, just remember: it's pronounced Joffe as in coffee or toffee!

www.ingramcontent.com/pod-product-compliance
Lightning Source LLC
Chambersburg PA
CBHW010823250626
47169CB00010B/2927